Origins Progeny

by

Diana Fedorak

Children of Alpheios, Book Two

Origins Progeny

Contact Information: info@thewildrosepress.com

Cover Art by *Teddi Black*

The Wild Rose Press, Inc.
PO Box 708
Adams Basin, NY 14410-0708
Visit us at www.thewildrosepress.com

Publishing History
First Edition, 2024
Trade Paperback ISBN 978-1-5092-5902-1
Digital ISBN 978-1-5092-5903-8

Children of Alpheios, Book Two
Published in the United States of America

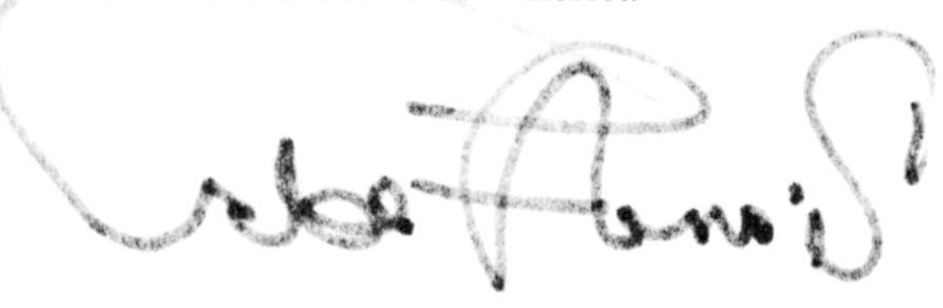

Dedication

For Cathy and Jerry

Chapter 1

When Alina heard the lullaby, a vise gripped her heart.

She stilled, trying to breathe. Across from her, three-year-old Mandin sat on their master bed of cot frames lashed together. Amid the rumpled sheets, he played with her link. Again, the familiar song emanated from her wrist piece. Rather than bring warmth to the stone walls of their underground home, the melody lodged itself under her skin like a splinter.

She snatched it from him. “No more.”

Her son pouted. “I don’t wanna nap.”

Already crabby upon returning from their trek, Mandin demanded to stay outside in the mild daylight of planet Eamine. Winter was the only season they could venture outdoors in their habitable zone, mostly composed of arid terrain.

She’d handed him her link so he’d stop complaining on their journey down to the cavern. While she liked music, that particular song disturbed old memories, better left untouched.

Before she could defuse her son’s resistance, a muffled voice came from the speaker in the outer corridor. A broadcast carried the community announcement.

“Stay here.” She flung aside the curtain that separated their bedroom from the living area and hurried by the creaky table and chairs. The front door panel squeaked as she slid it back on its track.

The speaker crackled. “Spartan, arriving.”

Her posture straightened. She rushed to her son. “C’mon, Kiean’s home. He always brings back a surprise.” She slipped the link on her wrist and shut off its musical mode.

Mandin bounded off the bed and clutched her hand. A wide grin spread across his face, mirroring her own. The announcement brushed away the old ballad from her thoughts, replacing them with hope.

In the corridor, the underground river trickled along, and they pursued the glow of the ground lights that illuminated the curving path of water. More polymer doors set into stone walls flashed by. As a physiographer, she was the primary surveyor of the underground town that they’d dubbed Evesborough and knew its structure better than anyone.

The hewn set of grand stairs marked the juncture with the main tunnel. Nine-year-old Syriah sprang out. “They’re back! Kiean’s back!” Her freckles seemed to dance at the news.

“Wait for us!” Alina followed Syriah’s trailing red braids. Up the steps Alina climbed, her thighs burning. Despite Mandin’s short legs, he was determined to ascend the grand staircase as quickly as he could.

Half-way up, the lights flickered. She paused to catch her breath. Underneath her climate suit, Alina grabbed a necklace fashioned from a thin strap of zepher hide. She rubbed the ring dangling from it. A gift from Kiean, the polished stone remained her tether.

They came upon the enormous hovercraft in the cavern’s main entrance. Daylight gleamed on the silver multi-story craft, the Triumph. People bustled on and off its main ramp to its common areas.

Lights flashed on the wingtips of the smaller expeditionary aircraft as it taxied into the cavern's mouth.

Breathless, she pointed. "The Spartan's here."

"I hope Kiean brought us something good." Syriah craned her neck for a glimpse of her older brother.

"He always brings gifts." Alina speculated on items available at the academy's supply outpost. Last time he brought back more meat sauce packets, making their meals tastier. A good thing, since she didn't cook. Through the crowds, she bounced on her toes as the craft's ramp lowered.

A figure strode down in an olive flight jacket, his strong features familiar. Kiean ducked his head along the bottom of the fuselage. A glow lit within her chest.

Mandin broke out of her grasp. "Da-da!" He ran through the throngs of people toward him.

Alina halted. The two children clambered around Kiean. He scooped up Mandin and draped an arm around Syriah.

Her son touched his face. "Da-da."

Kiean's eyes dimmed although he still smiled. He glanced at her, his once sandy hair more bronze from their time spent underground.

She drew in a deep breath. "He's excited you're back."

Kiean's gaze trailed over her face. "You're a welcoming sight."

"What did you bring us?" Syriah asked.

"We wrangled a metal laser 3-D printer. And some medications as well as more seedlings." Kiean bounced

Mandin in his arms.

Alina arched her back. “Tell me you brought another mattress. My back is sore from the one we have.”

He grinned as Mandin held onto his shirt. “I’ll make us new supports.”

Syriah cried out. “You didn’t bring back anything else?”

Kiean reached into his flight jacket pocket and held out shiny wrappings of candy. Syriah immediately swiped them from his hand. She sucked on the hard sweets, slurping them. Mandin squealed in protest, and Kiean passed one to him. Her son shoved the sugary morsel in his mouth.

“Just one. You still need to nap.” She reached for him.

“Noooo!” He clung to Kiean’s neck. “I want Da-da.”

Mandin’s words stung her cheeks. She didn’t envision having this conversation about his parentage so soon.

“I missed you too, buddy.” Kiean soothed Mandin by running his hand over his back.

Gulping, she tried to pry her son from his arms again.

“I no wanna leave Da-da!”

A flare of green distorted her vision, and a shove slammed against her mind. The cavern blurred, and she staggered. “Mandin, stop that!”

Kiean grabbed her arm, keeping her upright. “Hey, don’t do that to your mother. Be a good boy.”

Her son’s lips pressed together, his expression surly.

Kiean’s tone turned stern. “You don’t get any more sweets until you listen to your mama.”

Mandin's small mouth eased. "I sorry, Mama."

She rubbed her forehead. Lately, his telepathy seemed stronger, even with the herbal tonic that she used to suppress his seizures. While he wasn't naturally born like the rest of the Origins children, his powers would evolve as he grew older.

Kiean lowered Mandin to the ground. Observing Mandin's upturned face at Kiean's presence, she chewed her inner cheek. At some point, her son needed to hear the truth.

The emerald flecks in Kiean's eyes gleamed as they settled on Alina's face. No longer able to resist, she threw her arms around him. Her intimate half, finally home. Pressing herself against his sturdy frame released her misgivings. She inhaled his scent, notes of aircraft metal mixed with fresh rain. His absence had removed a sheen from her days.

He embraced her. "Sorry I didn't find a mattress. I brought you something better."

"Like what?" Maybe he brought scented soap, or a soft pillow for her.

"A visitor."

She searched his evenly proportioned features for clues. "Who?" Only an academy grad or instructor would venture out their way. No one else knew about Evesborough.

Footsteps thunked on the metal ramp. She gazed over Kiean's shoulder. Blond and wearing a dark climate suit tailored to his athletic frame, her brother stood before her.

Alina rocked back on a heel. "Gordo! What are you doing here?"

His green eyes sparkled. "Know where I can find the

lady in charge? Because I want to visit my big sis."

More muscular than when she saw him last, he appeared every meter the robust rogue ball player. Genetically engineered, he excelled at the game. She merely possessed good health as part of her design.

Now twenty years of age, he was four years her junior. As she hugged him, questions sprang to mind of how he made it to the outpost. He must have contacted someone at the expeditionary academy.

As she took in her brother's golden hair and fair skin, the resemblance struck her. A pang tugged at her gut with the realization that her brother had sought her out for a reason. Of all the days to hear that damn melody. Eamine was trying to warn her.

"What is it, Gordo? Tell me."

The sparkle left his green eyes, and he squeezed her arm. "It's Mom."

****

The hovercraft's flight room on the upper deck provided a quiet place. Alina listened from one of the armchairs in the front row. Gone was Gordo's red rogue ball uniform, and in its place, a thick black climate suit to combat the harsh winters back in Alpheios. His green eyes mirrored her own, although his hair was much lighter. Her hair resembled their late father, dark and fine. Gordo waited for her response on the raised platform.

"What's the prognosis?" Alina ran her hand along the armchair's arm, skimming the smooth fabric.

"Dr. Bellamy is keeping Mom's rash at bay, but it's been a struggle. She's trying to buy time until Genodyne comes up with a cure."

Her fingers curled into the chair's fabric. Thinking

of the biotech company, her nails left an indentation in the cloth. “How long will it take?”

“No one knows. Thousands took Genodyne’s product released a year ago called Revival. It was supposed to be an anti-aging tonic. Skin and joint rejuvenation, cellular turnover, even longer life expectancy. But they discontinued it after the deaths became undeniable.”

Alina frowned. “I remember the pitch. Does it affect everyone the same way?”

He leaned forward, elbows on his knees. “Depending how much of the product one took, survivors often suffer disfigurement. If you took more…” he shook his head. “Mom’s symptoms are fatigue and rash, but some days she still has energy. For now.”

Alina bumped the back of her head against the headrest. “And the riots you’re talking about—the council hasn’t moved against the chancellor?”

“Some have issued public statements of concern. But they haven’t moved to oust Jade Graylin. What the chancellor calls her ‘stability orders’ remain in place.” Her brother straightened, a spark flaring in his eyes. “Curfews are in place after sunset, and citizens are only allowed outdoors during daylight hours. They even cancelled last season’s rogue ball games. There’s a restricted zone around Genodyne, too.”

“Why?”

“The attendees at the games started booing the city council rep during opening ceremonies.” Her brother leaned back, half-smiling.

“But a restricted zone around the hospital?”

“No crowds are allowed to form in the plaza.

Genodyne will only accept patients on an emergency basis."

She rubbed a temple, remembering the last time she was trapped in Genodyne. "Jade Graylin will go to any lengths to maintain power."

"That's no help to Mom." A growl underlined her brother's tone. "Or to the other city residents."

Alina examined his face, ivory skin yielding to hints of peach, a reminder of their mother. Linette's vanity rested with her dewy skin, and the patent Genodyne granted her in her youth. She wouldn't hesitate in trying their latest advancement. Nor would she cope well if something happened to her enviable looks.

A small grain lodged itself at the base of Alina's throat, and she swallowed, hoarse. She'd missed Gordo when they first settled into Evesborough, thinking about him back in Alpheios. But she hadn't thought much about her mother at all. Nor bothered to contact her. Free in Evesborough, Alina's life would have taken a completely different trajectory if she'd listened to Linette's relationship advice.

As a pessimistic silence permeated the room, Alina allowed her curiosity to slip out. "Is Chance still Jade's Guardian aide?"

Her brother lifted his head. "Yes. He came to see me about a month after you took off and asked about you. I told him the truth. That I hadn't heard from you, and I didn't know where you were."

"What did he want?" Her voice flattened, like a rolling pin dropped on it.

"To know if you and Mandin were all right."

A twist wrung her stomach. She'd uprooted their lives because of Chance and his mother. "Has deep winter settled over Alpheios yet?"

"No, we have a few weeks left." Gordo fixed his gaze on her. "Are you thinking of visiting? Because Mom and Jakob's penthouse is safe, Lina. Still quiet there. It's the Falls District by Genodyne where the protests are usually held."

Gordo always called her by her childhood name, *Lina*, when he wanted something from her, or when he tried to please her. In this case, she gathered that he wanted her to come home.

The swish of the door opening announced another visitor. Kiean strode in with Mandin by his side.

"Bridge check shows systems are green, but we're getting some abnormal readings from the reactor. Tally is checking it out." Without his flight jacket, Kiean wore a long-sleeved brown pullover and pants with assorted pockets.

Her son climbed onto her lap, holding a computerized padlock. His dark lashes lowered to the contraption, and he punched in the code on the screen. His face filled with concentration as he manipulated the mechanism in his small hands. The lock clicked open, and a delightful expression overcame him. Again and again, he'd repeat the sequence, pulling open the locking bar.

She stroked his soft shoulders. "If it's not one thing, it's another." Mandin sat sweetly in her lap, yet just an hour ago, he'd unleashed his anger on her.

"Talley will sort it out," Kiean replied. The senior engineer had returned with him from their resupply run, indispensable as their connection to the academy.

Kiean and Talley led the others in keeping Evesborough running. Big Flint managed the place in their absence, but without the other two, small items would break here and there. The hovercraft was the nerve center of the village, cultivating their biomass to produce food blocks, purifying their drinking water, and supplying their electricity.

She'd helped Big Flint by conducting periodic checks on the environmental control system, but Kiean's steady presence anchored everyone. Evesborough seemed austere and less vibrant without him. At least with Kiean by her side, she'd sleep more soundly on their uncomfortable bedding.

Click went the lock again in her son's hands. "Mandin, do you remember Uncle Gordo?" Alina gestured to her brother.

Mandin's dark curls framed his round cheeks. He tore his eyes away from the lock and peered at Gordo.

"Remember me, kid?" Gordo winked.

Her son let out a soft giggle. "Gorda." He pointed at him.

Her brother chuckled. "Gorda makes me sound like a chubby girl."

She set her son gently on the floor, encouraging him to go to his uncle.

Alina motioned Kiean to the other side of the flight room. While Gordo entertained Mandin, she informed Kiean about Linette's condition.

"I don't want to leave." She checked on Mandin playing with Gordo. "Especially when you just returned. But he's her grandson, and I should bring him to see her before deep winter arrives in Alpheios." Alina stepped closer, inhaling a whiff of fresh rain.

Kiean braced his hand against the wall. "We took longer than usual because the expedition resupply crew mentioned they had to wait for a launch clearing, given the activity restrictions and Guardian patrols. If you return, they'll arrest you." His Adam's apple bobbed. "I'd rather you not go."

She took in a deep breath at his mention of the Guardians. The last time they pursued her, she'd escaped Genodyne. No use in avoiding the issue like she'd hoped. "There is a way to gain safe passage. I can send a letter to Chance." A knot lodged itself in between her shoulder blades. She wasn't used to talking about her ex. "His mother is still the chancellor. We can land outside Alpheios near Old Town, but I'll wait to enter until I receive word from him."

One of Kiean's brows raised. "You sure you can trust him?"

Across the room, her son showed the lock to Gordo. Mandin's dark curls and star-sapphire eyes were unmistakable in resemblance to his father. "No, but…he may want to see his son." Uncertain what Chance's reaction would be once he learned of her presence, she needed to contact him first. A bitter taste welled up in her mouth, and she bit down on her inner cheek.

Kiean straightened, dropping his hand from the wall. "I'll come with you. If your mother is feeling well enough, I'd like to meet her."

She blinked and tilted her head. "But I thought you didn't like Alpheios."

"I don't, but I can put up with it." His hazel eyes locked onto hers. "That is, if you're there."

Her shoulders relaxed. Grateful, she grinned. The lights overhead flickered. Kiean dipped his head to kiss her. Before she could reach him, a clanking from deep within the ship sounded, and the power went out, leaving them in darkness.

Chapter 2

From the third story window of Genodyne, Chance scanned the crowd below. Barricades separated the Guardians from the protestors pushing up the building's steps. He estimated nearly fifty people, loud and angry, demanding entry. One man threw a rock at an officer who ducked. The rock bounced off the top of his helmet. Three Guardians rushed the man, throwing him to the ground. One quickly tapped his baton near the rioter's arms, and crystalline tie cuffs surrounded his wrists. His men subdued the protestors, as Chance expected.

He touched his comm bar in his ear. "Sentinel, report status."

The lookout posted inside the main lobby of Genodyne responded. "All secure here. But…" the sentry paused. "If that crowd grows much bigger—"

Chance cut in. "Additional squads inbound. To push the perimeter back." He frowned, glancing at his link. Outside, two troop carriers arrived. Over a dozen officers poured out of them, many with their batons drawn. They herded the protestors back down the steps and into the plaza. A new line was established once the metal barricades marked the quad.

"All secure here, sir," the sentry replied.

"Hold the line. Chariot is still inside. Report any changes." Chance strode toward the elevator. The code name, Chariot, referred to his mother. He needed to brief her on the situation. The lift arrived on the first floor.

At the R&D wing, Chance punched the button for the underground elevator. It whisked him past the reproduction vault. He entered the tunnel. While brightly lit, the long passageway beneath the river was empty. His boots echoed along the white floor, and his shadow blurred by the white walls.

The tunnel opened to a large foyer that provided a view underneath the turbulent waterfall. The hidden facility was built into the mountainside behind the cover of roaring water. He maneuvered around the sculpted bust of Genodyne's former owner and city's founder, Duncan Ambrose. Monuments of the old man were ubiquitous throughout the facility.

At the far corner of the wing, Sergeant Rufalo who stood post greeted him. Chance waved his link on the cipher pad for access. The lock clicked.

Inside the laboratory, he found his mother, the executive officer of Alpheios. She conversed with Dr. Daxmen in front of the bay windows. Through the doorway of the control room, two technicians monitored several screens at a workstation.

Dr. Daxmen nodded. "Yes, Chancellor Graylin. We'll take a sample, but we could use some help."

"Go grab Rufalo outside. He can assist you," she replied.

"I'll explain to him what needs to be done." The doctor motioned to two techs. They exited, leaving Chance alone with his mother. She didn't like bad news but insisted that he tell her sooner rather than later, as she instructed that bad news never got better with time.

"Yes?" she asked.

Chance didn't inherit her diminutive stature. She

reiterated many times that she had genetically selected otherwise for him. But Jade Graylin, petite in her usual dark pantsuit, moved about like she owned the room. But he knew better, witnessing her occasional overreach up close. And her lies.

"Mother, the protests are getting worse by the day." Lowering his voice, Chance leaned in. "If Genodyne doesn't find a way to heal our residents from their Revival product soon—the one you approved—there will be violence again." He rested his hand on his baton.

"We're close to a solution." Her gaze traveled over his dark uniform. "Or is the crowd too much for Commander Zinyon to control? I've asked him to take an uncompromising stance as to avoid what happened a few weeks ago."

Grinding his back teeth, Chance recalled how the crowd nearly attacked Genodyne's board members as they were leaving the building, and the injuries the Guardians suffered in stopping them. "You clamp down further, you may provoke a worse response. We have a finite amount of manpower, and the entire city to secure."

The chancellor pin rested on her suit jacket, three peaks overlaid with gold atomic loops, surrounded by a wreath. As her aide, he wore a similar one, only smaller. For three years, he'd donned the pin. Three very long years, it seemed. "Release me from this assignment, and I'll help the Commander."

She turned her attention to the observation windows. "Not yet. We're so close."

His back stiffened. A flash of movement caught his eye. A stocky figure moved in view of the windows from the large laboratory. The pregnant humanoid appeared behind the metal gate that sealed off her quarters from the control room above. His hand itched near his microwave pistol, but Chance dropped his fist, reminded that the gate kept the room secure.

The door swung open, and Rufalo with the rest of the medical party reappeared. They passed through the control room and took the stairs down to the laboratory.

"Do they have a cure yet?" Chance asked.

"We'll soon find out." His mother kept her gaze on the unfolding scene below.

The laboratory contained assorted furniture that resembled a makeshift living area. The pregnant creature behind the gate scowled. Her skin glimmered traces of silver underneath, like the veins of giltspar mineral that ran through the stone walls. A dark gash appeared above her pantaloons, visible below her cropped tank top. It curved along the top of her protruding belly.

"What's that cut on her stomach? Was she injured?"

"Kora is almost done with gestation. It's been nearly one hundred days."

"They're already developed by then?"

"One of our requirements for surviving this planet was to speed their growth. Since she's able to metabolize giltspar, so will her offspring, so they can survive outside her body during the summer gamma storms. They're also capable of inhabiting all of Eamine, unlike us."

The medical party cautiously approached the gate. A growl emanated from the room, and Chance searched for Kora's male counterpart. Ash sat hunched over the bed, clutching his abdomen. His shoulder-length black hair fell across his face, and his skin reflected the same faint silver gleam as his mate, although it appeared mottled like a rash. He glared at the medical party, a storm stirring in his dark eyes.

"What's wrong with him?"

"Recent bone marrow transplant," she replied. "He suffers from a rare blood disorder."

Rufalo unlocked the gate. Kora's iridescent skin flickered, and her scales darkened. She hissed at them, her ice-blue eyes narrowing. Stout and well-built, she looked human, with her dark cropped hair and intelligent expression. But her skin rippled again, thickening into a brown hide, reminding Chance that she wasn't their kind.

Ash stumbled off the bed, arcs of electricity sparking from his hands. His scales flickered, managing to turn dark gray. His gait was weak, and he staggered toward the medical party.

"Stay back!" Rufalo held up his baton.

But Ash rushed him, holding out his palm. A bolt of electricity flew from it, but Rufalo swiftly pivoted. A scorch mark smoked on the wall behind him. Rufalo jabbed the baton forward, and Ash fell to the ground, stunned from its shock.

A male tech grabbed the female's arms and pinned her. She thrashed, her skin hardening further. Dr. Daxmen moved swiftly with a needle. He pinched the dark line across her abdomen and the skin gave, revealing a small flap.

"What on Eamine…" Chance's jaw slackened.

The doctor quickly jabbed the needle under the flap of skin, drawing blood at the top of her protruding belly. He stepped back, removing the needle. "Got it." He passed the needle to his female assistant.

His mother craned her head for a better view. "That's how she'll deliver the babies, near her stem cell reservoir. She develops a pouch near her midsection for birthing. Safer for her that way, and she can carry more offspring."

Kora kicked the male tech's knee. He winced and fell, struggling to hold onto her arm. Her pointed fingernails extended and slammed downward into his hand. He cried out.

Rufalo stood in front of Kora, holding his powered baton up in a threatening manner. She froze, never taking her eyes off him. The techs dashed back outside the gate, one of them hobbling. Droplets of blood from the male tech's hand splattered onto the floor. Slowly, Rufalo backed away from the gate. Kora approached him, a murderous expression on her face, her arm slung across her abdomen. Rufalo slammed the door shut and locked it.

"Leave my babies alone!" Kora's shrill voice rang out. Her hand groped to feel that she still possessed the little monsters inside her.

"Terrific beast you created, Mother." Chance didn't follow all the details of how Genodyne manufactured them, but understood they were chimeras. He vaguely recalled Daxmen's long-winded explanation about using the Origins children's genes as precursors and combining them with DNA fragments from the indigenous life.

"I told you, they're kronosapiens, not beasts." His mother brushed off her lapel. "Directed evolution for humanity is finally here. The Revival product was an interim step to mollify Genodyne since creating this new life form is very expensive. It's unfortunate the product didn't work as intended, but we've gained valuable information in the meanwhile."

His shoulders stiffened. His mother was spending

more time at the company as of late, instead of running the city. But to argue about her vision was futile. “So how are these kronosapiens different than the previous prototypes?”

“The others didn’t make it due to the difficulty of combining two species’ different reproductive systems. But I believe we’ve gotten it right this time.” She gestured to the window.

“Kora is more aggressive than her male counterpart so she can hunt. I wasn’t about to allow the burden of child-rearing to fall solely to the female—the council’s approval of Genodyne’s R & D was contingent on that. Ash is stronger than she is, which allows him to nourish and protect their litter once they are born. His teats are developing along his side.”

Repulsed, Chance shook his head. “What man would volunteer to become less aggressive?”

His mother fingered her pin. “It’s brilliant, actually. He’s loyal to Kora once he can scent she’s pregnant with his offspring, and we won’t have a scourge of unnecessary violence from males competing over females. The two sexes are co-equal and complimentary.”

“How many is she carrying?” Chance asked.

Dr. Daxmen entered the control room holding the needle. “Three krono-fetuses.” He glanced at Jade. “The blood from her womb should be rich in stem cells due to her pregnancy. We’ll test it as serum to treat the side effects of those who’ve already taken the original Revival formula.”

“Does that mean you’ll have a cure?” Chance asked.

“Hopefully. And a new product to promote.”

“You may need to come up with a new name for

branding." She stroked her chin. "Will the blood withdrawal fatigue her again?" She motioned at Kora who glowered up at them.

The doctor scratched his jowls with his free hand. "At this stage of her pregnancy, it should only last a day or two. Carrying offspring helps with her cellular renewal. And if she tries to shock anyone, her organs may suffer damage again. She'll be careful to keep the fetuses going and will restrain herself."

"And Ash?" his mother asked.

The doctor furrowed his brow. "The bone marrow from the sows is less effective than we thought. We don't have many donor matches left, and it'll take time to re-create more."

Chance swallowed back his distaste. Three curved bumps protruded from Kora's spinal column under her shirt, the organs that she used to generate electricity. Chance couldn't help but think they'd all be better off if this lot of kronosapiens passed away like the previous ones, weakened from their flawed start in life. Although he refrained from saying so in front of his mother. Otherwise, another argument would ensue.

She considered Kora and Ash a superior species that possessed characteristics of life organic to Eamine. His mother was determined to find a way to increase Kora's stem cell regeneration, so the creature could use her electric powers without internal organ damage.

Dr. Daxmen and the techs left with Kora's blood vial. Sergeant Rufalo resumed his post outside.

Chance faced the city leader. "Mother, release me from this post. I want to return to my men. I'm one of them, not an extension of you." Moreover, he was tired of being at her beck and call.

“May I remind you that I saved your career after that stunt you pulled three years ago.” Her words sharpened like a sword.

Heat flared underneath his chin. “I don’t need your help. I did what was right.” He tired of the same fight, and her recriminations of how he’d let their best opportunity for Phase Three slip away. If only they kept some of the Origins’ children to use as test subjects, she’d lamented. He’d disobeyed her orders to imprison the mother of his son. And he held no regrets about his actions.

“Hope it was worth it.” His mother snorted. “After Alina ran off with that Origins man.”

Flinching, he said, “I’m done with this assignment.” He spun on his heel toward the exit.

“Chance!”

Slowly, he turned back as her voice lowered. “The Revival product has complicated matters. I must get the serum right. It’s the only way to fix the situation.” Her brown eyes pierced his. “You *will* help me stabilize the city. Because you’re the only one I can trust.”

His jaw clenched. “Trust? You evidently don’t trust me enough to tell me the academy ship left to meet them again.” His finger jabbed the air. “You knew how much I wanted to send a message to Alina. Or have you forgotten about Mandin as well?”

His mother glanced at the window, but the kronosapiens retreated to the large bed at the corner of the room. “Because I didn’t want you distracted during the riots. I’ve pretended not to notice whenever the academy resupplied them.” She held him with her gaze. “We had a deal. I did not pursue Alina while you remained my aide. And I’ve kept my word.”

His knuckles tightened at his side. "But you would deny me a chance to hear any word of my son." Nightmares of Mandin's seizures still haunted Chance, and he wondered how Alina fared in caring for their son. Or if she ever thought about returning to Alpheios. Ever thought about what the two of them once shared.

His mother smoothed her suit jacket. "When they send a resupply ship again, I'll inform you. But I have more important matters that require my attention."

"Promise me. It's the only reason I don't walk out now." His hand itched to rip the pin off his uniform.

She scowled. "All right. I promise. If security is in place, I'd like to leave now."

Chance inhaled. While he won the personal battle with his mother, a larger one loomed ahead. Tensions in the city ran high, and many residents were calling on her to step down. He did not want to conceive of what could happen if the crowd outside broke through the perimeter and made it into the main building.

"Escort has the vehicle around back. I'll tell them we're inbound."

A slight smile from her, and she stepped closer. "Thank you." His mother lifted a hand and touched his cheek. "I knew I could count on you."

He opened the door for her and spoke to Rufalo. "Radio escort and tell them to have the engine running for Chariot's departure." As they led his mother down the hall, Chance checked the area for threats. He remembered the hostile expression in Kora's eyes. Perhaps after they finished the serum, his mother would come to realize that as chancellor, she should distance herself from Genodyne and focus on her citizens.

Chapter 3

Syriah heard the river rush into the slot canyon but couldn't feel the heat of the suns. The small waterwheel by the greenhouse gently turned with the flow of the narrow river. Everything got blurry when she floated through the greenhouse windows. Inside, Macy dug into a pot of herbs.

"Have you found her?" Dr. Olek's voice queried in her head.

"She's at the greenhouse." Shiny plants were all around. Syriah hovered by the pretty blossoms.

Macy smiled at her. The chieftain usually didn't interfere when Syriah exercised her powers, and gently encouraged her instead.

Danny's voice intruded. "I think you're wrong. I think Macy is in the great hall."

Everything faded, and Syriah found herself in a dark cavern room.

Dr. Olek sounded annoyed. "Don't interfere when she's projecting her consciousness. You'll disorient her."

Pushing back against the cavern image, Syriah concentrated harder, and the greenhouse reappeared. "Stop planting images in my head!"

Someone touched her arm. "Time to return," Dr. Olek said.

Syriah said good-bye to Macy, and the elder waved.

Syriah pictured her origin point, like the doctor had taught her.

Slowly, she opened her eyes, once again in the medical bay of the hovercraft. She was lying in a special medical chair with an overhead dome that glowed different colors. Her dizziness would leave in a second.

Dr. Olek studied a crystal screen. “You did very well. Only nine-years-old, and you projected yourself for five minutes.”

Danny smirked at her.

She pointed at him. “I could have done it longer, but he ruined my training!” Danny always tried to one-up her just because he was a year older.

“You were taking forever. It’s my turn now!” he said.

At the table nearby, Phoebe fiddled with a medical wand, her face slack. “Danny smells because he hasn’t bathed in over a week. Even his air is brown.”

Danny pushed his younger sister, and she nearly toppled from the bench.

“No fighting! You’re not a pack of sylins!” Dr. Olek said.

He hardly ever raised his voice. The tall doctor scratched the gray hairs around his temple, looking like he regretted his outburst.

Phoebe and Danny started arguing, but a buzz sounded, and the lights went out. In complete darkness, Syriah remained motionless in the chair. Sounds from others in the room reminded her that she wasn’t alone.

“The power just went out,” Dr. Olek said.

Syriah took in a deep breath. A humming vibrated the walls. One ceiling light panel illuminated. Shadows fell over her friends’ faces.

"Is training over now?" Phoebe asked.

"But I didn't get to go yet." Danny said.

The doctor pushed the power button on the chair. None of the dome lights turned on even though he clicked the switch several times. "Training is over for today." He glanced at Danny. "You'll go first next time."

Danny's face fell.

Syriah climbed out of the chair. Her powers strengthened a little more each training session. This was the third time that she astrally projected herself outside the cavern. The giltspar mineral in the surrounding walls always made it easier.

Phoebe widened her eyes. "Something bad… onboard the craft."

"Where?" Syriah asked.

"I don't know," Danny's sister replied.

They all watched the little girl, waiting for more information. Phoebe's chin quivered. She clapped both hands over her ears. A second later, a clanking noise shook the walls, like the ship was coming apart.

Shouts from outside reached them. Phoebe dove underneath the table. Dr. Olek crouched next to her. "Come now, Phoebe. Tell us what you saw."

Her long bangs covered her eyebrows. "It's Talley. He's hurt."

"Do you know where?"

"The reactor room."

Indeed, Syriah could sense the worry outside the walls. She was tempted to find Kiean since Phoebe's predictions, or what Dr. Olek called premonitions, often came true.

As he coaxed Phoebe out from underneath the table, Dulce opened the lab door. Her long ponytail fell over her shoulder. Syriah wished her own red hair was as dark and pretty as Dulce's.

Dulce said, "The power is out onboard the entire ship. The system is routing the generator to the most critical functions."

"Med bay should be on that list." Dr. Olek tapped the table. "Do you mind staying with the children? I need to find Talley."

"Of course." Dulce motioned them closer.

As he headed to the exit, Syriah stepped forward. "I want to go with you."

"Better you stay here."

"I want my brother." Whenever there was a problem onboard the hovership, the other grown-ups always asked for Kiean. Plus, he explained things to her in a way that she understood. "I know the shortcut to the reactor room. Kiean showed me."

Danny climbed onto the special medical chair. "Maybe this will turn back on again."

Dr. Olek gave his nurse a pointed look. Dulce reached for Danny. "Let's stay off the big equipment. But the wand here works on its own battery." She picked up the diagnostic wand on the table. "Do you want me to examine you?"

Both Danny and Phoebe hopped in front of Dulce. Although Syriah liked to watch the wand too, she'd seen Dulce use that trick before to distract them.

As the doctor grabbed his medical bag, Syriah asked again if she could accompany him. He sighed. "If you know the shortcut, lead the way."

They set off along the hallway, and Syriah led him down the back stairs. On the first deck, she cut through the dark cafeteria by following the lighted strips on the floor.

She stopped in front of the reactor room, and Dr. Olek knocked. Soloman opened the door. His brown hair was messy as usual. While grown up like her brother, Soloman acted like Danny at times. "No one is allowed in here. We're currently running on generator."

"If someone is hurt, I can be of assistance," the doctor said.

"Soloman, it's okay. This is *Doctor* Olek." Syriah gestured to her companion. Soloman was usually strict about rules.

"But no one is allowed in the reactor room. The equipment is very sensitive—"

She pushed the door open. "We heard Talley is hurt." Silly Soloman. He was suspicious of people he didn't know, and he didn't know Dr. Olek well.

Soloman scowled. "Okay, but just to help him." He fidgeted. "And don't touch anything."

The generator routed electricity into the reactor room. On the floor, Talley writhed in the corner. He held his shoulder. "Dang pump came apart, and the valve blew right through the glass." A piece of twisted metal rested by his feet. He was hurt, just as Phoebe predicted.

The glass along the top half of the wall was broken. On the other side, the fusion reactor remained dark and quiet. Soloman gazed at the instrument console as Dr. Olek tended to Tally.

Observing the engineer, Syriah tuned into his air. She was allowed to use her powers to help others, like Dr. Olek had taught her. The air's gleam gave her clues to someone's life essence and their mood. Tally's air sputtered red streaks. He was hurt bad.

Talley never showed any pain. Next to Big Flint, he

was one of the strongest men in Evesborough. But now the senior engineer winced. The atmosphere in the room felt slippery somehow, as if the adults tried to get a handle on the situation. Syriah closed her eyes. Kiean would know what to do.

Soloman interrupted her concentration. "What are you doing?"

She tried to focus on the bridge where Kiean often checked the controls. "Finding my brother." She swished through the ship's corridors and up the staircase. The bridge was empty. When Kiean wasn't working, he spent time with Alina and Mandin.

Maybe they were all together in the flight room. Syriah searched for Mandin's air, which usually glowed much brighter than anyone else's.

Someone grabbed her arm. "Stop that!"

She blinked up at Soloman who ruined her search. Dizzy from the abrupt change back to her point of origin, she rubbed her forehead.

"What's the problem here?" Dr. Olek asked.

"She's causing aberrations in the magnetic field." Soloman pointed at her. "She's the reason for the damage. Were you looking for your brother before the power went out?"

Heat filled her cheeks. "No. I was looking for Macy earlier. I didn't do anything!" She wasn't sure what Soloman was accusing her of.

"We don't know if she caused that," Dr. Olek replied.

Soloman gestured at the consoles. "But we do know. She's causing fluctuations in the electromagnetic fields. I'm playing back the readings, and they go wild whenever she uses her mind tricks."

Syriah clamped her lips together, stung by his betrayal. She and Soloman were supposed to be friends.

Talley spoke softly. "The reactor's magnets create a field to contain the plasma. The plates and tolerances are in perfect alignment. If they're thrown off—"

The door opened, and Kiean entered. Syriah rushed over and threw her arms around his waist. Finally, he'd come to make the situation right. He patted back her braids as she clung to him. "Just a power outage."

"Can you help me get Talley to med bay? I need to attend to his broken collarbone," Dr. Olek said. "And med bay should be listed a critical function that requires power."

"Done." Kiean examined the broken glass. "How's the reactor?"

"Toast 'til we fix the cryopump," Talley replied. "Think you can do it?" he directed his question to Soloman.

His assistant picked up the piece of metal by Talley's feet and studied it. "We don't have the materials or the machinery to manufacture such tolerances."

"We brought back a metal laser 3-D printer—" Kiean started.

"Can it generate this same alloy?"

"It uses a composite powder to make parts."

"But this alloy is made to withstand the temperatures of the plasma in the fusion reactor. The plasma can reach 100 million Kelvin." Soloman peered intently at the warped rod in his hand.

Syriah didn't know what they meant about the printer, but she backed away, to escape more blame.

Talley's chest expanded. "Maybe we can heat-treat the printer-produced part." He grimaced as the doctor finished the sling.

"But then it would have to be refined down to one-thousandth of a millimeter to create a valve that seals completely," Soloman replied.

Her brother's brow wrinkled as he gazed at the part in Soloman's hand. "This repair will take some time."

She was about to grab Kiean's hand, but he bent down to help the engineer stand.

As they left the room, Syriah trailed behind. When she'd looked for Macy earlier, she had floated through the first deck, passing by the reactor room to glide down the ramp. Had she changed the environment somehow, causing the senior engineer to get hurt?

Dr. Olek said to her, "It's not your fault. We're still trying to better understand your powers."

Syriah's chin dropped, and she studied the floorboards. Soloman usually told the truth, and everyone trusted him on the reactor. He'd memorized all its numbers. Twisting her fingers together, she knew Soloman blamed her. She hadn't meant for anyone to get hurt.

Chapter 4

Alina hopped up from the armchair in the Triumph's flight room. "You're not coming with me?"

"It's going to take at least six weeks for Talley's collarbone to heal. And we don't have a spare cryopump." Kiean stood before her. "I can't leave everyone in the dark."

A soft swish on the fabric a few seats away signaled Mandin trying to find comfort as he napped, curled upon an armchair in the dimly lit room. An illuminated panel kept the area from falling into total darkness, and she stepped closer to better view Kiean.

Through the shadows, the steady contours of his face emerged. The flight room walls insulated the noise from the ship, and it was even quieter without power.

She lowered her voice. "But why not let Soloman take care of it?" Even as she asked, Alina gathered that as attentive to the reactor as Soloman was, the Origins would balk on relying on him alone.

Kiean cocked his head. "Soloman can keep the generator running, but it'll require alternating power to the ship's various systems. I have to stay and find a way to fix the cryopump and get the reactor online again."

The tightening inside her chest grew deeper. "Big Flint can help him. People trust Flint."

"And he's kept Evesborough running while Talley and I were gone. I can't leave this mess to him, not while he's raising four kids."

Alina bit her inner cheek. Kiean's brown shirt was rumpled after returning from the reactor room, like he'd lifted a heavy object or person. He'd just returned to Evesborough, back for only a few hours. While she found his reasoning sound, she wanted him to accompany her to Alpheios. Especially if she had to deal with her mother.

"When do you leave?" he asked in a quiet tone.

She brushed a strand of hair away. "Gordo and I depart the day after tomorrow. I can ask Aurore to accompany us. She knows the Spartan better than I do."

"I'll fuel up the Spartan and program the route for you. Bringing Aurore is a good idea. She'll keep you company." He extended his arm out, hand against the wall.

His remark still didn't relieve the misgivings deep within her. Everything Kiean said made sense. As a meteorologist, Aurore could deal with weather while flying. Alina's geodesy skills made her a natural at navigation. So why the unease? She fiddled with the corded necklace that lay inside her suit top.

His smile faded. "You're not wearing it on your hand yet, are you?"

She stopped pulling at the cord but kept a grip on the smooth stone. "I keep it close to me. Where it matters."

"Or hidden away." His hazel eyes turned serious.

"You're already my intimate. As I am yours." She inched near him.

He dipped his head. "I won't rush you, but I didn't expect that reaction." He turned away and exhaled, running a hand over the back of his neck.

A flush rushed through her cheeks. "Why is it

important to you to have a public declaration?" She never believed in such archaic rituals. Whenever she pictured herself standing before him repeating some dreamy mantra in front of the entire village, her pulse shot up, and she inhaled deep breaths.

He pivoted back. "I don't care about a big ceremony if you'd rather have a small group of friends. I just want to make it official. And I was hoping it would be important to you as well." His forehead furrowed.

She drew closer. "You *are* important to me. What matters is how we show each other that over time."

He glanced away, his expression distant in the dark room. "That sounds like a no." His tone emptied.

"But I adore the stone you gave me." A flutter plucked inside her. "I just need some time to get used to the custom." She took in the skepticism on his face. "Don't you know how much I missed you?"

He released a small chuckle. "You're good at distracting me."

"How so?" She grinned. "Can't I have a kiss from my intimate half in the dark?"

A smile spread over his face, and he bent his head down, inches away.

The door swished open, and Gordo entered. She pulled away, and Kiean straightened. "Refrigerators are still powered on as well as the cooktops. But the big oven is down in the kitchen. Still managed to grab lunch, though." Her brother patted his stomach.

"Min essentials while we're on generator. Although I can check the programming from the bridge," Kiean replied.

She addressed her brother. "We can find a cabin for you." Glancing at Kiean, she asked, "Will there be power in the rooms?"

"The passenger compartments won't have power, but the flight crew cabins should."

"I wouldn't mind resting before we head back." Even though Gordo remained composed, his shoulders sagged as if he carried a weight.

"Do you mind grabbing Mandin?" she asked Kiean.

He gently lifted her son in his arms. Mandin made a "mmmmm," sound and rested his head against Kiean's shoulder.

She led them along the corridor by following the arc of the ship's walls. She stopped in front of the engineer's cabin. Usually, the flight crew quarters were off limits. "Do you have the code?"

Once Kiean gave her the combo, she punched it in and opened the door for Gordo. As she peeked inside the small but tidy compartment, an idea formed. She also needed to maintain commitments closer to home.

"Do you mind if we lay Mandin down for a nap with you? He's so tired, and if I bring him all the way down a hundred steps, he'll probably wake up."

Gordo yawned and stretched. "No problem. I plan on joining him."

Kiean rested Mandin on the bed and pulled the covers over him.

When Kiean started heading back the way they came, she tugged his sleeve. "This way."

"Where are we going?" He followed her until she came to the end of the hallway by a set of double doors, indicating a larger than usual cabin.

Stopping in front of it, she asked, "Do you still have the code to the captain's room?"

He raised an eyebrow. "The code…." A hint of

understanding entered his eyes as he punched in the sequence. Upon opening the door, the lights flickered on while he waited inside for her.

"Lights down," she said. As the overhead lamps dimmed into a gentle gold, she reached for him, feverish. His arms enclosed her, and his hand cupped her head. Her open mouth found his warm lips, and she crushed her body against his.

****

Alina rested her head on Kiean's chest, listening to his heartbeat. Sweat glistened off their skin in the captain's bedroom. He threw a sheet over her to protect her from the chill.

"Remind me why we don't use this mattress as our own?" she asked.

The plush cushion in the captain's suite curved around her frame, and she could feel the ache in her lower back abate. They were tucked away in the privacy of the bedroom, separated from the front parlor.

"Because then where would we sneak off to and hide?" Kiean's voice resonated against her earlobe.

She propped herself up on an elbow in time to observe his smirk. Prodding him in the ribs with her finger, she watched him squirm.

He grabbed her hand and dragged her close. "Is that what you want? A bed like this?" A rakish grin spread across his face.

"It would feel better than the contraption we have now." She ran a fingertip over the faint scar covering his sternum. Genodyne had performed heart surgery on him when he was an infant, before they dumped him with the Origins, among the naturally born.

He smoothed her hair back. "Done. What else do

you want?"

"Soft pillows. Ours are lumpy."

"Anything else?"

She rested her chin against his shoulder. "For you to come to Alpheios with me. We can celebrate your birthday there." He pretended not to care about his birthday, and this was the year that he'd turned twenty-six, but she couldn't resist adding the sweetener.

Kiean exhaled. "I wish I could."

Alina rolled onto her back. While she knew he needed to stay, the thought of returning to Alpheios unsettled her.

He turned on his side. "How long do you think you'll visit your mother?"

She closed her eyes and shrugged. "Long enough to fulfill my obligation."

"Meaning?"

Alina rolled over to face him. "She'll want to see her grandson. But I plan on returning before deep winter sets in Alpheios." As her thoughts drifted back home, she traced Kiean's bicep with her index finger. "Besides, I'm my father's daughter." *The wonderful man she left,* Alina thought.

"But what if her illness persists?" The emerald flecks in his eyes glinted against his amber irises like they always did when he was curious.

Her fingertip drifted over his shoulder. "I'll talk to Dr. Bellamy once I arrive. That's what Dr. Olek recommended."

"Is that her personal doctor?"

She nodded before flinging herself back onto the sheets. "Linette lives with Jakob Coughlin. He's one of the richest men in Alpheios, and better suited to provide for her than me." She bit down on her inner cheek, drawing the taste of iron in her mouth. "I suppose I'll find a way to help, but she'll probably be annoyed if I stay long." How she could prove useful, Alina had no idea, but she would latch onto something once she arrived.

"Promise me something."

"What's that?"

He propped himself up on an elbow. "That you'll be careful. And that you won't go anywhere near Genodyne."

"Not planning on it." She nearly laughed. "I certainly won't bring Mandin anywhere near there."

He cocked his head. "You think Mandin's father will call off the rest of the Guardians?"

She averted her gaze to the nightstand. Kiean didn't know about her last interaction with Chance. She found no compelling reason to discuss how Chance had aided her escape from Genodyne. "I'll ask if he wants to see his son." Repositioning herself closer, she asked, "Are you jealous?"

His mouth hovered over hers. "No. I trust you."

She brushed her lips against his.

"But I don't trust him." His voice growled.

"Aurore will be my bodyguard." She grinned.

"Enough about him." His forehead wrinkled as he gazed down at her. "But your mother—" he shook his head. "You'll go to the ends of Eamine for the people you care about the most."

"And that's a bad thing?"

"What I'm saying is that I'd like you to return back here to Evesborough. That's my birthday wish. This is your home." He reached for the ring on her necklace, turning over the small gem in his hand. "And Mandin's home, too."

She held her breath as he examined the gemstone that shined with giltspar. While she'd rather he accompany her, perhaps a break from Evesborough would snap her perspective into place, and chase away her qualms about a ceremony. She could even bring back a proper birthday cake from the bakery, since she'd burnt his birthday dessert the previous year. Cooking just wasn't in her DNA.

Her shoulders relaxed. "Well then, we agree. I'll tend to my mother, and you tend to the reactor. And I'll return by your birthday with more pillows."

He raised an eyebrow at her.

"I'll be careful. I promise." Her head sank back against the cushions.

His arm snaked under her torso, and he flipped her on top of him.

She squealed. "Are you trying to keep me from going?"

He traced her collarbone with a hand. "No, you're free to go. After I get one more good-bye."

As her leg glided across his body, a speaker crackled overhead.

"Kiean, report to the reactor room." Macy's voice meted out the command.

His head fell back. "It's the chieftain."

Alina watched as he threw his shirt over his broad shoulders and down his cut torso. She wanted to stay hidden away with him in the captain's suite a little longer. The polished furniture was arrayed comfortably along the walls, a welcome reminder of modern comforts.

A half-smile tugged at the corner of his lips. “What are you looking at?” He approached her side of the bed and draped his arm across her.

“Remember, you said yourself that I’ll go to the ends of Eamine for the people I care about the most.” She placed her hand over his. “That includes you. So please don’t worry about us.”

His face softened, and he sealed his departure with a kiss. The door quietly closed behind him.

She remained longer, allowing the warmth of his side to permeate her skin. The sheets still carried his scent, like the air after a fresh rain. Eventually, she flung off the covers and headed to the bathroom.

The shower contained a dressing area and tiled bench for relaxation. Their cavern home only held a small tub. As the hot water streamed over her, she remembered Linette singing to her while playing the keyboard. At six-years-old, she’d clung to her mother’s lap, entranced by her melodic voice, and the beautiful glow of Linette’s face while her mother sang a single refrain over and over.

Come back to me
So I can hold onto you my lovely
You’re my hope and my pride
My darling by my side
As long as you come back to me.

Alina closed her eyes as the shower drowned out all other noise. Tilting her head up, she allowed the water to drum down on her face, washing away the burning in her eyes. By the time she’d turned ten, she never heard that song from her mother again.

Chapter 5

Alina reached up and flipped a switch on the roof panel of the Spartan.

"I'll take care of it." Aurore examined the lit instrument from the pilot seat, her feline face wrinkled from concentration. "Your boyfriend was very specific on the checklist sequence." She pushed her black bang swoop out of her brown eyes.

"He's my intimate," Alina corrected her old classmate. "I'll check our supplies." She left the cockpit and made her way aft. She nearly bumped into her brother who slid onto a contoured bench wrapped around a table.

In the kitchenette, the cabinets held beverages and meals for their overnight journey to Alpheios. She turned a knob on a kitchen spigot to make sure they had running water. A few towels were available in the tiny shower. Their duffel bags were stowed underneath the bunks inside the wall cabinets, and she thumped each door, making sure they were secure.

In her own bag, she unzipped a quick access compartment to double-check its contents. Inside, she'd nestled extra packets of Mandin's herbal brew used to suppress his seizures, and his emergency seizure kit. She'd stashed plenty to ensure they didn't run out during their stay.

Satisfied they brought the required essentials, she

descended the ramp and gazed around the cavern one last time. Nearby, Mandin played with little Hudson, close to his own age. Ione watched the two toddlers, her brown hair cascading down her back.

Alina approached and said, "I'll bring back some fructose blocks for you and Cinda. Your pies are a big morale booster around here."

A gentle smile graced her friend's face. "You focus on your mother. I hope your presence brings her comfort."

She managed to avoid a grimace. "I'll try to return soon."

Ione tilted her head, her chestnut eyes resting on her. "She needs you. Nevertheless, we'll miss you and Mandin." She embraced her, and Alina allowed her chin to sink into her friend's soft shoulder. Ione often watched Mandin while Alina mapped new areas in their cavern and the surrounding desert. Tasty cooking aromas always lingered in her home, and she would invite them over at mealtimes.

Through the crowds, Macy emerged. The chieftain of Evesborough wore an embroidered gold sash trimmed in purple thread. A pattern of the distinctive bloomsun plant composed of trefoil leaves graced its fabric, a major herb used for health and longevity. Slung over Macy's gown, the sash signaled her authority. As the elder, she was selected as the village chieftain by an overwhelming majority of the Origins after they'd arrived.

"After Aurore conducts the pre-flight, we'll be headed out," Alina said.

"I'm sorry to hear your mother is sick," Macy said. "If you must stay for a while, we understand."

Alina tugged down the sleeve of her freshly cleaned

climate suit. "I may be back sooner than you realize." Her mother wouldn't tolerate her presence for long, and the feeling would be mutual. Instead, her plan was to reacquaint Mandin with his grandmother and speak with Dr. Bellamy. Then run an errand or two for her mother before she returned for Kiean's birthday.

Macy reached for her hand and pushed a small satchel into it. "For your mother."

Alina opened the pouch, revealing dried, grassy buds and a small tin.

"Dandlemane," the chieftain replied. "It helps soothe skin irritation. Immerse the herb in some warm oil overnight and add a few drops to the salve before you use it. That makes it more potent."

"Thank you. This is perfect." *Errand completed*, Alina thought. Her mother would love anything that could improve her beauty. Alina opened her thigh pocket and stuffed the pouch into it. Across the cavern, the Triumph's internal lights dimmed from generator power. "We'll bring back more essentials. Additional spices and different food blocks for variety." She smiled at her old mentor.

The village elder appraised her. "If you insist." Her head turned and followed the crowds that gathered near the fading daylight of the cavern entrance. "A power outage is never easy to contend with. Thankfully, it's mild enough for us to spend the days outside, but impatience will grow over time." Her gaze rested on Alina's necklace. "Thank you for leaving Kiean with us. He's a tremendous help."

"Of course." Alina gave her a tight smile. She thought she'd tucked her necklace inside her suit, but the collar formed a comfortable gap in front of her throat. "I know how much everyone relies on him. But you'll see—we'll be back before you know it."

The head of Evesborough tilted her chin down. "Our fate can be complicated by unattended wounds. To heal the future, one must confront the past."

"Meaning?" At times, she found it frustrating that Macy would speak in such opaque terms. As far as Alina was concerned, fate was illusory. Her choices would decide her future.

Macy smiled. "Good luck and have a safe flight. Be careful in Alpheios."

Alina hoisted Mandin in her arms. He was drooling, and crumbs surrounded his mouth. No doubt Ione had given the boys a tasty biscuit while they played.

Jostling him, Alina wandered forward and searched the crowd. Around the front of the x-craft, Kiean materialized, checking under the ship. His hand wrapped around certain surface attachments, tugging them. Mandin made a squealing noise when he saw him.

Her intimate half approached and wiped off her son's mouth with his sleeve. "You're all fueled up. I programmed the flight path. You'll skirt the edge of the active lava fields."

"But it'll take longer to get to Alpheios."

"Safer though if Aurore needs to divert for any reason. The AI will help with any changes." His arm reached up to grab a metal bracket overhead. "The ship will drop under surveillance coverage once it enters Alpheios's airspace. You'll land at the edge of the forest by the old mine a few kilometers from Old Town. It's a good place to hide the ship."

"Once I hear it's safe to enter the city, we'll take the rover through the woods direct to the penthouse," she replied. A saving grace of Linette's and Jakob's home was that it was located at the opposite end of the city from Genodyne.

Alina examined Mandin in his usual tunic, pants, and slip-on booties. She made a mental note to find him a climate suit like other city children. He possessed one warm hand-sewn jumpsuit and jacket that she'd packed for him. "At least we won't have to contend with gamma storms this time of year. Just the freezing winter."

"It's not deep winter there, yet. Message me when you arrive," Kiean said.

"Check the bridge," she replied, referring to the main hovercraft. While their links would remain out of range, the two ships had the ability to receive messages from one another using Eamine's magnetic field. Mandin abruptly leaned forward from her hold, his weight throwing her forward. Kiean hoisted him into his arms.

"Da-da, trip. You come on trip with us," her son said.

She fell quiet while Kiean smoothed back Mandin's curls. "I have to stay and fix the reactor. Your mother and uncle will take good care of you."

"But why you don't come with us?" Mandin asked.

"I'll see you again soon, buddy. Then we'll go on one of our hikes. You like hikes, right?"

Mandin's wide smile took over his face. "Yeah, I like the hikes." He giggled softly.

Gently, she pulled him back. "Say good-bye to Kiean." Her voice cracked. Soon she'd have to tell her son about his biological father, somehow.

Kiean's hazel eyes formed a questioning look. "Do I get a kiss?"

She took in his appealing features, tempted to ask him to accompany her once more. Instead, she nodded her assent.

His hand rested on her shoulder. “Do me a favor.”

“What’s that?”

“If the city situation worsens, just head back to the Spartan and take off. Get out of there.”

“We’ll be careful.” She lingered in his embrace. For a moment, she stayed rooted, not wanting to leave. When they separated, a slight tug weighed on her neck.

Kiean untangled her necklace with care, and his fingers slid the ring underneath her suit to her relief. “Would be a shame if this caught on anything onboard.” His palm laid flat over her chest. “So keep it close where it matters.” He ran his thumb across her sternum, giving her a flutter.

Her gaze lingered on his tender smile. Blinking, she turned her head away. A picture flashed in her imagination of getting stuck in molasses if she didn’t leave that moment. “I won’t be gone long.” Gordo waited for her up the ramp, and she joined him. Quickly, she hit the button to raise the apparatus.

She fastened Mandin’s seatbelt around him, placing him next to Gordo by the table. Another nutrient biscuit for her son would help keep him occupied. Up in the cockpit, she took station in the co-pilot seat next to Aurore. Her friend began taxiing out, following Kiean’s arm motions. He waved a marshaling light wand to guide them out.

When they cleared the cavern, Alina took one final look at Kiean. He stood out on the plateau, the breeze blowing his bronze hair crosswind. He winked at her and smiled. Aurore chuckled, and Alina could not help but grin. She waved to him, and he gave her a thumbs up before heading back to the mouth of the cavern.

Aurore set the auto-pilot controls. The ship vibrated during their short take-off, a sensation that Alina loved and hadn't felt since she left the academy. It only took a few seconds for the cavern to disappear, hidden safely from prying eyes. The first sun dipped low enough to touch the horizon.

The sunset broke over the barren tundra, casting blood-orange rays across the sky. Next to her Aurore chattered, running through the checklist. "Clear back in Alpheios. Just a meter of snow."

"We'll be back before the blizzards." A sip of water from her canteen helped chase away Alina's jitters. Soon the setting sun appeared on the pilot side of the x-craft as they headed north, and she studied the instruments. A swift trip would allow her to fulfill her obligations before returning back to Evesborough where she and Mandin belonged.

****

The interior lights dimmed late into the night. Alina crept into the Spartan's small kitchen to fetch a drink. Bringing the cup to her lips, the water sloshed over her suit as a pocket of turbulence hit the aircraft. She took a quick swallow, then set it down in the sink. Another bump rocked the craft, and she grabbed the edge of the counter. The aircraft shook.

Holding onto different surfaces, she stumbled back to the crew compartment. Mandin's long eyelashes were shut, and his chest gently rose as he lay asleep in his bunk. She clipped the bunk belt over him and left the night light on. As she stood, the Spartan's walls trembled. Bracing her legs, she left her compartment.

In the next cabin, the door swung open. Gordo poked his head out. "Is it supposed to be this bumpy?"

"I'm about to check. Do you mind staying with Mandin?"

As Gordo slipped into her room, she made her way up to the cockpit, pausing every so often as the aircraft was jostled in flight.

Blackness surrounded the windshield, and a rain of small particles pattered over the glass. Aurore peered at the monitor. A mass of wavy, red arrows flowed toward them on the weather radar.

"What is it?" Alina asked.

"Looks like a dirty ice front. We're running into a headwind flowing over the Hesperian mountains." Aurore checked the instruments. The Spartan flew a low-altitude route to terrain mask against the surveillance systems in Alpheios. They were one hundred meters above the ground.

"But we should be clear of winter storms, especially this time of year." Alina buckled herself into the copilot seat.

The patter of pellets intensified into a drumming onto the windshield. "It's high winds. Normally not a problem, but the snow melt mixes with heavy amounts of rock fragments on some of these ridges." Aurore scooped her bangs out of her eyes. "As it forms into ice, if the wind conditions are right, it starts carrying off the top few layers of muck, spewing a steady stream into the air. It can happen suddenly."

The AI's female voice interrupted them. "Foreign object damage detected in engine one. Engine one still at ninety percent thrust, but I advise deviating from the programmed flight path to clear the area as soon as possible to prevent further engine damage."

Aurore asked, "Lexi, how long will the front last on current heading?"

"By my estimate, until we clear the range, another twenty minutes. There's high risk that one, if not both engines, will suffer worsening functionality."

Alina's stomach leapt as the aircraft bounced. She keyed the intercom. "Gordo, buckle up. We're headed into serious turbulence."

Their flight path tracked over the terrain map on the monitor. "We can set down over the eastern edge of the lava fields." She pointed to the location, remembering Kiean programmed the flight path to give them a divert area. "The fields are inactive there, and we can wait for this to pass."

Her friend frowned. "The winds are from surface level up to ten thousand, so even if we touch down, there's still crud flying everywhere."

"But we can slip the aero covers over the engines." The drumming on the windshield turned into hail, and small rocks pelted the surface, obscuring their vision. Alina's arms tingled, and she gulped. *Work the problem,* she thought. They'd have to place the windshield cover on as well, which meant one of them would have to climb on top of the aircraft.

"You don't want to go outside in these conditions. Gusts are slightly over one hundred knots." Aurore chewed on her lip. "Hang on."

Alina turned to her. "What are you going to do?"

"Lexi, plot new course to Alpheios, high altitude to clear the range and this layer."

The monitor illuminated a string of light points in front of her. "New path calculated to avoid current weather conditions. We'll arrive about fifteen minutes ahead of schedule. Shall I execute?" Lexi asked.

Aurore said, "It's going to be a steep climb. Ready?"

"But won't surveillance detect us on approach to Alpheios?"

Her friend pressed her lips together. "If we don't get through this soon, the engines may be too damaged to return."

Swallowing, she glanced back at the divert location on the map. They were nearing the nav point rapidly, and given their airspeed, it was likely Lexi would take a sharp bank to turn them east.

A cockpit warning alarm sounded. The master caution light flashed yellow.

"More foreign object damage detected in engine one," Lexi said. "Engine at eighty percent thrust."

"We have to change the flight path before engine two gets hit," Aurore said.

Alina thought of Mandin still in his bunk. Neither she nor Aurore could hand fly well enough to terrain mask or land. They would be reliant on the AI. "Go ahead with the climb."

"Lexi, new flight path approved. Execute now." Aurore said.

"Copy, captain. Changing to new flight path. Please make sure you're buckled in."

Weight pressed on Alina's chest as they ascended. She inhaled a deep breath. A rock smacked into the windshield as the engines screamed, and the throttles moved forward. The aircraft shuddered as it climbed.

She held her breath. More rocks whacked against the fuselage. The Spartan bumped during its ascent, and the seat harness tightened around her. Her leg muscles strained. Finally, the pressure on her torso eased as they leveled out. The dark silhouette of the mountains appeared underneath them.

"All clear." Aurore eased out a breath. "Hope you have that letter ready for Chance."

"Of course I have it ready." Alina chewed her inner cheek. She wasn't sure how Chance would react to her note.

Chapter 6

Chance examined the projected message on his sleeve. The green letters glowed against his dark uniform. He clicked his link, turning it off. He glanced at Rufalo outside the glass doors of the director's office within Genodyne. "I want profiles of potential suspects sent to me as soon as they have any leads."

"I'll ask HQ to put together a lookout message," Rufalo replied.

"Good. Add any previously arrested protestors to the BOLO alert." Chance pointed at Rufalo's chest. "From this point on, no uncleared personnel around the chancellor. Tighten up visitor inspection protocols and vet everyone."

The message correlated with recent daily SITREPs. Small bands of angry residents still confronted patrols, throwing objects at them, and then running off.

Chance swept by the assistant manning the front desk in the waiting area and headed straight into the director's office. Inside, the spacious room held a small sitting area by a floor-to-ceiling window with a view of the waterfall. At the other end, his mother perched on a high-backed chair facing Dr. Daxmen behind his desk. Daxmen slumped back.

"Chancellor—" Chance said.

"A minute." His mother held up her hand, not taking her eyes off the doctor. "And Ash?"

Daxmen used a stylus to point at a translucent screen. “He’s experiencing GvHD, or graft-versus-host-disease from the second bone marrow transplant. The transplanted stem cells are attacking his body. I’ve adjusted his medication, and we’ll monitor him.”

Chance masked his face in stone to hide his disdain. After his mother publicly blamed the previous director, Ms. Silver, for Phase Three setbacks, Genodyne’s board replaced her with Dr. Daxmen, a man Chance deemed a chameleon who’d readily adapt to any situation in order to save his own skin.

She drew in a deep breath. “And Kora’s babies?”

“Chancellor, we have a situation.” Chance kept his tone respectful but firm. “I need to speak with you.” He wasn’t in the mood to sit by her side for another twenty minutes while she ran through an extended discussion with the doctor. Not when more important matters required her immediate attention.

Her lips twisted down. “Very well.” She followed him to a sitting area. “What is it already?”

He stood by the window. Outside, ice slurries were forming on the river in the gray afternoon. Lowering his voice, he said, “There’s been a political manifesto made public from a group that calls itself the Citizens Liberation Front. They’ve made several demands which if not fulfilled, will be met by violence.” He grabbed his baton’s handle. “They want the stability orders lifted. They also want you and the entire board here at Genodyne to resign immediately, to be replaced by their own representatives. That’s not all—they’re demanding a cure be made available to the entire city for free.”

“I don’t negotiate with fanatics.” Her tone hardened. “Find out who’s behind the manifesto and arrest them for treason."

She turned back toward the doctor, but Chance placed a hand onto her arm.

"Mother, this is a credible threat. The manifesto was found in the assembly room, just twenty meters away from your office. The fact they were able to slip through our regular security protocols is worrisome." He loosened his grasp once he had her full attention.

Her mouth twitched. "Don't we have cameras in the building?"

"We've tried reviewing the footage but there was some sort of interference that day which made large portions of the video useless. In the meantime, I've changed all the access codes to the building. You must take this threat seriously." He lowered his voice. "It could be an insider."

Her brown eyes narrowed. "Do you have leads?"

"Not yet, but the minute I do, you'll know."

She stroked her chin and stared thoughtfully out at the tumbling falls. "There are certain council members who would love nothing more than to take over my position. But not many who would have the guts to carry out such a threat."

He slid closer. "I've already asked Commander Zinyon for help. He has detailed one of his internal security officers to me."

"Keep me informed. I should also pay a visit to Commander Zinyon. See what further assistance his force needs."

"He would appreciate that. But we'll still have to tighten security around you." Chance's arm brushed his microwave pistol.

A weary expression crossed her face. "How so?

They already escort me to work."

He appraised his petite mother. While she wore boots, he was still a head taller. "We'll need to plus up security at your residence."

"But I already have a guard in the lobby." She pushed back her short hair. "I rather like my privacy."

"We need to place guards at your side."

"Outside the door." She folded her arms. "What else?"

Chance exhaled. He could stay at her home but decided guards outside her door would do. The only few hours he spent apart from her was at his own place. "I think you should take the group's demand seriously to make the treatment available for free."

She dropped her arms. "Genodyne won't agree to that. Not with the losses they're already facing."

He glanced back at Daxmen across the room. An urgency flowed into Chance's voice. "Then you *make* them agree. Genodyne launched Phase Three before it was ready. How many people have already died?" He swept his arm at the frigid river beyond the window.

She flicked at something indiscernible on her lapel. "Hundreds so far. But Genodyne paid those families a stipend and discontinued the product line."

"But thousands are already deformed, and more will eventually die. So once Genodyne has a treatment, make it free. It'll lower the temperature and nip any further support for this group. And it makes you look magnanimous as the leader of Alpheios." He waited, allowing the last sentence to take effect.

His mother rubbed a finger along her chin. "I might be able to convince the council to fund the treatment. First, we need an effective serum." Her eyes drilled into his. "Which we're in the middle of developing. Come along. You should listen to this."

"I have to concentrate on your security."

"Allow Rufalo to handle the security details. You're my aide, thus, I consider you an advisor. This way." She lanced the air with her finger in the direction of the desk.

"One second." He exited the room and gave the sergeant additional instructions. Back in the office, Chance rejoined his mother and Dr. Daxmen.

The doctor tapped the glass with his stylus. "The pregnancy kept Kora healthy, like we'd hoped. She's resting now that she's delivered the babies."

Video of the secret laboratory revealed the master bed and a cushioned bassinet nearby. Kora lay on her side, her hand stroking three tiny infants inside the bassinet.

Chance squinted. "They're so small." He could fit one of them within his palm.

"Yes, but they'll grow quickly. Two appear healthy, but one is struggling," Daxmen replied.

"Which one?" his mother asked.

"The smallest one. Poor blood circulation."

Chance spotted the infant on the monitor. At the end of the bassinet closest to Kora, a gray krono-baby cried, its fists waving. Two larger siblings wiggled awake next to it, their skin appearing healthier with a pewter glint peculiar to the species.

"Ash is feeding them, but the infant may not survive, even with intervention," the doctor said.

"Do you know what's wrong with it?" his mother asked.

"Underdevelopment of its pulmonary system." Daxmen scratched his flabby jawline. He then waved to a nearby silver cooler behind his desk. "I have his sample right here for testing."

Several vials were visible through the cooler's glass door. They contained a purple-crimson fluid. "Any chance the blood withdrawal damaged it?" Chance asked.

"I aimed for her womb. I was careful to avoid the fetuses." Daxmen's voice took on a defensive tone.

"Does she know that?" Chance raised his chin at the screen where Kora lay.

Daxmen's posture grew rigid, and he addressed the chancellor. "The withdrawal showed Kora's stem cells have great potential, but we need more self-renewal before we can replicate it on a mass scale for regenerative purposes."

"Meaning?" his mother asked.

The doctor tapped his stylus on the table. "The infants are rich in stem cells. If this one doesn't make it, we can use it by injecting its fluid back into her to give her a boost. That greatly increases the probability of a successful cure for those who took the preliminary product."

Chance recoiled at the suggestion. "Mother, that's high risk." Kora's anger nearly disabled one of his men.

The chancellor rubbed her forehead. "But if the baby dies…"

"She'll never forget it." He gestured at the monitor. "Think about that." While Chance didn't care about the kronosapiens, Daxmen's suggestion would cause unpredictable problems for his mother to deal with in the future.

The doctor shot back. "But it could help our own kind who are already sick."

Chance glared at him. While the blame had fallen on Ms. Silver for the initial Phase Three product, Daxmen was no better. The doctor was an ambitious conniver, and Chance relished the thought of punching him across one of his wobbly cheeks.

"Enough." His mother waved a hand. "The baby may live. We'll monitor it for the time being. In the meantime, prepare more bone marrow for Kora and Ash."

Daxmen twirled the stylus in his hand. "We have two sows left as potential donors. But we should wait and see if Ash can accept his current transplant before we try it on Kora. It's possible he'll overcome the GvHD."

On the screen, Ash appeared fatigued, although he propped himself up on the pillows, watching over Kora and his offspring. She handed him one of the babies to suckle.

"But you said we have two sows left," his mother said.

"Right, but if we do a transplant, we'll have to rule out gestating any other kronosapiens in the near term and freeze the rest of the krono-eggs. We went through nearly ten sows for these two to survive the lot." The doctor tapped the stylus on the table. "We must keep the remaining sows for reproduction and therapeutic purposes. For *us*."

"I understand." His mother rose. As Chance followed, Rufalo approached him. "Sir, the escort is ready around back. On heightened alert."

"Good. And her PSD?"

"Two men should be at her apartment upon her arrival."

His mother waited in front of the elevator. "Oh,

there's one more thing."

"Even more good news?" Chance punched the elevator button. He wanted to leave the bleak building.

She angled her chin. "An expeditionary aircraft has returned to the outskirts of the city. Quite unexpectedly since there was no flight plan, and the last record of its identifier was three years ago. They didn't respond to our calls. We're not sure who's on it, but I thought you should know."

Her words resonated in his ears. Could it be that Alina was onboard, bringing Mandin with her? Maybe she wanted to return home. Chance gave his head a slight shake. From his mother's serious expression, she was telling the truth.

"Thank you," he said.

She exhaled. "Now, don't get your hopes up. But it may—"

The elevator chimed and the doors opened.

"I'll take it from here." He held his palm over the edge of the door. Once his mother stepped in, Chance gestured for Rufalo to join them. As the elevator doors closed, Chance smiled at the first piece of good news he'd received in a long while.

Chapter 7

Snow blanketed the clearing around the Spartan, muffling any sound. Trees lurked like gray frost creatures as the first sun remained hidden behind the overcast sky. In the first few minutes of morning, Alina observed the lull, a breath of quiet before the sun's twin would join it. Beyond the woods, the city of Alpheios lay.

From the front of the aircraft, Aurore emerged. "Looks like the engines are fine. We can take off whenever we need to."

"You made the right call."

"I did what was necessary." Scanning the woods, she said, "Time to pull out the rover." Aurore traipsed up the ramp. She'd keyed a bunch of static into the mic when Alpheios control tried to hail them.

Alina stayed near the end of the ramp, gazing around. If control tracked them, they didn't send anyone to investigate. Maybe they simply thought it was an academy mission, given the Spartan's transponder codes.

She'd forgotten how the cold winters of Alpheios felt against her cheeks, like the burn of a razor if she stood still long enough. The snow touched the bottom of her calves.

Nearby, puffs of moist air left Mandin's mouth. He needed waterproof boots, but she acquiesced in allowing him to explore the area at his first sight of snow. They'd landed in darkness and chose to rest before daylight.

She turned up the heat on her collar while remaining alert. The rover rolled down the back ramp silent. Its engine off, her friend took the wheel with Gordo on the passenger side. She and Aurore donned expeditionary suits to deal with the climate outside.

When the rover came to a rest, Aurore gave Gordo instructions on its controls. The rugged vehicle could seat the four of them, but Alina had decided that Gordo would deliver her letter to Chance while she waited for a reply.

She pulled the small envelope from her thigh pocket and fingered its edges. It took her time to contemplate what to write. In the end, she restrained the hostility flowing from her fingertips and kept the message brief:

Chance,

I've recently arrived outside Alpheios city limits. Mandin is with me and is doing quite well as an inquisitive three-year-old. I've returned under rather unfortunate circumstances since my mother is ill. I ask that you allow us safe passage through the city so we can visit Linette. We can arrange a visit between you and Mandin during our stay if you so desire. Gordo will provide me your response should you have one.

Alina

Nearby, Mandin threw up a flurry of snow, laughing. She hadn't yet informed him of the identity of his real father, waiting to probe Chance's reaction to her letter first.

Aurore swished through the snow. "The curfew just lifted. Gordo will take the rover into the city."

Alina was tempted to tear up the letter. She wished

she could skip dealing with Chance. "And we're stuck waiting in the meantime."

Her petite friend shrugged. "We'll wait onboard the aircraft. If Gordo doesn't get an all clear by the last sunset, we take off."

Mandin brought his hand to his mouth and tasted the snow. He had removed his gloves. Alina bit the inside of her cheek. "Assuming Chance answers."

Aurore placed her hands on her hips. "He'll answer. Unless…" Her gaze narrowed. "You didn't insult him in the letter, did you? Maybe I should take a look at it."

Alina clutched the letter by her side. "I'm not dense." As she strode past, her friend snatched the envelope.

"Hey!" Alina lunged and grabbed the air as Aurore held the letter out of reach. "Give that back!"

Aurore flashed through the snow as Alina gave chase. Mandin chortled and ran after them, thinking it was a game. Alina's head verged on exploding. "Not funny!" She stomped a boot. But the little pixie was too fast. Aurore opened the letter behind the ramp. Her mouth hung open. "Gordo will provide me your response should you have one?"

Upon reaching her, Alina seized the letter out Aurore's hand. "Direct is best. And besides, Chance prefers honesty."

"Mama, look!" Mandin threw up a handful of snow.

"That's direct all right." Aurore tilted her head. "Have you thought of asking Chance how he's doing?"

Alina grabbed Mandin, and he squealed, protesting. "He's doing well. I'm sure of it." Her voice snapped. She hauled her son onto the walkway to examine his booties. They appeared soaked, and she wiggled a finger into the top of one. "We'll have to change your socks."

Mandin whined but she hoisted him onboard the ship.

Aurore was the only one who knew about her last encounter with Chance at Genodyne. Her friend gave her a curious look when Alina mentioned that he allowed her to slip away, but Aurore said nothing at the time.

As Alina heaved Mandin on the bunk and wrenched off his boots, his cheeks became wet. "Mama, I wanna go outside!" He sniffled while she rolled dry socks onto his feet. "I want to play in the snow. Please Mama! I be good."

She squatted by her son's feet. Mandin's nose ran. His mouth trembled.

Wiping his face with her thumb, she quieted her voice. "There's no need for such a fuss. You don't want to catch a cold, do you?"

"I not cold." Through the watery sheen in his dark eyes, sincerity shone through. "I warm, Mama. Please. Can I play outside?"

She rubbed his fingertips. "Mandin, your hands are like ice."

"But I not cold. I warm." His jacket and trousers shielded him against the wind, and his thick socks protected his feet. But his booties were made for trekking across a rocky desert with limited tolerance for moisture.

A sigh escaped from her, and she brushed a curl from his forehead. His face resembled his father's. "You do like the snow, don't you?"

He nodded at her, sniffling.

"Why don't I try to find you better boots? And a climate suit?"

Instantly, he perked up. Perhaps Gordo could bring

back cold-weather boots for Mandin upon his return. Although she'd have to entertain an energetic three-year-old onboard the craft while they waited. She reached for an extra pair of his shoes.

Asking Chance to grant a favor ate away at her insides. Maybe he wouldn't answer. She resolved at that moment that she didn't fly all this way to turn back around. Chance or no Chance, she'd find a way to visit her mother.

Boots thunked on the metal floor behind her.

"We've got company. It's the Guardians," Aurore said breathlessly.

Alina sprang up. "Can we take off?"

"They're already here!" Aurore dashed upfront toward the cockpit.

Bringing her fingers to her lips, Alina shushed Mandin. "Be very, very quiet. I want you to hide." His eyes widened as she wrenched open a nearby floor panel. "Here. Lie down and don't make a sound." It took a long time for her nightmares to stop about Genodyne wrenching him away from her arms when he was a baby. Her son shrank into the small storage area.

"Don't come out until you hear me."

"I hide." He huddled inside the floor.

She shut the floorboard and exited their quarters. Who would take care of Mandin if they hauled her away? She still had the letter and could insist one of the officers deliver it to Chance.

Slowly, Alina approached the open door. They couldn't take off with the ramp down. Her body flattened against the craft's interior hull. Male voices conversed outside. She recognized Gordo's voice. The phrase, "recent expedition" came from him.

The control button to raise the ramp rested on the other side of the opening. Aurore would surely be ready to raise it from the cockpit if given the opportunity.

Carefully, Alina poked her head out. Two officers were speaking to Gordo while another one walked toward the front of the craft. Behind the rover, the Guardians parked two all-terrain cruisers. One of the officers looked in her direction, and she quickly drew her head back in. A few seconds later, footsteps plodded up the ramp.

She dashed back to the kitchen. Upon landing, they had agreed that an expedition cover story made the most sense if anyone wanted to investigate them. She heated a kettle on the stove top just as the officer appeared.

He was young and wore a winter uniform cap. Its dark edges covered his ears but still flashed the Guardian insignia above its brim.

"Ma'am, how are you doing today?"

She put on a cheery expression. "Morning, officer. I was just making tea. Would you like some?"

He replied, "I'm Lieutenant Harding. Did you land recently?"

Leaning back, she kept her hand on the counter, inches away from the kettle. "Oh, I was asleep when we landed. Dreary outside, isn't it?" She'd been wide awake when they landed but sought to avoid giving away details.

If he moved to arrest her, throwing the kettle of scalding water in his face would buy her a few seconds. She'd sprint in the direction of the ramp, giving her an opportunity to push him off the craft when he gave chase. Gordo could fight off the others before making a break for the ship, and Aurore could lift off.

"Control tried contacting your pilot late last night but didn't get a response." He studied her expeditionary suit. "You a member of the crew?"

She swallowed. "Yes. What can I do for you?"

"Do you mind accompanying me outside? With the rest of the passengers for questioning?" Lieutenant Harding cocked his head.

The kettle beeped, and the sound of boiling water emanated from it. She gave the lieutenant a tentative smile, thinking of Mandin underneath the floorboards. "Right away." She exited the kitchen quickly, leading the Guardian away from their quarters.

Aurore appeared from the front of the ship, trailed by another officer. Beneath her long bangs, her friend's intense gaze met hers.

Outside, Gordo was still talking to the other officer by the rover. "And I just arrived to greet them. Waited for the curfew to lift, of course."

She gave her brother a terse smile while the officer chuckled. "Any rogue ball practices for you?"

Gordo grinned. "Winter break."

"Think you'll still play receiver once the games start back up? You can sure run with that oval."

"And bust through those attacks," another officer said.

"I just drop my shoulder into 'em," Gordo replied.

Leave it to Gordo to chat up the officers about his rogue ball games.

Her brother turned to her. "Was telling the guys I brought your son to see you once you landed from mission."

Harding glanced at her. "Your child is with you?"

"Oh, you know kids." She waved in the direction of

the Spartan. "They get all excited when they see the craft, and he's exploring inside."

"Who's the commander of this craft?" he asked.

Aurore took a step forward. "I am. Didn't find much in the great desert, but we got to escape the freeze here."

"Can I get everyone off the ship?" Harding asked. "For accountability?"

Alina thought of Mandin huddled beneath the deck. "I'll grab my son. He's probably upfront by the cockpit."

She boarded the aircraft. Upon opening the door to their quarters, she halted. The floorboards were pushed to the side, and the hiding space was empty. "Mandin?"

Silence followed, and she called out a few times. But no sounds came from anywhere within their compartment. In the kitchen, the bottom cabinets only held serving bowls. The red light on the kettle had gone out. Maybe he really did go upfront like she'd mused. At the cockpit, the seats were empty.

Crap. Where was Mandin? Goosebumps prickled her arms. As she racked her mind, Aurore yelled from outside. Alina wandered out on the ramp.

"Alina!" Aurore held Mandin's arm as he squirmed. "He's out here!"

How on Eamine did she miss him running off the craft? A flush hit her cheeks, and she picked up Mandin.

"Ma'am, I didn't catch your name earlier?" the lieutenant asked.

"Alina." She gulped. Her first name meant nothing.

"Alina…" His brows raised.

Her son for once, did not squirm as he gazed at the officers surrounding them. "DeHerte," she replied.

Harding's face brightened. "Alina DeHerte? Captain Graylin sent us here to find you."

The back of her neck tingled. Chance knew of her presence. They weren't sent to arrest her. But then why were they interrogating them? "How can I help?" she asked casually.

"Captain Graylin has asked that you and the rest of the passengers be escorted safely into the city. He would like a meeting with you." Harding flashed her a smile. "After you've rested from your journey, of course. But I'll take you wherever you'd like to go within city limits."

She blinked a few times. Aurore tried to suppress a smile. There was no need for the letter after all.

Gordo stepped forward. "We're going to our mother's. She lives in the Meander District. Care to follow us?" He gestured to the rover.

"Sure, if you're ready. Or—" Harding waved his arm in the direction of the Guardian vehicles "—if it's more comfortable for you, Ms. DeHerte, you can ride with us in one of the cruisers with your son."

Mandin squealed and tugged her sleeve. "Yes, Mama. Go for ride."

As she hesitated, Mandin became more insistent. She shushed him and decided it would be warmer in the Guardian cruiser. "Thank you. We'd like that."

"After you." Harding motioned to his cruiser. One of the other Guardians opened the rear door for her. She slid into the cushioned seats after Mandin bounced in. The Guardian shut the door.

She gazed around the vehicle. No grate separated her from the driver, and the distance between the rear-facing seats was rather roomy. Fizzy water bottles waited for them in the console. It was a distinguished visitor vehicle, aka, a DV cruiser, not a security one. The driver and lieutenant climbed into the front seats.

Her posture stiff, Alina leaned back into the seat and took in a breath to slow her heartbeat.

Harding's voice carried over to the back. "Just waiting for your captain to close up the ship and join in the lead car. We'll follow your brother."

Her mouth went dry. "Yes."

Mandin's little legs kicked along the seat. "We go for ride, Mama." His dark, star sapphire-like eyes shone, and he couldn't stop grinning.

She fastened the belt around his lap, trying not to think about why Chance had dispatched the patrol to look for her.

Chapter 8

The penthouse elevators opened. Alina stepped into the shiny hallway where diamond-shaped white tiles trimmed in bronze rested underneath her feet. The wallpaper had been redone in golden stripes with a long mirror lining the upper half of the corridor. It was a bit cool for Alina's taste compared to the temperate lobby they entered through. She turned up the heat on her suit collar.

Gordo carried their bags into the living area, an expanse containing gold-and-silver brocade couches and armchairs resting on a sand-patterned rug. Large, scenic tapestries of different views of the river hung on the stone walls to bring warmth to the room. Aurore had wanted to stay with her family so the Guardians had dropped her off prior to taking them to the penthouse.

Mandin wandered in the direction of the sofas but halted when a robot entered the room. He ran back and clutched her hand. She stroked his knuckles since it was his first run-in with a bot.

The silver bot was an advanced bipedal model with full hands and feet, unlike the clamps on older models. Undoubtedly another of Jakob's creations through his company, CynCorp. A curved screen wrapped around its head.

"Hello, Gordean," the female voice said. "I'm glad that you've safely returned. Who are our guests?"

Gordo gestured at them. “Alina and Mandin, meet Halle. She’s Mom’s personal assistant.”

A feminine face gazed at them from the monitor. “Hello, Alina and Mandin. Can I offer you a beverage or a snack?”

Mandin’s eyes enlarged like he saw a zephyr.

The bot was certainly more intelligent than the earlier models. “My son hasn’t had breakfast. Do you have a protein bar?”

“I understand it’s best for young children to have calcium. I can make him a dairy shake with protein. Would you like it sweetened?” Halle’s chin inclined toward Mandin.

He glanced at Alina who nodded. “Yes,” he said in nearly a whisper.

Alina stretched her neck. “Is Linette resting in her room?”

“Mrs. Caughlin is in the conservatory,” Halle replied. “She hasn’t taken visitors of late.”

It wasn’t lost on Alina that Halle used Jakob’s last name to address Linette. Her mother had married him after all. While Gordo’s earlier letters had mentioned it, her chest shrunk as she took the realization in.

Her brother said, “Halle, this is Mrs. Caughlin’s daughter and grandson. They’ve come a long way to see her.”

“I’ll check if there’s a good time to announce them.” The bot exited the room.

Gordo scratched his arm. “They married a few months after you left.”

A snort broke free from her. Of course her mother did. Linette usually did what she wanted. “A conservatory?”

"Jakob bought the other wing on this floor and renovated the entire penthouse for her." Gordo squeezed the strap of his duffel bag. "The humidity in the conservatory helps with her skin."

"Mandin and I should rest until Linette is ready." A tinge of sarcasm rolled over her words, and she crossed her arms.

"I'll show you to your room." Gordo carried their bags down the hall, and she and Mandin followed. "Mom will be happy to see you."

"I'm sure," she said under her breath.

Mandin clutched her hand, looking over his shoulder for the bot. His attention was diverted once Gordo opened the door to the guest bedroom.

Daylight streamed in, highlighting the silver bedding trimmed in blush. Pewter drapes remained open at the tall corner window, revealing the snowy riverwalk below. The Meander District was named for the broad curve in the winding river just beyond the banks. While the river in this location was not as fast-moving as the rapids area by the falls, the frigid water would still give someone hypothermia if they fell in. Mandin approached the mirrored chest-of-drawers, staring at his myriad of reflections among its different compartments.

"It connects to the guest bathroom." Gordo motioned to a door at the far corner of the room. "I can put his bag in the bedroom next door. It leads to the same bathroom if you need to access him in the middle of the night."

She turned in time to spot Mandin lifting open a blue beaded jewelry box on the dresser. "Don't touch that!" Her son breaking an expensive item was not the way she wanted to start her visit.

He snatched his hand away and wandered over to the periwinkle-padded bench at the foot of the bed. Mandin climbed onto the mattress and flopped on it, giggling.

"Mandin, you're still wearing your shoes."

He ignored her as he ran his hand over the fluffy bedspread.

She let out an exhale. "He won't sleep alone in a large bed. You can leave his bag here."

Gordo set their bags down by the closet doors. "Mom's room is down the hall at the corner. I'll let Jakob know you're here. He's probably in the study."

Before Alina could say she wanted to nap, he exited.

"Mama, how long we stay here?" Mandin asked.

Running her hand across the shiny bedding, she pondered an answer. "About a week." Or maybe less, she thought. A summer painting hung over the bed depicting the waterfall. The same waterfall that she nearly drowned during her last encounter with Genodyne. Maybe she could stow the painting in the closet when no one was around.

She unpacked their things, placing Mandin's clothes into the dresser. A silver frame by the nightstand gleamed. She picked it up.

The photo showed her father leaning back against a railing on the riverwalk. He held two-year-old Gordo in his arms. At age five or six, she clutched her father's hand as she pointed at the water. Her mouth was open, and the memory of her asking him questions about the river returned. Her fingers softly trailed over the edges of the photo. Her father's eyes would crinkle at the corners when he smiled.

"Hello, Alina."

Her back stiffened.

Slender with slick dark hair, Jakob possessed a smoothness about him as he stood at the room's entrance in a dark green templite sweater. His hands were in his trouser pockets. "A pleasure to see you again. Linette will be thrilled you're back. Is the room to your liking?"

Picking a speck off her sleeve she replied, "More than adequate. We won't require anything else." She motioned to Mandin, and he slid off the bed. "This is Mandin, now three years of age."

Linette's husband grinned and waved at him. "Hi, Mandin. I'm so glad you're here. Last time I saw you, you were just a baby." He held out his hands, palms facing one another, sizing a small object like a rogue ball. "I'm your Uncle Jakob."

She choked back an unpleasant taste in her mouth. Mandin's forehead creased as he exchanged glances between them. "Jakob is our host," she informed him. "Go say hello to him."

Her son marched up to him. "I'm Mandin."

Jakob held out his hand, and Mandin accepted it. Her son finally took to Kiean's teaching of the gesture. Her shoulders softened at Mandin's behavior, and she unfolded her arms.

"I'm impressed. That's a strong handshake you have there." Jakob gave him a cordial smile. "Are you hungry?"

"Halle is already making him a shake." She yawned and patted her mouth. "Afterward, he'll take a nap. I may join him."

"Mama, I hungry," her son replied.

The faint whir of a blender sounded somewhere at the other end of the penthouse.

"Come now, Halle can make the both of you a proper breakfast." Jakob gestured to the hall. "She can make you a crepe-thin or a riverside omelet. You'll find her meals quite tasty. What would you like? We have just about everything."

Mandin's expectant face thwarted her nap plan. "Breakfast would be delightful," she grumbled. The meals onboard the Spartan were infused with energy powder which gave all the dishes the same taste. "Omelet for me, please. And a fruit crepe-thin for him."

"Right away." Jakob wandered off.

Mandin stuck his head out the hall. "Will we see the robot?"

She opened the door to the guest bathroom. A spacious, tiled shower encased in glass greeted her. A deep bathtub rested next to it. "Wash your hands. Halle will serve breakfast."

As he made haste for the bathroom, she rolled her neck. They may as well enjoy the perks Linette and Jakob offered during their stay in Alpheios.

****

The sound of trickling water filled the conservatory. The air was temperate and damp. Natural light filled the large room through the carved slats in the outward-facing stone wall. Alina followed Halle along a mosaic path inlaid onto the floor, holding Mandin's hand. While he gawked at the sight of the azure foliage, Alina kept a grip on him. He wasn't used to this much vegetation back home, and she didn't want him running about. He would damage something she'd hear about later.

The space was meant to be soothing, but as she moved after Halle around a clump of leafy plants, her forearms tensed, and she kept Mandin close. They came upon a large fountain with a violet orb at its center, water pouring over the stone as it rotated. A few feet away in the corner where light spilled at her feet, Linette reclined on a chaise with a blanket pulled over her. Her eyes were closed, and her head turned to the side.

Alina shifted her weight to her other foot. "Hello, Mother."

Linette's eyes opened. When she turned her head in their direction, Alina sucked in a low breath. A hard, gray patch of skin covered her mother's right cheek. Pinker skin appeared along the length of her neck as if it had been scrubbed raw, although bits of scaly gray peeked through in spots. Her mother looked frail underneath the blanket.

Her eyes red and watery, Linette croaked. "Alina, you've come." She leaned forward, examining Mandin who stared back, then her hand flew up to the side of her face. "Halle, my hat, please."

"Of course, Madam. It's right here by your basket." The bot removed a halo hat from a wicker basket nearby. Linette immediately plopped it over her blonde hair and smoothed its mesh cover over her face. The back of her trembling hand was covered in the same gray scab.

Alina had prepared Mandin beforehand by informing him that her mother had a bad rash, but that he couldn't catch it upon touching her. Gently, she prodded him forward. "Say hello."

He took a few steps forward and smiled. "Hi, Nana."

Her mother's face brightened. "Me, Nana? I do like the sound of that." She held out her arms, and Mandin allowed her to embrace him. After squeezing him, her mother studied her. "You look…thinner. Have you been eating? And you look tired, too."

Alina gazed around the conservatory. Lush plants provided a tranquil atmosphere. The broad leaves were devoid of blossoms, though. Rather, the plants provided a gentle shield for whoever wanted to remain hidden within its garden.

Halle said, "I can bring out some vigor tea. Would you like that, Madam?"

Linette assented, and Halle left.

An extended pause stretched between them as Linette cuddled her grandson. The blue wooden frame of the chaise blended seamlessly into their surroundings. Its dimensions were designed in a custom-made fashion for her mother.

"You seem…comfortable. Your husband has provided you with everything you need." Her throat tightened, and she found herself looking more at Mandin.

Her mother's smile faded behind the veil. "Yes, we did marry. I know you weren't here, but it was a wonderful party. Where have you settled with my lovely—" Linette caught herself. "Where have you and Mandin settled?"

"There's a town in the desert. But we've made it our home." Alina grasped onto the question, wanting to avoid talk of the wonderful party.

As Mandin took a few steps toward the fountain, she said, "You can touch the water."

"The great desert?" Her mother placed a hand over her chest. "Why on Eamine did you go there? Gordean told me you were far away but safe."

"It's not that kind of desert." She faced her mother fully. "There's a cavern for shelter, and a flowing river."

"A cavern? You should have come to me sooner." Her mother plucked at her sleeves. "You can't raise

Mandin in a cave."

"Dad found it," she quickly replied. "And now it's a thriving community. Eamine doesn't revolve around Alpheios."

"I see." Linette stopped picking at her clothing, and her gaze shifted to Mandin who trailed a finger over the stone orb. "He looks like Chance, doesn't he? He's growing up to be just as handsome."

Alina's hands flinched. She focused on the sound of the fountain's trickling water, hoping it would soothe her.

"Have you thought about visiting Chance?" Her mother's voice held a soft yet probing tone.

"You would like that, wouldn't you?"

"Dear, I only want you to be happy." Linette adjusted the mesh in front of her face. "I seem to recall that Gordo said you had a paramour. Will you tell me about him?"

"Kiean is my intimate. We've been together for three years." Alina shifted her weight between her feet.

"And what's he like?"

She touched her collar but dropped her hand when she realized she was reaching for the ring. Her mother would instantly spot it and deduce Kiean's proposal. "He's a pilot. Hard-working, and kind to us." An urge to defend Kiean overtook her.

Her mother nodded in an approving manner. "That's important, isn't it?" Linette smoothed out the blanket over her lap. "That they make you feel *loved.*" Her mother peered through the veil.

Alina checked on Mandin who still held his hand up to the fountain. "He's also loyal, and a good role model for my son." She clamped her lips together. Not able to help herself, the remark flowed from her lips. Before she knew it, it came out as a comparison to her mother.

Linette exhaled. "You still possess that understated way of speaking, I see." She rubbed her arm with a scaled hand. "So why have you come now to visit me? To see if you could inherit anything after I'm gone? Don't worry, I've already asked Jakob to provide for you and Mandin in the event either of you ever returned to Alpheios."

Her words nicked Alina's face like a belt snapping. "I don't want your money. And don't talk like you won't even fight this disease."

"Then why are you here?" her mother demanded.

"I thought you'd like to see Mandin. And for him to get to know his grandmother." She fought to keep her voice even.

Her mother glanced at Mandin who played at the fountain, and a pained expression overcame her.

Alina reached inside her thigh pocket. "I also brought you this." She placed the tin of dandlemane balm that she'd prepared earlier on the side table by the chaise.

"What's that?" Linette scrutinized the tin.

"It may help with your rash."

"I'm not supposed to take anything without Dr. Bellamy's approval." Her mother held herself tight.

"Will you try it?" Alina gestured to the tin.

Her mother looked at it, unconvinced.

"What did the doctor say about your treatment?"

Linette quaked. "Dr. Bellamy will probably want to do another skin graft. But the procedure is rather unpleasant, and the pain medications make me nauseous."

Halle re-appeared carrying a tray. The bot set it

down on a side table. "Your tea, Madam."

Her mother didn't reach for a cup but rather drew the blanket close.

"But if the doctor recommends it, you'll do it, won't you?"

Linette removed her hat. She held it out to the bot and smoothed back her hair. Upon closer examination, the faint outline of another gray patch was forming on her mother's other cheek, and Alina understood then why her mother was spending so much of her time in the conservatory.

"Halle, I'm tired." Her mother lay back.

"Yes, Madam." Halle turned to them, and the bot's face behind the monitor formed a polite expression. "Mrs. Caughlin would like to rest now. I can make you and Mandin more tea if you'd like to accompany me to the dining room."

Her mother closed her eyes. Alina opened her mouth to speak but pressed her lips together. A burr lodged itself in her gut—this visit was proving more difficult than she thought. She grabbed Mandin's hand and followed the bot. Despite the beauty of the garden, her neck ached from rigidity, and she wanted nothing more than to leave the sanctuary.

****

Gordo poked his head into the dining room where Alina finished her fruit-and-protein tart for breakfast. "Dr. Bellamy is in Jakob's office. Want to hear the update on Mom?"

Alina wiped a smidge of yogurt off Mandin's chin and stifled a yawn at the long table with curved ends. She wiped off crumbs from the table. The sleek slab was inlaid with iridescent shingles reflecting the turquoise colors of Eamine's tumultuous oceans. She hadn't slept well with her son kicking her the previous night, despite the comfortable room Gordo placed her in.

"What do I do with him?" she asked, rather grumpy. There were too many expensive items in the penthouse he could break. Mandin's dark eyes gleamed, and no sight of any bags appeared underneath them. At least one of them slept well.

Halle who stood quietly in the corner of the room approached. "I can entertain him if you'd like." The bot's monitor flickered, revealing cartoons in place of her face. Mandin's mouth opened at the animation. He squealed as it played.

"Halle's good at that. He'll be okay," Gordo said.

"I'm programmed to entertain families and guests," the bot replied. "And I have additional safety protocols to keep humans, especially children, out of harm's way."

Alina pushed back her chair and rose. Following her brother out of the room and down the hallway, she rubbed her eyes. Down the tiled hallway her brother traversed, leading her to a corner room. He knocked before entering.

Inside, Jakob stood behind a sapphire-wood desk, gazing out the window at the city. A thin glass monitor with his company's logo, CynCorp, sat atop the massive bureau. Next to him stood a striking woman. Her platinum blonde curls cascaded down her back, gathered in a loose ponytail. "Gordo," the woman nodded before she set her luminous amber eyes on Alina.

Another Phase Two creation by the looks of her light-brown skin and slightly taller than average height. A rare gene combination, but the woman was stunning in her ivory climate suit. Alina realized that living with the Origins the past few years made the differences in appearance jarring. There were attractive types among the Origins, but not quite like this.

"Alina," Jakob said, waving her in. "I'm glad you've come. You slept well, I hope?"

She stopped in the middle of the room by a set of rounded chairs in front of his desk. Jakob stood with his hands in his pockets behind his desk, his posture relaxed. His silken shirt and pressed trousers were immaculate without any stray threads. Only the preoccupied expression in his eyes hinted at his worry.

She supposed her mother found his manners charming although Alina preferred her father's rugged looks and genuine smile. "I slept well, thank you." Faltering for anything more to say, she rested her hands on the back of the chair and squeezed the tufted material. She resisted going through the motion of exchanging pleasantries with him.

"This is Linette's daughter," he said to the woman. "Alina, Dr. Bellamy came over this morning to examine your mother. Why don't you sit down?" He gestured at the chairs. "You too, Gordo."

Her brother slowly took a seat and Alina joined him. The chair was rather comfortable against her back.

The doctor cleared her throat. "Linette's last skin graft hasn't yet fully healed, but the rash has already infected it. It's spreading faster now and will overtake the new graft soon."

"Is it a problem with the donor match?" Jakob asked.

"No. The match is fine. The disease has resurged, figuring a way to fight the new skin more effectively."

"What's next?" he asked.

Dr. Bellamy replied, "I can try another graft, but it's unlikely to work. It may, in fact, provoke a stronger reaction. I can't stop the rash from spreading now."

Alina said, "I have a dandlemane salve for her skin. I can give you a sample."

The doctor pinned her down with a stare. "Is that a herb?" A trace of skepticism lingered in her question.

"It has worked for skin ailments among the Origins." Alina straightened her posture and directed her remark to Jakob. "It can't hurt to try."

"The disease is persistent," the doctor replied.

"I'm open to anything at this point." Jakob gave Alina a grateful smile to her surprise.

"How long do we have until the rash takes over?" Gordo asked.

The doctor's voice shifted to a matter-of-fact tone. "In a few weeks, the rash will reach the point of no return once it spreads to her internal organs. Then Linette will have a month or two, at most. I can order some good medications for palliative care to make it more bearable for her."

"Palliative care?" Gordo's voice tapered off.

"It will make her more comfortable and lessen her suffering." The doctor noticeably swallowed. "I've tried everything in my toolkit. I'm sorry there's nothing more I can do." Her dark eyelashes lowered toward the ground.

The breakfast tart Alina ate gave her stomach a slight burn. "I'll get the dandlemane balm. Linette will take it if you recommend it."

Alina stood while Gordo hunched over. He stared at his shoes, his lips cramped together. She quietly shut the office door behind her as Jakob conversed in a low voice with the doctor.

Passing the dining room, she heard Mandin laughing at a rhyme Halle was chanting. She continued down the hall toward the bedrooms. In her guest room, the rest of the dandlemane balm sat in a small jar on top of the dresser. She'd followed Macy's instructions and used the entire packet of herbs, creating the tub of salve. Picking up the glass, she examined it. It looked like soap grease but smelled of nectar and Eamine, a rather calming scent.

She exited, but a noise came from the far corner wing. Slowly, she proceeded in its direction. In front of her mother's door, she raised her hand to knock. She would inform her mother that Dr. Bellamy would test the balm if it would help encourage Linette to take it. Another muffled noise stopped her.

Her nose nearly touched the door. A sniffle came through, as well as some ragged breaths. Her mother was softly sobbing.

Alina chewed her inner cheek. A ballast tugged down from deep within, tearing at her insides. She pivoted away and headed back to Jakob's study. Upon entry, she walked in as Dr. Bellamy was talking to Jakob.

"I heard from a colleague that Genodyne is testing a new serum that shows promise. I've already asked if they would consider human trials, but it's not quite ready. Told them you'd sign the appropriate paperwork, acknowledging the risk." She folded her arms over her chest. "That's our only other shot."

Clutching the jar, Alina stopped in front of her. "You trust Genodyne? It was their product that made her sick."

Dr. Bellamy spoke slowly. "I'm an independent doctor for a reason. But I've seen the preliminary test results. Their serum is working at the cellular level. It's worth a try."

Alina handed the jar to her. "Here's the balm." She glanced at Gordo. Her brother's chin tilted downward.

"I think I can get a sample of the serum," she said.

"How?" Jakob leaned against his bureau, his arms full of strain. "I've tried contacting everyone on the board I know. I'm getting a lot of sympathetic remarks, but all they say is, 'we're working on it'."

"There's one person the board will listen to." Alina took in a deep breath. "And that's the chancellor."

He straightened. "She used to take my calls but doesn't answer them anymore."

"She'll take her son's." Alina's hands curled into loose balls by her sides.

The doctor peered at her, an awareness overcoming her light-brown eyes as if she was measuring Alina for the first time.

Jakob's hands were on his hips. "Maybe we shouldn't mention this to Linette until you know for certain that you can get the serum. She's been through enough already."

Alina hadn't expected Linette's initial resistance to trying the balm. Perhaps her mother would balk at another intervention if she knew it came from her. "I agree. Now, if you'll excuse me, I need to contact the chancellor's son, who's also her aide."

Gordo's worried eyes met hers as she left. The lump in Alina's stomach ached, and she placed a hand over her belly. She would send a message to Chance as soon as she had a moment of privacy.

Chapter 9

Getting ready for Chance's visit that morning proved to be a nightmare. At first, Alina chose to wear her reliable, old climate suit. When her mother saw her in it, frown lines formed at the corners of Linette's mouth. Alina had informed her Chance was coming over to visit Mandin.

"Try honey for once, dear." Linette pulled her silk robe tight around her and waved wearily at her room. "I have some clothes."

A protest sprang to Alina's lips, but upon seeing the gray imprint on her mother's cheek, a pang developed under Alina's sternum. Later, after her mother departed for the conservatory, Alina admitted to herself that while her climate suit was perfectly functional, its seams were worn.

After rifling through her mother's racks of clothing for what seemed like an eternity, Alina settled on an emerald jumpsuit with a soft sheen. Chance used to like it when she wore green. Staring at her reflection in the mirror, Alina was filled with self-loathing and nearly tore the outfit off. But Mandin "aahhheed" when he saw her, telling her she looked pretty. *See mother?* she wanted to say. *I'm taking your advice. To use honey for once.* Closing her eyes, she let out a sigh. *So you can have the serum, too.*

As a show of defiance though, she wore the cord

with the ring Kiean gave her, visibly resting above the garment's V-shaped neckline. That was one item she would keep close, no matter the circumstance.

Shortly before Chance's visit, Alina waited on a gold-and-silver patterned couch in the living area. Mandin knelt at the gilded-mirrored coffee table, drawing on paper. Not used to the jumpsuit's soft material, Alina hoped she didn't sweat in it. The matching pointed mini-heels on her feet were her mother's as well. Rubbing the ring's stone between her fingers, she examined the silver keyboard at the long end of the living room. When had her mother obtained the instrument? Alina hadn't seen her mother play or sing in ages.

Gordo emerged, carrying a duffel bag over a shoulder.

"Where are you going?" She'd hoped Gordo would stay for the visit. He knew how to engage Chance and chat about rogue ball games.

"Arena gym," Gordo mumbled, his face pensive.

"The team's gym? I thought they were on winter break."

"I need to clear my head." His tone was clipped. "The facility is empty right now, the way I like it."

"Chance is coming over and—"

"I know." His voice returned to normal as he examined her. "Tell me about it later, okay, Lina? By the way, you look nice."

"Thanks." She dropped the ring, allowing it to fall against her skin. "Hey, Gordo?"

"Yeah?" In his dark climate suit, Gordo clutched his bag strap.

"When did Mom start playing again?" She pointed

to the keyboard.

"She hasn't touched it, but Jakob bought it for her when she first got sick. She would listen to Halle play while the conservatory was being built." His head down and his brow furrowed, Gordo left.

Alina rubbed her palms on the sofa. "What are you drawing?" she asked Mandin.

"You, Mama. And Kiean." He waved the paper at her.

A quiver took place inside when she saw the small figures and smiling faces. Earlier that morning, she had explained to Mandin that his father was coming over. Confused when she explained his father wasn't Kiean, he'd asked who Kiean was to him. After searching for an answer, she replied that Kiean was Mandin's stepfather who also cared about him very much.

Mandin seemed to accept her explanation and agreed to meet his "Dada" as he put it. "I be a good boy, Mama," he had promised her.

While waiting, she patted her hair back. The full braid held, preventing her from fussing with it. She covered her mouth as she yawned. Even after Chance answered her link message two nights prior, accepting her invitation to visit Mandin, she couldn't sleep. Staying in Alpheios brought back strange dreams.

The lift buzzer rang, and Alina shot into a standing position. Halle entered the room. "I usually accept the lift requests to screen visitors. You were expecting Mr. Chance Graylin today?"

Alina fiddled with her thin belt. "Yes. When he arrives, please send him in."

As Halle moved down the entryway, Alina clasped her hands in front of her. After a minute, she immediately recognized the easy male tenor speaking to Halle that floated in.

Chance strode into the room with his shoulders back, a warm smile enhancing his demeanor. "Alina, thank you for having me." Dressed in a black climate suit with royal blue accents, Chance carried a small satchel. Her son had glanced up at him but was mostly absorbed in his drawing.

As he closed the distance, Chance's eyes darted between her and Mandin. Reminded of how Chance towered over her, she quickly stepped close to the coffee table, avoiding contact. She gestured to the sofa. "Please, have a seat."

He swept his arm out. "After you." His pine-scented soap wafted in the air.

She took up residence on the far end of the sofa and released a breath when Chance settled on the other end. Straightening, she addressed the bot. "Halle, can you bring some refreshments for our guest?"

Halle gave Chance a courteous smile. "I have cucumber or orange fizz."

"Cucumber will do." He rested his elbows on his thighs.

The bot addressed her. "And for you, Alina?"

"Same here." She plucked at her sleeve. "And orange for Mandin."

When the bot left, she crossed her ankles, turning toward him. "Thank you for coming."

"Of course. I was very happy to receive your message." His dark eyes shone at her. She averted her gaze to her son who was heads down shading a sky over the figures he'd drawn.

"The lieutenant who met us after landing mentioned

you were looking for me. How did you know I was onboard the aircraft?"

Chance rubbed his hands together. "Just a hunch. That's why I sent the escort."

She forced a smile. "Thank you for the ride."

"Would you have told me you were here otherwise?" He focused on her, and she pulled her sleeve cuffs down. She never gave Lieutenant Harding the letter to deliver to Chance since she saw no good reason for it by that point.

"Actually, I was planning to contact you. For safe passage here in Alpheios." She smoothed the fabric over her thighs. "Linette is sick, and I've come to visit her."

"I'm sorry to hear that." He shifted in his seat, looking uncomfortable for a second as a crease appeared along his forehead. Chance studied Mandin who continued drawing.

"But you contacted us first, fortunately." Careful, she reminded herself. She needed to give Chance something first before she could ask for a favor in return.

"Mandin, can you come here a minute?"

He didn't answer and kept scribbling back and forth. She repeated her request, and he stopped. Her son silently examined Chance. His father smiled back. Mandin held out the drawing to her. "Here, Mama."

She took the paper and thanked him. While she kissed him on the cheek, she carefully placed the drawing face down over the arm of the sofa. Rubbing Mandin's shoulder, she nudged him in the direction of his father. "There's someone I want you to meet."

Her son clung to her knee but continued to regard her ex.

Chance held up a large palm. "Hi there."

"Mandin, this is your father, Chance Graylin."

While Mandin lingered near her, not moving forward, Chance opened the pouch. Out of the bag dropped a small toy replica of a Guardian cruiser. "Does this look like the vehicle that you and your mother came here in?"

Her son nodded and displayed a small grin.

"Would you like to see it?" Chance extended his arm out. "We call them GATVs."

Slowly, Mandin moved forward and plucked the toy from Chance's hand. Her son spun the knobby tires with his finger. "Mama, look." He held out the car proudly. "A GATV."

"The doors open. Who's in there?" For the next few minutes, Chance showed Mandin the little Guardian figurine inside the GATV, and how a lift sprung out to help the figure climb in and out.

Alina loosely held her hands in her lap as Chance showed their son the switch to light up the headlights with the siren's colors. When Mandin crouched to the floor with the toy, she said, "He enjoys figuring out mechanical things." She found herself telling her ex about their child's preferences and curiosities. And when Chance inquired about his health, she explained how Macy's herbal formula had eased reoccurrence of Mandin's seizures. Some of the tension dissipated within her as she found it was easy to talk about Mandin.

Halle returned and set down a tray of drinks on the table. When Chance leaned forward for a glass of cucumber fizz, Alina snuck a glance at him. Same noble profile and dark, piercing eyes. Eyes that she recognized every day when she spoke to her son. Although with Chance, there was a difference in him she couldn't quite place. A hint of restlessness came from him. Checking herself, she scooted a few inches away. A slight unsteadiness gripped her as his pine scent grew stronger.

She grabbed a glass of fizz as well. The bubbles tingled her throat.

"And how have you been?" Chance turned his long torso toward her, loosely holding the glass.

"Excellent." Her hand touched the back of her braid. Thinking of how Talley and Kiean fared back at Evesborough during the power outage, she took another sip. She offered Mandin the orange fizz, but he didn't want it, occupied with his new toy.

After placing the drink down, she swiveled her knees in Chance's direction. "I heard there are problems in the Falls District. I imagine it's keeping you busy at work."

He leaned back slightly. "There are some protests that occasionally turn violent. But it's nothing we can't handle." His tone held an edge. "I would avoid the area though and adhere to the curfew." A frown marred his features. "You're much safer here in the Meander District. Especially if Mandin is with you."

"People are upset at Genodyne, aren't they?"

"Genodyne is trying to solve the problem." He set the glass down and repositioned himself. "You've probably heard that Phase Three didn't exactly work out." His fingers flicked the air.

"Chance…" She licked her lips. "Linette took the original Phase Three tonic. The one that's been discontinued. We have a doctor for her, but recently my mother's taken a turn for the worse."

As he studied the mirrored table, she continued. "We can arrange another visit between you and Mandin.

For a whole afternoon."

She noticed he listened carefully, and she pressed ahead. "My mother is very sick, and the doctor thinks she only has a short time left until the disease turns fatal. I heard Genodyne has a serum that might help her. Please, is there any way I can get Dr. Bellamy a sample of it?"

He stiffened. "I'm truly sorry about your mother. I've always been fond of Linette. But the serum is….still being developed." He arched his brow. "Why would you give it to your mother after Genodyne's product made her ill in the first place?"

Alina slid a bit closer on the couch. "Because I have no other options." She grabbed her ring. "Anything to buy her more time."

When Chance's gaze fell to her necklace, she dropped her hand. He ran his fingers through his dark, wavy hair. He'd recently had a fresh haircut. "You don't know the implications of what you're asking."

"Then help me understand."

He glanced at Mandin. "You don't have to bargain with my son." Bitterness laced his tone.

"I thought you would like to see him while we're here." A flutter whirled in her core.

He shifted again and inhaled a deep breath. "I can't speak of Genodyne's research because I signed their NDA. Although I may be able to convince them to extend an NDA to you based on Linette being a volunteer test subject. Then they may give her a dose of the serum. But—" Chance locked his eyes onto hers. "It remains confidential. The public doesn't know about it."

Her heart galloped at the implications of his offer. A crawling sensation took over her skin at the thought of entering that building again. "I don't want to go to

Genodyne. Not after what they put me and Mandin through."

"There's no need to involve him. You mentioned safe passage? I can arrange that for both of you during your stay. No one will bother you. And I'll accompany you to Genodyne myself."

She contemplated his proposal. Every warning alarm rang within. Still, had anyone intended to detain her, they would have done so when she had landed. "All right, I'll go. But even then—I must inform Dr. Bellamy since she's treating Linette."

"Alina, if this gets out, it'll have enormous consequences for the entire city. You're to keep our conversations confined to these walls." His dark eyes bore into hers. "Promise me that. The safety of Genodyne's top personnel on this matter is already at risk. Your doctor should understand."

"You have my word." She despised that institution, but she could handle one visit.

"Then we have a deal. You'll get to see what's behind the curtain." A corner of his mouth turned up, and a spark of cockiness took over his eyes. "And only because it's you." He emphasized the last word.

Her arms tingled. Used to the climate suit that allowed her to control the temperature, Alina pulled at her fingers. "It'll be time for Mandin's nap soon. Why don't you stay a few minutes more with him until then? I have to check on Linette."

Her mother was probably napping in the conservatory, but Alina no longer wanted to be in the same room as Chance. Her stomach lurched as soon as his arrogance returned.

He gave her a bemused smile. "Two boys with toys

here to play with. We'll be fine."

"If you call Halle, she'll give you anything else you need."

"Anything?" He grinned wide.

She hopped off the couch. As she stood, Chance smirked. His gaze trailed over her, lingering on her body with an unsettling familiarity. A scalding bloom spread through her cheeks.

As she brushed past him, she resisted the temptation of kicking her pointed flats straight into his knee. No one owned her—certainly not him. On the way to the bedroom, she swore under her breath. She was taking off the stupid jumpsuit immediately. Halle could see Chance out.

Chapter 10

Standing behind his desk, Chance picked up the tool. “And you said a protestor was wielding this?” A twist crept up his back about the potential damage someone could do with such a weapon. His mother’s office was next to his own within City Hall.

Lieutenant Harding, the head of internal security, stood at the center of Chance’s office. “Yes. He swung it at one of our men who managed to pry it out of his hands. Unfortunately, the officer didn’t get a good look at him since the radical’s face was covered. Slippery outside with the melting snow when they fought. Rioter managed to get away.”

The metal gleamed in Chance’s hand from the outside light of his window. He gripped the tool’s handle and examined the broad, flat head. “It’s a chisel.”

“Correct. No prints on it since the sus was wearing gloves. I’m checking the different construction sites to see if they’re missing any equipment.” The lieutenant didn’t take a seat even though Chance had offered him one in his compact office.

“Good. Do a database search through their employment records to provide a list of workers who have prior arrests.” Chance set the chisel down on his desk.

“Already initiated that.” Harding tucked his Guardian winter cap under his elbow. “I’ve been checking on the council like you asked, but we're not turning up any unusual activity in their daily routines."

"Keep looking. Expand the investigation to their immediate families and close associates. That's all." Chance took a seat. Next on his list was a security update from Rufalo. City Hall had to be secured.

Harding lingered by his desk.

"Is there something else?" Chance intertwined his fingers loosely together.

"Just a follow up. Not that it's really any of my business, but the woman and child we escorted to the new penthouse in the Meander District..." Harding trailed off.

"What about them?" The chair allowed Chance to swivel toward the window behind his desk. Late afternoon light cast bright spots as well as shadows in his office.

"The little boy. His resemblance to you is rather uncanny." Harding lowered his voice. "If there's something I should know, I can help in the future."

Chance blinked and cocked his head, studying Harding. The lieutenant's observation sealed his assessment that Harding would make an excellent aide to the chancellor once he convinced his mother to release him. "Is that so?" Chance couldn't help but smile. "He's my son."

The lieutenant nodded. "If you want me to check on them and convey the meeting request again, I'd be happy to talk to Ms. DeHerte."

"No need, lieutenant. I've already seen them." Chance rested back against his chair. "Good update. Keep me posted on what the employment records turn up."

"You've got it, sir." Harding grabbed his cap from under his arm. He exited the room, pushing open the glass door with the justice seal imprinted on it.

The chisel rested in front of Chance on the desk. He picked up the instrument again and turned it over. Scrapes and indentations were scored on its metal edge. Its blade was cold to the touch.

Chance set the chisel down and scratched his jaw, recalling his meeting with Alina the day prior. She was thinner than when he saw her last, and the emerald jumpsuit showed off her slender waist. Her green eyes sparkled in her outfit. Remembering the defiant expression that she'd shown at the end of his visit, he chuckled. She rarely backed down when challenged. Her resistance to deference was one of the reasons he became intrigued with her in the first place. But beneath her strong-willed exterior, once Alina gave someone her heart, that person would have want for no other.

He drummed his fingertips. The ring that Alina displayed prominently on her deep neckline wasn't on her hand. As if the ring could deter him. She wanted the serum for her mother so he'd play her game. And Alina had donned that outfit to make a certain impression. Even if she couldn't admit it to herself, she still desired him. He was her first lover, after all. This time, he wouldn't make the same mistake again. His honor had lost her.

Alina and Mandin belonged in Alpheios, back with him. He needed to spend time with her where she could be reminded of their past. It would require careful probing on his part.

Chance smacked his fist onto his desk, jarring the chisel. Matters of the heart may as well be matters of war.

Once he was done, her fiancé would realize that Eamine had slammed the sky down upon him after it was too late.

Chapter 11

Syriah's tummy grumbled at the smell of meat pies baking in the kitchen. Danny stood next to her in the hovership's kitchen, watching his mother, Cinda, open the large door on the oven with a rag. Ione helped her sister set multiple pies on the counter. Behind them, a few women waited to use the oven.

Brown sauce bubbled up through the pies' golden crusts. Syriah's mouth watered. While the burners worked in their home in the morning and evening for an hour each, people started using the kitchen onboard the hovercraft to make large dishes that would last several days.

"All yours, ladies," Cinda said to the small group of women waiting as she hung the paddle back on its wall hook.

The women jostled one another as they rushed to the oven.

"It's already been four days. When are they going to fix the power?" Danny asked.

"Kiean and Soloman are fixing it. The generator is on in the meantime," Syriah replied. Tired of eating old bread with jam and dried meats that her father kept in the pantry, she knew the pies would have to cool first so they wouldn't burn her tongue.

How clever of Cinda to make meat pies. Their bellies would be full for another two days. She and Ione had made several pies to share among their families. Syriah got to roll out the dough. She pictured the happy looks on her daddy's and Kiean's faces when she showed them the pie.

Ione said, "Why don't we move to the cafeteria where we can eat?"

A few minutes later, Syriah carried the hot pie in thick oven mitts out to the long tables. She marched to her father and set the pie proudly in front of him.

"Ahh…" He lifted his nose in the air.

"Should we wait for Kiean?"

Her father handed her a plate. "We'll save him some."

At the other end of the table, Cinda served Big Flint and the rest of her family. Ione joined them with little Hudson.

As Syriah's dad sliced into the pie, his glasses steamed up from the heat rising from the pan. He removed his glasses.

The overhead lights flickered. "Uh-oh," he said.

The speakers crackled. "Hot water will be available for ten more minutes," Kiean's voice said. "It'll be available again tomorrow morning for two hours at the first sunrise, and two hours at first sunset."

A few mouthfuls later, Syriah rolled the yummy sauce along her tongue. Father scooped larger bites into his mouth next to her. Warm all over, she chewed the crust. Soloman entered the kitchen. Cinda waved him over and picked up a knife.

As she slid a plate over to Soloman, a man burst into the kitchen. "Dammit! Another day with cold showers. Line is too damn long."

Syriah stopped eating. While she tried to refrain

from using her powers since the reactor blew, she couldn't help but see people's airs. And the man's air was gray and angry. She'd seen the long line of people at the ship's bathing facilities when she first helped Cinda and Ione bring the pies onboard. Not everyone had a shower installed in their homes like her dad had made for them.

Her father swallowed his mouthful. "You can take a dip in the river outside tomorrow afternoon when the suns are shining."

The man scowled. "I don't want to wait 'til tomorrow." He strode to Soloman who stared down at his untouched slice and grabbed his shoulder. "Hey autard, turn the hot water back on!"

Syriah stopped mid-bite. She'd overhead some of the men say mean things to Soloman before, but they usually didn't touch him. And she knew Soloman didn't like that word, *autard*.

Soloman tried to wrench free. "I can't. We're rationing the generator's fuel to extend the kitchen time. Four minutes left for the water heater."

The man grabbed the front of Soloman's shirt. "I told you to turn it back on. You let it run for another hour!" His nose was close to Soloman's.

Big Flint stood. "Zaid, let him go. You gotta follow the rules like everyone else."

Zaid grabbed the knife next to the pie. "Shut up, Flint. I'm going to have a hot shower today." He held the knife up to Soloman's face. Soloman shrank back, but the man shook him. "You hear me, autard? You turn the hot water heater back on."

"I can't. Sorry."

Zaid pressed the tip of the knife against Soloman's

cheek. "I'll give you one more warning. You turn that water heater back on or you're going to find yourself with a scar and story to tell your friends. And you—" The man held the knife out to Flint. "Not another move. Or I'll cut him, I swear."

Syriah sucked in a breath. The man's air turned black as a storm. Big Flint inched toward them, but he wasn't quite close enough to stop Soloman from getting hurt. Cinda wrapped her arms around her kids while scooting them away. Ione had already pulled Hudson off the bench.

"Drop the knife, Zaid," Kiean's voice called out. He stood in the doorway with Hawk beside him.

Gulping, Syriah was filled with the urge to run to her brother, but her dad grabbed her wrist. "Don't move," he whispered. He squinted at his son by the door. He couldn't see very well without his glasses.

Kiean squared his shoulders, fire brewing in his hazel eyes. "You don't drop it, I'll ban you off the ship for a week."

Zaid's face pinched up. "Ain't fair, Kiean. We need more hot water. I've stood in line for the last three days and haven't gotten my turn yet."

"We're working on it." Kiean marched forward, accompanied by his best friend. "But I need Soloman's help with the reactor." He lowered his voice, but his words sliced the air like an axe. "You hurt him, and I'll tell everyone else you just delayed bringing power back for all of Evesborough. You'll be begging me to lock you in the brig where the crowd can't get a hold of you."

Zaid's jaw clenched, but he still clutched Soloman.

Hawk's dark eyes settled on Zaid. "I'm calling backup. Wilder is on duty." He touched his link.

Syriah glanced back at the doors for Hawk's younger brother. Both he and Wilder were part of Evesborough's security patrol.

Big Flint inched closer. "I'd listen to him if I were you."

Zaid glared at them.

"You want to bring Macy into this? Put away the knife," Kiean growled.

The man released Soloman.

Big Flint grabbed Zaid's arm and wrestled the knife out of his hand. Hawk pocketed the weapon.

Kiean approached Zaid. "Now, it's time you apologize to Soloman."

Looking between the men, Zaid said, "Sorry, au—I mean, Soloman." His tone shifted like acid. "It's not your fault you were born that way."

Her brother crossed his arms. "Soloman, come here."

His friend hurried behind him.

Hawk gestured to the double doors. "Kitchen's open for a bit longer. Go boil some water for your bath. Because…." A slow grin spread across his bronze face. "You stink."

As Zaid scratched his chin, he made an obscene gesture at them. His air smoldered as he left through the kitchen doors.

Hawk chuckled and slapped Kiean on the back. Her brother smirked.

Syriah couldn't bear it any longer. She flew to her brother, throwing her arms around his waist. Behind her, she heard Ione rushing to Hawk.

Kiean rubbed her hair and pushed it back from her face. "He's just crabby because he didn't get his bath."

The door to the cafeteria opened. Wilder stood in his light-blue uniform shirt as he clutched his security stick. Even more handsome than Hawk, Wilder's clove-colored eyes held an alert expression. A bit of sweat shone on his olive skin. "What happened?"

Hawk hugged Ione before answering his younger brother. "I'll tell you about it over some pie."

"I made us a pie, too," Syriah said to Kiean. "We all baked them." She tugged his hand.

Kiean's smile showed his teeth. "You save any for me?" He followed her to the table.

As they ate, Syriah's sat close to her brother, not wanting to leave his side.

Father asked, "How's the reactor doing?"

Kiean pushed food around his plate. "We need a new cryopump. Can't run the generator for both the 3-D printer and the hovership's systems at the same time."

"What about printing during quiet hours?" Dad asked.

"We've stayed up late the last few nights trying that." Her brother swallowed his food. "But Soloman is right. We tried to make a composite valve, but it can't withstand the reactor heat, even with treatment. The 3-D machine can make any other standard part—I helped Dr. Olek make Talley a custom mold for his shoulder. But this is different. We need the right alloy."

"Are you going to make one?" She ate the last crumb on her plate.

"No. I have to send a message to Alina and Aurore. Talley thinks they can get a cryopump at Alpheios."

"Where?" Dad's eyebrows curled inward.

Her brother's fork scratched against his plate. "The spaceship kept in the academy's hangar should have one.

It has a reactor onboard that's long been decommissioned, but the parts are still intact."

"How will you message her?" Syriah wondered if she could send a message, too. Alina often thought of ways to improve things for everyone at Evesborough. Syriah also noticed a sort of restlessness within her brother the last few weeks. He didn't speak of it, but she sensed it was about the ring he had given Alina.

Kiean rubbed his belly. "Terrific pie." He grinned at her. "The ships can talk to one another. I just hope she or Aurore checks for messages on the Spartan soon. We got their reply they safely landed."

Father pushed his empty plate away. "Thought folks would tough it out longer than this. Barely a week has passed."

Her brother shrugged. "There's bound to be a few whiners. In the meantime, Soloman is going to run a hoop of wire to the water wheel by the river. That way, we can keep the generator going once its fuel cells run low. Problem is the strong magnetic field here drains the power from the wires over longer distances, so we'll have to conserve it for the hovercraft's various functions." His fork turned over a piece of pie crust on his plate. "We can't run power to the homes. Although we can print some solar film for their lamps."

Syriah placed her head down on the table. "I miss Alina. When is she coming back?" If only Alina would hurry up and marry her brother, then everything would be all right. Alina's air was cloudier than usual lately, though. Syriah wasn't sure why.

Her brother rubbed her back. "Soon." While she was glad he ate with them, she could sense a slight uncertainty within him.

Chapter 12

Alina shivered in the darkness and reached for the temperature button on the collar of her expeditionary suit. Her link lit the cold metal path in front of them. Following her in the drainage pipe, Aurore buried her chin into her neck guard. “I don’t know why we’re breaking curfew.” Aurore was dressed similarly to blend into their surroundings once they reached their destination. “We could have gone straight to the hangar and avoided the Commandant.” A faint echo bounced off the pipe’s walls as she spoke.

“No one will see us this way.” Alina crept forward, careful to plant her boots on the slippery floor of the pipe where a thin layer of water had frozen over. She hugged a tool bag from the Spartan close to her hip, hoping the bag’s fabric would prevent the tools from rattling.

Their links were out of range from Evesborough, so Aurore checked and received a message from the Spartan. The message was sent via the Triumph from Kiean, urgently requesting a cryopump with instructions on where to find one. They decided to set out that night, and Alina had asked Gordo earlier to watch over Mandin after she put him to bed.

“But Talley said it’s likely the Commandant knows about the resupply ship that came to meet them.” Aurore blew out little breaths of condensed air. “Riley’s pretending not to know.”

"Which is why we should avoid running into anyone from the academy right now so we don't get them into trouble."

"If I had known we'd be skulking around in dark pipes, I would have brought the night vision glasses from the Spartan," Aurore replied.

Alina privately allowed that Commandant Riley may have granted her request for the cryopump had she groveled and showed sufficient remorse of leaving him high-and-dry without an instructor, namely her. After all, he went through the trouble of certifying her instructor emergency exercises, expecting she'd teach at the academy. Not only did she split shortly after her certification because of intervening events, she convinced Aurore and Talley to steal the Spartan and leave Alpheios with her and the rest of the Origins.

Talley had known the Commandant for a long time. She suspected that was why Riley allowed the resupply when Talley contacted his old coworkers for help. As for herself, Alina saw no need to beg Riley for a cryopump after not following up with him for over three years on her sudden disappearance.

"Over here." She stepped out of the pipe, hearing the rush of the river in the distance. Scooting behind the corner of a small utility building, she checked their surroundings for Guardian patrols. She didn't want to find herself in the position of asking Chance for any more favors. Agreeing to go to Genodyne with him was bad enough.

The academy was located within the industrial section of Alpheios. Across the way, warehouses and hangars sat quietly. No activity was visible, but a feathery coldness touched her nose. She looked up. Soft tufts of snow were silently falling. Standing still, she watched the flakes gently tumble down for a moment. After living in the desert cavern for three years, she'd forgotten what snow tasted like on her tongue.

"All clear?" Aurore asked.

"Yes."

They dashed across the cement over to the warehouses. Once they reached the buildings, they moved along the shadows. Alina poked her head out from behind a corner. In front of her stood a large hangar with the curve of the academy's sim dome behind it.

"Ready?" She pointed to a closed door at the hangar's side.

Aurore tapped her link. "I downloaded the entry codes from the Spartan. Hope they still work."

They sprinted to the door. A lonely light hung above it, and the snow descended more rapidly around them. Alina waited for Aurore to wave her link in front of the lock pad. The pad's light flickered red.

"Damn it," her friend muttered.

"Try it again."

Aurore held her link close to the pad. The light pulsed green. The lock clicked. "Got it." She shoved open the door.

Inside the blackness of the hangar, they stopped for a moment. Alina summoned the lights. Flickering on, the overhead lights illuminated the interior of the hangar.

In front of them lay a colossal ship shaped like a swollen missile with short wings toward its aft.

"Whoa…" Aurore said.

Alina had taken a tour of the ship for her historical exploration class, but her breath still caught at the sight of it. The word, FORTUNE, was imprinted in bold letters along its side panels. She couldn't help but smile. "My grandmother arrived on this ship." She remembered the story of how her grandmother had met her grandfather, a crew member of the ship.

The nose of the ship showed scorch marks from entering Eamine's atmosphere. Dents along the ship's side revealed the damage that had occurred upon its crash landing.

"There." Aurore gestured to a door behind the cockpit that was left open. She turned on the portable generator by the ship's nose so they'd have light onboard.

They climbed the steps to the first level. Past the main room that contained stacks of metal cryobeds, they made their way in the direction of the engines until they found a large steel door. It was labelled in black letters, REACTOR.

Alina clutched her tool bag close and pushed the door open. Behind a thick glass, the metal hourglass of a dormant fusion reactor lurked. A side door led to its interior.

"Show me the schematic again," she said to Aurore.

Her friend called up the green projection from her link against her sleeve. A sketch showed the outline of a cryopump situated inside the base of the hourglass that was the fusion reactor.

They shone their lights on the panels until Aurore zeroed in one. "Look, this is the cooling system."

Alina squinted, studying the label on the exterior panel. "Save Eamine, here goes nothing." While she was comfortable using tools, she avoided messing with the hovercraft's reactor. That was reserved for Talley's expertise.

She found the auto-screw in her bag. Kiean had sent instructions. As if all she had to do was follow a few steps and presto, they'd lug the pump back. After working the auto-screw, Alina removed the exterior panel. Inside was a metal pump similar to the diagram Kiean sent.

"You okay?" Aurore peered at her.

Catching her breath, Alina nodded. "What's the next step?"

"You're going to need an auto-wrench. Have to remove the bolts that keep it in place," her friend replied.

"I need more light." She dragged her sleeve across her forehead.

"Here." Aurore turned on her link and shone the beam into the compartment.

For the next twenty minutes, Alina worked the auto-wrench over each screw, angling it into position. Her wrist ached from holding the heavy tool but slowly, the bolts came undone. Except the last bolt that had rusted over. She sprayed it with some lubricant. After she tugged at it, the rusty bolt remained stubbornly in place.

"Now what?" She sat on the floor for a break and stretched her neck. A cramp was taking hold in her shoulders and upper back.

"Do you have a torch pen?"

She leveled an *are-you-kidding-me* stare at her friend.

"Stay here." Aurore scrambled for the exit.

As Alina heard her friend clamber around the hangar outside, she took sips of water from her bottle. Aurore emerged and held up a thin pointed rod. "Found one."

Aurore applied the flame to the bolt for a few minutes. Alina tried the auto-wrench again. A squeak came from the bolt, and she continued to grabble with the wrench, letting its auto-twist function go to work. Slowly, the bolt loosened through its thread. But when she tried to lift the pump out of its brace, she staggered forward.

"It's heavy," she gasped.

Aurore helped her lift it, but Alina's arms trembled like gelatin. Her link noted they had been inside the ship for nearly an hour. Aurore placed it an old sack and slung its straps around her shoulders. She gave Alina a high five.

Alina took another sip of water and trudged off the ship. She grinned to herself. *I just took apart a fusion reactor*. On the last step, she jumped off and her boots hit the floor.

A voice bellowed in the lighted hangar. "What have you stolen from me this time, DeHerte?"

Aurore bumped into Alina from behind.

A few feet in front of them stood Commandant Riley, his hands on his hips as he scowled at them from under his cap.

****

In the small room within the hangar, Alina clasped her hands under the table. Next to her, Aurore's bang swoop slid over her eyes as Commandant Riley spoke.

"I know about your hide-out and resupply from my crews." He paced in front of the small table they were seated at, the cryopump laying out in the open. "You going to tell me what's going on?" He stopped and stood in front of them.

Aurore remained quiet, and Alina's cheeks burned. Where on Eamine to start? She gulped. "We needed a part from the spaceship."

"From the fusion reactor?" Riley's mouth opened, then he snorted. "Oh that's right, the hovership took off the day the Spartan went missing, and never came back." He shook his head. "You know Minecorp went looking for their ship and its workers. Peter Mason was intent on finding them. Word has it that Jakob Coughlin paid him off, reimbursing him for the loss of the ship."

The tips of Alina's ears warmed. Jakob had stopped Minecorp from finding her and Kiean? And finding Evesborough? "He paid off…Peter Mason, the ex-chancellor?"

"Yes, I have a friend at Minecorp. Mason returned to his company after he was ousted by the city council."

Why had Jakob asked Minecorp not to look for her? The answer swiftly arrived. Gordo. He was the only one who knew about her escape and must have asked Jakob for his help.

The Commandant's mouth was still slashed tight. Her more immediate predicament demanded her attention. She had ruined everything by getting caught. They wouldn't be able to get the cryopump back to Evesborough where everyone suffered without power. Worse, if he turned her over to the authorities, she'd have to ask Chance to help her again. She grimaced at the thought of her ex's smug expression.

She straightened in her chair. "I should have come to you. I'm sorry." The only way to recover from the storm was to let it blow right through.

"Damn right you should have!" He shook his head and gestured at her. "You think you have a right to wear that uniform? Either of you?" His arm swept in Aurore's direction. "And you—" he grabbed the back of a chair and lowered his face to Aurore who dipped her chin into her neck guard.

"You have no idea what position you put me in once the Spartan went unaccounted for. The university withheld our exploration funding for an entire year." He pushed back the chair as he straightened. "When you see Talley again, you can tell him that I said that he—and this is on his shoulders since he was the senior instructor—ruined the experience of the students in class that year, depriving them of vital training they needed to further the mission of this institute." Fury sparked from his tight mouth, and Alina expected him to throw them out of the hangar, depriving them of cryopump for good.

"Sir, it was my fault. I asked them to help me because…" her voice faltered. Too much time had passed, too much to explain. She leaned forward. "Genodyne took my son. They took all the Origins' kids. We had to leave."

Riley grew quiet. "You mean that isolation order three years ago?"

She recounted how Genodyne wanted the children's DNA for Phase Three development. He grunted every so often at her explanation. When she finished, he said, "Fortunately for you, DeHerte, Genodyne has shown the city what kind of damage it can do so your story checks out. Unfortunately for the rest of us, we're stuck waiting on the chancellor."

A sour taste welled in her mouth. "She was the one who caused all these problems in the first place. It was her doing."

Riley crossed his arms. "And what would you suggest? A new chancellor?"

Aurore said, "Sir, we just need the cryopump. There's an entire community of folks who need it because the one in the Triumph's reactor blew. That's all we came for." She pushed her bangs out of her eyes.

The Commandant's face was still stern but his voice calmed. "You're telling me they have no power now?"

"Well, they're working off generator and a water wheel…." Aurore trailed off.

"You want the pump? Then this stops right now. No more sneaking supplies or stealing parts. You owe me a rundown of site B79, both of you. Another habitable site on Eamine changes everything, and you can't deprive this institution of that knowledge. Do you understand?"

She and Aurore exchanged looks. While Alina was reluctant to give up the site information, it couldn't be kept secret indefinitely, and they needed help in making Evesborough sustainable for the Origins. She asked, "What do you propose, sir?"

"Since they have back up power, they can wait another few days. Day after tomorrow, you two—" he pointed at them "—will return to the main building and document everything you know about the site. You'll download all the research you've done and brief me personally. Its geological composition, meteorological readings, everything. After that, you can have the pump." He waved at the cylindrical part on the table. "Deal?"

Aurore glanced at her. "We'll have to download the information from the Spartan."

Alina nodded. "I have my nav globes onboard as well. Once we have that, we'll brief you." Kiean would ensure Evesborough would be okay for just another few days.

"Both of you are breaking curfew. I don't know how you snuck over but go home." His thumb jerked at the door.

"Sir, I don't mean to pry, but why are you up at this hour?" Aurore asked. "Aren't you breaking curfew, too?"

He rubbed his face, the lines on it more apparent. "Working on a special project. Been spending some nights in the office." His shoulders sagged. "Go home, both of you. And try not to get caught."

As they stood, Alina caught the relief in her friend's face. However, she couldn't quite quell the rumblings within, feeling that the ground shifted once again underneath her.

As she and Aurore made for the hangar exit, she reminded herself that she should only stay long enough to get a serum sample for her mother, and to satisfy the Commandant so they could return back to Evesborough as promptly as possible. Otherwise, Alpheios was liable to suck her back in like quicksand, trapping her and Mandin for good.

Chapter 13

The sauce ladled over the meat smelled of cream and onions. Mandin scrutinized his gold-rimmed plate, not used to the rich dishes served in Alpheios, nor accustomed to dining rooms painted gold. At Evesborough, they grew plenty of biomass to feed the village, but sauces were used in small amounts or for special occasions.

They gathered around the iridescent dining table with her mother and Jakob on opposite ends. Alina chose a seat next to Mandin and across from her brother. Earlier that day, Halle requested Alina's presence at the announced dinner time.

Linette's ink-black long-sleeved top came with a high collar. She held her fork in a hand covered by black, finger-less gloves. Her mother's hair was neatly brushed, but Linette kept her chin downcast. Without her veil, the gray scab on her cheek was the sole visible reminder of her disease.

The spiral chandelier that suspended long pieces of crystal was softly lit, casting a glint on the aquamarine waves etched in the small shingles of the table, making the fine china appear as if it was floating on the sea.

Alina slid the fork in her mouth, absorbing the rich sauce with bites of translucent grain. Perched near the front of her seat, she wiped her mouth with a cloth napkin.

Gordo's fork clinked on his plate. His dinner disappeared quickly.

Her mother's dish while the same as theirs, was prepared without the cream sauce. Linette took tiny bites, chewing slowly.

The sound of eating and utensils covered the lack of conversation. Alina reached for her glass and took a sip of water.

Linette asked, "Halle can bring you white wine?" The bot left the room upon her signal.

While tempted since she hadn't tasted wine in ages, Alina replied, "No, thank you." Her stomach demanded water to accompany the savory dish instead.

"How's your dinner?" Jakob cut through his food with a silver knife.

Swallowing, Alina straightened. "Very good, thank you." She contemplated asking Halle to play some music to avoid speaking to him further. But the bot hadn't returned and instead, she lowered her chin toward Mandin. "Finish your supper."

He scrunched up his nose. "I no like this." Using his fork, Mandin pushed away a sliver of onion from his meat.

She brought her face close to his ear and lowered her voice. "Mandin!"

Jakob dangled his fork. "What's wrong with it?"

"Nothing. He's not used to the sauce." Alina glanced across the table at Gordo. Her brother carried an amused expression as he chewed.

"Perhaps he can try a few bites," her mother said. "That's what I used to do with you and Gordo when you were younger, to accustom your tastes."

"He's stubborn." Alina knew Mandin would make

gagging noises if he bit into an onion, or worse. He was liable to throw up another telepathic block at her. She didn't want to be embarrassed any further.

Her mother fell silent.

"He's a guest. We can't let him go hungry." Jakob touched his link.

Frowning, Alina was about to say she'd send her son to bed hungry to teach him a lesson. Before she could speak, the bot glided into the room. Mandin cheered at its arrival.

"Yes, sir?" Halle asked.

"Can you bring Mandin another plate without sauce?" Jakob gestured to him.

"Certainly, sir."

"Yeah," Mandin said, a note of triumph in his voice. "And no vegetables, either."

"Halle, keep the vegetables," Alina cut in.

"As you wish." The bot took his plate and departed.

Her brother leaned back in the chair and stretched. "I'm stuffed. It was delicious, Mom."

A smile peeked out from her mother. "I asked Halle to prepare fowl because I knew it was your favorite." She glanced at her. "And yours, too."

Although her mother managed to be accurate about Gordo's preferences, Alina's favorite meal was not fowl, but mutton. Instead of correcting her, Alina crammed another bite in her mouth.

Her mother put her fork down. "I have some news."

"What is it?" Gordo asked.

At the far end of the table, Jakob took a swig of wine as if he was preparing himself.

"We are leaving for a vacation to Tidewater in a few days. It would be lovely if all of you could join us," her mother said.

Alina swallowed her food. “Tidewater? You’re going to the ocean?”

“But I thought it was just a few observation stations out there?” Gordo traded glances with Alina.

“Tidewater has two stations that belong to the academy since it’s in our habitable zone. They’re set up on the high bluffs over the inlet, but it’s not really suited for visitors. While there’s no snow there, it’s still very windy,” she said.

“Well, there were only a few stations until recently.” Linette smiled across the table at her husband. “Jakob has built a cliffside refuge there, and it’s finally complete. And I’ve always wanted to visit the ocean. I’d like to go while I’m still mobile.”

Left unsaid was the pain Linette would be in a few weeks once her disease took a downward turn.

Alina turned to Jakob. “You built a dwelling there?”

He nodded, dangling his fork. “Yes. I had planned a get-away pad for some time. I have friends inquiring about a visit. A few of my associates are talking about building hideaways in the area, especially with conditions in the city as of late.” He raised his glass to Linette and gave her a slight smile.

Giving her head a shake, Alina turned back to her mother. “Shouldn’t you stay here, close to Dr. Bellamy? The medical care facility at Tidewater is bare bones.”

“We’re only going for a week,” Jakob interjected. “We’ll be back in time for Dr. Bellamy’s next call.”

Alina clamped her lips together. Did he have to answer for her mother about everything? Linette gazed at her expectantly.

“I can’t go. I have some errands I have to take care

of in the city." Chance had set up a date for her to visit Genodyne. The sooner that she found a way to retrieve the serum, the better.

"I see." Her mother glanced at her plate.

"Me, neither. Promised my teammates we'd train." Gordo leaned over and squeezed Linette's shoulder. "I wish you mentioned it sooner."

Alina blinked. Gordo usually went along with their mother on these ideas.

"Then we shall make it just the two of us," Jakob said, clearing his throat. "A nice, quiet vacation." He peered at Alina. "You and Mandin stay here and enjoy the penthouse while we're gone. I insist."

She shifted in her seat. Jakob's pointed stare showed he remembered their conversation in the office about her attempts to obtain the serum. She'd agreed to avoid instilling false hope in her mother. "Thank you," she mumbled.

Resignation flickered in her mother's green eyes. "Maybe we should go another time." Her voice was soft. "When they can accompany us." Linette lifted her head. "If you'll excuse me, I think I'll retire now." She rose out of her seat just as Halle reappeared with a fresh plate.

The bot placed the dish in front of Mandin. "Anything else I can get the young man?"

"No, thanks." Though there was still food in front of her, Alina's appetite vanished.

"I think I'll join my wife." Jakob wiped his mouth and left his napkin crumbled on the table.

Halle cleared their dishes while Mandin ate.

The three of them alone, she said to Gordo, "A refuge?"

Her brother shrugged. "I overhead them talking

about it last year. Jakob works hard to make her happy."

"I suppose he's wealthy enough to give her what she always wanted," she replied dryly. "Luxury."

Her brother's mouth turned downward. "There's more to it than that." He leaned in. "You don't remember how upset Mom used to get when Dad left on his trips."

"What do you mean?"

"You were studying at the library back then to get into the academy." Gordo rested his elbows on the table, his hands clasped together. "I came home after school. I used to hear them argue about it."

"So it's his fault that she left?" She threw a barb at his reasoning.

"No," her brother replied in a firm manner. "What I'm saying is that she felt neglected when he'd go on those long trips. He wouldn't quit or ask for another position, even though she'd begged him."

Alina shook her head. "He was an expeditionary commander. That was his job."

She was the one who'd comforted her brother after Linette left. Especially when their father was on a trip. She'd try to distract Gordo by encouraging him to focus on his athletics. He'd throw himself into those activities, hopeful his mother would return and be pleased with his progress. And she'd avoid mentioning that their mother had left them. That Linette had left *her*.

Gordo exhaled. "I know that." He took a gulp of water before standing. "I hope you enjoyed your meal. The only reason Mom organized dinner was because you and Mandin are here." Her brother left the dining room.

Staring at the table's display of colorful waves, Alina bit down on the inside of her cheek until she tasted blood. Next to her, Mandin played with his food.

"Eat your dinner." The cream sauce curdled in her stomach, and she grabbed the glass of water, wishing she chose wine instead.

Chapter 14

Chance climbed out of the GATV first, bidding Alina to wait. On the promontory, the familiar violet building loomed under the gunmetal gray sky that afternoon. Silver streaks of giltspar ran heavily throughout the structure. The waterfalls behind Genodyne mirrored Alina's internal turbulence. Every muscle in her body was on alert once they undertook their trip to the company. Perhaps Eamine would spare a favor so she could obtain the serum. Then she could return to Evesborough and put Alpheios behind her.

However, duty intruded on her desires. Chance sat across from her in the backseat, trying to ease into conversation. Remembering their last encounter, Alina kept her replies cool and succinct, and Chance stopped asking her questions. The more she had thought about how their last meeting ended, the angrier she grew. Chance had embarrassed her in order to provoke a reaction, and she refused to give him the satisfaction of one again.

A stumbling man approached Chance. Alina watched through the tinted window. Hardened, lead-like scales covered one of the man's eyelids, swollen shut, as he begged Chance to allow him through the barricade, his voice breaking. Chance pointed him to the side of the building, where the ER entrance was located. Alina gulped while the man limped away. She steeled herself for the visit.

Once the man was out of view, Chance opened the door for her. Stepping onto the ramp, she ignored his outstretched hand and hopped to the pavement. He unlocked a section of the Guardian barricade that surrounded the bottom of Genodyne's stairs.

Her heart sprinted as she followed him up the stone steps. They passed through the courtyard by a DNA metal sculpture, and she finally entered the building that she'd leapt off three years ago. That was during summer, and she had barely escaped the falls with her life. In winter, the river's water temperature would have overtaken her.

Chance stopped at the double glass doors. Noticing they didn't swish open for visitors like they used to, she waited for security to buzz them in. Behind them, the plaza was empty, although a few restaurant lights glowed in the bleak afternoon.

Inside the lobby, the prominent statue of Duncan Ambrose stood, staking his domain. She hurried by the city's founder. A Genodyne security watchman manned the information desk with a young Guardian alongside him. The young Guardian passed Chance a crystal tablet.

"Sign this." Chance handed her the tablet.

Glancing at the non-disclosure forms, she snorted. "Genodyne always has its secrets." She signed and passed him the tablet. "Who are we meeting with?"

"Dr. Daxmen," Chance replied, leading her through the tiled lobby.

She stopped. "Daxmen?" Chance had relayed beforehand that they would be speaking to medical personnel. Relieved that she avoided Jade Graylin, Alina nevertheless was stunned to hear Daxmen's name. She glared. "Doctor Daxmen took Mandin away from me." This was a mistake. She couldn't trust Chance about these matters.

His brow furrowed. "Ms. Silver is gone. The board placed Daxmen in charge of Phase Three."

"No wonder it's screwed up then."

Her ex angled his head. "He agreed to my proposal. Do you still want the serum?"

Alina glanced at the closed glass doors, remembering the man outside. Chance waited, standing tall in his black Guardian uniform. Impeccable as usual. The way he held his posture reminded her that he was in professional mode as well. She stepped forward, hoping their visit wouldn't take long. He led her down a long hallway toward the back of the building.

Chance utilized his link on the lock pad at the R & D department. After the doors clicked open, he led her to an elevator. A chill roiled her as it descended, and she avoided eye contact. When it opened, she faced a long, brightly lit tunnel.

"Where are we going?" She didn't recognize this portion of the facility.

"Non-public wing. Not much further."

The hair on her arms raised as she followed Chance through the tunnel. The only sounds were their hollow footsteps. They emerged in a foyer where they passed another bust of Duncan Ambrose. She shook her head. The founder of Alpheios had been a rather vain man.

At the window depicting them behind the waterfall, she gnawed on her inner cheek. She had survived being pummeled underwater before. Surely, she could make it through one visit to Genodyne's secret underground facility. Whatever lay ahead, it was carved into the side of the cliffs.

"What's in there?" She motioned to a thick, vaulted door with a red light shining over it.

Chance scowled. "Only Dr. Daxmen and board members have access to that room." His pace picked up. Chance's stiff back telegraphed displeasure.

He led her inside an observation room with large, angled windows. It was connected to a control room at the other end. Two techs in white Genodyne uniforms listened to a large man that she recognized. Dr. Daxmen gave them instructions on a monitor. Chance blocked her view of the control room and led her closer to the windows.

His voice dropped low. "Remember, the exchange is contingent on your cooperation." His lofty frame rose over her, and she took a small step back.

She crossed her arms. If citizens found out that Linette, a woman who lived in the Meander District married to one of the richest men in the city received a cure first, there would be an outcry of how that arrangement came about. "I signed the papers. Can we get on with it?"

He placed his hand on his baton and moved out of the way for a clear view of the lab below, surrounded by stone walls. Inside the room, a metal curtain of bars separated a living area from the exterior door that led up to the control room. At the far end of the makeshift quarters, a woman rose from the bed and stepped forward, gazing up at the glass as if she sensed their presence.

The stout woman's short hair was dark and slicked back. She peered up with arctic-blue eyes. "Who is that?" Just as Alina asked, the woman's skin rippled like an electric current disturbed it, darkening. Alina edged back from the window.

"Meet Kora and Ash," Chance replied.

Alina's mouth went dry. "Did Genodyne—"

"Kronosapiens, they're called. Hence, the change in her skin. They're supposed to be the next phase of evolution where humans transition into a species more suited to Eamine." Chance's face remained immovable.

"Your mother went through with it, didn't she?" A shiver crept up her back. She recalled her last encounter with Jade while she was trapped in the building. *Directed evolution,* was what the chancellor called it. "She created a new species of humans."

"It was never my idea." A frown marred Chance's face.

A bile-like taste spread through her mouth, like a bitter root. "And they had babies."

By the bed, a translucent bassinet held two krono-babies. The tiny things wriggled about, helpless. In the bed, a grown male rested. His gray skin possessed a mottled hue, unlike the female standing in front of them. A slight shimmer glinted off her skin.

"What's wrong with him?"

"He's not reacting well to a recent bone marrow transplant. Taken a turn for the worse." Chance waved to the female. "Kora is the one with more stem cells in her reservoir. The stem cells make up the serum that Genodyne believes will cure the side effects from the initial Phase Three product. She's recovered from birth now, so we can withdraw it from her."

Alina noticed three sizable bumps along Kora's spine when the creature turned and paced alongside the barrier. "Are you sure this is a good idea?" There were consequences in taking a sample from that—*creature*—a new mother no less.

The gray in Kora's skin reminded Alina of the gray patch on her mother's cheek. How Genodyne had formulated the initial Phase Three tonic fell into place. The product came from the kronosapiens.

"Would you like to speak with Dr. Daxmen?" Chance gestured to the control room.

She shifted her weight between her feet. "Yes."

When they entered, the doctor lifted his chin. Her stomach tightened as she stood near the man.

"Chance has explained the situation," the doctor said. "Mr. Caughlin consented on your mother's behalf. Dr. Bellamy will follow up with us on the results. So you see, it's a win-win for both parties." His tone rang haughty.

"Based on what happened previously, what assurances do I have that whatever you withdraw—" Alina glanced at the kronosapiens on the monitors "—won't worsen my mother's condition?"

The doctor gazed down his nose. "Ask Dr. Bellamy. She'll be administering it." He glanced at Chance. "If she doesn't want the serum, we'll find another subject. We won't have problems finding volunteers from the ER."

Her hands curled into fists. "Mr. Caughlin is good friends with most of the board. Isn't that why you agreed to provide us a test sample? Because you knew you can count on his discretion?"

The doctor studied her for a moment. "Very well." He turned to Chance. "My techs can use some help. Lenore," he gestured to a young female who chewed a fingernail, "is new since Zelda, my assistant, is out today. Buck's been through this song and dance before."

He nodded at the male tech who folded his muscular arms over his chest.

Chance touched the comm bar along his ear. “Corporal Martin, come down to the lab.” While they waited, Alina watched Kora roam the room restlessly, glancing back at her babies and up at the cameras.

About ten minutes later, the young Guardian from the front lobby appeared. Her ex pointed her to the observation area. “Wait there.”

“Why?” She wasn’t in the mood to be ordered around.

“Please, Alina. Just wait there.” He huffed and cocked his head toward the room.

She bit back a protest and repositioned herself in front of the windows. The sooner she got the serum, the sooner she could leave. And perhaps, the sooner Linette would feel better. Alina reached for the ring around her neck and stroked it.

As Chance gave instructions to Corporal Martin, Alina studied the lab below. The male lay listless, his eyes closed. The two krono-babies cried, but Kora stood by the gate, alert and watching the outer door. It was strange how the kronosapien seemed to know they were plotting against it, despite the tinted observation windows. Alina rubbed the stone on her ring, deciding to ask Chance afterward more about the kronosapien’s abilities. His mother had wanted a species more advanced than humans.

She overhead Daxmen’s remark. “Be careful. She’ll be stronger now since the last injection I gave her.”

Corporal Martin said, “I can stun her if she resists.” His finger rested above his baton’s electric discharge switch.

Daxmen replied, "Try to avoid that. We want her stem cell load as full as possible."

The small party exited down the stairs to the laboratory. Chance resumed his position next to Alina watching the scene below.

Kora growled at the party as they approached. As Buck unlocked the gate separating them, her skin rippled again and hardened like slate. The corporal unsheathed his baton. Daxmen waited behind with a needle in his hand, and Lenore hovered nervously next to him.

"Kora, we just need one withdrawal," the doctor said.

Buck swung the gate open.

The kronosapien lunged at the doctor.

Alina arced her neck back from the window.

Immediately, Buck attempted to grab Kora. She seized his arm and threw him against the gate. Corporal Martin thrust the baton over Kora's chest from behind, restraining her as she kicked wildly.

"Help him," Daxmen said to Lenore.

The girl rushed over and hoisted Buck to his feet.

"You took him!" Kora screamed at the doctor. "My baby is gone!" She contorted over, flipping the corporal onto his back.

"What does she mean?" Alina asked Chance.

"Don't know." He was absorbed in the unfolding brawl.

Daxmen backed away as both techs grappled with Kora. The kronosapien's claws protruded, and she dug them into Buck's arm. She twisted his forearm, and a sickening crack sounded. He screamed, and Kora flung him through the air. His back slammed into the wall. A jolt of electricity flew from Kora's palm and shocked

Lenore. The tech crumpled instantly.

"Stay here," Chance said to Alina.

"Wait!"

But her ex leapt down the stairs. In the lab, the corporal was on his hands and knees, shaking his head. Lenore remained unconscious on the ground.

"Stay back!" Chance said to Daxmen as he rushed by.

Kora kicked the corporal in the stomach. Martin doubled over. She turned and advanced in the doctor's direction with a murderous expression. Chance ducked as Kora aimed a bolt of electricity his way. She grabbed the doctor's lab coat and shoved him against the wall. Chance thrust his baton into her back. Crumpling on the floor, she released Daxmen. The doctor scrambled for the exit. Buck clambered after him up the stairs.

They stumbled back into the control room.

"Help them!" Alina gestured to the glass windows.

But Buck was holding his arm, grimacing. Sweat ran down the side of Daxmen's face. "We can't do the withdrawal until she's subdued," he gasped.

Kora was on her knees, rubbing her lower back. Chance clamped a baton over her throat and quickly dragged her through the open gate. He heaved her into the lab and slammed the door shut. The lock clicked. Shaking his head, he glowered at the empty space where the doctor once stood.

Corporal Martin was unsteady on his feet. Chance hauled him up the stairs.

Lenore blinked, and her eyes widened at her surroundings. Her foot was close to the metal bars of the gate near the kronosapien. Kora slowly propped herself up on one knee.

As Chance entered the control room supporting Martin, Alina dashed past him for the stairs.

"No, Alina!"

In the frigid laboratory, her pulse hammered away. Lenore's head rolled around, and she attempted to sit up. Alina crouched and pushed her shoulder forward. "Come, we must leave." She helped Lenore stand. "This way."

The woman hobbled to the stairs. As Alina followed, she felt a tug at her necklace. The cord cinched around her neck. A force yanked on the ring, throwing her back. She sailed through the air, helpless. Her head slammed into the gate, and Kora's hand wrapped around her throat. Face-to-face with the kronosapien, Alina gasped for air. She tried to pry away Kora's fingers but was lifted off her feet.

The creature studied Alina, her blue eyes curious.

A penetrating alien presence scraped at Alina's mind. Shoving aside her protestations, it swept over her recent thoughts, through Evesborough, through the tunnels and stopped on the children in the cavern's entrance. It zeroed in on Syriah and Mandin. Alina struggled to breathe. Her lungs were about to explode.

A wave of realization overcame Kora's face. "You're not one of us. But are you one of them?" She pointed her index finger, exposing a long claw.

Dizzy, Alina felt a sharp prick on her neck. Kora examined the blood on her claw's tip and slowly licked it. Her blue eyes narrowed. "Ancestor."

Alina's vision blurred. She thrashed but couldn't fight against the creature's squeeze. Suffocating, every cell within her raced, searching for any last ounce of energy. Kora kept her blue eyes locked onto Alina's face.

In her periphery, a flash of a baton thrust through the bars.

A jolt coursed through Alina's body. Every fiber of her being contracted in pain, and she screamed. As the searing agony reverberated, a curtain of blackness fell over her.

Chapter 15

The faint murmur of voices drifted into the room. Fluorescent lighting blinded Alina. Squinting, she recognized her surroundings as a hospital room. Swiveling her head to the side, a cramp shot through her neck. She cringed. Sensors inset on the solid bed rail pulsed blue from her movements.

Chance's voice came from somewhere outside. "Absolutely not."

"But she's a match…"

Alina's throat was parched, and small movements left a tingle in her limbs. An IV needle poked into her arm. Her head throbbed, and she moaned.

Footsteps sounded nearby. Chance entered and approached. "How are you feeling?"

She blinked a few times staring up at him. He was still in uniform. His brow wrinkled as he stared down at her.

"Like I was dropped off a building." Her throat hurt as she spoke.

Swiftly, he moved to the sink and filled a paper cup with water. He brought it to her lips. "Drink."

Her body lay stiff and heavy. "I can't sit up."

The motor in the bed hummed as Chance raised the upper half. She took the cup, and the water quenched her thirst. "What happened?"

He inhaled a deep breath. "I'm sorry about the

shock, but it was the only way I could get Kora to release you. I made sure that she took the brunt of it."

A freeze descended over Alina, chilling her core. The kronosapiens. Genodyne. Closing her eyes again, she remembered Kiean's warning about avoiding the company. She should have listened.

"What's the last thing you remember?" Chance asked.

"I was helping…" bits of images flashed through her mind. "How did Kora get a hold of me? I thought she was behind the gate."

Chance's fist was wrapped around a small object. "It was this." The cord she wore with Kiean's ring was in Chance's palm.

She took it from him and held it to her chest. "Why did you take it?"

His throat bobbed. "We didn't want to risk Kora hurting you again so I removed it from you. Her full powers caught all of us by surprise." He pointed at the ring. "We've never seen her move objects before with her mind. Based on how he designed her, Daxmen believes she manipulated the giltspar in the stone."

"Giltspar?" Her hand tightened around the ring.

Chance looked toward the foot of the bed, his expression distant. Then his gaze drifted back to her. "It's good to see you awake." A luster appeared in his dark eyes, and a corner of his mouth turned upward.

She took another swig of water and repositioned herself on the bed. "I wasn't supposed to be gone this long."

"Are you worried about Mandin? I thought your mother wanted to spend time with him."

"She did, but Halle is watching him." She'd hoped

that Gordo would help out. He disappeared earlier that afternoon.

A knock at the door echoed, and Chance answered it. She promptly slipped the ring into the chest pocket of her climate suit.

Doctor Daxmen came in. "You're up. Always a good sign." He moved to the foot of the bed and swiped the inset screen with a stylus. "Your vitals are normal. You just need some rest, and you'll be fine in a day or two."

Alina shifted again. Daxmen was an interloper, and she'd rather suffer in pain than have him touch her again, even for medical reasons. She glanced at Chance. "How long was I out?"

"About three hours," he replied.

She gazed at the doctor. "Can I leave now?"

"If you feel well enough to walk, you can leave. Or you can rest here for a little while longer. Although there is one other matter." The doctor raised his chin. Tucked under his arm was a crystal tablet.

"I said no." A broil underlined Chance's tone.

"What is it?" Alina asked.

The doctor cleared his throat, but Chance glared at him.

"She has a right to know," said a woman's voice by the door. The tap of boots on the floor announced Jade Graylin's presence.

Alina pressed her head back into the pillow. She swallowed as Chance's mother appraised her. Jade's gold state pin shone against her obsidian suit top. In her tailored suit, Jade's height came up to the doctor's shoulder, but she took up space with her posture, causing Daxmen to step to the side. The chancellor didn't care about Alina's health one bit. Chance's mother showed up for a reason, but Alina had no idea what it was.

"What do I need to know?"

Jade exchanged glances with the doctor. "Kora claimed you were a donor match for them. While you were unconscious, we took a sample to make sure you were fine, but also to confirm her assessment." The chancellor lingered near the foot of the bed. "She's correct."

A shiver racked Alina. She couldn't rid her memory of how Kora's cold blue eyes scrutinized her, how the kronosapien probed her mind. "I was nearly choked to death. I don't know what you're talking about."

"She took a blood sample when she had a hold of you," Daxmen replied.

Alina raised a finger to her neck. She touched a fresh scab with a trace of blood where Kora had clawed at her skin. "That's a lie. I have nothing in common with her. We're not even the same species." Even as she said the last word, a disturbing remnant of the last time she was in Genodyne emerged. "You didn't," she said to Jade.

"We had to finish the Phase Three program. And we salvaged what DNA was left from the Origins, and already had Mandin's genetic profile in Genodyne's database," Jade said. "We took the fragments that we thought would work. Which means some of the kronosapien's DNA is shared with yours."

Chance's hand tightened around the bed siding, interfering with the sensors that blinked rapidly. He spoke to the doctor. "You still have the other sows left. Use them."

"Given Ash's failure to adapt to the transplant, it's unlikely the other sows will do him much better."

Daxmen scratched his jowl, loose like pudding. “The tissue match for bone marrow tends to be one in a million per the general population. Usually from a relation’s donation.”

“What are you saying?” Alina asked.

Jade placed a hand atop the bed’s footboard. “Kora wants a tissue donation from you to save Ash. It’s an exchange. She’s agreed to give us a stem cell sample from her if you provide a donation.”

“Can’t you just…sedate her?” Alina asked.

“It interferes with her stem cell production—kills them, actually. You’ll want Kora as healthy as possible if you’re going to use the sample on your mother,” Daxmen replied.

“I’ll get a sample from Kora.” Chance straightened.

“You will not go near Kora and Ash unless I command it.” Jade’s tone sharpened. “With the strength she has now, it’s too risky.”

Alina tried to breathe. “She wants my blood?”

The doctor grunted. “Given that we’re dealing with another species, it’s a little more involved than that. The quickest way to save Ash whose condition is precipitously declining would be through a stem cell transplant, from a relative. Rather than using your blood, we’d harvest your bone marrow. He’s already suffering from GvHD so the bone marrow is the best option.”

Her mouth slackened. “You want my bone marrow?”

“GvHD?” asked Chance.

“Graft-versus-host disease. His body is attacking the previous transplants we’ve given him.” The doctor shifted his gaze back to her. “For you, the procedure is simple, although we’d perform it under local anesthesia.

We withdraw the tissue with a needle. Afterward, we'd keep you for a few hours to make sure your vitals have stabilized," Daxmen replied.

"But there are risks to that," Chance said.

The doctor shrugged. "It's a low-risk procedure, especially when the donor is young and healthy—" he glanced in Alina's direction "—like you are. There's fatigue and soreness afterward, but most donors recover within a week given our advanced post-op therapeutics."

"It's not worth it," Chance said to her, his dark eyes intense.

Jade cut her gaze to her son and pressed her lips together. She tugged down at her suit top and keyed in on Alina. "If Ash's body accepts your transplant, between him and Kora, we'd not only have enough stem cells to save your mother, but enough to replicate on a mass scale. We can save the thousands in the city who took the initial tonic. The choice is yours."

An ache spread through Alina's forehead, and she closed her eyes. Soon, her mother's disease would turn fatal. Her eyes moistened, and she brushed a hand over them. Taking in a deep breath, she set her gaze on Jade. "I'll do it."

Chance's face contorted with concern. "Are you sure? This isn't your problem to solve."

"But it is. And with so many sick in the city, it's your problem, too." She peered at Daxmen. "Under certain conditions. I won't stay overnight here. You discharge me after the procedure."

The doctor turned to Jade. "That's acceptable, but I'd want her to return for a checkup."

"I'll follow up with Dr. Bellamy," Alina said. "You'll also allow her to witness the procedure." She didn't trust Daxmen even when she was awake. He was liable to take something else from her while she was unconscious.

The chancellor gave her an approving look. "Very well. We have an agreement."

"At least allow her to recover from what happened this afternoon." Chance gestured at her. "She needs rest."

The doctor nodded. "We'll schedule the procedure for next week. It'll also allow Kora to replenish her stems cells from your," he looked at Chance, "shock of her. And I need to prepare Ash with conditioning therapy, anyway."

His mother lowered her voice in Daxmen's direction. "If this works, you'll need to rebrand the product like we've talked about. The name 'Revival' is now damaged in the public's mind."

"How about Restore? Has positive connotations, I think," Daxmen said.

Chance's mother nodded.

Another pang pulsed in Alina's head, and she winced. Her ex hovered over her.

"Please, will you take me home now?"

He drew his shoulders back. "Certainly."

The sensors flickered as she hunched forward. The headache intensified, and the pain crested in strong waves. She rubbed both temples with her fingers, and queasiness rocked her.

****

The last sun had already dipped below the horizon. Twilight hung over the plaza in front of Genodyne. A few officers manned the extended Guardian perimeter that sealed off the building from the area. Otherwise, the area was quiet. Waiting at the bottom of the staircase beyond the barricade was the GATV that Alina had arrived in. She rubbed the back of her neck as Chance spoke to the driver. By the looks of him, he was fresh out of the training academy.

Her ex opened the door for her. She stepped onto the lift and grabbed the handle alongside the body of the vehicle. A pang seized her lower back, but she pushed through and climbed in. Once she returned to the penthouse, she could lie down.

Underway, the driver navigated in the direction of the City Center instead of the main boulevard along the riverwalk. Linette's penthouse was in the Meander District, away from the City Center. "Why are we taking this route?"

Across from her, Chance replied, "The shoreline is closed off for curfew. We'll have to take the main boulevard."

She leaned back against the headrest. "Aren't we breaking curfew now that the suns are down?"

Chance gave her a broad smile. "We're essential personnel and can move around the city whenever we want. Relax."

Closing her eyes, she hoped her headache would go away. Sometimes it was just easier to allow Chance to take charge. It was what he loved to do, anyway.

"Are you sure you're feeling okay?" He leaned forward, his knee almost touching hers.

Alina nodded. "Just a little sore." When she tried to roll her neck, a sharp pain like a lightning bolt shot through it, and she sucked in a small breath.

"You should have taken the pain medication Dr. Daxmen offered." Chance held out a small pill bottle.

"I don't want anything." She nestled back in the

seat.

"Suit yourself." He tucked it into his chest cargo pocket.

Darkness encroached on the city, pervading like ink. She missed the frequent aurora borealis back at Evesborough on mild nights. The winter weather in Alpheios obscured the phenomena this time of year.

Outside, their vehicle approached the City Center. City Hall came into view. Exterior lights illuminated the majestic stone building. Grand carved columns supported the portico at its entrance. Across from the stone steps leading to City Hall was Ambrose Park. The large sweep of snow-covered grass was no longer visible, nor the obelisk at its center. Only tall trees marking the park's boundary lurked in the slide to night.

They stopped at an intersection. An old tree on the corner loomed, keeping its secrets close. Shadows in the surrounding area seemed to slink by.

A shout sounded from the park.

They looked out the GATV's tinted windows.

A small crowd of masked individuals had gathered at the base of the steps of City Hall. The building lights showed a band of officers swarming out, their batons drawn. One man with a scarf over his mouth threw an object over the heads of the officers. A boom echoed, thumping the air. Smoke covered the entrance. Alina's heart leapt as she tried to discern what was happening.

More masked people emerged from the park. Clouds of dust and smoke obscured visibility. A crowd of people massed at the stairs, and she caught glimpses of officers wrestling them. A full melee had broken out. Her grasp on the arm rest tightened.

"Get us out of here—now!" Chance said to the

driver.

With a click, the door locks secured them. The tires squealed, and the driver turned left at the intersection. The GATV rolled forward then screeched to a halt. Alina rocked forward.

"Put your seatbelt on," Chance ordered.

A flock of people poured from the darkness of the park. One pounded the hood of the vehicle. The GATV was quickly enveloped by a pack of masked figures. A hooded man smashed a rock into Alina's side window. Up close, half his face was covered by gray scales, and he sneered. She jolted back in her seat, squelching a scream in her throat. The shatterproof glass held although cracks appeared. She yanked the seat belt over her lap.

"Stay here." Chance climbed into the front passenger seat, barking at the other officer. "I said, drive!"

"I can't. I'll run them over," the young officer replied.

"Turn on the damn lights," Chance said.

In front of the vehicle, the headlights glared different colors at the unruly mob. A short scream of the siren startled the crowd. They hesitated in throwing objects for a moment.

Chance grabbed the receiver near the wheel. His ferocious tone broke out over the main speaker. "Clear out of the way of the vehicle immediately! Clear out of the way!"

The gang converged in front of them, and they beat the GATV harder.

"To hell with you, tyrant!" A protestor shouted as he kicked the vehicle's body.

Without a weapon, Alina drew her arms in, clutching herself. Covered faces with fierce eyes beat her window, screaming obscenities, within a breath of her.

Chance glanced over his shoulder, peering out the back window. "Reverse now!" His jaw tightened.

The GATV lurched backward, away from the mob.

"Turn here!" he said.

The powerful vehicle swung around and went back the way they came, then took a sharp right. Alina swayed in her seat. They picked up speed and roared through the street. She grabbed the ceiling handle.

"Up here, take Block 14 to 12." Chance touched his earlobe comm bar. "Come in, Sentinel. Say Chariot's position."

After listening, he said, "Do not bring Chariot to Lodestar location. I repeat, do NOT bring Chariot to Lodestar! Take her to Citadel. A riot has broken out at Lodestar."

Alina stared out of the windows, her heart hammering. Two more masked men slipped around the corner in the direction of the park. "Where are we going?"

But Chance was on the call.

Another minute or two passed, and faint signs of familiarity gleamed in the neighborhood. Residential stone condos flashed by.

"Stop here," Chance said.

They halted in front of a walkway a few yards from a stone high-rise.

He jumped out of the vehicle and opened her door. "Come on."

She leapt to the ground. "Here?"

"Yes, we need to get indoors." He stepped to the

driver's side. "There's an underground garage around the corner. Wait for me there."

The GATV pulled away.

Down the walkway, she rushed after Chance. Inspecting the building, she halted. An ornate wrought iron grate covered the double front doors that were all too familiar. "Wait, this is your place."

"It's where I can defend you." He placed a hand on her arm to urge her forward.

She pulled away. "I want to go back to the penthouse."

Chance exhaled through his nostrils. Every muscle in his body was rigid. "I need to find out what the situation is in the city before we drive into another ambush." He swung his arm toward the front doors. "You'll be safe here. It's temporary."

Whirling around, she searched the dark street. The GATV was gone.

"I don't have time to argue with you. Now please, you can wait inside until the riot dies down." The yellow light over the entrance highlighted Chance's face. His mouth was firm as he awaited her reply.

She swallowed, stuck for a second. Her blood flow still raced from the recent attack. The quiet of the neighborhood unsettled her compared to the explosion she'd heard moments ago. The only person outside was the man in uniform standing in front of her on the walkway. She could not ask Chance, as capable as he was, to fight off a sudden crowd.

"Just for a few minutes."

His link activated the lock opening. Once inside, he led her to the elevator. The lobby was well-lit and clean. A doorman at the front counter nodded at Chance.

"No other visitors tonight, Lawrence." Chance tapped the mounted crystal tablet on the counter and entered her name.

Lawrence? Alina stopped, gazing at the soft-spoken man behind the counter. More silver emerged in his dark hair than when she saw him last.

"Sure, Mr. Graylin. Heard there's a terrible ruckus by the park a few blocks away." He grinned at her. "Nice to see you again, Miss DeHerte."

Her cheeks warmed like she had been caught entering a private club where she didn't belong. She couldn't quite bring herself to smile back at Lawrence who had always treated her kindly. Instead, she nodded. Chance was holding the elevator door open for her, and she stepped in. Her stomach lurched as the lift climbed up five floors.

The doors chimed upon opening. Her skin crawled as she followed Chance down the hall to a familiar steel door. He waved his link at its entry keypad and the bolt clicked. He held the door open for her.

As he commanded on the lights, she blinked. In front of her was the living area where scarlet couches were arrayed. Alina stared at the furniture for a moment. Reminded of how they used to converse on them, she batted the memory away.

Folding her arms, she looked around. Familiar objects leapt out at her, like a tall black vase that stood in the corner. A floor-to-ceiling wall shelf held some books, an astronomical clock display with the local forecast, and framed scenes of the city. A long, stone countertop separated the kitchen from the living area.

Chance entered the kitchen and placed the medicine bottle on the counter. He opened the refrigerator and poured a sparkling clear liquid from a pitcher into a glass. "Do you want some fizz?"

Rubbing her arms, she acquiesced. He brought it out and placed the glass on the sleek serving table in front of the couch. "Sit down and rest. I have to make a few calls." He disappeared down the hall in the direction of the office.

She lowered herself to the couch. The fizzy water refreshed her, but her hands still trembled. Chance's low voice drifted into the room as he spoke in his Guardian tone. Taking another sip helped calm her jitters.

Gazing around, she noted not much had changed. Although the framed picture of them on the wall shelf was gone, replaced by a holo-base for entertainment instead.

She stood. Pacing, she made her way around the room, looking for new furniture or objects. The cream rug was still soft under her boots, warming the stone-tiled floor. But the tall glass that Chance served her fizz in was new, cut with beveled edges into the crystal. The wall shelf held some work mementos. One was a photo of his father in uniform, who died before Chance was born. Next to it, a photo stood that she hadn't seen before, of Chance wearing his new captain rank. In the picture, he wasn't smiling but possessed a stoic expression. A hint of cynicism appeared in his eyes.

It was shortly after Chance's promotion that Mandin was diagnosed with epilepsy. Her relationship with Chance crumbled shortly after that. As she studied the photo, she ran a finger down the shelf. It had been recently dusted. Chance always kept the place tidy, but the distrust in his expression the photographer captured was new. Prior to that, he often carried an upbeat disposition. Everything always rolled off him before.

That shift was new in him. She couldn't quite place it when he showed up at the penthouse. He'd entered the room with his usual swagger. But his voice at times held a muted, pessimistic shade, like he contained a dark roiling force within him, just underneath the surface.

The office door opened. She rubbed her forehead, turning away from the photo. Chance strode back in. "I have to stop by the Guardian headquarters. They've arrested some folks."

"You're leaving now?" She hovered by the wall shelf, exposed.

"I shouldn't be gone long. It's not far from here, if you'll recall." He cocked his head at her. "You're jumpy. Nothing will happen to you here."

"I'd like you to take me home when it's clear." Alina rested on a black, curved back armchair in the far corner of the room. Her gaze fell to a new game board with carved figurines on a small table. They rested over different spots on the underlying pyramids. Silence settled over the apartment.

Chance was studying her. "I'll check on the city situation." He moved to the holo-base on the wall shelf and flipped it over, checking its settings. Soft music emanated from the base, and he commanded the volume to lower. "I've programmed it to take commands from guests if you'd like to listen to something else."

She clutched the arm of the chair. "You'll come back soon?"

"I'll return before it gets late." A satisfied smile spread over his features as he straightened. "I'll tell Lawrence downstairs to keep an eye out." As he walked to the door, Chance pointed to the kitchen. "Please help yourself to whatever you'd like. Lock the door after me."

The front door softly closed behind him. Alina hurried across the room. After she hit the lock symbol on the keypad above the curved handle, she rested her forehead on the door and let out a deep exhale. Her skin chilled from its sleek steel exterior. Coated in a dark gray powdered finish, Chance had custom-ordered it. Now what?

The fizz dampened her headache, and she drank the rest of it. She twirled the empty glass between her fingers, allowing the last bubbles to tickle her throat. A soft melody wound its way around the room. Alina spoke, lowering the volume on the holo-base. Examining her surroundings, she turned around. If she was going to be stuck for a little while longer, she may as well snoop around her old quarters.

Chapter 16

Lieutenant Harding stood near the slender screen inside the interrogation waiting area. "Caught him as he barreled through our line at C.H. Strong as an avalanche. Almost made it inside until a corporal managed to grab his ankle. File shows he's clean—no arrests until now." He tapped the screen showing the prisoner's information.

Chance crossed his arms. He scrutinized the prisoner's photo. Remembering the crowd that they'd encountered while he was in the GATV with Alina, he swore under his breath. "Any weapons on him during arrest?"

Harding motioned to the objects sitting on the table. "He wore a respirator and had a gas grenade on him. Think he meant to set it off inside, which would have forced us to evacuate the staff." The lieutenant picked up a cylinder filled with a liquid. "Looks like a homemade device."

"Cunning plan. To target the councilmen right around curfew as they're escorted home." His own mother could have been at City Hall. Fortunately, Chance had already diverted her security team to her apartment while she was enroute from Genodyne. He squeezed the respirator's rubber head straps and turned it over in his hand. Scratches obscured the serial number on the metal filtration canister. "This is an industrial one."

The lieutenant switched to the video feed on the monitor. The prisoner sat hunched over at a table in the interrogation room. "I tried questioning him, but he didn't say much. They confiscated his link after he was subdued." Harding held out the silver wrist cuff.

Chance set down the respirator and cycled through the link's screen. "He zeroized it right before the attack." He placed it back on the table.

A nod from Harding. "Yes. They're practicing good OPSEC. Undoubtedly a Citizens Liberation Front attack. If they would have taken a DV hostage…" he gave his head a shake.

An ache permeated Chance's back teeth from clenching his jaw as he examined the evidence on the table. "What about the respirator's manufacturers?"

"AI returned three hits. One is a company that makes ours, so easy to rule that one out. Two other companies produce them. A construction company, and a mining one."

"Did you say a mining one?" Chance frowned, remembering the chisel. Then again, they would be in common use at construction sites as well.

"Yes. I'm already meeting with their reps tomorrow. For both companies." The lieutenant stood with hands loosely clasped behind him.

Gazing at the monitor, Chance studied the young man. "Check if they keep inventory records of who they hand them out to. I'll take it from here." He removed the baton from his belt. "Turn off the video cam."

"Yes, sir." The lieutenant tapped the translucent screen and deactivated the feed. Harding exited the waiting area.

Gripping the handle of the baton in one hand, Chance used his link to open the locked door leading to the interrogation room. The man kept his gaze glued to the table as Chance twirled his baton, taking his time in approaching him.

He rapped the baton on the table, but the prisoner refused to look up. Chance grabbed the opposite chair and reversed it. He straddled it and folded an arm along the top. "This is a rather unexpected surprise."

A scowl formed on the prisoner's face, but when his green eyes fixed on Chance, his head drew back. He gaped at the Guardian across the table from him.

"Hello, Gordean," Chance said. "It's just you and me now."

Gordo composed himself, but his forehead crinkled. Then he snorted. "Did they really think I'd talk just because they sent you in? You're wasting your time. You may as well lock me up now."

A small chuckle eased out of Chance. "Is that how you address an old family friend? But in this case, it doesn't matter. Because you're in serious trouble this time." He sharpened his tone. "You attacked City Hall, and they'll charge you for treason. Do you know what that means? You better give me something to work with. Because I'm the only one who can help you."

"You work for a corrupt regime. Your mother has killed innocent people in the city!" Gordo slammed his hand onto the table.

Chance stood and thrust aside the chair. With a flick of his thumb, he charged the baton until a spark arced out of its end, and he pointed it across the table. "You want to have a go at me? Because I have no use for traitors, no matter who they are."

"Screw you. I have nothing else to say." Gordo placed his outstretched arms on the table and curled up his hands. "Go on. Put the ties on me—do it!"

"Where did you get the respirator?"

Silence filled the room.

"I said, where did you get it?" Chance released the charge but kept the baton elevated.

Folding his arms across his chest, Gordo pressed his lips together.

The room was soundproof. With the camera off, no one would know what transpired in it. Chance would have his answers, one way or the other. He shook his head, lowering the baton. "You know who's going to be so disappointed once they find out you're here?"

Gordo's mouth twitched, but he remained silent.

Chance rubbed his index finger down his chin. "Your poor, ailing mother. To know her son has been charged with treason against the state." As he rolled the baton between his fingers, Gordo tracked his movements. "It's protocol we question all family members, especially with such serious charges." Grabbing the chair, he flipped it around to its proper position and sat down.

Alina's brother shifted in his seat. "Leave my family out of this."

"I'm afraid I can't do that."

He glared. "My mother and Jakob didn't do anything wrong! They know nothing about this." His forearm quivered as he pointed to his chest. "This is my fight, not theirs."

"But we have no choice. We can't take your word for it." Chance lounged back comfortably in the chair.

A sullen expression crossed Gordo's face. "You

know they're innocent."

Chance crossed a foot over his knee and loosely held his baton over his lap. "You're probably right about your mother and Jakob. But you didn't know your sister was in the GATV with me when that mob you were with attacked us, did you?" A tight smile etched its way across his face.

Gordo's head drew back. "I was on the steps…that wasn't what…" he gulped and shifted uncomfortably in his seat.

"How do you think she'll react when she discovers the crowd her brother was with nearly killed her?"

"Is she okay?" Gordo's shoulders sagged.

"Yes, thanks to me. But how awful for her to find out you were involved."

The prisoner quieted for a moment. "What do you want?"

"Information. Now, where did you get the respirator? We'll find out anyway, but if your story checks out, I might be able to convince the others to take an alternate route." Chance lowered his voice. "Help me, Gordo. Give me a way to spare your family from trouble."

"I don't know!" Gordo splayed his hands out. "We're given instructions over a secure channel about where the next event is going to be, and where to pick up equipment. I got the respirator from a warehouse. No one was there when I arrived."

"What warehouse?" Chance leaned forward in his seat.

"Some warehouse down in the Industrial District, number 149. It didn't have any welcome signs on it. They gave out a code to the door." Gordo shook his head.

"There was a bunch of equipment on the tables so I grabbed one, and the grenade."

"Who's sending out the messages?"

"I don't know. I got a private message from an unknown sender to join an encrypted channel."

A grunt from Chance. "Not good enough."

"You have the warehouse number. Go check it out." Alina's brother gestured at him.

"Is that all you have?"

"What else do you want?"

Chance contemplated the young man in front of him. Judging from his strength and speed, it wasn't surprising Gordo nearly forced his way into City Hall. Although no one would think him involved in such an act, not a young man from the Meander who was a professional rogue ball player. In that sense, Gordo was an asset. "We'll check the warehouse, but to leave your family out of this, you have to do something for me."

"What?" Gordo's voice strained.

Chance braced a hand on his thigh and angled forward. "Find out who's directing the attacks."

"How am I supposed to do that?"

"You zeroized your link, but you can figure out a way to regain contact with them. Ask for a meeting." Chance tapped his finger into the table. "Work your way into their inner circle. Get them to trust you. Volunteer to help them in whatever way you can. Make them believe you're wholly committed to their cause. Then, when you have some names, you come back to me. But you must keep it a secret and let no one—and I mean *no one*—know what you're doing."

"You want me to become a squealer?" Gordo's upper lip curled.

Chance rose and holstered his baton. "I want you to work for me now. It's the only way I can release you and call them off your family. May even buy you some leniency when it comes time for us to roll up the network."

Gordo's fists tightened. "I can't do that."

"Fine. But they'll detain both Jakob and your mother for questioning." Chance reminded himself that Harding already knew about Alina and Mandin. The situation called for delicate handling in order for him to leverage it.

"And as for Alina," he continued, "The government will force her to testify about the attack." Chance leaned a shoulder against the wall. "Treat her as a hostile witness if she refuses. They take treason charges very seriously. Because whatever she doesn't say, I'll certainly tell them."

Sitting back, Gordo grunted. "No wonder she left you."

Balling his fists, Chance examined his hands. His knuckles whitened. Any cordiality he once held toward Gordo fell away, but he quelled his temper. He needed results. "It gives me no pleasure to see this happen to your family. You expect me to be able stop my associates after you attacked them? I can help, but only if you cooperate."

Gordo's face clouded over. "How do I know you'll leave my family out of this?"

"Because…" Chance straightened. "I have too much history with your sister to cause her such pain. I want to get to know my son. And I never had anything but the highest regard for your mother." He flicked his wrist in a gesture toward him. "It's why Alina asked me to help her obtain a cure for her, and I agreed to her request. You do want that, don't you?"

Gordo grimaced. "If I do this, you'll help my mother?"

"You have my word that the minute Genodyne produces a cure, your mother will get the first dose."

"And my arrest?"

"We won't have to publicly release it. Therefore, your family won't know about it." Chance waited, letting his words take effect.

"Deal." The prisoner hung his head.

"Don't look so down. You're doing right by your family." *As I must now do for mine,* Chance thought. He couldn't allow such a movement to topple his mother. Such mobs were uncontrollable. He didn't want Alina angry with him for detaining Gordo, either. At the door, he glanced back. "Remember. No one else knows about this but us." He swung open the door and headed out.

Down the hall, Chance stopped by Harding's office. The lieutenant was scribbling a note on his desk but hopped up when Chance entered. He shut the door behind him. "Release him in the morning."

Harding's stare bore into him from behind the desk. "Say again?"

"He's our informant now. Delete his record out of the database but keep it in your backup files. The only people who know about this are you and me." Chance tapped the surface of the wooden desk. "You'll check on him from time-to-time, as a reminder. Don't tip off his family. They have no idea what he's been up to. Give him my direct line."

The lieutenant held his shoulders back. "If I do this, sir, I'd like to discuss my future assignment."

Chance studied him. He recalled Commander Zinyon's note about Harding when the lieutenant was detailed to him. "*Sharp officer. Obeys superiors.*"

"I know what you want. Do this, and you'll make my recommendation ironclad. That you should be the chancellor's next aide once we dismantle the Citizens Front. Understand?"

Harding nodded. "Yes, sir."

"Good." Chance took in a deep breath. "What's the city's status right now?"

"Squads are reporting back that it's all clear. We dispersed the crowd, and many of them are probably tending to injuries. Doubt they'll try anything again later tonight since we've doubled our patrols. They're not finding anyone outside."

"Who else was caught?"

"There were two others, but they were less useful. Just rabble who joined in at the last minute."

"Publicize the charges against them so it sends a message." Chance left the lieutenant's office and headed to the building's exit.

Chance had deactivated the news programming from the holo-base back at the condo to avoid alarming Alina, but now it presented him an unexpected opportunity. Alina would be unaware of the city's security developments.

By the lounge, the GATV driver waited for him. "Where to now, sir?"

Chance clasped the young officer on the shoulder. He grinned as he contemplated who anticipated his return. "Home. I'm done here for the night." Chance lengthened his stride as he followed the driver outside.

Chapter 17

Alina gently dragged her fingertip over the cord burn on her neck. Her wound still stung. The mirror's reflection showed the red mark across her throat where Kora had nearly strangled her. A shudder rolled through her. A fresh scab formed underneath her jawline. She gulped and opened the bathroom mirror.

The cabinet held Chance's toiletries. She decided against applying any lotion which could irritate her skin more. Her hand drifted from her collarbone down her climate suit. Inside the chest pocket, she gripped the hard gemstone of Kiean's ring. She couldn't bear to feel the strap around her neck at the moment. Best to leave the ring where it was, safely tucked away.

She left the bathroom and made her way to the guest bedroom. The door pushed open easily, and the lights flickered on upon her entry. She halted.

Inside the room was a large, blue wooden cube that Chance bought some years ago. Colorful pipes led in-and-out of the cube with different painted shapes a toddler could push through carved openings, matching and collecting patterns. Along the wall sat a sailor-blue bed with a sleek headboard and curved sides, designed for a small child. Slowly, she approached it. With care, she perched on the bed's end and rubbed her face.

He had kept the crib they bought but removed its rails to turn it into a child's bed. The eggshell-colored sheets were soft and clean. Swallowing, she walked over to the closet. No clothes were hung, but a few boxes remained around the floor. Taking a peek in one, she recognized her old clothes. Quietly, she shut the closet doors. She stopped in the middle of the room. The walls were still painted a cheerful lemon color. Light-headed, she exited.

She avoided the master bedroom. Instead, she ambled to the living room and reclined on the scarlet couch. While the temperature was comfortable in the condo, she turned up the heat on her suit a notch. Mellow music played from the holo-base, and she commanded it to air the news programming. There would be reports on what happened at City Hall. But the holo-base simply turned off the music and remained silent on its shelf. She gave up and folded her legs underneath her.

Her link showed it was getting late. She sent Linette a message, asking about Mandin. Her mother replied that Mandin had fallen asleep while Halle played him a bedtime story, and that the robot had made him laugh for hours. At least he was safe.

She sent a message to Gordo next. But her link queue remained empty. The weather forecast predicted snowfall later that night. It would be cold and treacherous, but the GATVs were rugged enough to navigate the streets during harsh conditions. Hugging a small pillow to her chest, she closed her eyes. There was nothing to do but wait.

Maybe Chance simply didn't get around to re-decorating the guest bedroom. He always worked long hours. However, the crib had been converted. And her clothes had been folded neatly and stored away. No feminine lotions or soaps were visible in the bathroom.

She curled up on the couch, clutching the cushion. Impossible. He wasn't a monk. There wouldn't necessarily be any signs of a date since he always kept the place clean.

The sleek couch cushioned her body comfortably. Hunched into a ball, fragments of their former lives nibbled at her mind. She sprang up and swiveled around the polished, black stone counter that separated the gathering area from the kitchen.

The cooler held a few protein blocks and leaf bundles. Fizz canisters were arrayed neatly on the bottom shelf. He must have canceled the catering service long ago. She wasn't really hungry, anyway.

A click from the front door sounded, and Chance entered.

"What did you find out?" she asked.

He armed the lock, punching in some numbers. "The city is unpredictable right now. Still reports of roving mobs so patrols are out."

Alina gripped the counter. "Can you take me home?"

"Sorry, it's not safe. Not until the curfew lifts in the morning." He breezed into the kitchen and ran a hand through his hair. Taking a glance at the untouched medicine bottle that he'd left for her on the counter, he frowned. He opened a cabinet, and a row of crystal goblets slid out on a rack.

"I can't stay here tonight." She brushed past him and stormed into the living area. "Call the driver. *Now*."

He placed a tall carafe on the counter. "Too much of a risk." Red wine from the carafe splashed into one of the crystal goblets. When he was done filling it, he poured more wine into another matching goblet. "Are you hungry?"

"No." She grinded her teeth. "You can't keep me here. I'll leave." Chance was always such a pompous ass. She would not allow him to control her.

He prowled out of the kitchen with the two goblets. "You'll do no such thing. I've already armed the lock with a code you do not have access to." He sipped a drink. "Want some wine? This used to be your favorite." His shoulders relaxed as he held out the crystal cup.

She brought a hand to her chest. "I have to check on my son—*our* son."

"Glad to hear I'm his father now." Chance set both glasses down on the serving table. "I'm going to change. Mandin is well taken care of at the penthouse." He headed toward the master bedroom.

"But I can't stay here."

Through the crack of the slightly open door, he called out. "You're safe here. That's what matters."

Alina's hands clenched into fists. She stood in front of the low table shaking, trying to contain the flames within. There was no way she would fall asleep on the scarlet couch tonight. Not with Chance in the next room over. Rubbing her forehead, she thought of the long walk back to her mother's penthouse if the M was shut down. It was completely dark with heavy snowfall. And if a patrol picked her up, she'd wind up back at Chance's apartment, or worse.

Chance strolled back into the main room, tying a knot over the front of his charcoal, drawstring pants. He had thrown on a black, comfortable shirt that opened at the throat. Eyeing him, she knew he usually kept a small backup key to manually open the door. There was a hidden pressure spring at a small opening near the lock pad. But he usually kept the key on his body, and she'd end up having to rifle through his pants pockets. She needed to switch tactics.

"Please, can't you call the driver? I want to go home."

His hands planted on his hips. "I'm tired from saving you multiple times in one day. Allow me to take a break tonight, and I'll save your precious ass again tomorrow." He approached, inspecting her neck. "You didn't take any of the medication, did you?" Exhaling, he shook his head. He brought a glass of wine to his lips. "Tastes wonderful after a day like today." The other goblet was in his outstretched hand, and his mouth curled into a satisfied smile.

She glared. "I'm not sharing your bed." Begrudgingly, she swiped the glass from him as he laughed. The fruity nectar rushed down her throat as she gulped it, not having tasted wine in ages. As the elegant liquid spread over her tongue, she savored its bold notes. She half-wanted to throw the wine in Chance's face, half-wanted to consume the entire glass. The hearty wine tasted delicious.

****

The lush bouquet of wine overcame Alina's caution, which had disappeared after the second glass. Now onto her third glass, she twirled the stem of the goblet in between her fingertips as the scarlet couch ensconced her. "Does the university still have winter lights?"

At the other end of the couch, Chance took a swallow, a knee pulled up beside him. "Not this year, given the curfew. They had it in previous years while you were gone, though."

"No winter celebration, then." They used to walk

through the campus during the milder evenings, watching the adorned buildings transform themselves into different colored light giants among the snow. The adjacent shops and cafes would remain open late, handing out spiced hot drinks and palm-sized pastries.

"The shops still open during permitted hours in the daytime," Chance said. "If you want to shop while you're here. At least you won't fall on a patch of black ice." He eased out a mellow chuckle.

Her leg was outstretched on the couch, and she nudged his hip with a socked foot. "The university should have cleared that!" Excited at the time among the crowds at the festival, she congratulated herself for taking a shortcut through a narrow alley to the shops. A moment later, she'd slipped on a dark sliver of iced-over pavement, her arms wheeling backward. Chance had grabbed her under her armpits, stopping her head from slamming into the frozen ground.

"A spot the clearing machine missed. Or maybe spiced liquor has that effect." He peered over his goblet at her.

Her mouth puckered. "You were awfully pleased with yourself as I recall."

"I saved you from certain disaster." Chance leaned toward the serving table and popped a baked crustette with meat relish into his mouth. He'd found a snack for them after scouring the kitchen.

A small giggle escaped from her. She unwound as her laugh curled around the room. Chance's loungewear fell gracefully over his powerful frame as he chewed the crustette. Still in her climate suit, she'd removed her boots after the first glass of wine. She may as well get comfortable on the couch if she was going to spend the night on it. The bed in the guest room was much too small.

The crystal goblet contained a diamond-shaped pattern etched into the cup, making it easy to grip. She reclined and took another sip. "I have a confession to make."

"Oh?" He angled toward her, dropping his leg from the couch to the ground.

She held the goblet close. "Thank you for this afternoon. How you intervened with Kora." She wiggled in her seat. "And in the GATV back at the park." The last of the vino swirled pleasantly in her goblet. "You saved my ass twice in one day." There was no sense in being horrid to him if they were going to be stuck in the same quarters.

A smile spread across his lips. "You're welcome." Then a mischievous glint appeared in his dark eyes. "You do have a pretty cute ass so it's hard not to keep an eye on it."

The acid of the wine roiled her stomach. "Stop that." Despite the danger signs, she finished the last gulp. "More, please." Her hand thrust out the empty goblet.

Chance gazed upon her thoughtfully. "I think you've had enough. Your cheeks are red."

A protest sprang to her lips, but he rose from the couch. He carried the flask of wine to the kitchen. She blurted out, "You're not the boss of me!" But she couldn't think of a time that he got tipsy like she did, and that irked her more. Eamine was begging her to hurl a boot at him.

He re-emerged with a carafe of fresh spring water and a crystal tumbler. "That, I'm definitely not." After filling the glass with water, he held it out to her. "It'll help wash down the crustettes. Sorry I don't have much food, but I haven't had time to pick up groceries."

Biting back a retort, she took the tumbler he offered. The cool water calmed her, and the crustettes helped ameliorate the rumblings in her tummy. They nibbled on a few more samples. As she chewed the delectable crumbs, she noticed that Chance switched to spring water as well.

"You ever hear back from your mother about Mandin?" he asked.

"Yes. Halle put him to bed." She stretched out her neck.

"The new personal assistants that Jakob makes are pretty handy. Thinking of purchasing one myself." He polished off another bite.

She finished her crustette and sipped more spring water. As the water took effect, the cloud gradually lifted from her mind. "Chance?"

"Yes?"

She ran a finger over the glass rim. "I noticed you kept the cube and kiddie bed."

Chance's gaze rested on the serving table. He shrugged. "A toy more for me. Sometimes, I push the shapes through the maze and collect the patterns. There's twenty-six in all, and I vary their sequence and see how many I can string together. Anyway," his throat bobbed, "Transforming the crib into a bed kept me useful during a stormy weekend."

Alina stopped breathing. The tumbler became slippery in her grasp.

Chance stood and ran a hand through his dark curls. "It's getting late. You'll find something comfortable in the guest room closet. I'll get blankets." He left in the direction of the master bedroom.

She set the tumbler on the console. It was a good time for a respite. The longer the night went on, the murkier her circumstances seemed. It was jumbling all together. Yawning, she covered her mouth. The wine left her slightly woozy, but the water reassured her that morning would be manageable. She made her way to the guest room.

The boxes in the closet contained clothing she'd forgotten about. Sifting through them, she remembered how she'd kept a few tailored pieces for their outings. Her hand pushed aside more intimate articles of clothing, digging deeper. Finally, she settled on a loose tunic and dark stretchers. A pair of thick stockings accompanied her feet, and she appraised herself in the mirror. Her limbs were covered, and at least she didn't look dowdy. Then again, who cared what she looked like? She shook her head and left.

In the gathering area, she hovered at the edge of the couch and rubbed her face. She bit her bottom lip. There was little choice but to stay for the night. It wasn't her fault that mobs attacked institutions throughout the city. She wrapped her arms around herself, thinking of Mandin sleeping alone in their bed at the penthouse.

Chance entered with an armful of blankets. She stood to reach for them, but he already snapped one out with a flick of his wrist.

"Thanks." She clutched a corner of the fluffy cloth.

Before she could grab the rest of it, he took up residence on the couch and spread the cover over himself. "Take the master bedroom. Get some rest, and I'll bring you home in the morning." He tucked a pillow behind his head.

The meat relish left a heavy taste on her tongue. “I’ll sleep on the couch.” She kept one hand on the blanket by his foot.

He rolled over to his side, facing out. “If you insist, you can sleep alongside me, but it might be a tight fit. Try not to kick me, please.”

Her mouth opened as he closed his eyes. “Chance, I won’t sleep in your bedroom.” She tugged at the blanket again.

Yanking it tightly over himself and out of her hands, he said, “Too late. I have the couch. Go to bed.” He yawned. “Lights down.”

The overhead lights dimmed with the exception of a low pilot light in the kitchen.

“Good night,” he said.

Gulping, she replied. “You shouldn’t have to sleep on the couch in your own home.” Her fingers pulled at one another.

“Like I said, you can curl up next to me.” In the faint light, a smile broadened over his shapely lips. “It’ll be warmer that way. Or you can turn up the heat and take the master bedroom.”

Standing in the dark, Alina plucked at her stretchers. She turned away. Down the hall she crept. She stopped at the thermostat outside the master bedroom and ordered it raised a few degrees. When she entered, a lamp softly illuminated the room. Surveying the bed, she released a long exhale.

The sheets were new. Onyx-colored, the top cover invitingly beckoned her with its thick, plush texture. She slid into the bed and snuggled the cover over herself. Her head found the pillow, a feather against her neck. She gazed around the lit room. The closet doors remained shut. A patterned pillow rested on the corner armchair. The soft sheets whispered at her to rest. She ordered the lights off.

Turning onto her side, the silky bedding glided over her body. Closing her eyes, Alina allowed sleep to overcome her.

****

A hand squeezed her neck until she couldn't breathe. Tighter and tighter, it gripped her, and Alina tried to scream. Only she couldn't make a sound, and the claws dug into her skin. Ice-blue eyes squinted at her, prying apart her mind. They settled on the children in the great cavern, carefully observing them. Blinking, the blue eyes rested on Mandin. They tracked his movements near the Spartan.

"Noooo!"

Someone shook her, and she cried out.

"Alina!"

Gasping, she flung away the cover, wrestling with the dark figure towering over her.

"You're having a nightmare!"

She blinked, the familiar tenor of the voice registering. Moonlight spilled through the window over the looming silhouette in front of her. One of her hands was hooked around Chance's muscular bicep. She froze, clinging to him.

"Are you okay?"

Her throat parched, she couldn't answer.

"I heard you from the living room."

She inhaled deep breaths. The dream had devoured her, wringing her insides tight. "I'm…sorry I woke you."

He drew her into his arms and rubbed her back. His hand stroked her hair gently, and his pine-scented soap filled her nostrils, leaving her dizzy. Lost and treading water, she imagined her head slipping underneath a wave. The room felt toasty all over from the heat being cranked up. Her chin buried into his shoulder through the thin fabric of his shirt. Fire engulfed her face, and she pressed a hand against one of the hard panes of his chest, nudging him away. “I’m fine. Thanks.”

As she rolled over, she caught the concern in his dark eyes.

“You sure?”

“Yes.” She clutched the covers tight around her shoulders.

“Be right back.” He padded out of the room.

A few minutes later, he placed a glass of water by the nightstand. “Get some rest.”

She waited until he quietly shut the door to lift her head. Her hand shook as she took a few gulps. If she drank enough water, maybe it would wash away the memory of Kora strangling her. She was safe, she reminded herself. Chance was in the next room if she needed anything.

About that, a tiny voice whispered to her. *You’re glad he’s here.*

Too weary to engage, she batted the voice away. She laid her head back onto the soft pillow. It was late, and useless to dwell on irrational fears. Her body found comfort in the bedding again. She deserved to rest until morning. When it was light out, she thought drowsily, she could return home. But notes of pine lingered in the room, lulling her to a dreamland of forgotten memories.

Chapter 18

Ice glistened on the bare trees lining the streets. While no one was out yet that morning, the rustle of the river nearby filled the air as Alina hopped off the GATV. The long walkway in front of her mother's penthouse was covered with a half-meter of white snow, pristine and not yet touched.

"The clearing machines should be out in a few minutes. Do you want to wait in the GATV?" Chance held the door open for her.

She shook her head. Chance had risen early that morning and already prepared breakfast by the time she woke. After drinking juice and taking a few bites of olein-covered carb toast, she announced she was ready to head back. He was friendly during their meal, but her cheeks still burned when she thought of how she'd clung to him the previous night. It was time to return to Mandin and her mother.

Chance scratched his head. "I'll clear a path." He started swishing through the snow in his black Guardian suit, but she quickly joined him.

"I'll make it."

Lifting her boots, she trudged through the thick snow up to her knees alongside him. She pressed her chin into the neck of her old climate suit. Puffs of air left her mouth as she plodded through the mass of soft snow. About half-way to the front doors, she tipped forward.

He lunged for her arm "You all right?"

She pulled away. "I'm fine." She could manage without his help.

They reached the lobby where the concierge inside waited. "Miss DeHerte, I would have called the clearer over if I knew you were out there," he said.

"It's no problem at all."

"Next time, don't hesitate to give my link a ping. Good morning, Mr. Graylin." The concierge remembered Chance from his visit the previous day when he picked her up in the GATV. Touching the crystal screen on his desk, the concierge entered Chance's name without her request. She turned away, biting her bottom lip.

Surmising that Chance wanted to see Mandin again by the way he hovered nearby, Alina allowed him to escort her up. When they arrived, the lift doors opened to the familiar entryway with gold-striped wallpaper and polished tiled floors. Mandin's laughter floated out from the living room.

On the gold-and-silver brocade couches, Halle entertained Mandin with a game depicting an animal hopping along a wooded trail on her face monitor.

"Mama!" He rushed over and clutched her waist.

Hugging him close, Alina smiled. His dark curls were soft against her fingers, and he looked rested, still in his pajamas. "Where's Nana?"

The animals disappeared from Halle's face, replaced by feminine features. "Mrs. Caughlin took breakfast in her room. She's still getting ready." The bot approached the entryway. "Good morning, Mr. Graylin. How nice to see you again."

"Hello, Halle." Chance's voice was amiable. "Your

hospitality programming is impeccable."

"Thank you for the compliment, Mr. Graylin."

"Did Mandin have his medication this morning?" Alina asked.

"Not yet. He said he usually takes it after he eats. He had a fruit frothy, and a sweet roll already." The bot formed a friendly smile.

Mandin's bottom lip thrust out. "Mama, I no need medicine."

"Yes, you do. You're supposed to take it every morning." She glanced at the bot. "Can you boil some water so I can steep his herbs?"

"Certainly, ma'am." Halle left for the kitchen.

"Where's Uncle Gordo?" At least her son's eyes were bright, and he was safe, even if her mother left the bot to watch over him.

Mandin shrugged. "I dunno." Still gripping her leg, he peered up at Chance who waited quietly.

She pondered Gordo's absence. He still hadn't answered her message from last night. The curfew had lifted so he probably left for the gym. But the snow hadn't been cleared, and it was pristine when they'd arrived. Perhaps he went out the back?

Rubbing Mandin's shoulder, she said, "Do you want to say hello to your father?"

Chance crouched and folded an arm over his knee to meet him eye-level. "Hi, Mandin. I've been thinking about you." His tone softened, a departure from its usual authoritative manner. "Do you still have that GATV I gave you?

His son broke out into a smile. "It's over here." He ran to the low table and picked up the toy. Alina noted he'd already left scratches on the crystal table with it.

"Can you watch him for a few minutes while I check on Linette?"

"Of course." Chance rested near Mandin on the brocade couches and beckoned his son to climb up on it with his toy.

Alina followed the hall down to her mother's bedroom. Covering her mouth, she stifled a yawn. She'd managed to catch a few hours of sleep after her midnight interruption and was somewhat recharged. When she softly knocked on the door, Linette's voice beckoned. "Come in."

Her mother's bedroom took up the corner wing where windows overlooked the river. The drapes were pulled back. Morning light shone on the enormous bed piled high with champagne-colored covers. In the sitting area at the other end of the room, her mother perched at her vanity. "Dear, how did last night go? Must have been very enjoyable since you didn't return." Still in her lilac peignoir, Linette grinned in the mirror as she picked up a hairbrush.

"Nothing happened." An itch grew underneath Alina's chin. "I had to stay at Chance's place because of the riot at City Hall last night."

"As you insist." Linette used careful strokes with the hairbrush, taming her medium-length golden strands. "There's nothing to be embarrassed about, Alina. He is Mandin's father."

"Mother, I'm engaged to Kiean." Alina approached Linette's good side sans rash.

"What?" Her mom placed the hairbrush down. "I don't see a ring."

Alina reached into her chest pocket. Holding the ring out, she noticed a small crease in Linette's brow as her mother studied the stone jewel on the lanyard.

"Why aren't you wearing it then?"

Alina's shoulders tensed. "Because I usually do, I just…" It was better to avoid telling her mother what had happened at Genodyne. Alina lowered her chin so the suit collar would hide the mark around her neck. "I didn't want it to get lost."

"Lost on your hand?" Linette shook her head. "Does Chance know?"

"Yes, he does." The itch had moved from Alina's chin up to her face, like insects crawling over her. She stuffed the ring back into her pocket and zipped it up.

Through closed lips, her mother ran her tongue over her teeth. Her voice lowered. "Is that what you want?"

Alina scratched her sleeve. "Yes. Chance is just here to visit Mandin." Giving her head a shake, she caught the reflection of her downturned mouth in the mirror. She didn't have the energy to discuss the last three years of her life with her mother.

"Congratulations, dear." Linette didn't look at her and resumed brushing her hair.

A bitter taste filled Alina's mouth. While Linette never met Kiean, Alina thought her mother would be excited for her, or at least pleased. Then again, why did she care whether her mother approved of her life choices? Close to the mirror, she scrutinized Linette. The gray patch on her other cheek had faded considerably with new skin appearing to take over its edges. Her neck was less raw, her face pink. "Your skin is getting better. Have you done something different?"

"It's this balm you gave me." Linette's green eyes brightened as she picked up the tin of dandlemane. "Dr. Bellamy tested a sample and said it was safe to apply.

Isn't it wonderful?" Her mother rose and smiled widely at her. "I can't thank you enough."

Linette's dewy complexion hadn't fully returned, but her movements appeared fluid again. Perhaps Macy's balm really worked?

Alina avoided engaging her doubts. Instead, she relaxed at the change in subject. "I'm glad you like it." Dr. Bellamy would know whether the balm could be used as a widespread remedy. While it was unlikely, maybe the bone marrow transplant could be avoided all together. "Has the doctor seen its effect on you?"

Linette waved a hand. "Oh, she'll stop by this week for her usual visit, but I feel better already. I should get dressed. Jakob wants to have lunch today in the dining room, and I think I shall. I've neglected him for a while now."

Alina smiled to herself as her mother moved down the hallway to the alcove that opened up into her wardrobe room. Her mother's morning routine always turned out to be an extended ordeal.

She left the bedroom, shutting the door behind her. In the hallway, she pondered how to ask Chance to leave. As she moved in the direction of the main room, her link beeped, and she checked the message.

It was from Aurore. Her friend had downloaded the data on Evesborough from the Spartan. They still needed to return to the academy and brief the Commandant on their findings so he would give them the cryopump.

In the living area, Jakob leaned toward Chance as the two men chatted about robots. Mandin grappled with the car in Chance's hands, playing tug-of-war. Her son squealed as Chance turned on the headlamps again, shining different colored beams. Both men rose when she walked into the room.

"Alina, what a relief you're here," Jakob said. "Have you seen your mother?"

"Yes, she's feeling better."

"I can't thank you enough for the salve." Jakob gestured toward her. "It seems to be working wonders on her."

"I hope so." Her arms twitched, and she cast her gaze to Mandin.

Chance released the toy to their son. "That's good news."

She gave him a stiff smile. "Thank you for bringing me home."

His dark eyes dimmed a bit. "Well, I should be going." He bent over and placed a hand on his son's shoulder. "Mandin, I have to leave now."

Her son looked up at him. "But why you leaving?"

Chance gave him a gentle smile. "I have to return to work. But maybe we can see each other again soon. Would you like that?"

Mandin jumped to his feet, the GATV toy still in his hands. "Mama, can I see Dada again?"

Her throat thickened from the carb toast she ate that morning. An insistence took over in Mandin's voice. "I want to play with Dada."

Jakob brought a fist to his mouth and coughed.

Mandin was used to playing with Syriah and Hudson back at Evesborough. In the city though, Alina couldn't think of anyone else to contact to keep him entertained. She wasn't sure when Gordo would return, and Halle couldn't fill the void the entire time. At times, Mandin took to certain people quickly. She suspected he knew when he could trust someone, like Syriah did.

"I have an errand to run tomorrow. Perhaps you can stop by in the afternoon if you're not busy." She shifted her weight to her other foot.

"Absolutely. I'll come by mid-day." Chance's grin reached across his face.

Her son smiled up at him. "Do you like the snow?"

"He doesn't have waterproof boots. Maybe you can take him to your apartment and show him the cube?" She smoothed a lock of hair forward to cover her neck.

Chance stepped closer. "I can take him shopping for boots. Then I can bring him to the courtyard where he can play in the snow." He straightened, his shoulders back. "I can also ask for the GATV driver to escort you wherever you'd like."

"That won't be necessary." The errand was for her and Aurore to accomplish alone. The GATV driver would report her movements to Chance. However, the courtyard was a safe place for Chance to watch over Mandin, walled off from the city's sidewalks. "He would enjoy the snow."

"Hear that?" Chance crouched in front of Mandin and touched a finger into his chest. "I'll pick you up tomorrow, and we'll get you the right gear for snow."

Mandin nodded and his grin widened. "I bring this." He held up the toy car.

"Sounds like it's all settled then," Jakob said, sliding his hands in his trouser pockets.

Chance squeezed his son's upper arm. "See you tomorrow."

Alina glanced around, but Halle had not returned. "I'll walk you to the lift." She followed Chance to the entryway.

He hit the elevator button and turned to her. "Thank

you. You don't know how much it means to me." His mouth closed, a reflective expression overcoming him.

"You're doing me a favor by entertaining him while I'm out."

"Maybe one day, the three of us can spend an afternoon together," he said.

Blinking, she tilted her face up to him. His dark eyes shone and fixated on her. Chance towered over her like he did the previous night, only this time he wore his uniform. A whiff of pine scent lingered.

The chime sounded and the lift doors opened. She stepped back. "See you tomorrow."

He entered the elevator. "Tomorrow, it is." Chance gave her a broad smile as the elevator doors closed.

She released a deep breath when he disappeared. While she was still embarrassed about the way she clung to him after her nightmare, she admitted Chance behaved honorably. Then again, he'd always been that way when they dated previously. Headed to her room, she decided on a long shower.

A thought about sending a message to Kiean via the Spartan's system occurred to her. Aurore would accompany her to the ship if she asked. But the snow was thick outside, and she wanted to bring him good news about the cryopump. She would obtain it soon enough.

Chapter 19

The crowd was restless in the great hall. Near the front, Syriah squirmed by her father. Kiean and Talley flanked Macy who stood on a flat rock that served as a platform. The stars in the night sky were visible through the gaping hole in the cavern's ceiling. Normally, Syriah loved gazing up at them, but she could sense the uncertainty behind her.

"When is the reactor going to be fixed?" a man in the front row asked.

Macy kept her hands clasped over the bottom of her gold sash. "We are working hard at it. Please be patient. This isn't a minor repair."

"You didn't answer my question."

Her face stayed soft. "We need a specific part. A cryopump."

"Do we have it?" someone else asked.

"We're working on getting it."

The crowd's air turned muddy. The cavern was thick with bodies. Frustration showed on the faces surrounding Syriah.

"When's the Spartan coming back?" A woman wondered aloud.

Macy's head turned to Kiean. He mouthed something to her.

"Soon," Macy replied. "In the meantime, we've run a line to the water wheel for the generator. The power will be used to run the Triumph's systems. It'll be ongoing based on the river flow, but we'll have no power for the homes starting tomorrow."

Murmurs broke out. People pressed upon Syriah from behind, and she grabbed her father's hand. He pushed back, holding his ground. Clutching his fingers, her heart hammered away. The mass of bodies cramped together in the room. She spotted Hawk and his younger brother, Wilder, moving along the wall toward Kiean's side of the platform. In their blue work shirts, the air around them turned cloudy, a sign of worry. Hawk gripped the special flashlight on his waistband.

"But how are we supposed to live!" A woman cried out.

Macy spoke louder. "We will sign up every household to access the Triumph's facilities on a rotating basis every other day for two hours at a time. It'll be posted at the main entrance of the ship. We'll also issue one solar-powered lamp per home that you can recharge outside."

"But I've got a family of six. How is that fair when there are those who only need to look after themselves?" Another man flung out his arm. He stood behind Big Flint, and Syriah noticed that Flint's eyes were cast downward. She looked for Danny or Phoebe, but they weren't with him. No other children appeared among the villagers.

Macy's mouth flattened. "The decision is final." She repositioned herself. "Use this time of year to enjoy the days outside. In another few months, it'll be too hot to venture outdoors. You can use water from the river and boil it as well. Don't forget the natural resources we have here. We still have plenty of biomass to produce food from the Triumph's kitchen. So there's no shortage of food."

"Not yet," a voice remarked from the back.

"Or you can allocate more power to those who built these homes in the first place," a loud voice demanded.

Syriah turned toward the speaker. The voice belonged to Zaid. Two other stocky men nodded around him.

Low whispers buzzed, and the room's air shifted to unease. She hoped Macy and Kiean would put a stop to everyone's bad mood.

The elder squinted at him. "The allocation is a temporary situation."

"But we blasted out dozens of tunnels for homes and removed the rock by hand," said a man next to Zaid. "And now you're telling us you're going to divert our power to some of these households who haven't contributed as much to building this community. Why should they get an equal amount just because they have kids?"

Syriah shrank against her father. "Who's that?"

"Ignasio." The corner of his mouth dipped down. "And that's his brother, Emilio, next to him."

Talley spoke, his back stiff from his shoulder encased in a ribbed mold. "Once we get the spare part, everyone will have power again."

A hush fell over the hall. "He's right," someone remarked.

"They've gone back to Alpheios." Zaid waved his hand. "Why would they return to this dump?"

Syriah glared. What a nasty man. Plus, what Zaid said wasn't true. Alina would come back.

Kiean stepped forward. "The crew will return soon.

They've acknowledged our message."

Zaid pushed his way to the front of the crowd, trailed by Ignasio and Emilio. A woman protested at being shoved aside.

"Is that so?" Zaid sneered. "You might be a pilot, but you're not in charge of the rest of us. I say we reward those who built this place. The rest can shelter outside using, er, natural resources as you so put it." He set his gaze on Macy.

"If you want power, I suggest you pull a maintenance shift onboard the ship." Steel underlined Macy's words.

"I ain't answering to him," Zaid lifted his chin in Kiean's direction.

Her brother stepped off the rock. "I don't want your help."

Ignasio and Emilio inched closer. Their air turned as dark as the river's bottom that flowed through the cavern.

Needles razed Syriah's neck. Her mouth went dry.

"That's enough." A sharpness gripped Macy's voice.

Father pulled Syriah toward the cavern exit. She resisted, but he dragged her. He stopped in front of Soloman. "Take her and leave." Father rushed up front.

People were surging toward the rock platform. Flint pushed his way up to Macy. The energy in the room turned to chaos. In her mind, Syriah screamed for her dad.

"Stay back!" It was Dr. Olek who yelled from across the cavern.

A few screams erupted.

Syriah could no longer find any of her family through the crowd.

“C’mon.” Soloman lifted her in his arms.

“No! Put me down!”

But he carried her away. A few women ran past them for the exit.

“Soloman, stop!” Syriah thrashed until his grasp loosened.

“Syriah, we need to leave.”

Hitting the ground, she disappeared deep into a darkness originating at her core. Her hammering heartbeat took over. Her insides burned like icicles plunged into her veins, and she fought back screaming. The cavern warped at the edges of her vision as she focused on reaching Kiean. A hum penetrated her ears. Into the blur, she zoomed to where she last saw her brother. Light appeared again.

Talley and Flint escorted Macy down a side tunnel where they left. But by the platform, a flurry of bodies grappled one another. When she found her brother, she choked back a sob.

On the ground, Kiean rolled over Zaid. Fists flew between them. Father grappled with Ignasio by the collar. The man thrust him away.

“Daddy!”

Her father’s glasses had been knocked off.

Wilder wrestled Ignasio to the ground, pinning his elbow behind his back. Auto-ties surrounded Ignasio’s wrist.

Hawk lunged at Emilio, his flashlight in hand. Sparks flew from the flashlight, and Emilio fell to the ground.

Kiean kicked Zaid off and rose to his feet. Zaid charged again, but Kiean kneed him in the guts and wrenched him away. Her brother’s right eye was red and puffy.

A few men separated them. They allowed Hawk to activate the auto-ties around Zaid's arms.

"Have a good time in the brig," her brother said. Wilder and Hawk hauled the criminals away. Ignasio cursed filthy words at them, and Syriah covered her ears.

The icy feeling drained away, but she stood stuck, trembling.

Dr. Olek stepped forward. "You better get ice on that eye. Let me examine you."

Kiean waved him away. "I'm fine."

"You're bleeding," Father said.

Blood trickled from the corner of Kiean's mouth. He wiped it away with his sleeve. "I'll survive. What about you?"

"Not a scratch. But I lost my glasses." Father squinted.

Dr Olek bent over and picked up the crumpled glasses as well as another object. He inspected them. "The lens popped out, but they're still intact. I can create a new frame for you now that we have the printer." He handed them to Father.

Kiean blinked, like he saw her for the first time. "What are you doing here?"

Tears overcame her, and she sprinted to him.

He wrapped an arm around her shoulders. "You shouldn't be here."

She buried her face into his shirt, trying to control her heaving. Relief filled her that he remained in one piece.

Father approached. "I thought I told Soloman to take you."

Soloman panted as he arrived. "I had her but…."

"But what?"

"She fought me and then…" He gazed at the wall lamps. "A flash of light overtook her before she vanished. Another one of her mind tricks."

Kiean rubbed her back. "She was scared." He lifted her chin. "Did you project yourself?"

Unsure what occurred, she shook her head. Her voice came out a mumble. "Maybe."

Dr. Olek peered at her. "I saw a glimmer of light when Soloman held you as well. Then you appeared here. But now you're flushed." He held out a diagnostic wand. She took a step away, waiting for him to use it on her brother, but the laser scanned her instead.

"Your heart rate is still high." The doctor's forehead creased. "Normally when you project yourself, you're much calmer, and it slows down. But your temperature increased, similar to your past projections." He scratched his temple. "Also, your brain patterns usually show a dissociative state. I'm picking up remnants of that."

"What does that mean?" Father asked.

"Somehow… I think her body is catching up to the spot where she's projecting her consciousness. There's no other explanation to how else she made it here so quickly. She couldn't have run through that crowd."

Soloman studied the silver-streaked cavern walls. "It's theorized that giltspar holds certain forms of energy. She might be harnessing some type of force field that connects to the electro-magnetic spectrum at certain points."

"That's logical, given that her powers are always stronger when surrounded by giltspar." Dr. Olek glanced at his wand. "The human heart exchanges electric signals with the brain, and the brain creates its own signals as well. We know it's closely linked to emotions."

"Is it..." Her voice came out small. "A bad thing I'm doing?"

"Not it all." He smiled. "I think it's a defensive measure and could prove quite useful in dangerous situations."

"But that means she's causing magnetic fluctuations again." Soloman scowled.

"Relax. The reactor is offline," said Kiean.

Syriah pressed her face into her brother's shirt. She'd only wanted to warn her brother to run. "Will they come back?"

Kiean brushed one of her tears away with his thumb. "Nah, they'll be in the clink until Macy decides what to do with them."

Soloman asked, "When's the Spartan returning?"

"Soon," Kiean replied. "They need time to get the part."

Her voice fell to a whisper. "I want Alina to come home."

Her brother smoothed her hair back. "She'll return." He hugged her close, but his air took on bleak gray. Syriah clung to him, not wanting to let go.

Shutting her eyes, she remained unsure of what powers she just unleashed. Never had so much fear consumed her, and it was the first time the icy feeling filled her with such dread. While her vision often blurred during her projections, this time, darkness overtook her journey. Until she'd reached her brother.

She couldn't convey her thoughts to others like Danny, but Syriah couldn't help but try. *Hurry home, Alina.*

Chapter 20

Commandant Riley stood over the hologram of Evesborough projected on the academy's conference table. His cap bill was pointed downward as he scrutinized the layout. The luminous sketch showed the different tunnels branching out from the main cavern and how the homes were arrayed.

"That's everything we've been able to gather about the site the past few years. It's rich with giltspar embedded throughout the entire system." Aurore had brought Alina's nav sensors from the Spartan which contained their mapping data. Next to her, Aurore was seated.

"What about this tunnel? Is it a drop-off?" He pointed to a small branch off one of the secondary tunnels.

"Yes. We haven't explored it yet because my probes stopped about one hundred meters down before returning as part of their failsafe. So I don't actually know its depth. We sectioned it off." Alina shifted in her seat. They had debriefed Riley for several hours on their new habitat. She had combed every inch of it, save the one tunnel. The Commandant missed nothing in these types of surveys.

He folded his arms over his chest. "But it's still too hot outside in the summer months for humans."

"Yes, sir. But the village is able to stock up and

remain in the cavern during that time." Aurore blew her bangs out of her eyes.

He pulled at the sleeve of his fitted top, revealing an in-line pocket and withdrew a small key. He wore a graphite-colored suit composed of a weaved fabric with a slight sheen that Alina hadn't seen before. She and Aurore had donned their academy suits.

"Thanks for this. We're going to have to dedicate more resources to researching zone nine." He tossed the key in Aurore's direction, and she grabbed it in mid-air. "You'll find the cryopump in locker six."

Her friend shot up out of her seat. "Do you mind if I grab it now?"

He angled his head to the door.

Alina rose to follow. She placed her hand at the junction of her shoulder and neck. Pressing into the muscle, she kneaded the area.

"I want to have a word with you, DeHerte."

She exchanged looks with Aurore. "Yes, sir."

After the meteorologist left, Riley shut the door. She braced herself as he approached. A lecture was forthcoming. "I know this site means something to you because of your father. I'm still mulling over why he didn't share this information with anyone but you."

Alina leaned back in the chair. "He knew about Genodyne's Phase Three plan at the time. He wanted this as a new habitable site for the Origins and their children."

Riley studied her for a moment, then removed his cap. Rubbing his hand over his short haircut, he exhaled. Plopping the cap back on, he said, "I would have given you the cryopump had you asked. You didn't have to steal it." He straightened. "Why didn't Talley contact me?"

"He was injured trying to repair the fusion reactor." Alina gnawed the inside of her cheek. A vexing contraction carved its way through her insides. Riley had given her a second chance at the academy when she had no other options. She didn't exactly repay him with gratitude. "We can set up a visit for you there. We've built some good infrastructure, but Evesborough could use the academy's help to really flourish as an alternate colony site."

"I'd like to visit." Riley then held out his arms, examining his uniform sleeves. "See maybe if this new suit works in that climate."

"Is that the project you've been working on?"

He nodded and gestured to the door. "Come with me."

Following him, she recognized the hallways leading to the equipment room. Upon their entry, lights shone on the inset wall panels where a few suits similar to the Commandant's were displayed.

He stopped near one of the smaller sizes. "These are a prototype of upgraded expeditionary suits. Fully waterproof, and they have an auto-regulated function for the wearer so no matter what season, it'll keep you at a constant temperature setting and you won't have to adjust its thermostat. This suit should withstand a more extreme range in weather."

A low wall panel swished open upon his touch. A shiny disk the size of a hand levitated above a circular base.

The metal disc gleamed, displaying a crystal at its center. "Giltspar?" she asked.

He flipped the suit over to its back. "Correct. It's an

energy pack that's generated from your body's movements." He slipped it into a silver-lined pocket on the suit's upper back and clipped the metal ring into three electrodes. "Feel that?"

Touching the new suit proved irresistible. She stroked the sleeve by the elbow covered by a solid black patch. "It's stiff here."

"That's where the bio-harvesters are located, and they transfer the energy to the disc via an embedded filament. You have them at both elbows and knees. Just keep moving to produce energy. The temperature conduits run through the seams."

Rubbing the fabric between her fingers, she noticed a shiny thread interleaved throughout the material. "What's this weaving?"

Riley replied, "That's the main advantage of this suit. You have a built-in deflection shield for radiation since giltspar is powering it. Now, I wouldn't stand outside in a gamma storm for a prolonged period of time, but it'll allow you a delay to get indoors and avoid radiation poisoning. Also insulated to protect you from the local wildlife should you stumble upon them, and they turn defensive."

"Really?" Her current suit regulated temperature upon a manual switch and was water-resistant. But it didn't protect anyone from the summer storms.

"Yes. I've been trying it out for the winter season since class isn't in session. You'll find compartments for a hood, face gaiter, and gloves." He paused. "Want to try one?"

"Are you serious?" A grin spilled over her lips. Her mind filtered through potential uses for such a suit back at Evesborough.

The Commandant raised a finger. "But you have to let me know how it holds up. Consider it a wear test for deep winter, and I need a female test subject. So I can make any adjustments before we start rolling them off the line."

"I'll definitely test it." Carefully, she slid the suit off the hangar. The stern lines on Riley's face had softened somewhat. "Thank you." Her voice came out nearly a whisper. A knot formed in her chest as she gazed at her old mentor.

A rare smile peeked out from a corner of Riley's lips. "Just remember to report back on its function."

Locking her knees, she took in a deep breath. "I won't disappoint you again. At least, not on purpose."

Chuckling, he gave her arm a soft slap. "Now go on. Get out of here and take the cryopump with you."

"Yes, sir!" She sped out the equipment room clutching her new loot, eager to find Aurore.

****

The new suit warmed Alina to the bone despite the temperature dipping to negative ten degrees Celsius. Its collar covered the mark on her neck although she fiddled with it periodically. Her ring rested safely in her upper arm pocket since the suit pulled smooth over the chest without pockets. She'd donned an academy ballcap instead of the suit's hood, pulling it down over her ears. She and Aurore walked past the bare trees glistening with icicles that lined the city's sidewalks. A single sun was hidden behind the layered clouds. Her link predicted it would snow later that night.

Up ahead, the stone buildings from the city's center sprouted into view. Her heart sped up as they neared the area by Ambrose Park where the GATV had been ambushed.

"We could have taken the rover," Aurore said, huffing. She'd already packed the cryopump away in it prior to their outing.

"It's only a few blocks," replied Alina. "Plus, I told Riley I'd try out the new suit." She didn't say aloud that she hoped the walk in the cold would clear her mind. She was grappling over her uneasy truce with Chance.

"Lucky." A grumble rumbled through Aurore's tone. "I didn't get a suit." Her friend shoved her bangs aside. "I need a haircut while I'm here."

Alina breathed out puffs of air while turning down a residential street. "If my mother wasn't so ill, I'd join you in pre-flighting the Spartan." Her stay in Alpheios was longer than she'd anticipated.

"I'll grab some supplies, then." Aurore rubbed her nose with the back of a gloved hand and cast a sidelong glance at her. "Maybe Chance will invite you over for another sleepover." Her voice sounded snarky.

Alina stumbled on a rift in the sidewalk that was hidden under a thin cover of snow. "I told you, nothing happened!"

"Are you sure?" Aurore's feline face twitched.

"Yes. It was because of the stupid riot I had to stay there." She sped up her pace, shaking her head.

"Hey, slow down! Don't you think that's convenient?"

She whirled around to face her friend. "You weren't the one who was attacked!"

Her arms trembled at the memory of the masked faces that pounded on her GATV window, centimeters away.

Aurore held up her gloved palms. "I believe you!

But I—"

Alina resumed her normal pace, trying to shake the memory.

"Do you trust him now?"

They entered the street where Chance lived. The quiet but well-secured condos blurred together in her periphery. "Why do you think I asked you to come with me?" She rubbed her forehead with a gloved hand.

No, she didn't fully trust Chance. Her cheeks toasted at how Chance's fingers touched her hair in the bedroom. But he left her alone, allowing her to sleep. Perhaps Chance just wanted a relationship with his son.

"Don't worry—I'm here!" Her friend took a jaunty hop. "Although we could ask for a DV escort on the way back to the academy." She gave her a wicked grin.

Alina shot her an exasperated look. "We won't stay long. I just need to grab Mandin." She pointed at Aurore's chest. "You'll take us home in the rover once we return to the academy."

Inhaling deep breaths, she led Aurore up the walkway to Chance's condo. The iron gate over the double doors loomed, and she braced herself. She depressed the ringer and shifted her feet. Aurore winked at her and pressed the buzzer.

"Clean off your boots."

Aurore rolled her eyes but joined her in wiping her feet off the coarse mat in the vestibule.

Inside the clean lobby, Lawrence greeted Alina from behind the desk. "Wonderful to see you again, Ms. DeHerte." Friendliness touched the smile he gave her.

This time, she smiled back at the older gentleman. "Can you let Mr. Graylin know that I've arrived?"

"He's out back with your son." Lawrence gestured

to a set of heavy doors at the other end of the lobby. "Believe they're playing in the snow."

She and Aurore headed for the courtyard entrance. The doors spilled out to an inner walkway, lined with carved columns that ran the length of the building's walls. A pavilion occupied the courtyard's center as a gathering spot, although it appeared empty given the weather. A squeal caught Alina's attention. In the far corner, Mandin tossed a handful of snow at Chance from behind a snow-made wall enclosure.

Alina's heart skipped a beat. Mandin wore a new charcoal climate suit with cardinal red accents on his sleeves, and red stripe across his chest. His cheeks were flushed a healthy pink, his eyes bright as he laughed. His wardrobe matched his father's outfit. Chance raised his arm to deflect the snow.

"Mama!" Her son spotted them.

Chance called out. "Want to join us in the snow fort?"

Her pulse quickening, she plunged across the snow. She could have sworn in her periphery that Aurore smirked, but her friend's heavy breathing accompanied her.

"Look, Mama." Mandin pointed at the walls. "Dada and me built the fort."

"Hi, Aurore." Chance raised a hand at her.

"Hey." Aurore flashed him a tight-lipped smile and folded her arms over her chest.

Upon reaching them, Alina appraised Mandin's snowsuit. "You didn't have to buy him an entire new outfit."

Chance replied, "He could use it in this weather. It's the latest style, but I'm afraid it's not as advanced as your expeditionary suits." He scanned her new outfit.

She knelt by her son in the snow. His small face peeked out from under the hood. His gloves were waterproof, and the thermostat button was tucked underneath his collar. His new booties kept his feet dry. "Thank you. This is durable material."

"Don't mention it. Had to try it out in the snow fort." Chance grinned, his hands on his hips.

"I'm afraid it's time to go," she said to Mandin.

Her son's face fell. "No! I want to play more. I want to play with Dada."

Chance touched his shoulder. "Your mother is right. We can do it again another time." His dark eyes settled on her. "Would you like me to ring the driver to take you back? He'll arrive within ten minutes."

Aurore made a grunting noise like she was clearing her throat.

Alina's boots wiggled in the snow. "We have an expeditionary rover back at the academy."

"That's several blocks from here. I can have the driver take you there if you want to pick it up."

She avoided her friend's stare. "We'd rather walk back." Her cheeks crackled from the cold. Chance had done her enough favors.

He motioned to the main building. "It's warmer in the lobby. I'll grab Mandin's daypack."

They trekked back inside while Mandin pestered her. "Please, Mama. I wanna play in the snow again."

She removed her gloves and rubbed his cheeks, cold to the touch. "Another time. We're done for today."

Chance spoke to Lawrence, and the concierge fetched a pack tucked away behind the desk. Her ex's red stripes flashed along his arms as he passed it to her. The suit clung to his tall frame, flattering across his broad shoulders, and tapered down to his waist.

He crouched to Mandin's eye-level. "Thanks for building the snow fort with me. I hope you had fun."

Mandin's grin spilled across his face. "Yeah, I did!"

A twinge plucked at her chest. Mandin's smile was as joyous now as when he hurled snow minutes ago.

Chance rose. "Thank you," he said in a quiet voice. "For allowing me to spend an afternoon with him. Maybe next time you can join us." He glanced at Aurore. "And you should come, too. I'll order hot stew for all of us afterward."

Aurore stuck out her chin and flashed him a toothy smile. Alina pressed her lips together. Aurore's attempts at sincerity were awful.

Alina stayed for a moment, basking in the warmth of the temperate lobby. "Perhaps one more outing since there's no snow where we live."

"I look forward to it." A grin graced Chance's face.

She admired his defined features for a moment until Aurore shuffled her boots loudly.

Chance escorted them to the exit. He held open the doors for them as they said their good-byes. When they burst out on the sidewalk, Aurore snorted.

"Hot stew? Like I'm wanted around," she said in a scoffing tone.

Alina slung Mandin's daypack over her shoulder. "He was trying to be friendly. Which is more than I can say for you."

"C'mon. I'd just ruin it by shoving a snowball in his face." Aurore scooted ahead of them. "I'll get the rover. You know, I would have been more friendly had we taken the escort!" She charged down the block to the academy.

"Can I see Dada again?" Mandin hovered by Alina's legs while they walked. Hope filled his large, dark eyes.

She grasped his hand, enclosed in mittens. "Yes, you'll get to see your father." She avoided adding, *before we leave for Evesborough.* The temperature dipped even more as late afternoon arrived. Her suit adjusted, but she could no longer feel the tip of her nose. Maybe she should have taken Chance's offer on the DV escort after all.

Chapter 21

The cord burn on Alina's neck faded, barely visible to a casual observer. Or so she surmised from her reflection in the bathroom mirror. Her new suit also hugged her frame comfortably, and its weave fabric carried a slight sheen. She pocketed the tin of dandlemane balm and exited her private bathroom.

In her bedroom, dim light streamed through a crack in the curtains highlighting the rumpled silver bedding. She pulled back the drapes to allow in more daylight, glancing at the winding river. An ice floe floated by. Given the penthouse's corner location, all the rooms facing the exterior wall contained a view of the river. She smoothed back the covers and straightened the pillows. After her breakthrough with the Commandant, she finally slept soundly in the large bed. Perhaps returning to Alpheios did afford some advantages.

Before leaving the room, she opened the blue beaded jewelry box on top of the dresser. She fished out the ring attached to the leather strap. Its smooth stone calmed her, and the giltspar sparkled from within it. She slipped it on her right hand. It looked lovely, but for some reason, didn't feel like her own hand. Quietly, she placed the ring back in the case and shut the lid.

In the hall, she bumped into Dr. Bellamy who was just leaving Linette's bedroom. The doctor's blonde hair was pulled back in a ponytail. Her winter-grade climate suit, thick and white, set off her brown skin and eyes.

"How is she doing?" Alina asked.

Bellamy gestured to the living room. "Let's discuss this somewhere more comfortable." As she followed, Alina's boots weighed heavy.

On the brocade couches, Gordo laughed alongside Mandin at a quip from Halle. When her brother saw them enter, he spoke. "Mom's skin really looks better. Is it safe to say she's recovering?"

A faint smile appeared on the doctor's lips as she gazed at Mandin who knelt on the couch, trying to touch Halle's face monitor. He was beckoning the robot to turn on its cartoons. "He's energetic this morning. How often do you play cartoons for him?" asked the doctor.

"I was waiting until he had his breakfast," Halle replied.

"Hear that, Mandin?" Dr. Bellamy asked. "You better eat breakfast if you want to watch cartoons."

"I not hungry." He reached for the bot again.

A sinking weight tugged at Alina's gut at realizing they should speak privately. "Mandin, go with Halle for breakfast. She can show you what they have to eat." She firmed her tone. "Or no toons."

Her son slid off the couch. "Okay, Mama. I go."

She waited until the bot accompanied Mandin out of the room, then took a seat next to Gordo. The doctor lowered herself into a curved back armchair.

Her expression turned serious. "The balm is a useful topical ointment, but its effects are temporary on your mother."

Gordo scooted forward. "What do you mean, temporary?"

The doctor shifted her gaze to him. "It's an anti-inflammatory ointment with some analgesic properties. That explains the improvement in Linette's appearance. It might have worked had we used it right from the beginning."

"What's her status, Dr. Bellamy?" Alina knew the balm was an unlikely cure, but she'd dared a ray of hope.

The doctor clasped her hands together loosely in her lap. "Please, my name is Jasmine. Dr. Bellamy is too formal, and I'm not that old. Or at least, not yet."

Alina's back tensed. "Jasmine, can you tell us what my mother's condition is?"

"The disease is spreading internally within her." Jasmine spoke slowly. "In about another week, her rash will return, but worse. The ointment won't make a difference. At that point, her organs will be affected." Her knees were angled to the side.

Alina pressed her thigh against Gordo's leg. Her brother cast his gaze downward.

"I'm really sorry," Jasmine said.

"You said about a week?"

The doctor nodded.

Taking in a deep breath, Alina studied the weave of the new suit covering her legs. The fibers in the fabric crisscrossed over one another, a tight mesh designed to protect its wearer. "There's one thing left we can try, but I need your help." She fixed her gaze on Jasmine. "Genodyne has used Phase Three to create a new creature. Several, in fact."

"What do you mean?" her brother asked.

The doctor crossed one leg over the other and clasped her hands atop her knees. "Go on."

Alina proceeded to divulge what she had observed about the kronosapiens. She described what she had witnessed about how their skin transformed, their powers, and how they reproduced. Her brother's expression turned incredulous. Knowing Gordo would react badly about news of the attack, she left out Kora nearly strangling her. Jasmine's posture remained upright as she listened, her face masked in concentration.

"The male isn't doing well. They're trying to save him, but his body seems to be rejecting a bone marrow transplant from the sows. The female is much stronger since she recovered from birthing."

Gordo's face contorted. "You're saying Genodyne is prioritizing these beasts over their own citizens?"

"It's long been a goal of Genodyne to create an advanced humanoid species." The doctor uncrossed her legs and leaned forward. "I can't believe they allowed you to witness their progress."

"Progress?" Gordo glowered. His hand tightened into a fist, resting on his lap. "Is that what you call what's happening to my mother?"

A fluttering broke loose in her gut, and Alina squeezed her brother's arm. "The kronosapiens may be the only way to save her."

"How?"

Inhaling a deep breath, she turned to Jasmine. "Turns out that I'm a donor match whose bone marrow can save the male. If I go through with the procedure, they can mass produce his stem cell serum to save everyone in Alpheios, including Linette."

Her brother jumped off the couch. "Did Chance put you up to this?"

The doctor extended two fingers in Alina's direction. "How are you a match? I'm not following."

"Because...Genodyne used portions of Mandin's

DNA to create them. They tested my blood sample while I was there."

A gleam filled Jasmine's eyes. "And Mandin shares fifty percent of your DNA."

Alina tugged her brother's sleeve. "It's not Chance's fault. He was trying to help us."

"Then tell Chance to turn over his bone marrow!" Her brother gestured at her. "Why does it have to be you?"

"Because Mandin's mutation came from me, not him. I inherited it from dad." Her breathing had quickened. "It's the only way, Gordo."

His teeth clamped together. "That company should be razed to the depths of Eamine, along with City Hall! That would be a kindness to them after what they've done to everyone else!" He shook his head and stomped out of the room.

Her suit warmed a degree to keep her steady.

Jasmine's head angled slightly, her expression thoughtful. "That's very generous of you, to offer a tissue donation."

"How can I not do it?" Alina's voiced quaked. "It can help save thousands of lives."

"You'll be under general anesthesia, so you won't feel pain during the procedure. The incisions for the needles are tiny, but there's a small risk of muscle or nerve damage. If you like, I can consult with your doctor. Who is?" Jasmine raised her brows.

Alina gazed at her amber irises. "I was hoping that you would be my doctor, and that you'd be the one to do it."

"I can do that." Jasmine leaned forward and grabbed her hands. "We'll make sure it goes smoothly."

"Thank you." She held onto Jasmine's comforting grip.

Laughter floated over from the kitchen. The padding of small feet sounded on the tile, and Mandin rushed back into the room. Crumbs surrounded his mouth, and he held up a pastry. "Look, Mama. Halle gave me a sweet cake."

The bot entered the room. "Mandin, you did not finish your juice."

His sticky hands pressed into Alina's lap, and she sighed. She allowed him to climb on her and cuddled him close.

"What's wrong, Mama?" His smile vanished, and he thrust his small face close to hers. He started to raise a hand to touch her cheek, but she pushed it down before he could use his telepathy. Instead, she brushed the crumbs from his face, his skin sticky with glaze against her thumb. "Nothing. I'm fine."

"You want some of my sweet cake?" Her son lifted the pastry to her lips.

"No. I'm not hungry." A pang roiled inside, flipping over her core. Slightly sick at the thought of returning to Genodyne, she nestled closer to her son. One task remained before her surgery.

****

Aurore shut the aircraft compartment lid over the cryopump. Alongside her in the cargo area of the Spartan, Alina secured the tool bag in another locker. Once completed, she held out a small cardboard box. "You'll make sure Kiean gets this?"

The box held Halle's sweet cakes that Alina found in the kitchen that morning. Inside the container was Mandin's drawing. She'd scribbled a birthday message on the other side of the sheet and enclosed a separate, private letter to Kiean.

"I promise not to eat the cakes on the flight home." Aurore's boots thunked their way out of the cargo bay.

Alina hovered outside the cabins while her friend stowed the box. She hoped Kiean would understand why she couldn't be at Evesborough for his birthday. Rather than focus on his potential disappointment, she imagined him sharing the sweet cakes with Syriah.

When Aurore reappeared, Alina followed behind. Her boots dragged down the length of the ramp leading off the Spartan. Surely, Kiean would understand once he read that she was undergoing a bone marrow transplant for her mother's sake. Perhaps he would come as soon as he installed the cryopump and be by her side as she underwent the surgery.

Outside, the suns hid behind gray clouds in the late morning, casting a dreary pall over the white-covered forest. Aurore hit the button beside the ramp, and the gears spun, raising the metal plank. Bits of ice fell from the craft. After the ramp sealed against the hull of the airship, Aurore made her way to the rover a few meters away. "I can drop you off before I leave," Aurore said.

"Thanks. Can you drive?" Alina didn't feel like navigating through the forest in the open-air ATV. But her new suit kept her toasty so she avoided complaining, particularly when Aurore griped about not getting a new suit.

"Sure." Aurore reached for her bangs out of habit, but they were recently cropped close to her forehead, with a slight curl above her eyebrows.

"It's nice to see your eyes for a change."

Her friend scrunched up her nose. "The lady cut

them too short."

"It looks good on you." Alina grinned. "I bet Wilder will notice."

"I can't live that down, can I?" Aurore swung herself into the driver seat. "One night of mercy and look what I get." She popped the ignitor to the fuel engine and gave it a moment to warm up in the cold.

Alina clicked in the safety belt and coughed at the exhaust fumes. "Are you sure it was just out of mercy?" She had witnessed Aurore's laughter at Wilder's jokes when they had stayed after dinner, hosted by Ione and Hawk. She and Kiean had chatted with their friends late into the night.

Aurore jammed her foot down into the pedal, and the rover leapt forward. "He won't leave me alone now."

"Maybe you shouldn't have encouraged him." Alina grabbed the roll bar overhead. "Although there's plenty of girls at Evesborough who would love his attention."

"Then he should stop pestering me. I'm not the velcro type." Her friend's knuckles tightened around the steering wheel. The engine roared as she gunned it.

The trees whizzed by in a blur. "No, you're not."

"Anyway, I don't know why he doesn't take the hint. I'm even mean to him." Aurore leaned forward in her seat.

"Why? I thought you enjoyed his company."

"Oh, it was hot fun and all, but I don't want him getting too attached." Aurore peered out at the terrain in front of her. "He tried to kiss me before I left, but I ducked and told him I needed to pre-flight the Spartan."

The wind gave Alina's cheeks an icy burn. "Why are you so rude?" She didn't say aloud, maybe it was her friend who feared attachment. It would only be met with vigorous denials.

"Because I don't believe in exclusivity. It's not realistic." Aurore maneuvered around a fallen trunk coated in a layer of snow. "Maybe he'll give Lyra a chance. She doesn't bother you or Kiean anymore, does she?"

Alina dropped her hand from the roll bar. "No. She keeps her distance." After they had settled into Evesborough, the seamstress greeted her in a civil manner whenever they passed by one another in the tunnels. Lyra carried a reluctant acceptance of Alina's relationship with Kiean. Alina had no desire to further wound the woman's feelings, although she doubted Lyra would have afforded her the same opportunity.

Aurore spoke over the motor. "I still see her chatting Kiean up every now and then. But he's pretty good about handling the attention." Her friend gave her a sidelong glance. "She may stop if you wear the ring."

The seatbelt tightened across Alina's chest as the rover hit a dip in the ground. She grasped the door's side bar. "Sometimes I wonder why the formality is so important to him."

"He was raised among the Origins. Maybe he wants everyone to keep their hands off you." A fiendish smile emerged on Aurore's face as her foot hammered down the accelerator.

"I'm already his intimate. Also, I thought you didn't believe in such customs."

Aurore lifted her shoulders. "I don't. But…"

"But what?"

The breeze tousled Aurore's short bangs. "Does Chance know about your engagement?"

The wind burned Alina's cheeks further and she

considered pulling out her face gaiter. "He saw the ring. I wore it quite prominently." Despite the new suit's coverage of her body, she felt exposed. "I don't have it on right now because of what happened with Kora." Her gloved hand went to her throat. The mark where the cord had cinched around her neck had nearly disappeared. She trembled though, at the thought of confronting Kora again.

"Whatever…" Her friend leaned forward to peer through the forest.

"Say it." The tall trees whipped by, devoid of leaves.

Aurore shook her head. "You've been flighty lately. It's not like you."

"Me? You're the one who can't be tamed!" The ATV's speed made Alina's stomach clench.

"Well, even though Kiean turned out to be the steady one, you're still my friend."

Alina kept a close grip on the side bar, but she smiled to herself. Thinking of the box of sweet cakes left back onboard the Spartan comforted her. Alpheios was a long flight from Evesborough. She wrote to Kiean about her surgery, mentioning that she'd be grateful if he could make it before the ordeal. It would chase away her jitters about the procedure.

She lost track of where they were in the woods. Listening to the wind and motor, she breathed in the crisp air. The ATV swerved, and the seatbelt tightened over her lap. "Careful!"

"Sorry, big tree." An impish smile peeked out from Aurore.

Her friend knew of her sleepover at Chance's place, but not the details—certainly not about the wine. Alone in the woods, just the two of them, she thought of confiding in Aurore about Chance's hug. She remembered how he gently stroked her strands of hair. And whether it meant anything—or if it was nothing.

Above the tree line, the city towers loomed into view. She shifted in her seat, deciding to leave the matter alone. Nothing inappropriate had happened between Chance and her. Was it so wrong that he was always dutiful, always the protector? Being a Guardian was ingrained in him since she knew him.

The riverwalk remained empty and devoid of pedestrians. A feather of dampness touched Alina's nose. She gazed up at the bleary sky, thick with gray. Another snowflake floated by. Along their way to the Meander District, the snow floated down. She checked her link, denoting the heavy snowfall that night. Deep winter had not yet arrived but was on its way.

By the time they stopped in front of the penthouse, snow flurries covered Aurore's hair. She pulled her hood on and Alina did the same.

"How long will it take for you to recover after surgery?" her friend asked.

"Dr. Bellamy said I might be sore for a week, but the procedure itself is simple." Despite the warmth of her suit, she wrapped her arms around herself.

Aurore's mouth twisted to the side. "I wish I could stay to help."

Alina shook her head. "They need the cryopump. I have Gordo and Dr. Bellamy here." Through the white tufts tumbling down, she gazed at her friend. "Now go, before the weather worsens."

Aurore embraced her. "I'll tell Kiean to send a message from the Triumph to the academy's flight center. I'll give him the codes to address you there."

Squeezing her friend back, Alina chewed on the inside of her cheek. “Thanks. Have a safe flight back.”

A sympathetic smile came from Aurore. “Good luck with the surgery.”

Alina unbuckled her belt and bounced out of the ATV. “Hurry now. It’s coming faster.” The sidewalk up to her mother’s penthouse was slippery, and she grounded her boots into the pavement. At the entrance, the doorman buzzed her in, but she turned for a final wave to Aurore. The ATV had already departed, no longer visible in the tumbling sheets of snow.

Chapter 22

Syriah and Danny traipsed alongside one another, following the curve of the underground river as daylight faded. Phoebe trailed behind them in the cavern's path.

"Why do we have to go back inside?" Phoebe pushed her bangs away.

Danny clinked his metallic rocks together. "I'm hungry. Don't you want lunch?"

A tickle reached her nose, and Syriah sneezed. Cool air swirled around her cheeks after they spent all afternoon outside climbing on boulders overlooking the river. While sunny and warm outdoors, the cavern temperature rapidly dropped.

Syriah knew when she wasn't wanted around. Kiean and Soloman were busy trying to install the cryopump since Aurore returned. But Alina was not onboard the Spartan when it landed.

Dragging her feet, Syriah wondered what was keeping Alina. Aurore was annoyed with Syriah's questions and didn't answer her. Nor did Syriah know the contents of Alina's letter to her brother. So Syriah stayed outside, to avoid bothering the adults. Taking Danny and Phoebe with her would keep trouble away from the reactor. Or at least, no one would blame her for causing anything else to break.

A few rocks slipped from Danny's hands. He stopped by the doorway of tunnel four. Crouching, he raked his fingers over the ground. “Hey, there’s more here.” Scooting forward on his hands and knees, he picked up pebbles.

Syriah’s tummy grumbled. She and her father finished their meat pies long ago. Maybe Danny’s mother, Cinda, would have some left.

A choking noise came from Phoebe’s throat. Her brown eyes enlarged. Slowly, Phoebe backed away.

“What is it, Phoebe?” Syriah asked.

“Bad.” The little girl shook her head. “It’s bad here.”

“Whadya mean?” Danny was still on his knees.

But his little sister ran off, in the direction of home.

“Phoebe!” her brother yelled.

A slight hum vibrated the padlock on the door. “Shhh…Danny, do you hear that?” A chill seized Syriah.

He stood. “It’s just the electric box in there.”

“No. It’s something else.” A crawling crept over her. An old entity, something she never felt before was on the other side of the door. “I think we should leave. Alina sealed off this tunnel.” She recalled Alina’s frustration at her sensors not returning data on this part of the cavern.

“That’s because there’s a drop off there after the electric box.” Danny clutched his rocks.

“No, it’s…do you feel that?”

The only sound around them was the whisper of the underground river. The wall light near the door was dim, casting shadows. Syriah closed her eyes. The entity that lurked beyond the stone wall was…vile. Her eyes flew open.

Danny’s face paled. He nudged her, and they sprinted down the path toward his home.

After the rounded the corner, she said, “You felt it!”

“Should we tell the others? Like Kiean?” He was

breathing hard.

The sensation disappeared as they put distance behind them. She slowed. "The door is locked."

"But whatever that was, it's not good. Did you get a solid sense of it?"

Syriah thought about informing her brother. After that chaotic night in the great hall, Kiean's eye turned purple. He also clutched his ribs at times. Ione had brought herb stew for him, and he'd recovered shortly thereafter. His energy returned around the time the Spartan landed.

"They're busy with the cryopump. We shouldn't bother them."

"But what if it comes back?" Danny turned down his tunnel. The wall lights in this area were brighter.

"It lasted only a few seconds." Gulping, Syriah tried to leave behind her alarm at the presence. She welcomed the sight of familiar doors around them.

They stopped at his home. Danny fixed his gaze on her. "Whatever it was…." His voice dropped to a whisper. "It wasn't… human."

Syriah swallowed. She could have sworn the presence was…aware. It wasn't dumb, like a sylin. But it was fleeting, and she wondered if she made another mistake. Shuddering, she said, "Just forget about it. We'll have power soon, and it'll go away for good."

He grimaced. "I hope you're right." He gripped the door latch.

Goosebumps covered Syriah's arms, and she rubbed them. She hoped to never encounter it, whatever *it* was, again. Quickly, she followed Danny inside.

Chapter 23

A double halo surrounded the twin suns in the late morning brought about by the ice crystals suspended in the clouds above. The white circles glowed while the suns appeared as pinpricks. Melting snow dripped from the trimmed bushes surrounding the courtyard that Gordo led them to behind the apartment building. The previous night dumped a meter of snow upon them, but it was still too temperate for it to last. Down the hill, sounds of the rushing river filled the area.

"How's this for fresh air? At least Mandin gets to run around a bit." He gestured at his nephew between them.

"I don't remember it quite this lovely." Alina inhaled the smell of wet soil.

"You only spent a few weeks here that summer. You moved in with Chance afterward."

She quieted, remembering her misery living with her mother. The constant sniping between the two of them, given that the penthouse was Jakob's home. The pavement was wet under her boots, although the mover had already cleared the slush away. She gripped Mandin's hand. "Careful, it's slippery."

"The pergola should be dry," Halle said. "While my components are weatherproofed, I prefer to avoid wet areas if I can help it."

They followed the bot's advice and took up

residence on a bench underneath the shelter.

"Mama, can I play there?" Mandin pointed down the path to small garden pond ringed with stones. He wore his snowsuit and booties.

"The water may still be frozen." Her link showed barely above zero degrees Celsius.

"He might be able to spot the krulls moving about underneath the surface. They keep a flow into the pond where the krulls accumulate," Gordo said.

"Would you like me to accompany him there?" asked Halle.

"All right." She watched Halle move after Mandin as he trotted to the pond. He'd enjoy seeing the krulls. The tiny, shiny fish had long, iridescent whiskers that glowed when they were excited.

Her new suit adjusted to the outdoor temperature, and she listened to the winding river beyond the courtyard alongside her brother.

A beep sounded from her link. The message read:

—For your procedure tomorrow, please be ready at noon. I'll pick you up via escort. I'm looking forward to seeing both you and Mandin again. Affectionately yours, Chance.—

Affectionately yours. She pondered that phrase. Chance used it when they first met ages ago. Perhaps he lapsed into old habits.

"Anything important?" her brother asked.

"It's Chance. They're ready for my procedure tomorrow."

Gordo glanced at her link. "Does Kiean know about your surgery?"

"Yes." She shut off the message. "The reactor must be keeping him." Her chin dipped to her chest as she listened to Mandin's babbling in the distance.

She recalled Mandin's question earlier that morning. He asked if Kiean and Syriah were moving to Alpheios, too. His face seemed long when she'd explained that they'd return to Evesborough after Nana felt better.

"Are you sure you want to go through with it?"

She nodded.

"I don't know why you trust Genodyne." Gordo scowled. "This is their fault."

"I don't. Dr. Bellamy will be there with me the whole time."

Her brother hunched his shoulders. "You going to tell Mom?"

Alina stiffened. "I'd rather that she not know."

"But why?"

"I just—let's wait to see if it'll work." Alina thought back to the last few days. Her mother was visibly weakened, her hand trailing on the wall at times to hold herself steady whenever she came out of her room. It was a sharp contrast to the luminous woman that Linette once was.

"I think you should talk to her."

"We agreed not to cause her further stress. Or false hope." Alina gripped the bottom of the bench. "Jakob thinks so, too."

Her brother leaned back. "You agree with him for once."

She pushed away a strand of hair. "Out of necessity. Thanks, by the way, for watching Mandin while I'm in surgery. You're a better fit for him than Jakob."

"No problem. Look, Lina, I know Jakob isn't Dad, but he does care for Mom. He found Dr. Bellamy as soon as Mom's skin started changing."

Alina dug her boot toe into a crevice between the stone tiles. "Are you trying to ruin my morning?"

"No. You don't say much around him, though." Gordo furrowed his brow.

"I'm civil. What else is there to say?" *That Jakob didn't care that Linette had a family when he started an affair with her*, she nearly remarked.

"So Chance is taking you to Genodyne?"

"Yes. I'll need help getting back after the procedure so he's going to escort me." *The procedure will be over in a single afternoon*, Dr. Bellamy had reminded her. Nevertheless, she shifted in her seat a few times.

"Is he that indispensable? Can't someone else bring you back?"

She blinked. "What's gotten into you?"

"Nothing, sorry. Just…thinking." His head tilted down.

"About what?" She nudged him. "Is it about Mom?" Her brother's green eyes met hers. A cloud of turmoil roiled Gordo's expression.

Halle's voice broke through their moment. "No, Mandin! Come back!" The bot receded down the crest of the hill past a large tree.

Alina jumped off the bench and hastened down the pathway. Gordo's footsteps crunched in the snow after her. At the top of the hill, a few scattered trees below blocked her view of the riverwalk. "Do you see him?"

"There!" Gordo pointed. Mandin's small figure crouched near a drainage pipe at the edge of the water. Boulders and shrubbery were strewn across the soil. Ice floes from the river streamed by.

"Mandin, stop!" She dashed down the hill.

Behind her, Gordo called out, "Halle, secure him!"

The bot clamped down on the back of Mandin's snowsuit and hoisted him away.

Alina skidded around the trees lining the riverwalk. The snowy sludge of the riverbank slowed her pace as she fought to maintain her balance.

Mandin swayed from Halle's hand, yelping as his legs dangled off the ground. "Put me down!"

The bot swung him on top a large boulder nearby. "Don't move."

His eyes rounded as Halle set him on the rock. An expression of awe overcame him as he appraised the bot.

Gasping, Alina halted in front of the pipe by Halle. For once, she outran her brother. Before she could demand an explanation from her son, a caution light flashed from Halle's monitor.

"Alina, be careful of the sylin!"

A tentacle lashed her ankle. She whipped around just in time to feel a jolt in her boot. A blue current rolled up her calf then dissipated outward in a wave. Down by the mouth of the pipe, the angry face of a brown sylin with its tentacles extended appeared. She leapt back.

Halle said, "You've been shocked! I'll alert emergency services!"

A ring of green overtook Alina's vision, and iciness spread throughout her chest. Mandin's fear poured into her, and she shook her head to snap out of the daze. She swore she heard his small voice crying out "Mama!" in the depths of her mind.

Gordo grabbed her arm. "Are you okay?"

"I'm all right. Gordo, did you hear that?"

"Hear what?"

Collecting herself, she stretched her arms out in

front of her and flipped them over. She ground her feet into the soil. No pain or burn coursed through her limbs. The only sign of the sylin's attack remained a small sting by her ankle. She rubbed it. "I'm not injured—don't call emergency services."

"An adult sylin's shock is no small matter. Especially in wet surroundings. It could have temporarily immobilized you," Halle said.

Gordo knelt in front of the pipe. "Empty. Must have ran off."

Alina ran her hands down her sleeves. "This suit—it must have protected me." A fragment of the Commandant's description returned about how the suit kept its wearer safe from animals.

"Goodness, you're lucky!" the bot replied.

"Hold on." Over the silver bot's shoulder, the large boulder came into view with no little boy sitting on it. "Where's Mandin?"

"Why, I set him on the rock out of harm's way."

Alina checked behind the boulder, but only a patch of snow lay on the ground, imprinted with the outline of a small boot. "Gordo, do you see him?"

"No. I'll check the pond." Her brother sprinted back up the hill.

She ran alongside the curve of the riverbank, her heart hammering in her chest. No one could survive for long immersed in the river, given its temperature. She thrashed through a few shrubs. "Mandin!"

Another boulder loomed. She scrambled onto it and cupped a hand around her mouth. She shrieked her son's name. But only the gurgle of water was audible. Scanning the river bend, she looked for any hint of Mandin. More ice floes drifted by.

From the top of the hill, Gordo called out. “He’s not here!”

She yelled, “Halle! Help me find him!”

The bot’s head swiveled around its axis. Then Halle quickly zipped across the riverwalk and stopped by a large tree. “I found him!” Behind the trunk, she pulled out Mandin by his upper arm.

Gordo reached them first. “Alina! He’s having a seizure!”

Gasping, Alina nearly slipped on the wet riverwalk pavement.

When she arrived, Mandin stood frozen, staring into space, unaware of his surroundings.

She grabbed his shoulders. “Mandin!”

Her son blinked a few times, and after a moment, he shuddered. Recognition of her returned to his face, and he choked back a sob.

Fighting back tears, she embraced him and rubbed his back. Bile rose up her throat.

The bot held out her hand “Can I scan him?”

“Go ahead.”

They waited while the blue laser from Halle’s palm traced over Mandin’s face and body.

“His vitals are returning to normal. He’s unharmed,” the bot said. “I’ve recorded the event.”

“He shouldn’t be having breakthrough seizures.” She tried to catch her breath. “I have to adjust his medication.

“Mama, you hurt?”

She wiped the tears from his cheeks. “No, I’m fine. You can’t run off like that. And don’t touch wild animals. Sylins can electrocute you.”

“They usually remain underground this time of

year," Halle said. "It must have come out to hunt since it's a little warmer today. He spotted it from the top of the hill."

Gordo scratched his head. "How did he end up here with no one noticing? I ran past the tree and checked the courtyard."

Alina kneaded his shoulder. "Mandin, do you remember what happened? We couldn't find you."

Her son trembled as he clutched her. "Mama, I sorry. I scared."

Glancing at Halle, she asked, "How did you find him?"

"Behind the tree. I used my infrared scanner," the bot replied.

"Infrared?"

"Yes. He wasn't in the visible light range, so I switched sensors. I detected him, immobilized."

"What do you mean?" Gordo asked.

Alina hoisted up her son. His arms wrapped around her neck, and she nuzzled his soft cheek. "It means…I think it means Mandin couldn't be detected with the naked eye. That he was having an episode that may have triggered…some change in the light spectrum around him. Thank Eamine that we have you, Halle."

"It's been an eventful day. Perhaps you two should rest," Halle replied. "I can make warm scones and tea."

Her brother rested a hand on her arm. "Halle is right."

Alina shifted Mandin, allowing his legs to wrap around her waist. "Want some sweet scones?"

He nodded, and they trudged toward the courtyard. Gordo stayed close to their side.

Smoothing back Mandin's hair, she remembered the

small cry in her mind. When Mandin was petrified, he immediately telegraphed his fear to her. But this was the first instance she heard him speak to her mentally. And watched him vanish. Wait—he disappeared by the Spartan when they landed that day. Had he had another seizure then too that she hadn't been aware of?

Dr. Olek last adjusted his herbal formula over a year ago. The possibility grew that his powers were overtaking it. She kissed his cheek. When her own medical ordeal was over with, she needed to tend to her son. Developing from a toddler into a little boy, his powers manifested in different ways than she'd imagined.

****

Dr. Bellamy tucked her diagnostic wand in her bag by the armchair. "I'll talk to your mother now." She gave Mandin a soft smile.

Alina squeezed her son's arm. "Why don't you find Halle?"

He ran out of the living room, grinning widely.

She exhaled and settled back on the sofa. "Thank you for coming so quickly. He looks fine now, but just this morning, he had an episode. Gordo saw his seizure, too."

The doctor peered at her. Her blonde curls were pulled back in a low ponytail. "You said Mandin has a pediatric neurologist?"

"Yes, Dr. Olek. He suggested we wean him off his tonic soon. But with his seizure…" Alina rubbed her forehead. They'd adjusted his dose over a year ago with no problems, but the setback had wrenched her insides.

Dr. Bellamy trailed her fingertip along her chin. "You said he hasn't had a seizure since he was a baby?"

"Yes, that's right. The herbal tonic has suppressed them. Till now."

"Based on Halle's recording of the seizure, and your description of his fear beforehand, there's a possibility it might be a psychogenic seizure."

"I'm not familiar with that," Alina said.

A thoughtful expression came over Dr. Bellamy's face. "Psychogenic seizures are non-epileptic. They're often in response to intense, physiological events, like distress, or trauma. They can mimic absence seizures, or other forms of epilepsy, but he'd have to be admitted to Genodyne for an EEG to verify that."

Alina recoiled. "He already had an EEG as an infant. It confirmed his epilepsy." She didn't want Mandin anywhere near Genodyne. "Can you do the EEG?"

The doctor shook her head. "I don't have the equipment."

Rubbing her forehead, Alina contemplated how much longer she'd have to stay in Alpheios. She had the bone marrow transplant tomorrow, and then there would be a recovery period. "Dr. Olek has a portable one, but it's… back home."

Dr. Bellamy leaned forward. "If you'd rather wait to consult with his neurologist, I brought you a different medication for Mandin. The thing is…" Her mouth turned down at the end. "If it's psychogenic, his episodes might be resistant to standard anti-convulsant meds. In that case, cognitive behavioral therapy may be more useful."

"Therapy?" Alina's mouth hung open. She'd provided her son with everything he needed. She cuddled him close at night, making sure he knew he was loved. Dr. Bellamy must be mistaken. What would her three-year-old need therapy for?

The doctor replied, "You can try the medication for now. If there's a breakthrough episode, I would definitely bring it up to his neurologist. I focus mostly on internal medicine and general surgery." Her hands clasped together in her lap. "But the reason why children are often weaned off seizure meds is that the likelihood of another seizure is minuscule if they haven't had one in several years, especially if they're healthy otherwise. Children's brains are highly plastic, and they change as they develop." She shrugged.

"So Mandin is all right otherwise?" Alina found her pitch was raised.

Another nod. "Physically, he's a healthy little boy, as far as I can tell."

"He isn't different from other children. He hasn't suffered any abuse or major life trauma..." Her hands curled into loose fists on top of her thighs, and a slight tremor overtook her voice.

The doctor placed her hand over Alina's. "I'm not saying he did." Her voice was gentle. "Why don't we try the meds for now? If it *is* an absence seizure, not a reaction to an emotional event, those tend to be more benign. But for safety reasons, it's good to stop them."

Swallowing, Alina nodded. "Yes, please."

Dr. Bellamy reached for her bag. She pulled out a bottle of syrup and relayed the dosage instructions.

Alina took the bottle. "Thank you, doctor."

"I told you to call me Jasmine." She grinned. "And how are you doing? Are you ready for tomorrow?"

"Me? Oh, yes." Alina waved a hand like it was no big deal. "I just...want to get it over with."

A chuckle eased out of Jasmine. "I don't blame you.

Don’t worry, I’ll be gentle.”

“How long will the procedure take?” Alina scratched her arm. She didn’t really want to talk about the surgery.

“I’ll be there early to sign their NDA, but the surgery itself will last less than an hour.”

“Then I better have a good dinner tonight since I’m not supposed to eat before the anesthesia tomorrow.”

“Clear liquids are okay, up to two hours prior. Bone broth might help if you’re hungry.”

Alina stood. “Thank you for coming doc—I mean Jasmine.”

“Try to relax.” Jasmine touched her shoulder. “I’ll see you tomorrow.”

Taking in a deep breath helped somewhat. Alina walked Jasmine to the lift.

After her departure, Alina set off to find her son. Mandin and Halle weren’t in the kitchen. Maybe he was watching toons with the bot in the bedroom. She would sleep easier if she knew he took his proper dosage before her surgery. Passing her mother’s bedroom door along the corridor, the blur of her tasks piled high.

Chapter 24

Syriah watched as her brother threw clean clothes in his gear bag on top of the master bed in his room. The cavern walls were lit by the overhead bulb that dangled from the ceiling. Power flowed to the entire village since Kiean installed the cryopump.

"Why can't I go with you?" she asked.

"It's unpredictable in Alpheios right now. Safer for you to stay here." Kiean pressed on the mattress. "What do you think? I redid the springs. Alina wants a firm bed."

She bounced on it. "I think Alina will like it. But you should take me with you." She yawned and covered her mouth. For a second, she thought of curling up on the bed since she'd was tired from not sleeping much lately.

Using his thumb, Kiean wiped a strand of hair from her face. His right eye was no longer puffy, but a purple half-moon rested high on his cheekbone. The split in his bottom lip was healing thanks to Macy's dandlemane balm.

"Soloman can run the reactor now. I have to get to Alpheios to help Alina before deep winter hits the city." His voice calmed her, but she tugged his hand anyway.

He cupped her chin and gently lifted it. "Promise me you'll be good and listen to Dad. And I'll bring you back more candy from Alpheios." His fiendish grin delighted Syriah. Her brother always knew how to make her feel better.

"I want more sweet cakes."

"Yeah, me too." For a second, a shadow rippled across Kiean's face. Barely a hint, but she caught it. It came and went since he read Alina's letter, and Syriah sensed his faint worry. Alina was not present at his birthday dinner that Hawk and Ione had made for him. He tried to sound upbeat, noting his birthday could be the previous week for all he knew. Dad had used the date that Genodyne brought Kiean to their door as a baby, but he wasn't certain of his exact birthday as a newborn.

A knock at the door sounded. She followed him to the main room. Aurore whirled in, breathing hard. She'd returned from Alpheios with her long bangs cut short. Her normally bright orange air was flickering. While fun to be around, Syriah sometimes sensed Aurore's surface wasn't that deep. For it to be wavering showed something really bothered Alina's friend.

"Hawk is missing. He told Ione that he'd return after checking on a vibration reported down tunnel four called in by several residents, but that was several hours ago. Wilder went to check on him, but he can't find him anywhere."

A crease developed in her brother's forehead. "Tunnel four branches off to that steep drop that's sealed off, by the electrical junction box."

"Yes, but the lock on the door has been removed." Aurore's hands jutted out to her sides. "Wilder thinks Hawk might have removed it to investigate the vibration."

"Where's Wilder now?"

"He's at Ione's. She's worried."

Gulping, Syriah tried not to remember the presence

she felt around the door of tunnel four earlier. She wasn't even sure what it was, or how they'd react to her description of it.

"We still have those nav globes onboard the Spartan?" Kiean's mouth dipped at the edges. "Last time Alina used them down the drop, they returned with no readings. That's why she blocked it, out of caution."

"Yes. I can try to change up the settings." Out of habit, Aurore reached for her bangs, but dropped her hand.

He nudged Syriah. "Go to Dad's."

His face was set in a mask, but Syriah could feel his concern about his best friend.

"Can I help? Maybe I can sense him." She hadn't used her powers since the cavern incident, but little Hudson would wonder where his father had gone.

"It might be better if you stay with your father," Aurore said.

Syriah's heart fell. No one trusted her since the reactor broke. They all blamed her. Even Dr. Olek was too busy to train her, saying he had many patients to attend to during the power outage.

Her brother placed his hand on her shoulder. "She might be able to help." He gestured to Aurore. "Grab the globes and meet me at the entrance to tunnel four. Bring as much rope line as you can."

Syriah's hopes soared. If she could help them find Hawk, maybe they would forgive her for breaking the reactor. She hurried after Kiean outside to their corridor.

****

Syriah trailed after her brother, Wilder, and Aurore around the curve of the underground river. Equipment bags swayed from their belts, and Aurore lugged a large cable wheel on rollers. Up ahead, the wood door was open revealing a gap in the stone walls, its padlock dangling on its lever. They stopped, and Kiean turned on his headlamp.

"I asked the residents further down in tunnel four if they undid the padlock, but everyone said they did not. They all felt a strange vibration coming through the walls." Wrinkles marred Wilder's forehead. "Hawk must have opened it to investigate."

"Look." Aurore ran her hand over a bolt and D-ring anchored just inside the tunnel's entrance. A lanyard was attached to the ring. "He used a safety line. Probably when he checked the electrical junction box inside." She plucked at it. "It's still tight. No slack."

Kiean hunched over and checked the electric box. Standing, he called out his friend's name. No sounds returned.

"Should we just haul up the line?" Wilder asked.

Kiean gave the safety line a tug, but it held taut. "Feels like it's caught on something." He shook his head. "There's nothing wrong with the electrical box." Craning his neck, he peered over the ledge. "I can't see the bottom—too dark. He might have lost his footing."

Wilder's dark eyes flickered to Aurore. His mouth tightened.

As Aurore handed out comm bars to the men and set up the antenna, Syriah placed her hand on the wall. A faint life force touched her fingers, fleeting. She pressed her hand flatter, hoping it would return. "Hawk was here but…." A rock pitted her stomach. "I can't feel him anymore."

Aurore pulled two nav globes from her bag. "Wait," she said to Kiean. "Before you go, let me try to get some readings." Red lights from the metal spheres glowed, and she released them. They flew down into the darkness.

While they waited for the globes, Kiean pressed his comm bar to his earlobe, and synched it with his link. After they tested their comms, Wilder's hands curled and uncurled by his sides. He was not as tall as Hawk, but with magnetic dark eyes and a constant smile against his olive skin, he closely resembled his older brother. No wonder Aurore was drawn to him. Although at the moment, Wilder wasn't smiling. Neither was Kiean. His face was like stone as he waited.

A presence crept up over Syriah, the same darkness she'd felt the other day. A slight vibration touched her chest. She stepped back. Opening her mouth to speak, she stopped when the two spheres popped back up, hovering.

Aurore examined their readings. "They never got past one hundred meters."

"It's the same problem Alina had with them." Kiean stepped into a harness. "We'll have to rappel down." He faced Wilder. "Help me with the top anchor?"

"Standby." Hawk's brother slipped on work gloves. He hammered the studs into the feet wells of the cable wheel on a thick portion of the ledge. Kiean held it steady and helped him secure it.

Her brother gathered the rope and glanced at Aurore. "Can you keep track of our depth? By the rope?"

"Wait." Syriah stood frozen. The presence vanished, but her insides turned to ice. "I don't want you to go."

"It's okay. I'm strapped in." Kiean turned toward the ledge, but she grabbed his hand.

"What is it?" he asked.

She didn't know how to explain the cold blackness

that passed through as they all gazed at her. It was like no other animal she'd encountered. The presence was something very old. As a force, it was foul. But it lurked down in the depths of the darkness. She shuddered. "Don't go. Something happened to Hawk."

He knelt in front of her. "I have to help. He may have fallen and could be hurt. I need to bring him back, you understand?"

She flinched at Aurore kicking a pebble. Her brother touched her arm. "I'll return. I promise." He glanced at Wilder. "Ready?"

Wilder tugged the ropes on his own device and gathered the bundle in his fist. "Think we have enough line?"

"I brought the hoist cable from the Triumph. And attached it to the one on the Spartan. It's the longest we have," Aurore replied.

"We'll soon find out." Kiean slapped Wilder's arm. "I'll go first."

"I'll track the length." Aurore said. "Please stay up on comm." A yellow light showed from the lamp that she had set up on the ledge, casting eerie shadows.

Kiean tapped on the beam from his link, giving him extra light in addition to his headlamp. He stepped close to the edge.

Syriah clutched her arms over one another as her brother slowly dipped below the ledge. As his head disappeared, she held her breath. Wilder followed him.

Aurore stuck her head over the ledge, then glanced at her link from time-to-time. She spoke into her comm bar. "About twenty-five meters down."

The girl closed her eyes, focusing. Her mind branched out. Kiean's presence was strong in the tunnel.

Beyond him, she searched for Hawk. A faint trace of Hawk was still present near where they stood at the opening. But nothing deep from the tunnel, other than total silence, so thick that she couldn't view anything. A chill ran through her, and her arms trembled.

The old, foul presence from earlier had withdrawn from the area. She opened her eyes, choosing not to follow it. Taking in a breath, she hoped her brother would hurry before it returned. Waiting, she rocked back and forth on her feet.

The metal wheel groaned as it spun out the cable. A joint in the line slid past the ledge.

"Past one hundred meters." Aurore touched her comm bar on her ear. "You've made it farther than the globes."

Syriah chewed on a fingernail.

After a few minutes, she asked Aurore, "Where are they?"

"Touchdown. They hit the floor." Aurore touched her comm bar. "No, wait. They're on another ledge." She sucked in a breath when she glanced at the colored markings on the cable. "Over two hundred meters down."

"Did they find Hawk?"

But Alina's friend didn't answer, checking her link.

Syriah crept up to the edge of the ledge and peeked over.

"Careful!" Aurore pulled Syriah back out to the walkway. "Stay there and don't move." She touched her comm bar again. Aurore's dark eyes widened. Her usual perky expression disappeared. "It's time for you to find your dad and stay with him."

"But I want to wait until Kiean comes back."

Thirsty, she thought of asking Aurore for water from her canteen but didn't want to annoy her. "I'll be good, I promise."

"Your brother wants you to find your father and stay with him." Aurore chewed her bottom lip.

An ache spread through Syriah's tummy. "Please, let me wait for my brother."

Aurore touched her shoulder and lowered her voice. "You have to go." She gave her shoulder a small push. "Go on."

"But what about Kiean?"

"He's fine. I'll tell him you're waiting for him with your dad, okay?" Aurore blocked the ledge with her body. "Now go." She placed her hands on her hips.

The little girl turned away and brushed the tears from her eyes. No one wanted her there, not even her brother. She had failed them in finding Hawk.

****

Kiean leaned over the control panel of the Triumph's bridge, typing a message. Syriah had never witnessed her brother so glum. He stared for a while at the message that he wanted to send to Alina. Syriah brought her knees into her chest while resting on a seat. She dug her chin into her knees.

Nearby, Danny played with magnetic stones. *Click, click,* they'd go every few seconds as he allowed them to pull together in his hands. *Click, click.* It was the only sound in the room, and it was starting to bother her.

Syriah wrapped her arms around her legs. The adults whispered more than ever the last few days, but she knew that they'd found Hawk's body. Kiean refused to discuss with her what happened except to say there had been an accident. But she overheard fragments of "bite marks" and "attack" from the adults. The presence that she'd sensed, an ancient and foul entity lurking somewhere down tunnel four, had ended Hawk's life.

She'd never seen her older brother cry. While no tears came to Kiean, at times, he held his head in his hands. He seemed lost, unlike himself. Lost without his best friend.

If only she had searched for Hawk sooner. Maybe she would have found him. Then Ione wouldn't be crying so much at home, holding little Hudson close.

Click, click, went the rocks in Danny's hands.

The door swished open, and Big Flint entered the bridge. Danny hopped off his seat and ran to his father. Flint wrapped an arm around his shoulder while Danny pressed his face into his side. Hawk was Danny's uncle-in-law. After telling him to quietly sit down, Flint approached Kiean.

"Funeral will be in five days. Ione has decided that much."

Her brother barely gave him a nod. "What arrangements need to be made?"

"Cinda is taking care of Ione and Hudson as far as making sure they get something to eat. But…" Flint glanced at Syriah and Danny over his shoulder. "Maybe we should take care of the…logistics for moving the crate to the memorial and then onto the burial site."

Her brother straightened, but he winced. "Whatever she needs. I already boarded up tunnel four."

"Thanks. One less thing for her to worry about." Flint rested a hand on Kiean's shoulder and left the bridge. Her brother turned his attention back to the panel in front of him.

Click, click, went the rocks. "This place sucks,"

Danny said.

Syriah closed her eyes. Her brother hadn't spoken much the last few days. Maybe Alina would hurry home once she received the message. Alina was close friends with Ione and wouldn't want her to be so sad. Syriah went still, and her mind branched out. Focusing hard, she silently projected herself behind her brother near the panel to read the message he was sending.

The green letters glowed against the black screen.

—Alina, I regret that I can't come to Alpheios sooner. There's been an accident involving Hawk down tunnel four. Funeral arrangements are being made in his honor. Once the memorial is over, and the weather clears, I will fly to Alpheios to explain everything. Flint and Cinda are supporting Ione and Hudson during this difficult time, as am I. I'm sorry I can't be there for your procedure. I wish you and your mother the best Eamine can deliver. Yours always, Kiean—.

A voice intruded into Syriah's mind. *You knew about the beast. Why didn't you tell anyone? It's your fault.*

She recognized it as Danny's voice. *Stop it. Leave me alone.*

Your fault that Hawk is dead. You should have told them what you sensed.

Stop! Syriah gnashed her teeth as she tried to eject Danny from her mind. *Get out and leave me alone!*

The rocks fell to the floor.

She stopped projecting. Uncurling from her chair, she glowered at Danny. He glared back.

"Stop it!" she said.

Her brother rose.

"He won't leave me alone!" Her eyes moistened as

she pointed at Danny.

Kiean lifted her up, and she rested her head into his shoulder. Gasping, she could no longer contain her tears.

"I'm here." Her brother rubbed her back as she released all her fears into his shoulder.

He twisted, and she lifted her head. "What is it?"

His forehead crinkled. "Did you do something?"

"No!" Please, she couldn't possibly have done anything else wrong.

"The message is gone." Still clutching her, he gazed down at the panel. "I was about to transmit…" He touched the screen. "There's a signal wave. Did it send it?"

"Syriah botched it again." Danny had picked up the stones and held them in his fist, as if he was about to throw them at her.

She shook her head back and forth. "No! I swear, I didn't do anything!'

Her brother hugged her close. "It's okay. Hey—" he directed his words at Danny. "It was an accident, what happened to Hawk. No one's fault. Do you understand me?"

It was the hardest she heard her brother's voice over the past few days.

Danny's eyes enlarged at Kiean, and all he could do was nod.

"Time to get off the bridge and take a break," her brother said in her ear. "I can use a nap, too. Want to come home with me?"

She nodded, sobbing harder.

Carrying her, he strode toward the bridge's exit. "C'mon, Danny. Time to go home."

Hanging onto her brother tight, Syriah couldn't stop

her tears. It wasn't her fault, was it? She didn't know Hawk was missing. Phoebe had not given her any premonitions, but simply ran away that day they'd passed the tunnel.

She hated Danny in that moment, hated him. Why did he have to be so mean to her?

Outside the bridge, they passed Soloman who held a device with a screen in his hand. The little needle in it jumped around. "Kiean, I'm getting strange magnetic readings—"

"Not now." Her brother carried her away, much to her relief.

Macy called her talents a gift. *Use them wisely,* Macy said. But lately, all they brought was harm, rather than good. Syriah wished she was like all the other children, normal. She cursed being born different. If she was normal, no one could blame her for anything bad happening ever again.

Chapter 25

Alina pulled the hospital sheet over her waist, gazing at her toes poking through the clean fabric. While smooth to the touch, she didn't find the blanket particularly comforting. She leaned forward in the medical bed, plucking at the cloth. The sensors in Genodyne's bed flickered at her movements.

Chance settled on a stool by her bedside. "Sure you want to do this?"

Swallowing, she nodded.

"I'll stay until it's over." His shoulders angled toward her, his arms resting on his thighs. In his uniform, he had escorted her to Genodyne. She had contemplated walking through the ice and snow, to experience the cold's harsh reality so she could think. Given the recent attack on their GATV though, she accepted his offer to bring her to the hospital instead.

"Thanks." She noted his serious expression, the hint of concern on his face.

"Does your mother know you're doing this?"

She rolled her lips inward. "No. And I prefer she didn't." If the transplant didn't work, Alina would never hear the end of it from her mother. Better that Linette think that they used Genodyne's latest therapeutics without knowing the details of how it was manufactured.

"And Gordo?" His gaze intensified.

"He's not crazy about it either, but he agreed to

watch Mandin while I undergo the procedure." Goosebumps prickled her skin through the thin hospital gown. She wanted to rip it off, but hunched over and rubbed her arms instead.

Chance rose, and his lofty frame hovered over her.

A tremor quaked within. She willed herself to stay motionless. Maybe if she didn't move, she'd absorb some of his confidence.

He rested a hand on her shoulder, easing the strain within her. "I won't leave you." A slight smile spread across his lips as he held his shoulders back and steady. His dark eyes gleamed. Chance seemed to contemplate a thought. "You should know—"

The door opened. Dr. Daxmen and Dr. Bellamy entered.

The corpulent doctor cleared his throat. "We're ready for you."

Chance's head swiveled between the two doctors.

"This is Dr. Bellamy." She gestured to Jasmine whose platinum locks were tucked into a neat roll.

He extended his hand. "A pleasure. You are…Linette's doctor?"

"Correct." Jasmine's tone was efficient. "And Alina's now, as well. You can call me their family doctor, I suppose." She gave Alina a comforting smile.

Grateful for her presence, Alina looked pointedly in Daxmen's direction. "I'd like some assurances that after I do this, we'll get the serum from the kronosapiens."

"I'll assist with the withdrawal." Determination permeated Chance's voice as he shifted into Guardian mode.

Daxmen smoothed the lapel of his doctor's coat. "That won't be necessary. Kora said she'd do the withdrawal herself. That she prefers it that way."

"Then I'd like to witness it." Iron stiffened Alina's spine. She tried not to think about encountering Kora again, but she needed to verify that Genodyne would uphold their end of the bargain.

"Alina—" Chance began.

"I'll stay in the control room." She drew the sheet tight across her lap. "If you'll accompany me."

"You'll be quite fatigued afterward." A warning underlined Jasmine's voice.

Chance said, "Why don't I verify it instead, with Dr. Bellamy? You can rest."

Alina nodded. Chance had only helped her since her arrival in Alpheios. "Then I'm ready." A breath loosened from her. She turned to Jasmine, searching for reassurance in the doctor's amber eyes.

Dr. Bellamy patted her forearm. "This won't take long."

Daxmen called in two attendants. They maneuvered Alina's bed out to the hall, following the doctors. Chance kept his hand on the bedrail, walking alongside her as they guided the bed toward the operating room. A blur of ceiling tiles passed by as she gazed up. As they rotated her bed to enter the OR, she glimpsed a surgical team with masks over their faces standing by.

Chance gave her hand a squeeze, his thumb rubbing her skin. "I'll be right here the entire time in the recovery room."

His touch was reassuring. "Thank you." She lingered in his grasp for a few seconds longer.

The automated doors swung shut behind her. Both doctors traversed behind the window of a washroom to prepare for the surgery. Another medical attendant in scrubs lowered the head of her bed until it laid flat. Overhead lights glared from above, and Alina squinted.

Turning her head to the side, her gaze fell upon the instrument tray. Several metal needles rested upon it, longer than the length of her hand. A mallet rested by them, next to what looked like a T-shaped plunger.

An attendant held up a breathing mask. "Just try to relax."

Blinking, she allowed the attendant to place the mask over her nose and mouth. A blur softened the ceiling lights, and the room faded from view.

****

The plastic bag of crimson blood sat within the metal tray on the scale. The numbers flashed a liter-and-half worth of bone marrow. Chance turned away. They said they wouldn't take much from Alina, but the bag full of her fluid made his stomach churn. Nearby, Dr. Daxmen updated a new male tech on Ash's condition by the monitors. Chance deduced that Buck, the other tech, was still recovering, waiting for the bone to heal that Kora had broken.

The door to the outer room clicked open. Chance left the control area to investigate. Dr. Bellamy strode in, and he met her by the observation windows.

She said, "I just checked on Alina. She's sore, but I gave her a medication to help mitigate that."

Chance frowned. "She's awfully pale. Is that normal?" He'd waited by her bedside in the recovery room. She appeared groggy but recognized him when he called out her name. A wave of relief had filled him when her green eyes focused on his face. He stayed until she emerged out of her haze. The first thing she'd asked for was a drink of water.

"She needs rest, and then she'll return to her old self in a few days. I withdrew the bone marrow from both hips so she may want to avoid walking around too much." The elegant doctor nodded at Daxmen. "He cooperated during the surgery."

"So now he'll do the same for Ash?"

"Actually, he'll run an IV line into the recipient. The fluid will flow to his bone marrow cavity and the stem cells will reproduce there." She approached the window and peered down. Kora hunched over the bassinet, checking on the growing babies, her three bumps visibly protruding on her spine. "Fascinating creatures, aren't they?"

He shrugged, not as taken with the kronosapiens as the woman who stood next to him. Dr. Bellamy was younger than he expected, but possessed a skilled demeanor that was reassuring. She proved to be a much better choice than Dr. Daxmen to conduct the procedure. "About those creatures, doc—"

"Please, call me Jasmine." Her light-brown eyes penetrated his.

He paused. "All right. Jasmine."

"Are the babies twins?" she asked.

"The kronosapiens are capable of carrying multiple babies." Chance had pondered over the different scenarios about what had befallen the third infant. He never followed up, for he didn't want to confirm his worst suspicions. Sometimes, it was better not to ask such questions.

Daxmen called out from the control room. "We're ready. Doctor, would you like to accompany us?"

"Yes." She stepped forward, but Chance blocked her from advancing.

"I'd rather you observe from here," he said. "They're dangerous."

Surprise flashed across her eyes. "I need to see this."

"Jasmine, I'm asking you to stay." The memory of Alina's encounter with Kora was imprinted on Chance's mind, and how terrified he had been that she'd harm Alina before he reached her. He couldn't afford a similar situation with Dr. Bellamy, not when she attended to Alina.

"Kora has promised to allow us to do the transplant," Daxmen said. "She wants Ash to get better."

Dr. Bellamy studied Chance. "We both told Alina we'd verify the exchange. You'll accompany me."

He ground his jaw and gestured to the stairs leading down to the laboratory. "After you."

The two doctors led the way, followed by the male nurse who carried the transplant bag in a tray alongside some other supplies. The laboratory was a few degrees cooler than the observation room. Chance's hand itched by his baton, but he kept it sheathed. Kora pivoted upon hearing the door open.

Daxmen stopped in front of the gate. "We have the transplant ready for Ash. Can we enter?"

Kora narrowed her eyes at Chance. "He is not welcome."

"Then no transplant." He hardened his voice.

"Stop." Jasmine placed a hand on his chest. Her forcefulness surprised him.

"You can wait out here." Not an ounce of fear appeared on Jasmine's face.

"Kora?" Daxmen said.

The kronosapien's expression was marred with suspicion. She glanced at the tray the nurse carried.

Kora's head tilted back, and she sniffed the air. "Enter."

Daxmen unlocked the gate and traversed to Ash's bedside. The nurse set up the IV while Daxmen gave Ash a cursory exam. He explained in a low voice Ash's condition to Dr. Bellamy who seemed mesmerized by the patient. Kora hovered by her babies, never taking her eyes off the doctors.

Chance leaned against the doorway, resting his hand on his baton handle. The team hung the bag of dark, red fluid on a medical pole. As the blood flowed toward the bed, Daxmen checked the tubes. He nodded at Kora from across the bed. "It's done. After this bag, if it works, he should be feeling better within days." He took the syringe from the tray and rounded the other side of the bed where Kora waited.

"That's far enough," she said, moving in front of the bassinet.

"For you." He held out the syringe. "Two vials. Based on our arrangement."

Her upper lip curled at the instrument in his hand. She swiped it from his grasp. She turned her back to them, facing the bassinet.

Kora was bent over with the needle, her spinal bumps protruding. Chance angled his neck. He glimpsed the needle, pointed at Kora's midsection. As she withdrew the fluid from herself, one of the krono-babies made a noise like a squeak. They were much bigger than when Chance saw them last, filling up the entire bassinet space. They were now the size of human babies several months old. Just how fast did these creatures grow?

The female kronosapien faced them again and revealed the full vials in her palm.

As the doctor took the needle and vials, a snort of

contempt resonated through her nose. “Leave us.”

The medical party scurried for the gate. Daxmen locked it after exiting, and Chance followed them up the stairs. He glanced back at Kora who watched them, her mouth pulled back in a smug smile. The sooner this ordeal was over for the city, the sooner he could transfer out of his thankless assignment.

Back in the control room, he asked, “When will the serum be ready?”

“I’ll look at it under the scope before curfew. Once I confirm the results, I can pass it to Dr. Bellamy here. Mass production will require the board’s approval.” Daxmen instructed the nurse to take the syringe to the R&D section.

“I’ll deliver it myself to Linette first thing in the morning.” Jasmine’s smooth voice interjected. “In the meantime, I can discharge Alina.”

Chance contemplated the timeline. As soon as Linette was cured, and Alina recovered, she’d leave Alpheios, taking Mandin with her. He could feel her barrier toward him drop a little each time they were around one another. Soon, her stay in the city would come to an end. He had to move quickly.

Chapter 26

Steady tufts of snow tumbled all around. Alina peeked out the GATV. The walkway to the penthouse was already buried, as if someone had spread a white coverlet on the ground. She had glided out of the hospital in a chair-lev, but the nurse returned it to Genodyne after they loaded her into the vehicle. While Alina's head had cleared somewhat, her energy had been sapped. It was as if her life force had gone on strike. Her body nudged her to rest.

Snowflakes landed on Chance's Guardian cap as he held his hand out to her. Alina grabbed the door handle and rose. Fatigue permeated her limbs, and her entire backside was numb from Dr. Bellamy's medication. Upon taking a step onto the lift, she winced. A jolt of pain coursed through her lower back. Chance's arm encircled her waist. He swept her up in his arms, and a small squeal broke free from her. Her heart skidded in her chest.

"You don't have to carry me." Exhausted, she shivered. Chills wrung her core as if to warn of an oncoming fever.

He kept a secure grip on her as the snow fell around them. "It's slippery. Hold onto me."

For a second, she lost herself in the soft gleam of his dark star-sapphire eyes. Her arms surrounded his neck, and her cheeks flushed. Swallowing, she reasoned there was no sense in being stubborn. Chance was already deeply involved in her current predicament. Her body ached too much to demand any protest.

He carried her to the door, away from the hum of the GATV. The only sound was the crunching snow under his boots while he carried her along the walkway. Heated air in the lobby circulated around them upon entry. The doorman rushed to the elevator when he saw them. Alina's cheeks warmed over. A chime signaled the doors opening, and Chance stepped in with her.

She could hear the strong thump of his heart as the lift ascended. "I can stand."

Gently, he set her down. "How are you feeling?"

Every small pang yelped in her back and hips. She leaned back against the wall and took in a deep breath. "I need to lie down." Nausea tickled the back of her throat. She swayed, and Chance grabbed her.

"You're breathing hard." He lifted her again before she could object. Wooziness filled her stomach, and she laid her head onto his chest. His torso was warm, and she pressed her body into his to sap some of his heat. Taking a deep inhale, she smelled brisk pine. The doors opened to the familiar tiled hallway.

Chance marched into the bright penthouse where they were greeted by Halle.

"Alina, are you hurt?" the bot asked.

"She slipped outside in the snow," he replied.

Alina lifted her head and blinked. She had confided in him that Linette did not know about her operation, but no excuse arose of her condition. He smoothly deflected the inquiry, and she was grateful for the small lie.

Mandin slid off the couch. Her brother stood when Chance carried her into the room.

"Mama!" Mandin ran over, his small face squished with concern. "Are you okay?"

"She fell down outside, but she'll be fine. She needs to rest."

Her son placed a small hand on her arm. "Mama?"

"I'm fine, sweetie. I just want to go to bed." She fought back another wave of nausea.

Gordo's face was pinched. Strife clouded his green eyes. While he'd agreed to watch Mandin, he didn't hide his thoughts about the situation.

"I should scan her." Halle held out an arm, and her monitor flickered to a vitals screen.

"Dr. Bellamy will come by in the morning to check on her." Chance's voice was firm.

"Are you sure? If she hit her head, I'd rather check her for injuries," Halle replied.

"Not her head. More her back. She needs to lie down."

"Then I'll bring her a relaxing tea." The bot scooted in the kitchen's direction.

Her son followed them to her brightly lit bedroom. Chance threw back the bed cover and rested her on the soft sheets. She withdrew her arms from his neck, suddenly cold. As she crawled into bed, he pulled the curtains shut.

"Dr. Bellamy will bring the serum tomorrow," he said.

"You saw the exchange?" She glanced at Mandin who would not understand what they were discussing.

"I did. They went through with it." He smoothed the covers over her shoulders. "Rest for now."

Mandin's small mouth turned down, worry filling his dark eyes. "But Mama no feel good?"

“I told you, she needs to rest.” Chance rested his hand on Mandin’s shoulder. “Why don’t you come with me for an overnight? Let your mom sleep while we play in the snow?” He turned to her. “I’ll keep an eye on him so you can sleep.”

Still slightly dizzy, she’d assumed Gordo would watch him. His expression in the living room when he saw them gave her pause. Mandin thrust his face close to hers. “Can I play outside in the snow?”

A smile crossed Chance’s face as he waited for her reply. She bit her bottom lip at the thought of denying Mandin the opportunity to spend time with his father. And Chance would see to it that their son remained safe.

“You’re sure it’s not a bother?”

“Of course not.” Chance took his son’s hand. “Mandin, why don’t you get your shoes on?”

She lifted her head in the direction of the closet. “His suit is there.”

“I’ll take it from here.” Chance led their son out and grabbed his snowsuit from the closet. He instructed Mandin to pick up his shoes strewn on the rug. Alina watched, noting how in the short time that Mandin knew Chance, he never challenged him as he did with her, but rather did as he was told.

Once the door shut, she let out a deep breath. Her head swam, and a fire burned the back of her thighs. She curled up under the covers, pulling them tight around her shoulders. Alina drifted off before tasting any of Halle’s tea.

****

The next afternoon, Alina rested on the brocade couch in the living room twirling a glass of fizz in her hand. She’d slept straight through morning like her body had given out on her. When she woke, she ditched her climate suit for an outfit that Halle left out for her. The rose-colored pullover was butter-soft on her skin, and the muted gold stretchers encased her legs in a supple material. After getting dressed, Alina threw her hair back in a loose ponytail. She took a few more sips of the delectable citrus fizz and smoothed the peacock-patterned throw over her lap.

Dr. Bellamy entered the room from the direction of the conservatory carrying a kit. She wore a fashionable white climate suit that contrasted against her bronze skin and upswept blonde curls. "The serum sample looked good under the scope, so I gave Linette an injection of it. I'll return soon to check her progress. I'm supposed to tell Daxmen how Linette does before he recommends mass production of the serum for distribution." She took up residence in the striped chair across from Alina. "How are you feeling?"

"Better, but still sore. Sometimes, I get dizzy when I stand." Alina plucked at the throw, impatient at her lack of mobility.

The doctor opened her kit and held up a wand scanner with a circular head. "I'd like to take a look, if you don't mind. Please lie back." Alina obeyed as Dr. Bellamy hovered over her. A blue light pulsed from the head of the scanner and trailed down Alina's body.

Jasmine studied the readings. "Your vitals are good. Don't try to stand suddenly. Take your time." She bent over her. "Where are you sore?"

Alina pointed to the side of her buttocks. Jasmine's hands gently lifted Alina's chin and peered into her pupils. "That's where I withdrew the bone marrow. I can give you a stronger prescription, but it may make you groggy." She touched her gently, prodding and asking if there was pain in certain areas.

"I'd rather be awake." The prescription Alina was on dampened the pain although it didn't completely rid her of aches.

A smile graced the doctor's face. "Then I'll give you something different to help with recovery." She tucked the scanner back into her kit and produced a small bottle of capsules. "Take two in the morning, and two in the evening with food. You'll feel better in a day or two."

The doorbell rang, and Alina pushed herself up.

Jasmine took her kit and headed for the tiled hallway, meeting Halle along the way.

Chance's voice carried into the room as he exchanged friendly pleasantries with the doctor. The sound of the elevator chime signaled Dr. Bellamy's departure. Mandin strolled into the room followed by his father.

Alina's heart softened when she saw her son. Mandin's grin showed off his baby teeth, and he carried an orlind bloom, but he did not rush her as expected. Instead, he glanced back at Chance as if to seek permission.

"Go on, but remember, no climbing," Chance said.

Mandin approached her. "Mama feel better?"

"Yes, now that you're here." She held out her arms, and he stepped into them. Squeezing him, he smelled like a mixture of snow and a grape-scented bath. He handed her the plum-colored blossom.

She rolled the stem of the lush flower between her fingertips. "Where did you find this? They grow in the mountains."

Chance reclined next to her. "That's our secret. We

didn't climb any mountains, but he accompanied me on an errand."

The flower's delicate, sweet scent imbued her with hope. "Thank you. It's lovely."

"You're welcome." Chance's voice dropped a mellow octave. "You look much better. How are you feeling?"

"Bruised, but I'm taking it easy. Doctor's orders." She squirmed, wishing her energy would fully return.

Halle glided into the room and set down a tray with a pitcher of pink fizz, extra glasses, and herb-infused biscuits. "Doctor Bellamy seemed very pleased with your progress when she left. I dare say you'll be active again in no time."

"I hope so. Halle, do you mind putting this in water for me?" She handed the bot the flower.

"Certainly." The bot left the room.

Mandin grabbed a biscuit off the plate and nibbled at it.

"Orlinds symbolize vitality. It was a thoughtful choice." Alina rubbed the soft sleeves covering her forearms.

"They're also rare. Like you." Chance's face became serious. He sat close to her on the sofa.

Her cheeks flushed. She watched Mandin eat his biscuit.

The bot returned carrying the orlind nestled in a bud vase. When Halle set it on their tray, Mandin asked for the lemonade-infused fizz, and the bot obliged by pouring him a glass.

Halle beckoned him across the room where he sprang up onto a matching sofa. A note of joy rang out from him as the bot flashed a rogue ball game across her monitor. In between bites of the biscuit, Mandin pointed at clips of Gordo carrying a ball tight against his side and streaking across the indoor field.

"Gordo showed him rogue ball?" Alina asked.

"Yes, while you were out with Mr. Graylin. Your brother taught him the rules, and now Mandin enjoys watching his games." Her monitor displayed Gordo leaping into the goal zone. He knocked over the defending goalie.

"See? Uncle Gordo scored!" Mandin pointed at Halle's screen.

Alina chuckled.

Chance swiveled his head around the room. "The rogue ball champ isn't here?"

"He's been training lately." She nestled back into the couch cushions. While her brother seemed to enjoy spending time with Mandin, he didn't say much to her these days like he usually did. A gym bag slung across his climate suit indicated that he was headed out in the mornings, and a determined expression would appear on his face.

"How's Linette?" Chance asked.

Alina relayed to him details of Dr. Bellamy's visit. "And she said these pills should help me recover in a day or two." She wrapped her hand around the bottle in her lap.

"I have an idea. That is, if you're up for it after your recovery." A glint filled his dark star-sapphire eyes. "We can take Mandin on a city tour via the maglev this weekend. Make a stop to grab some hot chocolate by the university. Has he been on the M yet?"

She kneaded the cozy throw. Lounging around the penthouse for the next few days would keep her in close proximity to Linette. Small gray patches still lingered on Linette's skin, and her mother kept to her suite lately. A day out would give her and Mandin a needed break.

"Not yet. It's a good idea before deep winter is upon us." She could relax during a maglev ride. And Mandin would enjoy spending time with his father.

"I can meet you both here before we start," Chance said.

"Then it's settled." She reached for a biscuit, but her movements were stiff. Chance's long arm reached for the plate and held it out in front of her.

"Thanks." The savory crumbs rolled over her tongue, and she took a swallow of her fizz.

"Are you hungry?" he asked.

"I can use some soup." The biscuit while yummy, left her eager for more. She had eaten only a yogurt parfait for breakfast that Halle had served on a bed tray while Alina sat propped up on pillows. Halle had insisted on a calcium and antioxidant laden breakfast.

"Halle, do you mind a hot soup and sandwich lunch for them?" Chance rose. "I can help you in the kitchen before departing."

"Why Mr. Graylin, no help required at all. It would be my pleasure." The bot's female face smiled at him. "I have a root-and-vegetable broth that's very flavorful and healthy. Melted cheese over meat sandwiches will make a good accompaniment."

"Chance?"

He glanced back at Alina.

"Why don't you stay for lunch?" She removed the throw from her lap, the velveteen cloth smooth between her fingers. Her throat resisted her request for help but she managed to force the words out. "You can accompany me to the table."

"Absolutely." He strode across the room to her side.

Halle left for the kitchen, and Mandin trailed after her, telling her what type of sandwich he wanted.

Chance held out his arm. Alina reached for his elbow and bracing herself, slowly stood. Her socked feet took a few steps forward. The aches lingered, but she could walk without sharp pain. Leaning into him kept her steady.

"You'll be good as new in no time." His words were a soft buzz in her ear.

"As long as I have sustenance." She curled her hand around his upper arm. Her pulse raced as she held onto his bicep, her fingertips pressing into his firm muscle. She was pleased that he accepted her invitation to stay.

Sunshine filled the dining room, and she looked forward to Halle's vegetable broth with the three of them.

Chapter 27

Alina's fingers touched the academy's console in front of her. The lights blinked, and she scrolled through the screen for messages. Pulling her seat closer, she studied the monitor, one of many arrayed in front of her.

She arrived at the academy in the afternoon, taking the maglev directly from the penthouse two days after her surgery. While Dr. Bellamy's medication helped her move about, perhaps traveling across the city so soon was a mistake. On her way over, she nearly slipped on the icy sidewalk, and grabbed a nearby fence. The motion twisted her lower body, and jolts of pain spread through the back of Alina's thighs.

Still, she hoped to hear from Evesborough. On her way in, the Commandant mentioned he was running off to a meeting and left her alone in the large flight control room. The room temperature remained chilly for the electronics equipment. The large wall screen normally depicted a map of the academy's mission locations but remained dark, off for the winter break.

No new messages appeared at the console before her.

Alina tried again, adjusting the date range. Kiean would have responded by now, nearly a week after Aurore's arrival back at Evesborough, especially at Alina's mention of undergoing a bone marrow transplant in her private note to him. Aurore wouldn't have forgotten the sweet cakes. But the message bank remained empty.

She rested back in the chair seat for a moment then straightened. "Give Spartan's last flight route." The AI assistant would know if Aurore ran into problems flying home.

A trace of dots blinked on the screen. "As requested, Instructor DeHerte," the female voice replied.

"Topographic map," Alina said.

The dots blinked along the flight route and disappeared as expected by Evesborough. "Spartan altitude is consistent with flight descent," the AI said. "Spartan landed by sight B79. Last known location of the ship."

Once Aurore taxied the Spartan into the cavern, the system would have difficulty detecting the locator beacon. It was one of the reasons that she and Kiean had moved both the Triumph and Spartan inside shortly after their arrival three years prior. It kept Evesborough hidden from those who would search for it.

However, the Triumph contained a more powerful communication system that could transmit through Eamine's magnetic field to the city's flight centers. They no longer needed to hide its transmissions from the academy, given that she'd already shown Riley its whereabouts.

Perhaps Kiean was still working on fitting the cryopump to the fusion reactor. But wouldn't he have informed her of a problem or delay by now? Or Aurore would have returned in a hurry to grab more parts. Radio silence was unexpected.

"Show encrypted messages."

"Date range?" the AI asked.

When Alina gave the required parameters, the program replied, "No encrypted messages received."

She chewed on her inner cheek. An uneasy wave built in her stomach. She checked the forecast again. The winter storms would descend on Alpheios soon.

"Show any ship detected within the last twenty-four hours enroute to Alpheios."

The program displayed codes of a few hover-jet taxis within the city. She checked the flight schedule for expeditionary craft. As expected, no flights were programmed over the deep winter break. No other large aircraft showed up on the screen.

Vexing pangs permeated Alina's lower back. She slumped over and rested her arms on the console. The hard equipment dug into her flesh. Maybe he was in no hurry to get to her, given her hesitation about his proposal. She'd likely be stuck in Alpheios over the winter.

Rubbing her forehead, she squashed her doubts. "Transcribe message."

The AI replied, "Ready to transcribe."

"Kiean…" The cursor moved across the screen spelling out his name. What was she to say? Exhaling, she decided to confide in him about her surgery.

"My bone marrow donation went well and…" The cursor blinked, awaiting her voice. *And I hoped you would have arrived by now*. But she didn't want to say it like that. Not if there was still a problem with the reactor.

So what else? *That I slept over at my ex's house and am spending more time with Chance*. She couldn't write that, either.

The sound of the door opening jolted her out of the seat.

Commandant Riley strode in his new suit. “Did you find what you needed?”

“Oh—yes, sir.” She touched the screen to delete the incomplete message. Dang. She wore her old suit which was broken into, choosing not to squeeze in the fitted suit he gave her. “I have to go, actually.” Not looking her mentor in the eye, she hurried past him.

“Alina?”

In the hallway, she glanced over her shoulder. “Sir, I’ll check out the new suit during the storm and give you an update afterward. I told my mother I’d be home by now.”

A puzzled expression appeared on his face, but she marched toward the exit despite the burning in the back of her thighs. Dr. Bellamy’s medication was waiting for her back at the penthouse.

Chapter 28

The aches in Alina's hips faded as she gazed out at the glistening, white city. The suns gleamed in their wedge formation through the maglev window, brightening the afternoon. Already cooped up for several days, she reveled in their maglev ride. Mandin pressed his nose against the glass while she and Chance pointed out city landmarks to him.

For just a few hours, she wanted to leave behind her concerns and enjoy what the city offered them. It was likely one of their last mild days before deep winter arrived. They disembarked at the university station. Precipitation dripped from the trees. Toasty in her new suit, she inhaled fresh air.

"Careful, it's wet here." Chance held out his arm for her. He wore a steel-gray flex suit for their outing.

To avoid slipping, she tucked her arm into his. Their closeness warmed her further. Mandin held onto Chance's other hand as they walked to the row of shops lining the university's campus.

"Right on time," he said as they stopped in front of a polished door.

"And this place is?" She didn't recognize the establishment.

The stone building held no windows. No sign adorned the shop that might indicate its business.

"I made a reservation for us." He grabbed the sleek

silver door handle.

"But I thought we were just getting hot chocolate?"

He grinned and swept out his arm. "You'll see."

Inside, a large patch of synthetic sea-blue grass and shrubbery beckoned. Children handled knee-high flower petal puzzles at one end. Others climbed inside a hollowed-out tree. In the center, kids ran through a maze of trimmed shrubs. Giggles, shouts, and laughter emanated from the children. The little playground had been transformed into a beckoning nature spot for them to wander about.

"Mandin, look!" She pointed at the curved ceiling that was painted in gorgeous colors.

Overhead, a depiction of the second sun rising in the blue sky gleamed. The sunrise cast a golden glow on the picturesque play area. Mandin's mouth slackened as he stared upward.

"Save Eamine, where have you brought us?" An unexpected thrill wound its way through her like she'd discovered a forgotten fairytale.

"I confess, they serve more than just hot chocolate." Chance's dark eyes shone while he watched their reactions.

"Mr. Graylin," called out an older woman. She moved toward them in an elegant silver sheath, smiling. "Is this your party?"

"Mrs. Vernita, may I introduce Alina and Mandin?" He placed a hand on his son's shoulder.

The woman stepped forward. "A pleasure. Is this your first time here?"

Alina could not help but smile back. "Yes, it is."

"You're in for a delight. Follow me." Mrs. Vernita led them around the perimeter. Curtained booths furnished with plush materials held patrons. One boy attacked a large bowl of heaping caramel cream, enough for three people. Parents occupied other booths, sipping hot drinks while their children explored the playground.

The proprietor flourished her arm toward an empty booth surrounded by midnight-blue curtains. "As you requested, Mr. Graylin. The corner table."

Mandin clambered onto the upholstery. Mrs. Vernita touched the holo-stand upon the smooth table. A menu projection appeared.

Chance and Alina slid in at opposite ends of the booth, bracketing Mandin. Their son peered at the pictures of different delicacies before him.

"May I recommend the tri-flavor special?" Mrs. Vernita pointed to one of the menu items. "It's made with toffee, whipped cream, and berries. A customer favorite, and large enough for you three to share. Or if you'd like something lighter, our spiced pudding is scrumptious with a burnt sugar top and dollop of cream."

"Mama, I want that!" Mandin pointed at the picture of the mounds of caramel cream the boy they had passed was eating.

"I think your mother should order," Chance said with a chuckle.

"The pudding sounds wonderful. He hasn't eaten dinner, yet." A small indulgence wouldn't hurt Mandin. Alina also craved the texture of custard on her tongue.

"Excellent choice. Tea for you two? Our in-house tea is a very nice compliment." Mrs. Vernita's arms were loosely crossed behind her back.

Alina agreed, settling back on the comfy cushions.

The shopkeeper winked at Mandin. "It's quite safe in our garden. That's what we call it." She motioned to the expanse of grass. Nearby, there was a little circular gazebo containing a blackboard floor. Children scribbled with colored chalk on top of it. "We took care in selecting the materials for their size, and the floor is padded underneath." She disappeared in the din.

"How did you find this place?" Alina relaxed in the cozy booth. High-pitched titters emanated from the garden nearby.

"Quite by accident." Chance's arm sprawled along the back of his seat. "I was shopping a few doors down one weekend and left hungry. Saw folks entering this place and decided to follow them. Mrs. Vernita whisked me away immediately," he said with a laugh. "Can't say I resisted."

"It's charming." Alina gazed at their fairy-like surroundings.

"Can I play?" Mandin wiggled between them.

"After we eat," she replied.

"You want to play?" Chance held out his hand, urging him to grab it. He taught Mandin the sylin-shocking-game based on speed. When Chance poked him in the ribs, Mandin squealed.

Their son insisted on another round. After a few giggling fits, Mandin turned to his mother, challenging her with an outstretched hand.

His father swept away his hand. "No, your mother is still recovering. Leave her alone."

A wave of relief swept over her, and she mouthed her thanks to Chance.

They studied the table patterns which held illustrations of different animals under its clear veneer. She pointed out the zephyrs and dragons to Mandin. He queried her on other creatures.

Mrs. Vernita returned with a tray that held a glass dish filled with pudding. “Enjoy.” She set down three dessert spoons for them. Mandin immediately grabbed one. Next came the silver teapot and two teacups.

Mandin shoveled a spoonful of pudding in his mouth.

“Slow down,” Alina said.

“Leave some for us.” Chance slid the dish over in her direction.

She dipped her spoon into an unbroken spot of burnt sugar, and the top film cracked, giving way. Notes of cinnamon and vanilla coated her tongue as she tasted the delicate pudding. Another bite proved irresistible. She reveled in the creamy texture as they took turns eating. Once the dish was empty, they all rested in their cushioned booth.

“Can I go now?” Mandin asked.

She wiped a smidge of cream from the corner of his mouth. “Yes. Have fun.”

Chance opened up the space on his side, allowing Mandin to slide out. Their three-year-old ran to the garden.

“You’ve managed to find time to enjoy yourself despite work.” She drew the teacup closer, its heat pleasant against her hands.

“Not really.” Chance closed the space that Mandin left between them. “But I made time once I knew you had arrived.”

Alina studied her steaming cup, and she took a sip of the hot tea. Its scent was fragrant with an earthy smell. The tea spread inside her tummy, balancing the sugary ingredients. “You must relax somehow. What do you enjoy outside of work?”

He fiddled with the handle of his teacup. "I've been playing Method in the evenings against the AI. Do you know how to play?"

"I've played a few times." She recalled the checkered board and figurines in his apartment. Years ago, she had learned to play at the academy, although the AI beat her more often than not. But Chance didn't know that. "I can hold my own."

"It quiets my mind. Helps me think." He lifted the cup to his lips.

"What's your signature move?"

A thoughtful expression appeared on his face. "You make sure to use your chevalier to fight any advances your opponent makes toward the empress. Once the chevalier vanquishes the other players, your empress goes in for the kill and takes the emperor's throne."

"Now I know how to beat you." She drank more tea, slightly giddy from the sugar. At the playground, Mandin was wriggling about inside the tree.

"You're welcome to try. I should warn you, though, I've learned other advanced tactics you might find difficult to counter."

"Challenge accepted." Her fast response was instinctual, even though she was uncertain if she could beat Chance at the game. She planned on asking Halle for some tips and running practice sessions with her.

"Then we must play soon." A wry smile extended across Chance's shapely lips. "Want to wager on it?"

Already in over her head, she nevertheless barreled forward. "What are the stakes?"

"The loser must entertain the winner with a five-course feast. Since you're a terrible cook, that means you'll have Halle help you concoct a suitable cuisine."

She scowled. So what if cooking wasn't her forte? She had more useful skills in her quiver. "And do I get to choose my menu when you lose?"

"I'll cook for you myself if you win."

"Done." She drained the rest of her tea. "Just so you know, Mandin prefers poultry."

"I meant dinner for the two of us, alone."

Despite the smooth tea, a jitter careened about inside her belly. Chance was close enough that she breathed in his pine aroma. She fiddled with her link. Earlier that morning, an alert warned of an incoming winter storm. A longer stay in Alpheios was inevitable. The harmless challenge would occupy her.

She checked on Mandin, noting he was no longer at the tree. "Where did he go?"

"He ran into the maze. He's having a good time."

On the ceiling, the first sun was setting. The colors dimmed to a golden pink. She blinked. "The suns move across the ceiling, don't they?"

"Yes. They'll cycle back to morning once the second sunset is complete." He downed the rest of his tea. "There's more, though." He moved out of the booth and reached for the curtain.

"Where are you going?" She arched her back.

He closed the midnight-blue curtains around their booth. "Don't be so impatient. Watch."

Cloaked in the dark booth, she waited. Ensconced by the heavy drapery, she caught glimpses of Chance's silhouette as he returned to his seat. Gradually, her eyes adjusted to the blackness.

A soft illumination rippled through the curtains. Stars twinkled in their folds, enveloping their booth all around, and overhead. She drew in a breath. "This place has all kinds of surprises, doesn't it?"

"Do you like it?"

"I've never seen an establishment as beautiful." A buoyancy surged in her at their splendor, like they were tucked away in the arm of a hidden galaxy. The stars shimmered, welcoming her into their own private universe.

"There must be hidden wires in the curtain. Did Mrs. Vinter give away the secret?" She shifted toward him.

Chance's face was a breath away in the midst of the darkness. Her heart skidded to a halt. He drew closer until his lips pressed onto hers. A soft tingle spread through her chest as the stars receded. His kiss was smooth like their dessert, but flavored with hunger. He cupped her face, drawing her in. Warmth rushed into her, and a glow lit from within.

"Mama, where are you?" a small voice said.

She abruptly separated from Chance, her cheeks broiling. Blinking, she watched him rise and draw back the curtains. The booth brightened again. She gathered herself when Mandin's curious face appeared. "I'm right here. Your daddy—" she pushed back her hair "—was showing me the curtains."

Mandin placed his small hand on her knee. "You okay, Mama?"

Her vision tinted green as he channeled into her emotions, trying to discover what had flustered her. She couldn't allow him to witness the upheaval inside her, like a tectonic plate had shifted. Fighting to compose herself, she gently removed her son's hand. "I'm fine. Why don't you go play?" Her link showed daylight fading outside. "Because we'll have to leave soon before the curfew."

Her son tilted his head, watching her. She nudged him in the direction of the garden.

"Okay, I wanna do the maze again." He dashed off back to the grass.

Next to her, a smile tugged at Chance's lips. "I'm sorry we were interrupted." He leaned closer. "I hope you won't back out of the challenge."

"No! I have to prepare, though." She checked her link again. "You'll give me adequate time, at least a week."

His eyes outlined her facial features. "Are you all right?"

As he gazed at her longingly, she quivered inside. "Yes. Why do you ask?"

His mouth turned up in an amused expression. "You're blushing."

"Am not." She rested her palms on the side of her cheeks, as if the gesture would banish how her face baked all over. Dropping her hands, she tugged down the sleeves at her wrist. The suit fit her snugly, resisting her pulls.

He appraised her. "Maybe fresh air will help. I'll grab Mandin."

A touch of relief overcame her as Chance left the booth to find their son.

Standing when they came back over, the ceiling sunrise dazzled her. Vertigo hit, and she clutched the edge of the table. Her hips no longer ached, but her blood pressure must have dropped. Chance flicked his link over the holo-base, paying for their meal. On the way out, he rested his palm on her upper back, guiding her out.

****

Outside, a gossamer-like veil fell over the world as

ice crystals fluttered in the blustery wind. The diamond dust glinted in the last rays of light, a portent of a change in the weather. Mandin chatted endlessly about the maze as Chance listened, responding to his enthusiasm. Across the street from the university's pavilion, they entered the maglev station.

She clung to the escalator banister as it took them up to the embarkation level.

"Where are we going now?" Mandin asked.

"Home," Chance replied. "But would you like to go back to that shop?"

Mandin hopped off the escalator with both feet pounding the platform. "Yes! I wanna go back!"

A pod slowed in front of them under the maglev track. They clambered through the open doors, and she took a seat. The river streamed through the valley, turbulent and freezing as they chatted around her. Frost coated the trees. Mandin perched on his knees, his hands leaving imprints on the window. She tugged at his jacket. "Careful. I don't want you to fall back."

"I've got him." Chance stood Mandin on his lap, his hands holding his son's waist so he could look out the window.

The patter of ice tinkled against the pod's window. They disembarked at the Meander District stop, and she summoned her last bit of energy to walk the block to her mother's. Chance accompanied them. The doorman greeted him and called down their elevator.

Slightly dazed, she leaned back against the elevator's railing. Mandin clung to Chance's hand, asking him when they could return to the shop.

"Hopefully soon." Chance exchanged a look with her. "Maybe after your mother gets some rest."

The elevator doors opened, and Mandin bounded out to the polished hallway.

She straightened, debating how to leave. Chance reached for her waist, and he swept her close. A charge coiled through her. Her inkling of a friendly hug evaporated at the sight of his dark star-sapphire eyes. Her arms surrounded his neck. Everything glimmered like the stars when their lips met. She was transported back to the booth.

"I had fun today." His voice was low. "I'll message you later."

"To see Mandin?" Why was her face on fire again?

"To see *you*. For our match, remember?"

Alina nodded. She had a hunch that Chance would be difficult to beat, although she'd work with Halle to put up a fight.

"Good." His smile widened.

She exited the elevator. Chance raised a hand as the doors closed. The apartment's furnishings were a warm and cozy sight.

Halle skimmed over to her. "I'm making a roast for dinner. Care to join us shortly?"

While the bot's voice was pleasant in her ears, Alina's appetite vanished. "I'll take it in my room later." A desire to spend the evening alone overtook her.

"Very well. I'll request Gordean eat with Mandin when he returns any minute now from the gym. He's always famished after his work-out."

Alina headed to her bedroom. Upon entering it, she shut the door and exhaled. The bed provided a needed break. After curling up under the covers, she touched her lips again.

Her inner resistance had crumbled around Chance in

a way that overwhelmed her. His kiss was of a different nature from when they'd first dated.

In the booth, she had felt that he fought back crossing a boundary, like he'd devour her if given the opportunity. And for a moment, a thrill had roared within her. Still light-headed, she closed her eyes and hugged a pillow. Exhaustion crept over her limbs. She welcomed a nap to sedate her jumble of thoughts.

Chapter 29

Chance's link warned of freezing temperatures, and he held no desire to take the maglev back. He called a GATV from the penthouse lobby, and a driver promptly pulled to the curb. Satiated from his outing with Alina and his son, he leaned back against the seat. "To C.H.," he said to the young Guardian driver upfront.

"Yes, sir. Did you have a good visit?"

"I'll say." Chance's careful planning had paid off. He bounced his hand on the bench in a gesture of satisfaction. Having confirmed Alina's affections for him, he smiled to himself. Thank Eamine for the incoming storm.

He'd ensure that she'd experience an exciting game of Method but would allow her to beat him. She took such challenges seriously. A game at his place would extend late into the night.

Up the block, a familiar figure carrying a bag strode in the direction they just left.

"Pull over here," Chance said.

The driver complied and Chance lowered his window. "Get in."

Gordo glanced over his shoulder before climbing into the GATV. He took the seat across from him.

"Need a ride back?"

Alina's brother shrugged.

"Circle around the business area, then return us to

the penthouse," Chance said. As the GATV headed toward the colorful shops of the Meander District, he scrutinized the criminal in front of him. Gordo's posture was tense. While Chance would rather return home after such a glorious outing, business reared its head. "I hope you have information for me."

His passenger looked out the window. "I met someone from the Citizens Front. She goes by Maggie and is bringing me to a meeting next week to meet the others."

"Do you have a last name?" Chance's elbows touched his thighs as he clasped his hands together.

"I'm not even sure Maggie is her real name," Gordo replied. "A few years older than you, with dark eyes and hair. She keeps a long braid. Petite, but she knows how to handle herself. I made sure she understood that I was keen to help them depose the current government." A spark of anger flashed in his green eyes, and a mocking smile curved across his face. "That's what you wanted, right? For me to ingratiate myself for more information?"

Chance leaned back. "I look forward to finding out about the leadership."

"I get the sense that she is one of the leaders."

"How do you know that?"

"The way she talks and carries herself."

"Where did the respirator come from?" Chance didn't bother hiding his annoyance. Lieutenant Hardin's meetings with the two companies produced little in the way of identifying the origins of the respirator since both company reps admitted they procured it from a single supplier. When the lieutenant visited the supplier, he had complained of a box of respirators being stolen the previous month.

Gordo cocked his head. “Minecorp.”

“Minecorp?” Chance blinked. “But we ran the database on the warehouse owner. It was listed under a deceased businessman, a dead end. We found nothing when we searched the warehouse. They must have cleared it. How do you know?”

A snort came from Gordo. “Maggie had a snow cap on the last time we met. She kept it folded down to cover her ears so it looked like a plain black cap. But when she left, it had crept up her head, revealing a symbol.” He extended his arm and activated his link projection. “It was this.”

The small orange carat symbol was underlined from its right leg onward. Minecorp’s trademark logo loosely resembled the shape of its excavators.

The implications ignited Chance’s danger meter. This wasn’t some ragtag bunch of disaffected residents with utopian ideals. His mother’s enemy was much more powerful and organized. He took in a deep breath. “You sure?”

“Yes. I matched it as soon as she left. I knew I had seen it before.”

“I need to know when and where their next attack is planned. Operational details to include the target, weapons, and number of participants.” One hand over the other, he rubbed his knuckles. Outside, they departed the shopping area and headed back the way they came.

The projection disappeared as Gordo touched his link. “I’ll see what I can find out.” He tugged down the bag strap slung across his chest. “For someone so interested in the Citizens Front, you seem to spend more time with my sister than your office at City Hall.”

Chance's hand fell to his side, curled into a fist. He had relied of late on Lieutenant Harding to investigate. "You wanted the serum for your mother, and your sister made that possible with my help. You saw Alina. She needed help recovering."

"That's not the only reason you're at the penthouse." Gordo's mouth was tight.

"Am I not entitled to see my own son?" Chance fought to remain calm. At one time, he and Gordo were on cordial terms. But that all evaporated back in the interrogation room. If it was any other felon but Alina's brother, Chance would have cuffed him hard as a reminder of who remained in charge.

His passenger glanced out the window before turning to face him. "She's engaged, you know."

"She doesn't want to marry that guy." The words spewed from Chance like venom.

"Even so, it should be her choice. She doesn't need anyone manipulating her." Gordo's cold stare drilled into him.

Chance held his own piercing gaze. "She can make her own decisions." He grabbed the overhead handle and leaned close. "I would tread *very* carefully." Lowering his voice, Chance sharpened it like a sword. "Or your whole family will know you're a traitor. You're fortunate I'm fond of your sister to extend such an offer to you. The choice is yours." He repositioned himself and called out to the driver. "Stop here."

The GATV pulled over within sight of the Meander metro station. Two blocks remained to reach the penthouse.

"You can walk home," Chance said.

Gordo grunted and flung open the door. Upon

touching the ground, he slammed it shut.

"Back to C.H.?" The driver asked.

Peering at Gordo's back as he walked away, Chance unclenched his fist. The deal was meant to insulate Alina and her mother from this ugly business. But it didn't mean that Gordo would avoid prison. Her brother could prove to be an unwelcome hinderance if he was free on his own accord.

Chance gave his head a shake. It was nearly curfew, but a meeting with his mother was in order immediately. "Yes. To C.H."

****

His mother was speaking with her female assistant when Chance entered her office. The twin windows flanked her massive bureau. Soft light streaming in showed daylight was fading. "Chancellor, I must speak with you."

Jade Graylin gave her head a shake but dismissed the young woman. The assistant smiled at him on her way out.

When the two of them were alone, his mother stood. "Curfew is nearly here, and it's time to dismiss my staff. I hope this is rather important for you to keep me late." She waltzed out from her desk in her signature dark sheath top and slacks. She headed to the seating area composed of two sofas facing each other. Her gold chancellor pin glinted on her lapel.

Chance spoke before she could lower herself onto a sofa. "Mother, we have a tip on who's leading the Citizens Front."

She looked sharply at him. "Who?"

"Minecorp employees are involved."

His mother stiffened. "Are you sure?"

"I'm working an informant for more proof, but it's a solid lead."

Her mouth tightened. "Peter Mason. That son of… I did oust him a few years back when I put forward the emergency declaration." She paced in front of her desk. "He wasn't exactly enthralled that the council voted me as his replacement. Although the vote margin was razor-thin."

"I don't have anything linking him to the attacks yet." Chance shifted his weight among his feet. Peter Mason was his old boss and didn't seem like a man who would foment chaos in the city. He had returned to his company, Minecorp, after Chance's mother replaced him.

"You worked for him for only a few weeks," she said.

"True, but…" Chance grasped for words, a rarity for him. "I don't know if he's aware of who's planning the riots."

"He was always an idealist." She stopped at the front of her desk peering at him. "He must be involved."

Chance remembered Mason's talk of making Genodyne subservient to the government rather than an ally, which was reality. It was easier to treat Genodyne as a partner in the city's success than to battle them for control. "I'll bring him in for questioning."

She brought a clenched fist to her mouth. "Do it." She dropped her hand. "But not for questioning, for an arrest." Her stare sharpened. "We must move quickly."

He rocked back on a heel. "An arrest? If you want that, we'll need to show he knew about the attacks to hold him in custody."

"Then provide the evidence." Her voice resembled

spilled acid, like vinegar on an open wound.

He studied his mother's pinched face, contemplating the ramifications of her order. The Guardians fell under the chancellor's office. But the arrest of Peter Mason left a burr in Chance's gut. "Do you plan on bringing the matter to the council?" If the council closed ranks behind his mother, Chance knew it would put Commander Zinyon more at ease about such a high-profile arrest.

She clutched the back of the sofa. "He still has some allies on the council who would back him regardless, like Councilman Shah." She straightened. "I'll need Councilwoman Lacey's support moving forward. She's the swing vote."

"Think you can get it?"

"She's still sore at me for removing her niece from Genodyne." His mother brushed a speck off the top of her shoulder.

"Ms. Silver was her niece?"

"Yes. I'm sure Lacey would love nothing more than to affirm a no-confidence vote in me for payback." She placed a hand on her hip. "I'll have to work out a deal with her."

"What did you have in mind?"

"I'll call the board to see if they'd take Ms. Silver back."

He gave his head a shake to make certain that he heard her. "Didn't they fire her publicly, blaming her for Phase Three side effects?"

"It'll have to be done discreetly." She held her elbows together loosely. "Dr. Daxmen will want credit for the cure, now that we're so close since Alina underwent the bone marrow transplant." His mother raised a finger, waving it. "I'll need to leave him in place as the director of operations. Which means I'll have to convince the board to give Ms. Silver a different role."

"Like what?" Chance transferred his weight from one foot to the other. From his three years as her aide, he observed that loyalties in the government shifted quickly after momentous events.

"Special advisor to the board. That isn't a public position. Plus, that gives Lacey insight into Genodyne's developments, so she'll back me. She owns quite a few of their shares." His mother glanced at him. "I need your full attention on Minecorp."

"You have it. I'll start now." He started to leave, but his mother spoke.

"I mean it, Chance. Now is not the time for you to be distracted with Alina." She looked as if she bit into a sour fruit.

His mother's words were like needles razed across the back of his neck. "She's the mother of my son. And she's saving your position by giving Genodyne the keys to a cure."

"I admit I've underestimated her resolve." Her lips twisted to the side. "But she's not one of us."

"I'm not asking your permission." He imparted a warning growl to his voice. "I care about her." He found it refreshing that Alina wasn't the type of coiffed robot that his mother would prefer to see him with.

"You can do better." She peered intently at him.

"You should focus on shoring up your support with the council. My business is my own." His jaw clamped shut. He wouldn't allow her to dissuade him like she had done that fateful night three years ago. Chance knew shortly afterward that he'd made a terrible mistake leaving Alina and Mandin at the hospital. The suggestion of giving Mandin up for adoption had been his mother's idea. Sickness spread within him for weeks. He wouldn't abandon his family again.

She exhaled and leaned back against her desk, nearly sitting on it. "I need Peter Mason in a cell."

"An arrest may enrage Mason's followers. Or have you forgotten that night I had to divert your motorcade from the riot at City Hall?" His arm swept across her office.

She straightened. "He has motive. Some of his employees took the Phase Three product after the mining accident."

"The accident last year?" He recalled a scheduled blast at one of the mines had malfunctioned, hurting a small site crew. Once the Origins left Alpheios, Minecorp recruited workers from the Inland District. Most of the Inland residents were born of Phase One only, unable to afford Genodyne's Phase Two. "How did they get the tonic?"

Jade rubbed her sleeve. "Mason purchased it for them. They were some of the first to take it. But it didn't work out as planned."

"Why didn't you tell me this before?"

"Genodyne thought their product would work." She straightened and tugged down a fold on her suit top. "So you see, Peter Mason must be arrested."

Chance shuffled his feet. Her mouth was set. Despite her stately office, the situation confounded him. It was too slick to grasp, like it could careen suddenly in another direction.

Her voice deepened. "Is there a problem?"

He swallowed. "No. I'll arrange the matter."

"Time, son. Do not take long." She turned back to the schedule on her desk.

He pivoted to exit. He ran through a list of instructions to relay to Lieutenant Harding. A former leader intent on toppling his mother would be a disaster. As much as Chance wanted out of his current position, he couldn't allow her to be usurped.

Chapter 30

The next morning, Alina awoke to the aroma of baking bread. Vigor filled her legs, the effects of the procedure finally wearing off. She was ravenous. After breakfast, she'd test the suit for the Commandant. Given the previous evening's outing with Chance, she desired a few hours outdoors, alone.

In the kitchen, the whir of the blender wiped any sleep fog left in her head.

"Want to try this? It's a protein-cruciferous shake." Gordo held out a glass filled with thick, green goop.

She grabbed a carb roll from a basket. Still warm, she brought it to her mouth. Halle must have prepared them. "Is it tasty?"

He poured the rest from the blender into a small glass. "Fresh with zero sugar."

Cautiously, she took a sip. "Definitely fresh." The crisp rawness of the ingredients rolled over her tongue, chalky and devoid of any saccharine. A distinct change from the pudding that she, Chance, and Mandin shared yesterday afternoon.

The cooler held a container of olein spread. She craved some fat. "Where's Mom?" She smeared the spread over her roll and took a bite.

Her brother leaned back against the counter, taking a gulp of his shake. "Conservatory."

Alina stopped mid-chew. "Is she feeling okay?"

"She's tired." He brought the glass to his mouth and paused. "Her face looks better, though. That balm you brought her really cleared up her skin. It's gone from her hand, too."

Swallowing the roll, she washed it down with another swig of the shake. "But shouldn't the stem cells give her more energy?"

He finished a sip. "Dr. Bellamy said it may take a little more time to clear the disease from her system. I'll get Halle to make us an iron-rich stew tonight for dinner."

She contemplated checking on her mother after breakfast when Mandin trotted in. "Mama, I wanna play outside."

Bites of bread filled her mouth. "Later. I'm eating right now."

"Can Dada come?"

Nearly choking on the shake, she placed the glass on the counter. "Mandin, I'm busy today." She shoved another piece of the roll in her mouth.

"But I'm bored!" He flung his arms by his sides. "Can you ping Dada?"

"No."

Her son stomped his foot. "But I have no one to play with here! Syriah and Kiean aren't here!"

"Hey bud, as soon as I finish my shake, I'll play with you." Gordo raised his glass. "Teach you more rogue ball, okay?"

Mandin studied his uncle.

Alina pointed to the doorway. "Wait for Gordo to finish his breakfast."

Her son sulked as he left.

Gordo settled back against the counter. "He couldn't

stop talking about your outing yesterday with Chance. Guess he had a good time. Did you?"

She studied the remaining green concoction in her glass, debating whether to finish it. "It was fine. Listen, I have to test a new expeditionary suit outdoors. Can you watch Mandin for a few hours?"

"There's a winter storm inbound." Gordo's eyebrows curled inward.

"I know. I'll return before it gets late." As she downed the rest of the drink, her forehead tingled from a surge of its vitamins.

"Are you sure you want to test it now?" Her brother glanced at his link. "The forecast expects—"

"I have my link. Perfect time to test the suit." She strode out of the kitchen.

In the living room, Mandin was laying on his belly, his chin propped up as he gazed at Halle's monitor. The bot played cartoons.

Back in the bedroom, Alina slipped into the new suit. Tying her hair back, she itched to leave the penthouse. As she laced up her boots, she thought of where she could go. A location clicked in mind. She checked to make sure the suit contained the rest of its accessories and strode out.

Later, she'd check on her mother when she returned.

More squeals and music emanated from the living room. Mandin was absorbed with the animals hopping on the bot's screen.

"I'll be back soon," she said, but Mandin didn't seem to hear her.

She jabbed the lobby button. As the doors closed, she released an exhale at the lull. The outdoors would help her make sense of the last night's events. Her fingers gently grazed her lips. She stood in the very spot that Chance kissed her hours ago. And she was still trying to make sense of her response. She'd kissed him back, admitting that she enjoyed it.

Chapter 31

The clouds in the sky were the color of slate, the suns barely visible behind them. Alina's link protested a storm warning beep, and she picked up her pace, crossing through the frost-covered blue grass toward Old Town.

She needed somewhere quiet to think. An urge overtook her to visit the place where she and Mandin found sanctuary several years ago. Just a brief visit, less than an hour, before she'd head back. The maglev had whisked her to its last stop, and she'd disembarked for the trek the rest of the way.

By the time she arrived in Old Town, the old park with its abandoned log beams and homemade fort was empty. No children's laughter emanated from the area like it once did. She waded into the large meadow, leaving civilization behind. Eventually, the mountain homes came into view. Stone globes protruded from the hillside, impassive and silent.

She climbed the staircase carved into the mountain, taking care to ensure her boots gained traction. Up three flights, she ascended. Finally, she arrived at the house at the end of the row.

The wooden door gave when she pushed on it. Inside, the house was cold, but daylight shone through the small window by the stove. The woven, colorful rug greeted her.

She removed her hoodie and gloves. Pushing back a lock of hair, she looked around. Macy's old home still held the blue wooden table and chairs. Dried herbs remained hung over the old stove, their leaves disintegrating into fragments. A sweet, putrid scent of rotten perishables lingered. That, combined with a layer of dust made Alina sneeze.

At the table, she entered her observations into her link. She noted the twin winter solstice was nearly upon them, days away. The suit held during her walk over. Temperatures dipped to negative twenty degrees Celsius, but she made it.

She lifted the curtain that marked the entrance to the bedroom. The quilt on the large bed was thrown back, and the pillows shifted around. The last time she was here, they left in a hurry. Kiean had tried to help her and Mandin escape.

The icy wind during the trek proved draining. She slipped into the large bed. Pulling the quilt tight, she closed her eyes. Memories of what transpired between the walls lurked.

Three years ago, Chance had searched her out toward the end of summer, asking her to return home. He'd reminded her that he was Mandin's father. How angry she'd had been with him for leaving them that night in the hospital, she could understand that in retrospect. Even after his apologies, she'd refused him. After all, she'd found Kiean.

Kiean had fought for her during that terrible moment when Genodyne had seized their children. She burrowed deeper under the covers. Why hadn't Kiean sent a message? During their arguments back at Evesborough, he sometimes left and tinkered onboard the hovercraft.

Despite her doubts, he always returned home. The dust tickled her eyes and nose, and she sneezed again. He was unhappy that she wore his ring around her neck instead of on her hand. Although as of late, she didn't wear it at all.

A pang deepened inside her core. He knew about her surgery. Aurore would have informed him. She reasoned that the reactor must be keeping him. And yet…the whispers in her mind persisted. He did not come to Alpheios.

Maybe what she dreaded occurring was finally happening. Everyone always left. Her defects were carved into her, like a knife taken to wood.

Heat flushed through her, and she squirmed. She gripped the patchwork blanket over her head. A dull ache wound its way through her chest.

May Eamine forgive her mothering mistakes.

She gradually fell asleep.

****

The shrieking wind roused her. Stumbling out of bed, her boot caught in the loose rug. A clatter of hail rattled the small window in the kitchen. A sliver of daylight was still visible. A whirl of snow flew by the pane. The storm had arrived.

Her link held two messages. Both were from Gordo, looking for her.

Her suit had adjusted to the ambient temperature indoors and kept her warm, allowing her to sleep. But the air gave her nose and cheeks an icy burn. She glanced around the room. A single log lay by the stove. She could stay until the storm passed, but it was likely to last several days. She couldn't leave Mandin that long.

While the indoor temperature was stable at zero

degrees Celsius, her link noted it was already negative forty outside. Humans typically entered a dangerous state of freeze at those temperatures within ten minutes without proper attire. She chewed her bottom lip. A growl emanated from her stomach.

The rotten stench of perishables indicated she'd have no food. Although given the snow, she'd have no shortage of water. Perhaps she should stay. The walk to the maglev took nearly an hour under normal conditions. Tufts of white flew by the window over the stove.

She checked her link again. Nightfall would arrive soon. Thrusting her hands in her pockets, she grabbed her hoodie and face gaiter. *Deal with it. You promised to test the suit.* Her face now covered, she composed a reply to her brother, telling him she was on her way home.

Taking in a deep breath, she threw open the door. As she pulled on her gloves, the wind shrieked at her.

****

Her knee aching, Alina pressed her hands against the hard object she'd tripped over. Snow hid a log in her path. Shivering, she rubbed her knee. Blackness surrounded her. She squinted at her link in the dark. The numbers glowed back. It was nearly negative sixty degrees Celsius outdoors.

She'd cleared the woods but wading through the accumulating snow had lengthened her travel time. The snow was up to her knees and would continue to rise. Gasping, she peered through the curtain of whistling white all around. She wasn't even sure she emerged at the right spot out of the woods where the dirt path led back to the city.

Uncertain of her whereabouts, she tried to activate the link's other features. "Show my location." But the howling wind drowned out her voice, and the link blinked back, "ERROR." She tried again. "Light." But her link did not register her command.

Crap. She could remove her gloves and fiddle with it, but her fingertips were numb. Her body shook as the suit struggled in its fight against the elements. Her stomach had shrunken into a pit. Although her face was covered, she couldn't feel the end of her nose. She wiggled, feeling a coil inside her suit. Did one of the battery lead wires disconnect? If the other two leads held, she still could make it back.

Had Gordo received her message? No response from him. How long would it take until he called her in missing? Touching the corner of her eye, she winced. Windburn scraped at the small amount of her exposed skin. She could call Chance. He'd find a GATV to search for her. A small relief grew within her at knowing he wasn't far. Her link might not even tolerate much more of the freeze. But the GATVs would have to drive slowly in this weather, and by the time he reached her…

How long would it take to travel back to Macy's home in Old Town? No, she was already two-thirds of the way to the city. The edge of the woods marked it for her. That is, if she exited in the right direction.

Rooted in the spot, her insides trembled. White flecks whirled around in the darkness. What if she'd stumbled off course and exited in the wrong direction? How long then would it take her to reach Alpheios? She imagined Commandant Riley's face, surprised at the news when they'd finally find her. His perplexed expression at her judgement.

Sorry. I meant to test the suit. But look, I found its tolerances at about negative fifty. The suit still puttered along, providing some heat, just not enough. She should log that. They'd peel her link off her wrist when they found her stiff and cold. Her slog wouldn't be all for nothing. That is, if she could wiggle her fingers. Icy pinpricks pierced her toes in her boots.

Recalling the Commandant's instructions, her old academy voice returned. *Move.* Its tone was pitiless. *Don't stop moving.* She dragged her feet forward. Five more minutes, she'd give herself five minutes to find her bearings. If she couldn't figure out how to get to the city by then, she'd message Chance. And ask Eamine for favors that she'd last until he arrived.

Trudging through the banks of snow, she struggled to lift her legs. She flailed and fell again into soft snow. Glancing over her shoulder, the view was the same. Blackness peppered with white flurries. The scream of the wind taunted her. Her teeth chattered, and she crossed her arms over her chest. She was certain she took the right path… didn't she? Blinking, she froze.

Was that a flicker of red light?

She rubbed her eyes. In the distance, the flicker appeared again. She lumbered in its direction. Steadily, it came into view. The maglev line! It must be. Red lights marked the top of the maglev rail structure by its stations. That meant she wasn't far from the edge of the city.

Maybe the maglev was still running. It usually limited its operations during deep winter, but it wasn't that late, yet. At the very least, the station would provide shelter. Her heart hammering in her chest, she plodded along as quickly as she could toward the light.

Chapter 32

Chance placed his hands on his desk and leaned forward. “You have nothing?”

Lieutenant Harding’s fingers twitched by his side. “Sir, Peter Mason is coming up clean. I don’t have anything linking him to the attack on C.H. or your GATV.”

Shaking his head, Chance set his hands on his hips. “What about the woman, Maggie?”

“Her real name is Min…” He squinted at his link. “Lou.”

“How’s the last name spelled?”

“L-i-u.”

“That’s pronounced like l-e-o.”

“Min,” Harding paused, “Liu,” pronouncing it correctly, “is a longtime employee of Minecorp, and their supervisor of operations.” His winter hat was tucked under his arm. “She’s been spotted at several protests. And she traveled to Mason’s home last week, but we didn’t get any convos due to interference in the background.”

“Interference?”

“Sounded like classical music, sir.”

Chance frowned. He needed to show his mother he had a case against Mason.

He opened the bottom drawer to his desk and

retrieved the chisel. His thumb ran over the scratches on the blade. “Supervisor of operations?” He held it out. “See if you can match this to any Minecorp equipment. If confirmed, arrest her. I’ll start working up an arrest order for Mason.”

Harding took the chisel. “On what basis?”

“Conspiracy to commit treason. You have surveillance footage of her at previous protests, right?”

“Yes. We might be able to hold her for a while, but I don’t have video of her attacking anyone. And that night at C.H., everyone was wearing masks.” A drop of sweat formed along Harding’s hairline.

Chance waved the concern aside like he was brushing away lint. “Confirm that’s Minecorp’s equipment, and that’s enough evidence to bring her in.” He held the lieutenant’s gaze, lest Harding falter on him. Chance held no use for weak or indecisive men.

“If you want this job, you must be prepared to protect our leaders. Bring her in quietly to avoid tipping off the Citizens Front. I’ll interrogate her myself. Then we’ll have our evidence on Peter Mason.” He pushed an exhale through his nose. “Anything else?”

“No, sir.” Harding pulled his shoulders back. “I’ll run this against her DNA sample from Genodyne to see if any matching cells show up on the handle.”

“That’ll be all, lieutenant.” He watched as Harding exited his office.

Hopefully, he’d stiffened his replacement’s resolve. Chance touched the sound-disc on his desk. The internal call system was for the private use of City Hall officials.

“Number 5-8-1.”

The call routed to the adjacent office. “Yes, Captain Graylin?” His mother’s assistant answered.

"Is the council meeting scheduled as planned later this week?"

"Yes, the last day of the week. The chancellor would like you to accompany her as usual."

"Tell her I'll attend."

The sound-disc clicked off.

His mother would turn irate if he didn't make the arrest before the council meeting. He spoke to the monitor to his desk. "Pull up all records on Min Liu."

The cursor blinked, then a green roll of words appeared. Chance leaned forward to study the files. After a few minutes, he leaned back in his chair, pressing his fingertips together. The lieutenant had done his research. Most of what he stated was reflected in her files.

A fragment of his mother's last conversation about Minecorp emerged, reminding him of the mining accident. "Show me the names of those in the mining blast incident last year."

The AI responded with a list of about a dozen names.

Chance homed in on a particular name: Bo Liu.

"What injuries were sustained by Bo Liu?"

The assistant replied, "Minecorp insurance reported paying a stipend for a crushed hand along with persistent migraines."

"Any relation to Min Liu?"

"Bo Liu is Min Liu's uncle. Appointed her legal caregiver since Min was age nine after her parents died when their mining vehicle overturned."

Chance straightened. Her uncle would be liable to have information on Min Liu's whereabouts. "What is Bo Liu's address?"

"200 Inland Way, but the member was reported

deceased as of six months ago."

He fell back against his chair. Bo Liu's crushed hand would have made him a prime candidate for Genodyne's Phase Three product since the company had advertised joint rejuvenation as one of its benefits.

"Do Minecorp records show who received the Revival tonic?"

"I show seven units purchased."

That was enough to hold Min Liu after an arrest. What Chance was still uncertain of was whether Peter Mason was linked to any of the attacks. But as the head of Minecorp, it was more likely than not that he knew of his employees' activities. Chance rubbed his forehead.

Mason was selected as chancellor precisely because the city had tired of Ambrose's iron reign. Chance stretched his neck. Regardless of his own thoughts, he needed to focus on operations. His mother would handle the politics. Once he arrested the main leaders of the Citizens Front, it would be a good time for him to request release as her aide. She'd have the cure, the city would be stabilized, and he could return to a leadership position under Commander Zinyon.

That would give him a final opportunity to cement his relationship with Alina. She was within a breath of entering his life again. Their evening of playing Method would allow the last pieces to fall into place.

Chapter 33

Frozen and stiff, Alina took a moment to thaw in the warm penthouse as she stepped out of the elevator into the hallway. Her suit adjusted quickly, regulating her core temperature back to normal limits. It was well into the night as she heard her son's and brother's voices spilling over from the living room.

She removed her hood, hearing Mandin's querulous tone. "But I no wanna take it."

"You have to, kiddo," Gordo replied.

Alina stumbled in the direction of the living room when Halle spotted her. "Alina, we're so glad you're here! How did you get back?"

As Alina found comfort in the surrounding heat, Mandin leapt in her direction. "Mama!" He threw himself at her, and his arms encircled her waist.

She peeled off a glove and tousled his curls. "It's good to see you, sweetie."

"Hey, you made it!" Gordo rose from the couch. "What took you so long? I was about to call the academy."

Although Commandant Riley would have lent a hand, the academy wasn't in charge of the city's emergency response—that responsibility was the Guardians. Odd that Gordo wouldn't have called Chance. "Well, I tested the suit." Too tired to explain her delay, she wrapped an arm around her son who still clung to her.

"You must be famished. Would you like a protein-and-root-vegetable stew?" Halle asked.

"After I wash up." She looked down into her son's beseeching eyes.

"Next time, you take me with you to work," Mandin said.

"What?" She glanced in her brother's direction.

"Oh, I told him you were at the academy." Gordo scratched his arm. "That you were working on a project. And I told Mom the same thing, too. So she wouldn't worry."

She closed her eyes a moment. Rather than chastise her brother for his fibs, she should be grateful he tried to calm the rest of the family. "I'm sorry. I didn't mean to be away so long."

"You didn't tell me!" Mandin's eyes turned watery.

"I had to take care of a few things." She wiped his face. The sight of his tears pierced her sternum. "Now, what were you arguing about with Uncle Gordo?"

"He doesn't want to take his new medication. The one you asked me to give him." Her brother motioned to the bottled syrup on the crystal coffee table. "He's been spitting it out."

"So he hasn't had any of it?" Alina cupped Mandin's chin. While her son's mouth was downturned, his grip onto her was strong.

"He's put up a fight since you left." Exasperation dragged down Gordo's lips.

"Mama, I big boy. I no need medicine. I no wanna take it!" Her son stomped his foot.

Exhaling, she crouched to meet him eye-level. "Mandin, Dr. Bellamy said you should take it. Please, I don't want you to have any seizures."

"But I was trying to find you!" His bottom lip trembled, and he reached for her arm.

Her vision tinted green, and an overwhelming sense of abandonment seized her chest. He channeled all his emotions into her, his call outs, his persistent search of her while she stayed in Old Town. He'd tried to use his gifts, but she had been too far for him to reach her, and yet, he'd refused to give up.

"Oh, Mandin." She hugged him close, breathing in his sweet breath, feeling the sticky coating of a pastry on his cheek. The green haze faded away. "You're everything to me, you know that?" She squeezed his shoulder. "I'm sorry I didn't tell you. It won't happen again."

As she stood, he asked, "Where are you going?"

"To take a long, hot shower." She smiled at the view of the tapestries of the river on the walls, a welcome comfort. "Can I do that?"

Mandin slowly nodded. "You eat dinner, too, Mama."

"Yes, I'm hungry. But after I get cleaned up." As she disentangled herself from him, she motioned to her brother.

Gordo accompanied her down the hall to her bedroom.

"How many times did he spit out the medicine?" She smoothed back her hair.

"I managed to have him take a spoonful on the second try, then I caught him spitting it out in the sink." Her brother stopped at her bedroom. "He's pretty sneaky."

"Have Halle make a dessert smoothie and mix in the

syrup. Don't tell Mandin it's in there," she said.

"You've got it, sis. Gotta say, he was really upset while you were gone." Gordo leaned against the doorframe. "I tried entertaining him the best I could, but he kept asking for you."

"Thanks. He didn't have any reaction to the storm?" It was the first time Mandin had been exposed to a blizzard. He'd never encountered one at Evesborough.

"He didn't have any seizures." Gordo rubbed the back of his neck. "But that's when he'd look for you the most. When the storm was the most severe outside. It's like he knew, even though he didn't listen to the forecast like we did. Oh—he had this in his fist, too." Her brother dug into a pocket and held out Kiean's ring.

The lanyard was gone. But the stone was cool against her fingertips, and the giltspar mineral sparkled within it. Mandin's powers were stronger with the mineral, and a flutter touched her chest at the thought of him frantically trying to reach her.

"Thank you." Clutching the jewel, she stepped into the elegant bedroom. The blue beaded box remained on the bureau. The ring warmed her welcome back, and gently, she placed it in the box for safe keeping.

Alone in the pleasant heat of the bedroom, she wriggled out of her suit and removed her boots. In her underwear, she rested hunched over at the end of the bed and rubbed her face. She removed her link when a new message on it blinked.

—Once the storm passes, I look forward to our game of Method. You didn't forget, did you? Affectionally yours, Chance—

Her fingertips twirled the slim device in her hand before she set it on the bureau next to the beaded box. A shower would reinvigorate her, chasing away the mist that floated into her mind as of late.

As the hot water streamed over her aches, Mandin's search for her lingered. She thought of Dr. Bellamy's words. *Cognitive behavioral therapy.*

Could it be that Mandin finding out Kiean wasn't his father proved traumatic? Doubts grew. She'd kept Chance from Mandin for over three years out of necessity. Her son's health and safety were always her priority, ever since he'd been born. *Or perhaps you rationalized fulfilling your own desires,* a little voice whispered to her.

She tilted her face upward, allowing the hot water to drum down, hoping it would wash away the dirt and grime from her.

Chapter 34

Peter Mason's new home resembled a large, stone gallery set in the foothills of the Inland District, with opaque windows overlooking the city below. While Minecorp's office was located in the vicinity of the City Center like many other companies, records showed that Mason sold his former penthouse and moved after his company's mining accident. While the Inland was a quieter area with smaller, multi-story family units, it made little sense to Chance that Mason left his former city home if he wanted to win his seat back.

Chance marched up the gravel pathway to the broad steps before the front door, leading a squad of four men behind him. Min Liu had proven elusive, and no longer stayed at her residence. Due to Harding's delay in locating her, Commander Zinyon had been skeptical of his mother's order to detain Peter Mason. The commander remarked that if Chance was so sure of Mason's guilt, to lead the arrest himself.

Chance looked around. Few neighbors surrounded the large home, although small towers loomed just over the hill crest. Although his men handled the protests in the city, they were getting injured, and he did not want any witnesses to a spectacle of an arrest. The situation could turn unpredictable.

At the front door, he turned to Sergeant Rufalo behind him. "Stay professional no matter what happens."

Rufalo straddled the front step. "Yes, sir."

Some of the men appeared apprehensive but steadied themselves at hearing Chance's order.

He jabbed the buzzer near the heavy front door. After hearing the ringing echo through the house, Chance rapped on the door planks with his knuckles.

A bot answered the door. The silver machine was similar to the one that Alina's mother possessed. "Good afternoon. I'm Dexter. What can I do for you?"

"Is Peter Mason here?" Chance asked.

The male bot's lens that made up its eyes adjusted a few times, scanning them. "He's occupied. May I ask your business for a follow up later?"

Keeping his voice level, Chance replied, "We have a warrant to detain him."

"But I'm afraid that's not possible. You're mistaken." The bot started to close the door, but Chance wedged his foot in the entrance and flung the door back. "You're not to interfere with official security forces. You know that."

Dexter retreated and hurried off to find his master. Chance followed the bot into the spacious entranceway and through a considerable dining room. A great room with fireplace and large chairs remained empty, and the bot scurried through an archway at the far end.

Chance arrived with his men at the entrance of a sunken library where the afternoon light faded on the stone floor. Tall bookcases lined the walls, and a desk was placed at the far end.

"Sir, I tried to stop them, but he insisted," Dexter said, standing in the center of the room.

Walking toward Chance was a tall, fit man. Peter Mason's craggy face showed no sign of trepidation.

Rather his deep-set, dark eyes scrutinized the squad. Small patches of white appeared in his dark beard, and his haircut took on a peppered look. "What can I do for you…" He squinted and angled his head. "Chance, is that you?"

Behind Mason on his desk lay large design prints, although Chance couldn't quite view the schematics. He avoided the trap of his old boss trying to put him at ease.

"Yes, Mr. Mason. I'm here to inform you that I have a warrant for your arrest for conspiracy to commit treason." Chance squared his shoulders. "As it's a rather serious matter, I hope you'll cooperate." He motioned to the men behind him. Two of them formed a line, blocking the exit. Sergeant Rufalo and the other flanked Chance.

"Conspiracy to commit treason?" Mason raised an eyebrow. "On whose accusation? The justice department hasn't contacted me." His smooth voice betrayed no sense of worry.

Chance opened the zipper on his chest pocket. He plucked out the warrant with the seal from the judge his mother directed him to find for signature. "Here, as it's your right to see the charges."

Mason took the paper and bowed his head, reading. He furrowed his brow. "For meeting with Min Liu? She's my supervisor of operations. Tell me, do you usually arrest people for speaking with their employees?" He flung the warrant out. "She requested a leave of absence from work which I granted."

"She's been implicated in the violence and will be detained as well." Chance tucked the warrant away. "If you know her whereabouts, that will prove useful to your case."

"I would think she's at home," Mason replied.

"We checked, and she has disappeared. Surely you can find out. As you just said, you are her boss."

"As I was once yours." Mason's eyes rested on Chance's insignia pinned to his chest. "You're still working for your mother, I see."

"That's correct. Now sir, I have to request—"

"You tell Jade Graylin that her sword will miss its mark." His voice turned acerbic. "And that her actions will only rebound in a way that will knock her off her throne." His gaze penetrated Chance. "I know nothing of the protests or violence except what I see, like all citizens of Alpheios." He cocked his head. "But what does she expect, after she's allied herself with a company that cares nothing for their lives? Or the fact that she has shut down all public access to council meetings? Are you really surprised that people in the city are desperate?"

"There's no excuse for violence." Chance's voice flattened. "You know the city cannot tolerate that." He ignored the churn in his stomach, even though he had skipped lunch earlier, too preoccupied with planning this event.

Taking in a deep breath, Mason peered at him. "You seemed to be rather fair-minded when you worked for me."

"I'm a servant of the city, sir." Studying the man in front of him, Chance wondered if his mother had overreached. During the short time he'd worked for Mason years ago, he saw no nefarious activity from the man, although he hadn't known him long enough to judge otherwise. What he observed in the short time that he assisted Mason was that many in the city respected him, and Mason enjoyed engaging his citizens.

Then again, the ex-chancellor wouldn't be fool enough to leave a trail for them to follow. He was an intelligent man who must have developed insight into his subordinate's activities, at the very least. Or if he really didn't know, Chance didn't want to conceive of what might occur next.

"You understand that we all have a duty," Chance's hand swept to his comrades, "to defend the city." He kept his voice steady. "If you know nothing of the riots, then that evidence will emerge during your trial."

Slowly, he unsheathed his baton, ignoring the pang of regret coming from within him. "Now I must ask you to cooperate."

A corner of Mason's mouth dipped down. "I'm retired from government service, as you know. My attention has been focused solely on my company."

As Chance took a heavy step toward him, Mason held up his hand. "I shall come with you. There's no need for that, Captain."

Inwardly, Chance released a breath. While the men would do as he ordered, he did not look forward to a physical confrontation with his ex-boss. He motioned with his head.

Rufalo and two other men bracketed Mason. "Sir," Rufalo said softly. "Please come with us."

Turning to Dexter, Mason said, "Call Hugh Steward, my attorney. Tell him what has transpired."

"Right away, sir," Dexter squeaked out.

Chance stepped to the side and swept his arm toward the exit. "After you, sir."

As Mason passed him, he said, "I think we're past the pleasantries, Captain Graylin." The biting tone took hold again. "But I appreciate being able to walk out of my own home instead of being dragged out."

His men escorted Peter Mason out. Chance approached the last man standing at the door. "As soon as Mason is secured in the vehicle, send a man back to help me search the house. Two are to stay with Mason at all times, do you understand me?"

The young officer affirmed the order and hurried after the others.

Turning back to the room, Chance drew in a deep breath and strode to the desk. He ran a hand through his hair. There must be some clue, some stronger evidence, to tie Peter Mason to the riots. He started leafing through the design prints and sketches on the desk.

Chapter 35

Icicles hung from tree branches the morning after the blizzard abated. Alina left the Channel District's M station clutching Mandin's hand, accompanied by Halle before the second sunrise. Temperate weather was unusual during deep winter, and her link showed conditions would worsen again after a brief break.

"But why isn't Dr. Bellamy coming to our home?" Mandin asked.

Our home. Alina noted his assumption. "Because Nana and Jakob are leaving on vacation as soon as Dr. Bellamy clears her. They're leaving from Jakob's work in the company's hover-jet. We're meeting them there." The frigid air nipped at her face.

"Also, I must plug into CynCorp's systems for my update before I accompany them," Halle said.

"Are we going, too?" her son asked.

Although the sidewalks had been cleared, snow walls lined the streets. Flecks of dirt and soil were embedded in the snow mounds, like a spoiled dessert. She contemplated showing Mandin the sea, for he hadn't visited it before. The climate, while windy, would be more pleasant than Alpheios this time of year. But a deep reservation stirred from within, like a vacation would permanently uproot them somehow.

"No," she finally said.

"But why?'

"Your father wants to spend time with you."

She stopped at the corner. A thin sheet of ice stretched across the intersection where they were supposed to cross. It must have formed after the movers already cleared the streets before dawn. While she dressed Mandin in his new climate suit and boots, Alina didn't relish the idea of potentially slipping.

"Would you like me to carry him? I have extra traction on my base contact points," Halle said.

"Yes! Mama, can I?" Her son's dark eyes shone, despite the overcast day.

"Go ahead."

The bot lifted Mandin in her metal arms and plunged forward. "Here we go!"

Mandin laughed as the bot carried him. Alina stepped on the thinnest part of the ice where it cracked under her heel. Carefully, she took a wide berth, sticking to the edges of the ice in her new suit. She shook her boots free of slush upon reaching the sidewalk. "Hey, slow down!"

Halle's silver body glinted from the end of the block. The bot moved swiftly with Mandin while he egged her on.

As they moved toward the Channel District of the riverwalk, Alina noted that a few residents took advantage of the lull in the storm. Most businesses were still closed due to the solstice winter break. A few windows in the office buildings stirred with activity.

The violet tower that was CynCorp loomed. The high rise was the tallest building along the Channel District set, a gleaming structure that overlooked the river of Alpheios. They approached the wide steps and terrace leading up to the building. The pavilion was lined with silver polished spheres, the same metallic color as Halle's arms that carried Mandin.

Alina considered her son's inquiry about the vacation. She would gain no benefit in waiting around for word from Evesborough. Tapping the comm bar on her ear, she instructed the link to send the observations she'd gathered about her new suit to the Commandant. At the end of the request, she paused, wondering if she should ask for any messages. She ended up transmitting the readings. No sense in muddling her observations with more questions.

She climbed up the stone steps after the bot and her son. Gordo was also staying behind in the city. And she'd promised Chance a game of Method the following evening. Wiping her boots on the doormat, she reminded herself she needed to practice the game after Halle received her systems update. A tingle spread in her stomach at the thought of her next rendezvous with Chance. One thing she knew for certain was that she did not want to be beaten badly at Method.

Halle set Mandin down by the entrance. The large glass doors slid open. They approached the information desk. A woman sprang up when Alina requested Jakob's office. She wore a gray climate suit with CynCorp's blue logo on her chest. Otherwise, the lobby was mostly empty.

"Ms. DeHerte, right? He's expecting you." The woman led them to the elevator bank. Mirrored lift doors surrounded them, but she stopped at a set of glass doors nestled at the end. Stamped on the doors was CynCorp's symbol, a blue gear with curved edges.

Alina studied the logo with the company's title

stretched alongside it. “Cynthetic Choices Corporation? I never knew that was the company’s full name.”

“Most people don’t. CynCorp is easier to say.” The woman swiped her link in front of a pad, and the doors opened. “This will take you directly to the executive suite on floor twenty. Mr. Coughlin’s assistant is expecting you.”

As the transparent elevator whisked them up, Mandin’s mouth hung open. He crouched, pointing at a few pedestrians on the riverwalk early in the morning. “Look Mama! Look how small they are!”

“Yes. We’re going to the top floor.” As they ascended, the river came into view. She explained to her son how this portion of the river broadened from the falls, and pointed out the Channel pedestrian bridge over it. Across the bridge lay the desolate woods leading to Old Town. Most residents took the bridge to access the colorful Arts District nested in the hills further upstream by the falls.

Alina’s ears tickled with the change in pressure as they passed more floors. Finally, the lift came to a gentle rest.

They stepped out, facing a curved desk with a stately brunette behind it. Her head was down as she examined her glass monitor, swiping it as she spoke into her comm bar. Alina approached her.

“I’m Kyla, Mr. Caughlin’s assistant. Dr. Bellamy is already here. I’ll announce your arrival.”

While Kyla spoke into her comm bar, Alina took Mandin’s hand again. “Be good,” she said in a low voice. “Don’t touch anything.”

Her son nodded, but his legs twitched with energy. Kyla led them to a set of doors at the end of the corridor.

Gordo burst out from the office, his posture rigid.

"Gordo, what's wrong?" Alina stopped.

Dark fury masked her brother's face. "I gotta get out of here." He whizzed by, but she scurried after him.

"What is it?"

He punched the elevator button. "Ask Dr. Bellamy. That procedure you did…" He grimaced. "I know you were trying to help, but…"

A weight dropped in her stomach. "Tell me."

Gordo stepped into the elevator. "You should hear it from the doctor. There's something I have to do." He hit a button on the control panel.

"Wait!"

The doors closed before she could get an answer. Her link beeped a message. The sender showed it was from Commandant Riley. Rattled, she turned back to the office. Kyla, Mandin, and Halle waited for her near the office double doors. She'd check the message later. Gulping, she composed herself for Dr. Bellamy's update.

****

Jakob stared out the expansive windows overlooking the river when Alina entered with Halle and Mandin. Linette rested on a sofa across from Dr. Bellamy in a sitting area at one end of the long office. While her mother's skin was clear of gray patches, her face was drawn, and her mouth wrinkled downward.

The doctor stood in a violet climate suit, her blonde curls tucked into a bun with a few tendrils framing her bronzed face. "We were just talking about you, Alina."

Why? Alina wondered. The office was all stone and glass. The seats were fashioned of curved chrome frames, embedded with slim, black cushions.

Jakob turned around, his hands in his pockets. He

motioned at a seat near Dr. Bellamy. "Why don't you sit down?"

A buzz from Alina's link reminded her about the Commandant's message. Silencing it, she glanced at Mandin. "Should he listen?"

Her mother's husband made what sounded like a noise of exasperation. "Halle, do you mind?"

Alina pulled her shoulders back. She refused to slouch or apologize. Mandin was not some inconvenience to be managed. The bot led Mandin to the far side of the large office where life-sized photos of robots adorned the walls. Halle explained the different models, pointing out their features.

Dusk brewed in her mother's green eyes, and Alina halted. "What is it?"

Linette's voice came out a low rasp. "You had no right."

Alina stiffened. "Meaning?"

"I told her about your bone marrow transplant," Jasmine said, her voice soft. "She needs to understand her condition, so I told her everything."

"And?"

Jakob sank into a chair by Linette, and his gaze fell to the stone floor.

A warning flare shot off within Alina. "Will someone explain what's going on?"

Jasmine's lips pressed together. "Your mother got better at first, and I thought the serum was working. But some of the cells have since mutated." She pushed aside a hair coil. "I took another look at them under the microscope, and it turns out there were fetal stem cells mixed in with Kora's adult stem cells."

"I'm not following." Alina clutched the back of the

closest chair to her, her hands wrapped around its cold metal frame.

"The fetal cells mutated to cancer cells, reversing the progress." She shook her head. "The initial cell cultures didn't show any problems, but there was no time to observe them over a long period given your mother's condition. It's a rare mutation, but sometimes fetal cells behave this way." The doctor gestured to Linette. "Now, Genodyne does have therapeutics to fight cancer, and I've administered them to your mother. I was able to stop the cancer from spreading."

"But is she cured?" The chrome frame felt slippery under Alina's grasp.

The doctor's shoulders hunched over. "Unfortunately, no. The underlying disease will spread again."

Linette was dressed in her travel best, an all-weather black climate suit with curved white stripes along her arms and torso. She rose her chin and gazed at Alina. "You shouldn't have offered your bone marrow without asking me first."

"Darling, she wanted to help," Jakob said.

"And you knew about it and didn't tell me." Her mother's voice strained.

"We had to try something." Alina wiped her palms on the side of her thighs. She reached for the manual button on her suit to cool off but dropped her hand. The suit adjusted automatically and wasn't malfunctioning, but heat nevertheless clawed at her neck. Had her operation been all for nothing?

"I never asked for your help!" Linette cried out. "How dare you keep this from me." Her hands curled in her lap.

Flames seared Alina's cheeks. "I didn't do it for just you! There are many others who are sick! But that would require you to acknowledge someone other than yourself." The remark hit like a dart aimed for its mark. Linette winced.

"Stop, please. This isn't helping." Jakob leaned forward in his seat. "It was a low-risk procedure, hon." His gaze shifted to Alina. "And she didn't mean what she said. Right?"

Alina didn't want to reel back her words, despite her mother's refusal to look at her. She was *not* sorry for what she said. How could her mother be so ungrateful?

"It's unacceptable." Linette's bottom lip trembled. "A parent is not meant to outlive their child. She could have suffered damage to herself, or it may affect her in the future." Her mother touched her forehead. Her skin paled.

Her husband took her hand. "Maybe we should hold off on the Tidewater trip."

Linette leaned into his grip. "I'll never see the ocean, will I?"

The room quieted as Jakob stroked the top of her hand. Alina's throat closed off, and she walked past the sitting area to the windows. A sting took hold in her eyes, and she crossed her arms. *Now you care?* She wanted to say to her mother. *You weren't even home when Dad died.*

She'd been the one to receive the news about her father from the Commandant. She was the one who had to tell Gordo, still a child at the time, because her mother had already left them. It took her several days to track her mother down. She found her in a fancy hotel in the Arts District, staying with Jakob. Mustering her restraint from hurling history in her mother's face, she knew it would do no good. Alina chewed on her inner cheek instead. The pain helped her to focus on the view.

A large hover-jet waited on a tarmac pad at the ground level, not far from the river. Jakob always kept the latest models. A sheet of ice expanded over the river's surface and extended underneath the Channel bridge.

"I want to go home." Linette's voice sounded weak.

"Please lie down." Dr Bellamy firm tone broke through.

A rustle of movement took place.

Alina whirled around. Her mother's face appeared ashen, then her skin rippled. The gray spot reappeared on her cheek. Jakob stood over her, helping her recline.

"What's wrong?"

The doctor checked her mother's pulse on her neck. "She's feeling faint." Her fingers gently touched Linette's chin and raised it. "Try to rest and don't get up until you're ready."

"Do you want tea or water?" Jakob's forehead creased.

But her mother didn't answer. Her eyelids closed.

"Water may help," the doctor replied.

Alina rubbed her face. A coil snaked through her gut. Her insides trembled at the sight of the gray scales covering her mother's cheek.

Jasmine straightened. "There is one last thing we can try."

"Yes?" Jakob asked.

"Alina's bone marrow transplant was given to Ash. Dr. Daxmen noted Ash is rapidly improving. His stem cells won't have fetal cells mixed in with them." The doctor scratched the sleeve of her violet suit. “It could cure her, along with the thousands in the city who initially took Phase Three.”

“Does that mean you have to get a withdrawal from Ash?” Alina balked at the thought of facing the kronosapiens again.

“Daxmen already has samples from follow-up.” Jasmine grabbed her messenger bag. “The kronosapiens allowed him to take a few vials hoping to confirm that Ash was getting better.” She slung the bag over her torso. “I’ll need one vial to check under the scope to confirm his stem cell count. And one more to administer the serum. But time is short. She needs it right away.”

Swallowing, Alina willed her breakfast to stay put. “Do you need any help?”

Jasmine studied her link. Her forehead crinkled. “I’m getting a message that Genodyne is on lockdown.”

“Why?”

“I’m not sure. Last time they did that, it lasted until the next morning before they gave the all clear announcement.” She twisted the link on her wrist. “I usually can access the emergency entrance, but I’m not sure it’s open during a lockdown.”

Linette lay listless, her face wan. Turning to Jasmine, Alina said, “I’ll go with you. And help you find a way inside.” She didn’t have a plan on how they’d enter the building, but she’d broken into Genodyne before.

“Alina…” Linette’s voice wavered.

“It’s only vials we’re fetching.” She avoided gazing at her mother’s slumped figure and fixed on Jasmine. “Everyone needs it.”

“Thank you,” Jakob replied.

“Can I leave Mandin here?” He held onto Halle’s

hand, pointing at the photos. Under no circumstances would she bring him to Genodyne or anywhere near the kronosapiens.

Jakob's chin rested in between his thumb and index finger. "Halle can watch him."

Alina approached her son and instructed him to stay and wait for her. He smiled and grabbed the bot's hand.

Her stomach was tight when she followed Jasmine to the elevator doors. The doctor plucked at the leg of her violet suit as they waited. The translucent doors opened, and they stepped into the lift.

As the lift slid down the shaft, the icy river came into view. Alina's legs tensed at the thought of their destination. But she had to retrieve the vials—there was no other way.

Chapter 36

Syriah glanced up at the tall purple building, shielding her eyes. The second sun rose in the late morning. “This is where Alina is staying?” She tugged at the hem of the oversized jacket that Cinda had given her as a hand-me down.

“According to Aurore.” Kiean made his way to the shiny doors covered by metal swirls.

She followed her brother along the wet walkway, cutting through the snow-covered grounds. It had been so long since she played in the snow that she was tempted to stick her gloved fingers into it.

He pushed the buzzer at the entrance. Kiean wore a hooded expeditionary suit that Talley gave him. Her brother had prepped the Spartan for flight as soon as he saw the break in the weather. His face had almost completely healed from the fight in the great hall, although a dark splotch still appeared by the corner of his eye from the faded bruise. He’d stopped icing his face after Hawk’s accident.

Syriah could still hear little Hudson’s cries for his father, and Ione’s soft weeping. Shock wound around the entire village from Hawk’s death. Big Flint and Cinda cooked hot meals for everyone. As for herself, Syriah was glad to take a break from the gloom and accompany her brother on his trip. She heard much whispering among the adults and kept quiet, lest anyone blame her for Hawk's death. To her relief, no one seemed to notice her.

The building doors swung open, allowing them in.

As the heated air swirled around them, Syriah relaxed. Once they found Alina, everything would be better. Syriah knew from Kiean's air how miserable he'd felt for many days as they waited for the blizzard to pass.

The tile was shiny under her boots, and the lobby was clean. A doorman waited behind a round desk. The gold elevator doors reflected back their figures. She didn't know Alina and Mandin were staying at such a fancy building.

Kiean approached. "Alina DeHerte, please."

"Is she expecting you?" The doorman asked the question like he wouldn't believe the answer. His silver air dimmed from suspicion.

Her brother shifted. "Just tell her Kiean is here."

"No one is home at the penthouse. I can take a message, but the Coughlin family left earlier this morning." The doorman rested his arms in his elbows.

A shadow of disapproval crossed her brother's face. "Do you know where they went?"

"For the security of our guests, I can't provide that information."

Kiean led her out of the lobby back outside. A plucking pulled at Syriah's stomach like when Danny would sometimes pinch her. They had flown all this way but failed in finding Alina.

"You said you sent her a message." She hurried after her brother on the walkway.

"I sent it to the academy, but I'm not sure if she saw it." A puff of air escaped from his mouth. "Problem is I don't have a link to find her."

Syriah fell quiet. Her brother had accidentally smashed his link into the stone cliff face when he tried to hoist Hawk's body up the line. Maybe here in Alpheios, far from Evesborough, she could prove her powers could do good. Although it would be difficult without surrounding giltspar walls like the cavern. Still, the tall buildings would provide help if she concentrated. "Why don't we take the maglev over the city?"

"What good will that do?"

"I can try to find her."

A corner of her brother's mouth lifted into a half-smile. "Okay. It's better than hanging around here waiting." He took the sidewalk in the direction of the M.

She trekked beside him. "Do you think Alina will be happy to see us?"

"Hope so." Kiean's arm fell across her shoulders, and he hugged her to his side. "I'm glad you talked me into bringing you, you know that?"

Her chest lifted like a balloon. If she could find Alina and Mandin, then she could tell Danny back at Evesborough how strong her powers were.

****

Syriah gaped at the tall silver bot in the office. Halle played a cartoon for her and Mandin.

All that searching. Syriah had finally done something right with her powers. While riding the maglev, she'd spotted Mandin's glimmer through the glass elevator as it rose up the side of the building. It dazzled her in a way it hadn't before. She pointed it out to her brother, and Kiean found the office. Jakob invited them in to wait, explaining they just missed Alina, and she would return shortly.

On the couch, Kiean spoke to Jakob's wife. Syriah

stared when she first saw Alina's mother. Even for city people, her mother was beyond lovely, despite the gray patch on her cheek. But her pink air was weak, fading into yellow. It signaled a waning life force. Alina's mother touched her forehead again, flashing a gray patch on her hand.

Jakob walked into the office. "The repair port is ready. We can upgrade Halle's systems while waiting for Alina and Dr. Bellamy."

Kiean rose. "Your wife isn't feeling well."

Jakob rushed to her side. Then he touched a speaker on his desk and called his assistant.

On Halle's screen, the cartoons continued. When Mandin pointed with his finger again, his hand was wrapped around a small object.

"What's that?" Syriah asked.

He hid his hand behind his back.

She pried open his fingers; he whined. In his palm was the ring that her brother gave to Alina. "You're not supposed to be playing with this!" She snatched the ring away. Alina would be very upset if her giltspar ring went missing.

Jakob spoke in a low tone to Kiean. "I should stay with Linette. I was hoping to upgrade Halle today, though."

"I can conduct the upgrade for you," Kiean said.

Jakob appeared grateful. "The bot module is on the ground floor, across from the tarmac. We'll take the company hover-jet home afterward. There's room for all of us, and my assistant will let Alina know."

"I'll tell your pilot to get the jet running, too."

"Thank you." Jakob checked his link. "They should be back shortly."

Syriah slipped the ring in her pocket as her brother approached them.

He grinned. "We're going to upgrade Halle. Be good, and don't touch anything." He bounced his index finger off Mandin's nose, and the little boy laughed.

Syriah examined Jakob's air. Dark blue in its seriousness, the company man seemed private, the way he stood with his hands in his pockets. But she detected no meanness in him.

Kyla from the front desk glided into the room carrying a platter with cups on it. "Mr. Coughlin, you requested fizz for Mrs. Coughlin?"

"Yes, please." Jakob waved her over. He stroked Alina's mother's back and whispered in her ear. Syriah watched as his air softened being close to her. Alina's mother nodded, and Kyla served her.

Syriah gripped Mandin's hand to make sure he was extra good. She wasn't sure what changed about him, but his air was much shinier than usual.

Once Alina returned, all would be better. The adults would help Alina's mother. Then Alina would board the Spartan with Mandin. And her brother would take them back to Evesborough before the launch window closed, and they could all go home.

Chapter 37

Chance grabbed a detection wand from the desk and departed his office. He traversed down the hall to the assembly room to prepare for the council meeting. The doors already stood open.

A young female aide in a burgundy suit and long, dark hair was setting down citrus fizz bottles and glasses on the curved table perched on a dais. The seal of Alpheios hung on the wall behind it, bearing atomic loops over the three peaks, surrounded by a wreath.

He greeted the aide whose turn it was to run the meeting logistics. “What’s the snack today, Elba?”

“Floral biscuits.” She gestured to the gold-rimmed plates with bite-sized cookies on them. Petals pressed into the cookies glinted in different colors.

“Did Councilwoman Diamante suggest them?” he asked. Elba was Diamante’s aide.

“Yes. Would you like one?” A delightful smile broke over her face. “They’re quite good, not too sweet.”

“No, thanks. If you don’t mind, I’ll conduct the security check now.”

Her smile disappeared. “Of course.”

He had contemplated a while back asking Elba to dinner at his place. She was always eager for conversation. Sure that she’d agree, he nearly sent her a message via link. But Chance ultimately discarded the idea, foreseeing that they’d run into each other frequently at work. He maintained a cordial, but professional relationship with her instead. Besides, he was no longer interested now that Alina had returned.

Chance initiated the wand. Running it underneath their seats, he conducted a sweep for explosives and listening devices. After the manifesto had been found, he took the task upon himself rather than rely on the building security team. The spectator area below the dais would stay empty, but he descended the steps to search the area anyway. The council had closed off their proceedings to the public based on his mother's direction. He conducted a final check under the chairs along the wall where the aides usually sat.

Satisfied, he returned to his office where he stashed the detection wand. Then he opened the adjacent door to his mother's outer suite. Her assistant smiled at him and waved to one of several comfortable chairs. He checked the messages on his link for updates.

After a few minutes, the inner door to the chancellor's office opened. His mother emerged in a shiny, black pantsuit. Her gold chancellor pin gleamed against her lapel.

He followed her down the hall toward the assembly room. "Standard update?" Chance often found the meetings dull. Lately, the council discussed the state of the city, but demurred on any action.

"I'm introducing a resolution to fund Genodyne's Phase Three cure," she replied.

He straightened. When any of the five members made a proposal, it was often debated and voted upon. Most council members did not bring up a proposal if they didn't think it would succeed. They risked repercussions in voting against her as the chancellor. As the city's administrator, she controlled the Guardian forces. "You should get it, I hope?"

Her arms swung by her sides as she strode. "I'll have to give them an update on the bone marrow transplant and its promise."

"Have we gotten an update from Dr. Daxmen yet?"

"A few days ago. It was working on Linette." Her voice lowered into a growl. "The council will fall in line behind me once they fund the cure."

"Linette is cured?" he asked.

"Son, you have to move fast on these matters."

Upon the chancellor's entrance to the assembly room, the four other council members who had already arrived rose to greet her. They all displayed their council pins, although only his mother's pin was encircled by a wreath. After she exchanged greetings with them, she was ready for the center seat. Chance took up his usual place against the wall next to the other aides.

"Good afternoon." She opened the meeting. "I have promising news from Genodyne. They now have a cure for the side effects from the earlier versions of Phase Three."

Councilwoman Diamante to the right of his mother smiled and tucked her brown hair behind her ear. Raised in one of the wealthiest families within the Arts District, she wore a maroon-and-tan striped suit that draped her angular frame.

His mother continued. "The female kronosapien's birth of several offspring has resulted in a rich batch of stem cells. It's working to counteract the initial side effects of Phase Three."

At the far end, Councilman Sonora's stocky build leaned forward. His tan face expressed interest.

"They've tested it already?" Sonora was from the Industrial District, sparsely populated. His seat was a new one recently added to the council by the previous chancellor. Sonora oversaw the fusion reactor and the infrastructure projects for the city.

"Yes. A human subject has recovered from Genodyne's new serum. And to top it off, the male kronosapien is recuperating, no longer ill. Genodyne found a bone marrow donor who was a match for him." Jade Graylin waved her hand in the air as if she was a conductor.

"And how did they find a compatible donor? The kronosapien project wasn't supposed to be public." Councilman Shah sat at the end of the dais closest to Chance. His blue climate suit was trimmed in a gold weave along his collar and cuffs that offset his thick, dark hair.

Shah often spoke up during the meetings, representing the Inland District. His mother would gripe in private that he was a constant headache. While Chance couldn't quite view the expression in Shah's blue-gray eyes, his tone implied skepticism.

"They found a volunteer who does not know where the serum came from." Chance's mother smoothed down the front of her suit top.

"How fortuitous they found a match," Shah replied.

"Perhaps we should hear more about the cure." Councilwoman Lacey spoke with a deliberate cadence. In a bright yellow winter suit with short hair that resembled wheat, she gave Shah a polite smile.

"Yes," Councilwoman Diamante said quickly. "I know my district is hoping for good news." She fiddled with her gold link.

Chance took Lacey's remark as a good omen. While he found himself adept at reading people, Councilwoman Lacey remained an enigma to him. A successful businesswoman, she represented the newer Meander District.

"It's quite simple," his mother replied. "Kora's pregnancy has succeeded in producing enough stem cells to stop tumors from spreading in laboratory tests. Further, it has the effect of shrinking them. I have some images of the cell cultures we can view."

His mother touched the inset table controls. "Exhibit One." A close-up of a slide containing stained cells showed on the screen.

"This first photo shows a skin culture from a patient sick from Phase Three side effects. You can see the dark cells outnumber the healthy, red ones," she said.

As his mother continued her update, Chance's link flashed. It was a new message.

Lieutenant Harding—*A large protest has grown outside CH. I've directed the other squad to join Sgt Rufalo's line.*—

Chance gripped the edges of his link as he stared at the message. He'd already doubled the size of Rufalo's squad weeks ago.

Chance—*Size?*—

Harding—*Est 300*—

With the remaining squad in the building called to the front, he'd have no personnel security for the council when they adjourned. But he couldn't allow a breach of the building.

Chance—*Stdby.*—

Commander Zinyon's number was at the top of his scroll list, right under his mother's number. The link activated the call, and he touched his comm bar.

As the council discussed the slides, he lowered his voice. “Transmit code 2-7-1, Lodestar location. Authorization Charlie, Golf, Two, Niner.”

Elba turned to him, a questioning look on her face. But he didn’t have time to explain and sent the transmission.

Chance—*Alert BN activated.*—

“I believe a resolution funding Genodyne’s mass production is in order, as use of their bioreactors is a rather expensive process,” his mother was saying. “They want to know that we’re behind them before they distribute the serum.”

Harding—*Will coord with alert BN CC upon arrival.*—

Chance—*Rgr*—

His mother wouldn’t like being interrupted, but the council must know about the situation outside.

“And what of the kronosapiens and their offspring?” Shah asked.

“Genodyne plans to utilize them as a showcase for their new reproduction program,” his mother replied.

Chance stood. “Chancellor?”

Shah’s tone sharpened. “Our residents need time to be fully healed first.”

“Chancellor?” Chance raised his voice.

“Yes?” The corner of his mother’s mouth curved downward.

“We have a security situation outside.” He gripped the handle of his baton.

All the council members turned to him. “The crowd size at the front of the building has grown to a large degree. I’ve requested that Commander Zinyon mobilize the alert battalion. For everyone's safety, I recommend the council remain here until the battalion and its commander arrive. After our forces push back the perimeter, we can escort each of you home with added security." He stopped, awaiting further instructions.

His mother took in a deep breath. "How large is the crowd?"

Shouting carried over from the outside.

"Around three hundred."

"How long until the alert battalion arrives?"

Outdoor noise reverberated through the walls.

"About ten-to-fifteen minutes." He estimated that while the Guardian headquarters was not far from the City Center, it would take the officers a few minutes to don their riot gear.

Councilwoman Diamante's chin lifted. "What's that sound?"

Chance listened. A dull roar wound its way by the assembly room. The noise was coming from the front of the building.

He cracked the door to investigate. A phrase was being shouted again and again. Chance allowed the door to close behind him and ventured a few steps, straining to hear.

"May-son! May-son! May-son! May-son!" The crowd chanted.

He swore under his breath. As quiet as Chance tried to keep Mason's detainment, the news must have broke. He touched his link to contact the lieutenant. "Protestors' demands?"

Harding replied, "They want Mason's release from prison. They also want the chancellor to step down."

Chance said, "Send out a BOLO for Min Liu. If

she's spotted, arrest her."

Upon his return to the assembly room, his mother spoke. "Do we have a problem?"

"The crowd is protesting Peter Mason's arrest and confinement." He hesitated, knowing she wouldn't like the rest. "They're calling on you to step down."

Chance scanned the stunned faces Councilwoman Diamante and Lacey. Hesitation rippled through Sonora's face.

His mother narrowed her eyes. "I will not be blackmailed by an unruly mob. Particularly when we have government business to vote on."

Councilman Shah asked, "On what grounds was Mason arrested?"

His mother's mouth tightened into a slash. Mason's new home in the mountains was in Shah's district.

"We have evidence of his conspiracy to commit treason," she replied.

"What evidence?" Shah pressed.

Chance's link flashed another message.

Harding—*Alert BN inbound. ETA five minutes.*—

"Officer Graylin, can you please explain what the Guardians have found?"

He addressed Shah. "We have a confidential informant embedded in the Citizens Liberation Front. The informant has revealed that one of Mason's female employees from Minecorp is one of the operational leaders of the movement. A weapon recovered at the recent attack on City Hall also belongs to Minecorp. Mason has met recently with her." While Chance didn't find further evidence at Mason's home, he was waiting to hear back from the forensics team about the contents of Mason's computer.

Shah studied him. “That implicates her, but it’s not clear to me that Mason is fomenting violence. Do you know the particulars of their meeting?”

His mother immolated Shah with her stare. “I suggest we allow the Guardians to conduct their investigation without meddling.”

Shah frowned.

Sonora said, “This is a grave matter. However, we require more information.” He gestured to Shah. “Let us await the official charges. In the meantime, we can vote on the chancellor’s resolution.”

Minecorp owned some buildings in Sonora’s district, Chance observed. Although it was typical that Sonora avoided conflict and tried to please everyone.

“Yes, Mason’s treason is quite shocking.” Diamante fiddled with her thick necklace and turned to his mother. “But the Phase Three presentation was quite informative. I, for one, am hopeful about Genodyne’s breakthrough.”

Lacey gave a slight nod, signaling her agreement.

The chancellor quieted for a moment. One by one, Jade Graylin took in the expressions of the council members. Chance noted that she was likely to have Diamante’s and Lacey’s votes, which meant Sonora would fall in-line even if Shah voted against the resolution. Sonora often voted last and agreed with the majority of the council, never being the odd man out.

“Councilman Shah,” his mother crooned, “I understand your concern about this matter with Peter Mason. I was surprised to learn about it myself. But please, don’t let this delay Genodyne in providing relief for the people who live in your district.”

Shah’s fist curled on the desk. “I expect us to address Mason’s arrest very soon showing evidence for his detainment." His voice trembled in anger.

Chance's link flashed.

Sentry—*Both k.s. escaped GD. Dr. Daxmen KIA. Situation dire.*—

Damn. The alert battalion couldn't be diverted. The crowd outside posed an immediate threat to his mother.

Chance—*Loc of k.s. babies?*—

"Of course we shall update you," his mother was saying. "Let us now turn our attention to the resolution and introduce it into the record."

Sentry—*K.S. parents took them. Whereabouts unk. Bldg lockdown.*—

Sentry—*Please send squad to GD ASAP.*—

Chance faced little choice. Once the battalion arrived, he would need to send a few men to Genodyne. He stood again. "Chancellor?"

"What is it now?" Her voice sliced the air.

He took a deep breath. "We have a situation at Genodyne. The kronosapiens have escaped. And I'm afraid that Dr. Daxmen is dead."

Everyone fell quiet, absorbing the news. All the council members' heads swiveled in his mother's direction.

Finally, she spoke. "That's regrettable news about Dr Daxmen. However, there are other members of his team that can still mass produce the cure."

Lacey's link lit up. She relayed the message while everyone leaned in her direction. "My niece, Ms. Silver, is currently at Genodyne and has confirmed your aide's news. It appears other members of Daxmen's team have been injured. She's also gathering an emergency meeting with the board to discuss whether they want to activate the Phoenix Protocol."

A slight gasp came from Diamante.

Chance did not know what the Phoenix Protocol meant.

His mother's upper body visibly tensed. "I will see to this myself after the meeting. We must protect the cure at all costs."

After an uncomfortable lull, Lacey replied, "Maybe we should table all resolutions until the situation has been brought under control."

Councilwoman Diamante and Sonora exchanged glances. The atmosphere in the room reversed itself.

The chancellor's lips disappeared into a thin line. "We shall adjourn. I'll call all of you once I find out more."

Diamante said, "You're not going over there now, are you?" Her mouth fell open, and she touched her chest.

"I am." His mother's steel gaze fell upon Chance. "My aide will see to my security."

Chance composed himself, lest the council sense his alarm. He did not want his mother anywhere near Genodyne. He wanted to ferry her to a secure location, which meant her home where the entryway and exits could easily be controlled at the condo.

"What about the crowd outside for the rest of us?" Lacey asked.

He said, "If you'll just wait here a few minutes, I'll have security details plussed up and arrange for your departure out the back exit."

Shah snorted. "We'll scurry out the back like scared yezirds."

His mother stiffened. "Meeting adjourned." She shot out of her chair and hurried out.

Chance tapped his comm bar to call Harding and relayed security instructions.

Out in the hall, Chance lengthened his stride to catch up to his mother who was already half-way to her office. When he arrived by her side, she said, “Get the GATV immediately. I want to go to Genodyne now.”

“Mother, it’s not safe. We don’t know where the kronosapiens are and have sealed the building. I urge you to reconsider.”

“I must stop Ms. Silver!”

He swung open the door to her outer suite and stepped in after her. “What is the Phoenix Protocol?”

She shook her head. “Not here. I’ll explain there.” She flapped her hand at him. “I said now! I must leave right away!”

Chance took a step back, stung. Her assistant looked at them, distressed.

Regaining his composure, he inhaled a deep breath. “Yes, Chancellor.” He touched his comm bar and activated his link. “Harding, give me a two-man escort plus driver to meet me out back. We’re taking Chariot to Pantheon location. Do it now, before you handle the other council members.”

His mother stalked to her office. “Come get me as soon as we’re ready to go.” She slammed the door behind her, and the thud vibrated the walls.

Chapter 38

Alina's breath left a small cloud on the maglev windows. It blended with the frost covering the window's edges. Beside her, Dr. Bellamy said, "That's a big crowd. I wonder if it has anything to do with the Genodyne lockdown."

The pod soared over Ambrose Park which contained the spillover of a mass of people gathered in front of City Hall. It was unusual to see so many people out during the twin solstice break. Most stayed inside for the holiday, hosting meals for friends. The scene was hardly festive.

Her fingers tingling in her gloves, Alina gulped. Several GATVs arrived, and Guardians spilled out of the vehicles in their riot gear. Trudging through the snow, they burst through the crowd. "Did you try contacting Dr. Daxmen? He might be able to let us in the building."

Jasmine shifted the strap of the small bag slung across her torso. "I sent him a message. I'll try again." She tapped her link.

Outside, a canvas of snow draped the city while the pod passed between stacks of amethyst high rises. Frost clung to trees and lamp posts.

As the maglev swung over the wide rail arc that transitioned to the Falls District, Alina sucked in a breath.

"What is it?"

"Look." She pointed out the window. Above the

river, an expanse of ice covering the cliff face gleamed, suspended vertically over snow-covered boulders. "The falls have frozen over."

They gaped at the falls across the promontory that housed Genodyne. Alina had seen the falls partially frozen before, but never quite like this. Except for a few narrow streams of water gently cascading downward, the bulk of the water remained an immovable block of ice.

Slowly, the pod descended and the falls left their view. The doors slid open at the Falls District stop, and they disembarked.

Jasmine's forehead crinkled.

"What is it?"

"Daxmen still hasn't gotten back to me. I even sent him an update so they don't administer Kora's serum to anyone else."

They strode out of the maglev station. Cold air sliced Alina's cheeks like a razor, knocking her awake. "Do you know where he keeps the blood samples?"

The doctor nodded. "In his office, but I'll need to confirm them under a scope."

They hurried across the empty plaza toward the steel Guardian barriers that separated Genodyne from its surroundings. Most of the cafes and stores were still closed from the twin solstice break.

They approached the hospital's terrace but stopped in front of the metal barricades anchored tightly across the pavement.

"The ER entrance." Dr. Bellamy motioned to the corner of the building.

Alina followed her around to the other side. They dashed up a ramp to the glass entry, but the doors refused to open. Dr. Bellamy flashed her link on the keypad, but a red light blinked in response.

"Ugh." Her mouth curved downward. Jasmine tried her link again and pushed on the door. "It's not giving me access."

The far end of the ramp wrapped around the corner of the building. "This way." Alina dashed along the ramp's path to the front terrace.

As they approached the glass doors to the main entrance, a Guardian officer in an armored vest emerged from behind a metal DNA strand sculpture.

"Stop!" he said. "No one is currently allowed inside the building."

"But I'm a doctor and need to meet a colleague here." Jasmine's voice was breathy.

"The building is on lockdown. You can't enter right now." Sweat dribbled down the side of the officer's face from under his helmet. His hand rested on his baton.

"When does it reopen?" Dr. Bellamy demanded.

"Yancey!" Another Guardian at the other end of the terrace waved. "Chariot is inbound."

His head snapped in that direction. "Now?" He grimaced. "You ladies have to leave. For your own safety, go back to your domicile and remain indoors."

"But I have to help my mother!" Alina flung her hands to the side.

"Go!" He pointed to the stairs, his mouth set.

Gulping, she dragged her boots down a step as he watched them.

"Escort ETA is fifteen minutes. I need a detail." His colleague called out.

About halfway down, she glanced in his direction. The officer's back was to them as he already walked to his co-worker and they were both deep in conversation.

The lobby doors slid open, and another Guardian hustled out to join his peers congregating at the far end of the terrace.

"Come on." Tugging Jasmine's sleeve, Alina bounded up the stairs.

Alina ducked behind the DNA sculpture. She waited until the Guardians huddled together, discussing their next task. "Now!" She ran toward the glass doors with the doctor. The doors started sliding shut. They swiveled sideways just as the doors closed behind them.

Inside, a blue ceiling light blinked. An intermittent alarm sounded in the lobby area. Every few seconds, it whined into a crescendo. They stopped behind the life-sized statue of Ambrose to catch their breath. The information desk was empty.

"Why the lockdown?"

"I don't know." Jasmine wiped her brow. "But Daxmen's office isn't far." She hurried in the direction of the elevator doors.

When Jasmine punched the lift button, the doors opened immediately. Alina hopped in beside her.

Once they arrived at the third floor, Jasmine led her to the main office suite with a floor-to-ceiling glass entryway. The wall sign indicated it was the Genodyne's director's office. The alarm faded, but a blue light still flashed overhead. The assistant desk remained vacant.

"Where is everyone?"

"Who knows, but we won't be long." Jasmine barreled into the inner office. It was empty, and the lights brightened upon their entry.

"Now what?"

"Daxmen kept the vials close." The doctor brushed a strand of hair back. "After we did your bone marrow transplant, he brought me up to his office so we could discuss the kronosapiens more."

Jasmine ducked behind the desk and opened a glass fridge. As she reached in, Alina gazed out the windows at the far end of the room. Small trickles of water coursed over the frozen falls. Water still gushed into a pool, but further down by the bridge, a thin surface of ice covered the river. The current still flowed underneath.

She checked her link. It was negative twenty-three degrees Celsius outdoors. While it was still early, eventually, the second sun would appear.

"Got it!" Jasmine held up two vials containing purplish-red fluid.

"Are you sure those are Ash's?"

"Yes. Daxmen labels everything. But I still have to check them under a scope."

"Where do we find one?"

Jasmine looked around the office. "I bet he didn't travel far."

Alina poked her head out by the assistant's desk. A closed side door was visible. "Out here."

They entered a small kitchenette. On the far counter rested a curved white microscope with a small glass monitor above it.

A smile lit up Jasmine's smooth face. "I told you he wouldn't travel far." She opened a drawer underneath the microscope. "Now I need some slides." She fumbled around as Alina checked her link. They had been in the building for about fifteen minutes. Jasmine found a dropper and carefully applied some blood from one of the vials to a glass slide.

"I should get the kronosapiens medical files while I'm here as well," Jasmine said as she placed the slide underneath the scope. "If I had them in the first place, I could have better predicted the results of Kora's blood sample on your mother."

"Where does he keep them?"

"His office computer. But I don't know the pass phrase."

"I'll try to access it." Alina left the small kitchen. Back in the office, she touched the monitor. It brightened.

"Pass Phrase?" The female AI assistant asked.

Alina mulled through the possibilities. "Kronosapien."

The screen flashed and the female voice replied, "Denied."

She licked her lips. "Revival."

"Denied. Another incorrect password will require biometrics authentication."

Alina straightened. She would be locked out completely in a moment. She pondered her previous encounters with Doctor Daxmen. When she awoke in the hospital room, he was there. Then Jade showed up. At the end of their conversation, Jade had mentioned rebranding of their product. And Daxmen had made a suggestion. Alina took in a deep breath. "Restore."

"Access granted."

A rush of adrenaline filled her as the monitor blinked, waiting her next command.

"Retrieve all files on the kronosapiens. Ash and Kora."

The green file logs scrolled up on the screen. Fumbling with her link, she called up the transfer frequency. "Transmit to 143.79."

"Transfer downloading."

She fidgeted as the dots on her link blinked. The size of the files were rather large. After a minute of the transfer in progress, she chewed on a fingernail.

"Transfer complete."

Alina glanced at her link. As she thumbed through the files to make sure all the information downloaded correctly, an unread message indicator flashed. Tapping it, she commanded it to project on her sleeve. She read the message.

—Alina, I hope this message finds you and Mandin well. Aurore has predicted a break in the weather tomorrow at Alpheios. I've prepared the Spartan for flight and plan on taking off tonight so Syriah and I can arrive after the cold front passes through. Thank you for the sweet cakes. I've missed you and Mandin and wish for all of us to be together again. Yours always, Kiean.—

He was on his way to her. A twinge wound its way around her chest. He sent the message the previous day, but Commandant Riley probably didn't check the flight control room until this morning, which is when he forwarded the message to her.

She rubbed her forehead, remembering the last time they'd spent together at Evesborough, locked away in the captain's room. She raised her hand to her collar to lower the temperature but found no button. Sweating, she dropped her hand; she was in the automated suit that the Commandant had given her. The suit was functioning normally, but heat plagued her.

"Shall I return to sleep mode?" the female AI asked.

"No." Alina leaned close to the monitor and lowered her voice. "Search files back twenty-six years ago for a male baby born here with a heart condition."

The screen cursor blinked a few times. "One file

meets those parameters."

"Open it." She peered closer to view Kiean's actual birthday. The least she could do was to bring him confirmation. The file contained the requisite matching information. Listed was the same month and year as recalled by his adopted father, Connor, that Kiean was delivered to them. All she needed was the actual day.

The file revealed the entire lot of babies did not reach full gestation due to the sow's system-wide organ failure, except one. A male fetus born premature who required heart surgery. She squinted at the screen. The names of his biological parents were listed. A small gasp escaped her.

Hospital director has informed parents that the fetus expired during the operation. Offered a new implantation with a different sow at no charge.

She took a step back. Kiean believed that his biological parents had abandoned him. Instead, Genodyne had lied to them. Rather than working with them to care for their premature son, they washed their hands of Kiean after the operation when they delivered him to the Origins. The company must have not wanted to deal with the anger of his parents, nor did they want their reputation for producing healthy babies tarnished.

"Alina!"

She committed his birthdate and parents' names to memory. "Close all files. Sleep mode." She hurried to the kitchen.

The doctor's platinum-blonde head lifted up from the scope. The video monitor depicted a mass of blue cells with red dots at their center.

"This is good!" she said. "Genodyne can replicate these colonies for everyone."

"Will it work?"

Jasmine grinned. "It's exactly what Linette needs." She shut off the microscope and dropped the two vials in her small carrying case. "I can inject one directly into your mother and save the other for mass production. Did you get the files?"

"Yes, I have them." Once she got Dr. Bellamy to her mother, she could finally absolve herself of the weight that pulled at her.

They hurried out and waited by the lift door. As the blue light still flashed overhead, Alina's mind leapt ahead, thinking of her future. Everything would fall into place once they reached CynCorp.

The elevator whisked them several floors down. Alina stepped out. The alarm was louder on the ground floor. She ducked around the corner to a large hall that led away from the lobby. Beyond the front doors, the Guardian officers waited.

"ER exit?"

"Yes," Jasmine replied.

They hastened around a corner and dashed to ER wing.

As Alina crossed another corridor, two figures approached them from the opposite hall. She halted.

An unfamiliar woman with a long, dark braid scrutinized her. But her companion was unmistakable. Blinking, Alina said, "Gordo?"

"Alina! What are you doing here?" Her brother caught up to her and grabbed her elbow. "We need to go."

Jasmine waited for them at the turn that led by the ER entrance, her eyes widening.

The woman, slightly out of breath, checked her link.

"Two minutes left."

"I came for the serum." Alina hurried alongside her brother.

"I thought it didn't work."

"It's a different one." Walls blurred by as she tried to comprehend why Gordo ended up at Genodyne. "What's going on? And who's your friend?"

"No time for questions! I'm Min, by the way." She broke into a run and yelled at Jasmine. "Get out of the hospital!"

"Exit is this way." Jasmine neared the end of the hall and turned right.

They rushed around the corner straight into the ER area. Gordo pulled Alina harder, and she crashed into a nurse.

The woman yelped as she swayed.

"Sorry!" Alina called out.

Gordo's grip tightened around her arm. "C'mon!"

Glass doors loomed ahead.

"Why are we running?" She gasped as they hurtled out of the building. Sunlight seared her eyes. She bent over to catch her breath.

"Can't stop! We need to get away from the building," Gordo said.

"But the Guardians—" Jasmine replied.

"Screw them!" Min cut in.

They sprinted across the plaza in the direction of the cafes. Alina dared not look back for she was sure they were visible to the sentries outside.

As they passed by the eateries, Jasmine tripped on a loose stone in the pavement.

Alina stopped. "Are you okay?"

"Yes," the doctor replied, holding her bag close. "I

didn't want to break the vials." She lifted the flap and peeked in. "Still intact."

"Alina!" Gordo waved from across the street corner near the M entrance. Min was jumping up and down, motioning frantically with her arm.

"What's the hurry?" Jasmine asked.

"I don't know." Alina glanced over her shoulder. Across the plaza, a GATV was parked at the foot of the stairs leading up to Genodyne. She squinted. If it was a DV vehicle, it could only mean…

Her brother yelled her name again. Gordo's eyes met hers, his expression frantic. A pang grew in her stomach. What had he done?

A thundering crack reverberated through the air. Alina whirled around, looking for lightning. But the ground shook, and a deafening roar overtook her ears. A blast wave punched her in the chest. She fell to her side, covering her head. Jasmine was on the ground next to her. A few seconds later, dust and small stones rained from the sky down on them.

Coughing, Alina couldn't hear herself. A buzz grew in her ears that turned into a high-pitched ringing. She shook her head. Tugging on her earlobes cleared one ear but the other still rang.

Jasmine was saying something to her.

"Alina!"

She rubbed her ear again, and the ringing abated.

"Are you okay?"

Dust tickled her throat. She brought her fist to her mouth, coughing. "I think so." Rubbing her eyes, she heaved herself up.

Across the plaza, black smoke poured out of the corner of Genodyne's top floor.

Chapter 39

The elevator doors opened. Chance stood in front of his mother while Sergeant Rufalo and Corporal Martin flanked her. Chance had left Lieutenant Harding to deal with the protest at City Hall once the alert battalion had arrived. The underground tunnel leading to Genodyne's research area stretched before them. A blue light flashed overhead, but the alarm faded.

Chance stepped out cautiously. He touched his comm bar by his ear and spoke to the Guardian he posted in the lobby. "Tunnel clear. Any sign of the kronosapiens?"

His comm bar crackled. "Sir, there's a breach inside the reproduction vault. Lights indicate forced entry. Do you want me to send a team to check it out?"

Chance cursed to himself. He barely had enough manpower to secure the building perimeter, leave a look-out, and keep a personnel security detail close to his mother. "Check-in with Lieutenant Harding for C.H. status. As soon as he can release a squad, have him send it over."

The vault lay one level up from their location, directly underneath the building. Chance tried not to think about what kind of havoc the kronosapiens were causing in the vault, but at least they were not on the same floor as his mother. "Move out and clear the area," he said to Rufalo.

The sergeant obeyed and signaled to Corporal Martin to withdraw their microwave pistols from their holsters. Martin's movements were jerky since they entered the building, but Chance selected him after the stint in the laboratory a few weeks ago, and his knowledge of the kronosapiens. After the incident with Kora attacking the medical team a few weeks prior, he'd also issued his team maximum force weapons.

As the men hurried up the tunnel, Chance fell in step alongside his mother. "Tell me about the Phoenix Protocol."

"Come. I'll bring you to the cryo chamber." She hastened her stride.

"Cryo chamber?" He furrowed his brow. The cryopods were used long ago for spaceflight and had no medical application that Chance knew of at Genodyne. Or at least he didn't see any all the times that he accompanied her inside the building.

His team went ahead of them and rounded the corner by the tunnel's exit, momentarily out of sight.

"It's the sealed room beyond the foyer. We have to stop Ms. Silver from going in there," she said.

He glanced over his shoulder, checking that no one followed them. "Cryo room? What are they using it for?"

She lowered her voice. "This has to stay secret. It's where Duncan Ambrose is kept."

Chance halted. "What on Eamine are you talking about?" *The founder is dead,* he told himself. "His public memorial stated that his remains would be interred behind the waterfall."

"Well, the facility was built behind the waterfall—" she gestured ahead "—but he specifically requested cryosleep during the twilight of his life until Genodyne found a way to revive him."

Shaking his head, Chance bore his gaze into her. "Then why have the memorial?"

"It was his idea since Phase Three research was kept secret and could take decades to come to fruition." She snorted. "He still had time left, according to doctors, but Ambrose thought resurrection would be less risky if he wasn't too weakened."

"That's what Phase Three was all for?" Chance's jaw opened. *Revival* was the original name of the product, he recalled.

"Initially. But I developed my own vision, and Genodyne's board agreed with my plan." She shook her head. "I should have never asked for Ms. Silver to be reinstated." His mother resumed her pace. "She's trying to sideline me and tilt the field toward Genodyne. That woman is getting back at me for laying the early failures at her feet."

He slowed near the tunnel's exit. "Are you telling me what I think you're implying?" The blue light in the tunnel flashed, throwing an occasional strobe over the white walls.

His mother sniffed. "Yes. The Phoenix Protocol is meant to awaken Duncan Ambrose when Genodyne finds a way to extend his life. And the Phase Three supply of stem cells is that solution."

They arrived in the foyer, and Chance held up his hand. His mother stopped. As he waited for the other two officers to return, he gazed at the bust of Alpheios's founder. Ambrose's statue peered out the window at the solid ice wall. Chance gave his head another shake, trying to comprehend the enormity of his mother's revelation.

"Damn," she said.

"What is it?"

"We're too late." She pointed at the sealed door with light overhead. "Look."

The thick, metal vault door was still shut, and its lever flushed against the wall. "The light is green. Isn't it usually red?"

"Yes. The revival sequence has begun." Her gloved fingers pulled at one another.

The two officers appeared from around the corner. "We found Daxmen just inside the doorway of the observation room. Looks like he was trying to escape," the sergeant said.

Martin gulped. "He was attacked badly."

"Any other casualties?" Chance asked.

"One attendant is still alive. She's unconscious in there," Rufalo said.

"Sign of any of the baby kronosapiens?"

"No, sir," he replied.

Chance pointed at Martin. "Come with me to help the attendant. She'll tell us what happened." He faced Rufalo. "Stay with the chancellor. Do not leave your post."

"Chance, I must—" his mother said.

"Do *not* leave this area." He summoned his sternest voice. "Stay with Rufalo for just a few minutes. You need one of Daxmen's techs to run the Phase Three mass production, remember?"

She scowled and crossed her arms. His mother tapped her heeled boot on the floor.

At least she listened to him for a change. Chance swept around the corner with Martin.

At the entryway to the observation room, he

carefully stepped over Daxmen's corpse. The doctor's shirt was heavily stained with crimson, and a small pool of blood had formed under him. The stench of iron floated into Chance's nostrils. A gash in the doctor's neck bore deep claw marks.

Through the bay windows, the deserted lab below showed a warped metal gate wrenched away from the far end of wall. Clumps of rock surrounded the gate's anchor points. The bassinet was also empty.

A female attendant lay in the doorway of the control room. It was Zelda, Daxmen's assistant. A bruise covered her cheek. Chance crouched and snapped his fingers in front of her face. While her chest rose lightly, she didn't respond.

"Check for ammonia inhalants." Chance pointed at the nearby medicine cabinet.

Corporal Martin rummaged around the drawers. "Here, sir." He handed over a thumb-sized capsule.

Holding it over her nose, Chance snapped the capsule and brought his other elbow across his face.

After a second, Zelda's eyelashes fluttered. Slowly, she moaned. He helped her sit up, and she rubbed her head.

"Do you remember what happened?"

Her hand shot out, and she grabbed his arm. Gasping, Zelda tried to speak.

"It's okay. We're here now, Zelda." His arm supported her back. "Do you remember what happened?"

Her eyes roamed over him and the other officer. "Ash and Kora…" she said breathlessly.

"They're not here. You're safe now." Chance kept his voice even. "What happened?"

She twitched. “Ash. The bone marrow transplant was a success. But he’s so much stronger now since he recovered. He was able to use his powers to crack the giltspar rock around the gate, and then he forced it open. But Kora…” she shuddered.

“Kora what?” Chance prodded.

“Kora went right for Doctor Daxmen. Ash wrapped the babies in a sheet and took them. I thought she’d kill me after she was done with him. That’s all I remember.” Zelda clung to his forearm, trembling.

“Do you know where the Phase Three serum is? The one containing the kronosapiens’ blood work?”

She nodded. “Daxmen kept the vials in his office.”

“Can you mass produce it?”

“I…I don’t know.” She rubbed her forehead. “It’s a rather complicated process that requires use of our bioreactors.”

He helped Zelda up. When she stood, Martin handed her an ice pack that he found in a cabinet. As she pressed it against her cheek, Chance said, “You’ll check that the vials are still in Daxmen’s office so Genodyne can carry on his work. Corporal Martin will escort you. Many in the city are still sick, you understand?”

Weary, she nodded. “Yes, I know.”

He signaled Martin. “Rejoin once Daxmen’s office has been secured.”

Martin helped Zelda hobble out. At the doorway, she winced and looked away from Daxmen’s body.

They left the lab and entered the foyer. As the officer led the tech down the tunnel, Chance swore. His mother was gone. Rufalo stood in front of the cryo chamber door.

“I told you not to leave your post!” Chance said.

"Sir, I didn't!" Rufalo motioned to the door behind him. "But the Chancellor insisted on entering the room and asked me to stand guard." Sweat moistened Rufalo's scalp through his short buzz cut, and he wiped it away. "She's got a mind of her own."

Chance ground his teeth. Of course his mother didn't listen to him. She cared more about the awakening of their relic of a founder than bringing calm back to the city. "I'm going in. Stay alert and come get me immediately if you hear of any movement from the kronosapiens."

"Yes, sir. No one else will pass."

Taking in a deep breath, Chance lifted the metal lever and swung the heavy door open.

****

In the small cryo room, swirls of frosty air bit at Chance's face. The entire room was like a large meat locker. A long, metal capsule lay at the front of the room with its lid open. His mother and Ms. Silver hovered nearby. An attendant leaned over the capsule and lifted a scrawny old man in a hospital gown. The tech set him down on a nearby diagnostic chair.

Ambrose's bald head and pinched mouth were recognizable. He blinked rapidly.

Chance slowed his gait and approached his mother's side. "Mother," he whispered.

She lifted a palm, and he quieted, uncertain of what would come next. Ms. Silver held a triumphant smile.

The old man croaked. "Do you have the remedy?"

Ms. Silver said, "We do, but there's been a complication."

"What complication?" Ambrose's voice was scratchy as the sensors on the diagnostic chair turned blue.

"We created a new species for directed evolution," Jade said. "They generate enough stem cells for tissue regeneration and life extension."

"Directed evolution?" Ambrose's face resembled a pickle, wrinkled and grooved throughout. "A worthy endeavor. But what is the complication?"

His mother fingered her suit hem. "The new species—kronosapiens—have escaped their holding area. We'll have them back in short order, I assure you."

"But our operations director who oversaw the program, Dr. Daxmen, has been killed by one of the kronosapiens," replied Ms. Silver, giving Jade Graylin the side-eye. "It appears they're much stronger than us."

Ambrose's head rested back, and he sighed. "Nothing worthwhile is without sacrifice. You've awakened me at an opportune moment."

"His vitals are returning to normal," the tech said to Ms. Silver.

Her smile grew. "Do you hear that Mr. Ambrose? You're recuperating nicely." Her tone dripped of honey. "The board thought we could use your leadership for the final stages of producing and distributing the final cure."

The founder lifted his head. "And you may tell them as soon as I've recovered, I'll return to my leadership post as head of the company." His gaze rested on the gold pin of the chancellor's suit. "So Jade, you turned out not to be completely worthless."

She hissed through her teeth. "No thanks to you."

Chance stepped forward. He wouldn't stand by while this artifact spouted insults at his mother. "Perhaps you should rest. We'll handle the kronosapiens." As soon as the alert battalion dispersed the crowd at City Hall, he would prepare a team of men with Lieutenant Harding to hunt them.

Ambrose's sunken eyes settled on Chance. "Well, who do we have here?" His head turned back toward Jade. "Is it possible you made some decent decisions with my lineage unlike that conniving geneticist who raised you?"

A rush of blood descended into Chance's head, and he shifted his weight. "Mother, what is he talking about?"

Her mouth twisted. "Chance, do you remember I told you that my mother raised me?"

"You said your father abandoned you." An ache grew in his gut.

"He did. Chance, you are your father's son. A Guardian, as I've always told you." She motioned to the old man. "But your grandfather—"

"Don't say it." His stomach pitted. "Are you about to tell me the inconceivable?"

"You haven't told him, have you?" Ambrose said. "Then I shall."

Chance swallowed hard. Maybe the old man would tell him the truth.

"Your mother wasn't the typical product of two parents. I used several sponsors' DNA to produce the best child. The majority of the DNA, of course, was my own since I had no heirs." He plucked at his hospital smock. "But the geneticist who was supposed to oversee the program and raise the child lied to me. I wanted a son, but she wanted a girl." He jeered at the last word.

His mother's voice was shrill. "I've succeeded where you have not."

"Have you?"

"I advanced this biotechnology as chancellor of this city, and history will credit me for it." She pointed at her chest, her voice a barely controlled rage. "I'll be responsible for humanity transcending its limitations here on this planet."

A swell of sickness gripped Chance. His father was a courageous and admired Guardian commander. But his mother…he placed a hand over his stomach. Save Eamine. How could she lie to him about his grandfather?

Ms. Silver said coolly, "We should focus on the cure, which is now in jeopardy." Her hands behind her back, she turned to Ambrose. "I will advise the board to prepare themselves for your leadership. They will welcome your counsel now that we are so close."

"I'll deal with the security situation." Chance stiffened. At the moment, he'd rather fight the kronosapiens than stay in this refrigerator of a room. "For the good of the city."

A crafty grin emerged from the old man. "Ahhh…perhaps you are a worthy descendant. I look forward to getting to know you, Chance. That is your name, correct?"

Chance's head jerked in his direction. "Yes."

His mother pushed back her bob. "I was about to tell you—"

"Save it." His voice went flat. "I've sent Corporal Martin to help Daxmen's assistant secure his office since he kept the serum in there. Once we confirm it, you can inform the council that the company is ready to mass produce it to save the city."

"I will be the first to receive it," Ambrose interjected.

Ignoring him, Chance battled back bile rising in his

throat. He blinked, focusing on the woman who raised him. "Please, Mother. The city needs you right now." His voice strained. He would deal with Ambrose's disclosure later. No feelings of kinship fell over him about the old man. Ambrose was an elderly, sharp-tongued stranger to him.

A gleam of composure overtook Jade Graylin, and she squared her shoulders at Duncan Ambrose. "Ms. Silver will attend to you. I have a city that requires healing." Exhaling, Chance followed her to the exit.

"Don't forget, I run the company! I get it first!" Ambrose squawked.

Neither of them turned around.

****

When the elevator arrived at Genodyne's ground level, an incoming call from the lobby sentry buzzed Chance's link. He touched his comm bar by his ear.

"Sir, a squad from the alert battalion has arrived. They've entered the building."

"Good. Send them down to the reproductive vault."

He exited the elevator with his mother and Sergeant Rufalo.

"The motion sensors in the reproduction vault have ceased picking up movement. Do you still want me to send them in?"

Chance slowed his pace to the lobby. "Any reports of the kronosapiens location?"

"No, sir."

The creatures still had to be somewhere in the building. All entry points and exits had been locked down. "Have them conduct a sweep, starting with the vault. The tunnel is clear, we just came from there." He pointed at Rufalo. "Check out the lobby, and ready the vehicle."

The sergeant hurried ahead while Chance scanned the corner and hallway. "Mother, get behind me." For once, his mother complied, and he drew his microwave pistol from his holster.

He touched his comm bar. "Martin, status."

A voice replied, "Sir, on the third floor. Daxmen's office is secured. But…"

"But what?"

"The assistant said Ash's vials are missing. Kora's blood work is still here, but the ones that belong to Ash are gone."

Chance's hand twitched. "Copy. Rejoin in the lobby."

"What is it?" His mother asked.

His gaze swept the hall as he moved forward. "Some of the vials are missing, specifically from the male, Ash. But we still have Kora's stem cell blood."

His mother rubbed her head. "I'm going to have to recommend someone to replace Daxmen. Or Ms. Silver will get to the board first and install someone loyal to her."

He glanced back. "Later. I want to get you out of this building and home to your residence where Martin and Rufalo can stand guard."

She replied, "All right. But Chance, I want you to come over later so we can discuss Duncan Ambrose."

A pang developed in his forehead. He didn't need this distraction right now. "I have to take care of the security situation first."

Up ahead, the hall opened to the tiled lobby. Rufalo waved at them. Chance touched his mother's arm, and they hurried in that direction.

At the lobby, the squad arrived that Harding had dispatched. The group swept past them, their helmets and vests on, and weapons drawn. "We'll find them, Captain," one of the men called out as they headed for the corner stairwell. "We'll sweep bottom-to-top until we do."

Rufalo stood by the information desk manned by the sentry. He touched his comm bar, confirming a message. "Sir, they have Chariot's GATV ready."

"Good." Chance secured his sidearm. The squad would take care of the threat. His last task was to get his mother home.

The elevator doors at the far end of the lobby opened, and Corporal Martin emerged. He strode toward them.

The sentry looked up from the alarm panel. "Sir, I'm getting movement on the top floor."

"Top floor?" Chance ran through the implications. Did the creatures move through the stairwells?

"That's where the board meets," his mother said. "I should speak with them if they're still here."

Chance whipped around. "That's not a good idea."

"Son." She placed both hands on his arms. "I need to ensure Genodyne can still produce the cure. You said yourself the city needs it."

"Ma'am, the board left a few minutes ago. They adjourned," the sentry replied.

"Redirect the squad to the top floor," Chance said to the sentry. "Mother—"

A deafening boom erupted. Rufalo ducked. Chance shoved his mother behind the information desk. Shielding her with his body, he crouched as ceiling debris hailed down on them. The entire building shook.

A rain shower dampened his hair, and a different alarm sounded.

A shrieking tone resonated throughout the lobby. Sprinklers in the lobby ceiling activated. Dust and ceiling particles covered the tiles. Both Martin and Rufalo hunkered by the desk. But the area was clear.

He stood and waved at his men. “We have to go.” Chance’s voice echoed in his hearing. He ground his jaw, clearing his ears. He’d find the perpetrators that did this while his mother was in the building.

Chance led everyone toward the glass doors. His mother needed to get into the armored vehicle ASAP.

Chapter 40

Columns of smoke billowed from the top floor of Genodyne. Alina faced her brother who waited across the street by the M stop. His mouth was set, his green eyes reflecting angry satisfaction. The explosion was no accident.

She shook her head and mouthed a single word to him. *Why?*

"C'mon!" He swung his arm overhead again, urging her to leave. Min tugged at him.

Around them, a small crowd trickled into the plaza. They were shouting and pointing at Genodyne. A few carried signs.

"Where did these people come from?" Jasmine asked.

"It must be some of the protestors from City Hall," Alina replied.

On the front terrace, a Guardian was frantically speaking into his comm bar. It was the officer who'd tried to stop her and Jasmine from entering earlier. Two of his squad hurried to the plaza to stop the protestors.

While the men yelled at the gathering crowd, trying to disperse them, another Guardian hustled out the glass doors of Genodyne. The red stripe on his arm indicated that he was a sergeant.

She sucked in her breath at the next person who emerged from the building. Chance held Jade Graylin's arm, urging her to the steps, where the GATV waited at the bottom. Another young Guardian flanked Jade. The officer-in-charge of the perimeter ran over and stopped Chance, gesturing at the building. As Chance spoke to him, the sergeant and young Guardian escorted Jade Graylin down the stairs.

"Look!" Min's arm raised up.

Through the rising smoke, a figure materialized on the roof. A woman approached the edge. Alina began to sweat in the warming day. Kora stood atop Genodyne in the same cropped tank top and loose pants she wore back in the lab. Her skin gleamed gray. The kronosapien watched the scene below, her blue eyes aflame.

Alina cupped her hands around her mouth. "Chance!"

He did not hear her, focused on his animated co-worker by the DNA sculpture.

"Who is that?" A protestor shoved one of the squad members and was wrestled to the ground. His comrades beat the officer's back.

"Chance!" She lurched a few steps forward and stumbled.

His head lifted, and he gazed out at the plaza.

Alina called out again. "The roof!"

His brow wrinkled. He still couldn't hear her.

She pointed, and he glanced up. But he was too close to the building to view Kora.

The sergeant opened the GATV door for the chancellor. She was still climbing down the stairs with the young officer next to her.

Kora leapt off the roof, her knee high in the air. Her sturdy figure landed with a thud in front of the GATV.

A woman among the protestors shrieked.

The sergeant slammed the door shut and rushed Kora. A blur of motion between them, and his body hurtled through the air over the hood of the vehicle. He bounced off the plaza stones.

"Save Eamine!" Jasmine covered her mouth.

With a hop, Kora was on the same step as the chancellor and young Guardian.

Chance drew his microwave pistol and aimed at Kora.

She held out a palm. A jolt flew his way. He ducked behind the DNA sculpture, firing.

Her skin hardened to dark brown. His shot missed Kora by centimeters and skimmed the top of the GATV. The vehicle vibrated.

Screams broke out. People shouted and ran out of the plaza.

The kronosapien kept her hand raised. She directed it toward the sculpture. Another jolt. The helix glowed and sizzled. Chance fell back, stung from his proximity to it.

Alina yelled. "Chance!"

On the ground, he twitched and rolled onto his side.

She sped toward him, but a man dashing out of the plaza clipped her shoulder. She staggered and threw her hands out.

The young Guardian raised his baton and swung. Kora blocked the weapon with her forearm. Her other fist plowed into his chest. He gasped as he fell back.

Jade scrambled to reach the vehicle. Kora's skin returned to gray, and she snatched the back of Jade's suit. The kronosapien wrapped her hand around the chancellor's throat. Kora lifted Jade Graylin high overhead.

The chancellor's legs thrashed as Kora squeezed her neck.

Alina's hands went clammy.

"The M!" Jasmine urged her. "We have to get out of here."

But Alina sprinted toward Genodyne. She had to help Chance survive. He was getting back up on one knee.

About halfway across the plaza, she heard it. A disgusting crack as Kora broke Jade Graylin's neck.

Alina halted.

The kronosapien released the chancellor. Her body fell onto the steps, limp. Chance's face contorted. A harrowing howl emerged from him.

Jasmine grabbed Alina's sleeve. "Stop! She's too strong for us!"

Alina's pulse raced. "But Chance—"

Gordo had sprinted across the plaza and caught up to them. "He can take care of himself! We have to go!" He clamped his hand over her arm.

A smug smile appeared on Kora's face. She leapt again, touching down on the nearby sidewalk. Her arms a blur, she ran and disappeared in the direction of the riverwalk.

Chance was on his feet, clambering down the steps to his mother.

"I'm not kidding. We have to move." Gordo's firm tone caught Alina's attention.

Speechless, she glanced at Jasmine. Worry filled the doctor's face, her hand on the messenger bag slung over her torso. *The serum*, Alina thought. She could not abandon her mother.

Across the plaza, Min hung back, throwing her

hands up. The implications of what her brother and Min had done—the Guardians would immediately arrest him once they learned he was a suspect.

Robotically, Alina nodded and scampered to the station with him and the doctor.

After she crossed the street, she paused outside the M station.

On the steps, Chance hovered over his mother, cradling her head. His neck tendons strained, his face full of wrath.

"Alina!" Her brother waved at her from inside the M entrance.

Chance rose to his full height, his fists balled by his side. He bolted off the steps and sprinted in the direction that Kora left.

Her heart hammering, she joined her brother.

****

In the maglev pod, frantic whispers were exchanged between Min and Gordo. Numb, Alina glanced at Jasmine next to her on the bench. Pewter-colored dust trickled from the doctor's hair.

Blinking, Alina wiped drywall fragments from Jasmine's purple suit along her shoulders. Plaster bits and tiny pebbles covered Alina's suit the Commandant had given her. Her throat ached from inhaling ash, and from her screams across the plaza.

Gordo's hand tightened around the overhead strap. He steadied his green eyes on her. "You didn't tell me about the other serum."

She rose and faced him. "Why?"

"You know the answer to that." His tone was gruff.

"People could have been killed. They *were* killed." The snap of the chancellor's neck still rankled her ears.

She held zero affection for Jade Graylin, but Chance's expression in that moment was seared into her mind.

"We waited until the board left." He held out a palm as if to stop her.

"They didn't deserve to get off easy—that was your idea." Min folded her arms. "But bonus points for getting rid of the chancellor."

Quivering, Alina grappled with restraint. She wanted to grab Gordo and shake him, to yell until he submitted to reasoning and sense. "What were you hoping to accomplish?"

"A change," he replied through his teeth.

The slight bump of the pod rocked her back on a heel. How could she say she was any better? Especially after the rebellion she took part in three years ago?

"But there were patients in the ER," Jasmine said. "Innocent people."

"Yeah? My uncle was innocent, too." Min's voice trembled. "He trusted Genodyne. But he didn't matter to them. All the doctors did was dull his pain at the end." Her tone grew bitter. She stepped closer to Jasmine.

Alina blocked Jasmine, glaring at Min. "I don't know you."

"Enough." Gordo sandwiched himself between them. "They're not at fault," he said to his companion.

Min raised her chin. "They're going to expose us."

"No, they will not." Gordo swiveled his head back. "You won't, will you, Lina?"

Grinding her teeth, Alina's insides twisted. His stare bore into her, but a slight pleading appeared in his eyes. "Don't tell Mom."

She scowled. Dammit to Eamine, he deserved a thrashing. But he knew she would never betray him.

The pod lurched to a stop at the City Center, and the door slid open.

Min hopped onto the platform, followed by Gordo.

“Where are you going?”

“Tell Jakob and Mom I’m staying with teammates for a training camp, okay?”

“Gordo—wait!” Alina’s hand braced the door.

He gave her a slight smile. “You get the serum to Mom. You always know what to do.” Gordo motioned his head to Min, and they disappeared from view.

The door bumped against Alina’s hand again. Releasing it, she allowed it to close. Recalling all those times Gordo left with his gym bag, she realized where he was going. The public didn’t have access to his team’s athletic facilities. He could hide Min there.

She resumed her seat. “Jas—”

“You don’t have to say it. I heard nothing.” The doctor clutched her bag. “I just want to get this to Linette.” She gave her head a slight shake. “I have to do this now, or I can’t reverse her condition.”

Closing her eyes, Alina pressed the back of her head into the window. One more stop until the Channel District.

She saw Chance again holding his mother. Her arms prickled. Strong and unharmed, he’d chased after Kora. A sour slick churned in her gut. Taking in a few deep breaths, she leaned forward.

“Are you okay?” asked the doctor.

Outside the pod, both suns climbed high in the afternoon. CynCorp’s violet tower swung into view. It glistened, its glass elevator sparkling as it ascended. The ice-covered river behind the building anchored the city. She glimpsed the edge of CynCorp’s tarmac with a few small figures near the parked hover-jet.

“Mandin?” A tingle ran through her. She pressed her cheek against the glass, but the tarmac vanished as the pod descended to the Channel District station. They disembarked and took the escalators down to the street.

****

Outside the M station, Alina shielded her eyes from the brightness. Plunging forth into the slush, she crossed the street. Dr. Bellamy accompanied her. Unease gripped Alina, and she inserted her comm bar into her ear. Checking her link, she noticed a message from Jakob’s office. She dialed his direct number.

He answered. “Yes?” A mechanical noise hummed in the background.

“We have the serum. Where is my mother?”

His voice was hard to hear. “At the LZ. We’re taking her home. By the way, Kiean is here.”

She halted. “Kiean is with you?”

“Yes. He’s with the children.”

“Alina?” Jasmine waited a few paces ahead of her.

Swallowing, Alina said, “We’ll meet you there in five.”

Kiean was here. In Alpheios. And Jakob said “children,” meaning, Kiean brought his sister. Rubbing her forehead, she confronted how on Eamine she would explain her circumstances to him. The memory of Chance’s kiss lingered. Her cheeks flushed as they approached the Channel District buildings.

Icicles from the trees dripped as they hastened along the sidewalk. The CynCorp building loomed on the corner.

A small clump of residents headed for the riverwalk. Alina and Jasmine hurried across the street and trailed them. CynCorp's building stood the tallest, its silver spheres marking its broad pavilion.

Someone from the crowd shouted.

The glass elevator on the CynCorp building was descending, and a woman stood atop it. Kora surveyed the area below.

"Come on!" Alina dashed to the stone steps of CynCorp, and they scrambled up past the silver spheres.

Kora landed five meters in front of them. Panting, Alina's chest tightened. Nothing she could use, nowhere she could hide came to mind.

People pointed at the kronosapien from the street.

Kora tilted her chin and observed Jasmine. "You. You were there."

The doctor backed away, shaking her head. "I was just observing."

Smoldering blackness overtook Kora's face. "He took my baby. You were there." Razor-sharp claws emerged from her fingertips.

Unable to speak, a bead of cold sweat dribbled down Alina's back. She stood before the creature. Perhaps if Kora attacked her first, Jasmine would have a chance to escape and get the serum to Linette.

A command echoed from across the street. "Don't move, or I'll shoot!"

Kora's skin thickened into a brown hide as she spun around.

A surge from Chance's energy pistol hit Kora. The kronosapien screeched and staggered by a silver sphere.

A groan of metal reverberated, and Kora hefted the sphere above her head. Facing the street, she hurtled it toward Chance.

Alina grabbed the doctor's arm, and they barreled to

the front doors.

Jasmine tugged on the handle. “It’s locked!” She pounded on the glass.

“Security must have locked down.” Alina glanced over her shoulder.

Kora was gone.

Gulping, she craned her head. No sign of Chance, either. “Around back.”

They crept around the corner, staying close to the walls. The glass elevator remained empty resting on the ground floor. Alina stopped when she saw the silver orb lodged in a recessed doorway across the street. A glimpse of a black uniform peeked out. They darted over.

Chance lay unconscious behind the object, a lump already forming on his forehead. He must have ducked into the area when Kora threw the sphere.

Alina touched his arm. “Chance?” Unresponsive, his chest still rose. She called his name again.

The doctor touched his neck. “He’s unconscious.”

“Where’s his weapon?” Alina searched the pavement, but no pistol lay nearby.

“Not sure. But I can help him.” Jasmine opened her bag.

A man yelled something from behind the CynCorp building, from the direction of the LZ.

Alina lowered her voice. “Stay here.” She scrambled to the other side of the doorway.

A familiar scream pierced the air—it was her mother.

Alina’s gut wrenched. A narrow ladder rested against CynCorp’s elevated landing platform. A few seconds later, a man’s body hurtled over. Jakob hit the ground, dazed.

Climbing up, Alina saw the hover-jet on the LZ, its nose pointed at the river. Larger than the regular jets, its body took up most of the platform. Still at rest, it levitated about a meter off the ground. An auxiliary power unit was plugged into the rear of the craft, humming.

She rounded the tail and nearly collided into a hydraulic unit. On the other side, Kiean held her mother's arm near the jet's open door. Alina's heart leapt. He stood there reassuringly, urging her mother onboard. The pilot motioned at them. Linette trembled all over. Syriah and Mandin fidgeted nearby.

Kora emerged from around the nose.

"Kiean!"

He glanced in Alina's direction.

She frantically motioned with her arms. "Behind you!"

Syriah shrieked at the sight of the kronosapien. She pulled Mandin, and they fled underneath the hover-jet.

As Kora stalked Kiean, her skin thickened into a dark hide. Kiean shoved his hand into a nearby tool bag underneath the craft. He swung a wrench at her head.

She batted it away and punched him in the stomach. He fell to a knee. Linette stepped back and tripped, ending on her rear. Her raised arm blocked her face.

Alina crossed the pavement, trying to reach her mother. Kora stood over Linette and raised her palm. Her skin darkened into slate, and an arc of electricity danced on her hand.

Her skin. Kora's skin changed as a defensive measure. "No!" Alina threw herself in front of her mother. Flinching, she closed her eyes the moment Kora cast out a jolt.

Her teeth grinding together, Alina blinked. The current rippled down her suit in a blue sizzle and dissipated. Her suit carried its own protection. The Commandant's words came to mind. *Will also protect you from the local wildlife should you stumble upon them, and they turn defensive.*

Kora's blue eyes widened, then flitted to the gray patches on Linette's face. "Is this to whom my blood was given? This weak, pitiful human?"

Alina's throat hurt. "She's my mother."

A small clanking noise came from the power unit on the other side of the hover-jet. The creature's head craned in that direction, then a dangerous smile crossed her face. "Who do we have here?"

"We mean you no harm."

"I sense…their air." Kora passed her by. She strode in the direction of the tail, but Kiean was on his feet.

He fired a torch pen into Kora's shoulder. A flame burst forth, and she screeched. She whirled around, but he fired the tool again. Kora leapt back. She took cover by the craft's rear, out of sight.

"Mom, are you okay?"

"Yes." Her mother's face was ashen. "Who was that? Jakob tried to remove her."

Kiean helped Linette stand. "Where are the kids?"

"Get my mother onboard!" Alina sprinted after Kora. CynCorp's glass doors were about ten yards behind them. If she couldn't get them on the craft, perhaps they could get indoors.

Tripping on the end of a hydraulic hose, rough asphalt slammed into Alina's kneecaps. Pressed on the deck, she glimpsed behind the power unit where the children huddled on their hands and knees. Her giltspar ring gleamed on Syriah's index finger.

Kora loomed above the children. Mandin screamed and grabbed Syriah's hand. The immediate daylight around them rippled, and the children vanished. Aching, Alina stood by the craft's tail.

The kronosapien gazed at the empty spot. Her eyes met Alina's. Shaking, Alina inched closer. Even if she bought the children a few minutes to escape, it was worth it.

Kora frowned. "Where are they?"

"I don't know."

A small yelp came near the front of the jet. The tool bag shifted, and the children materialized as Mandin stumbled underneath the fuselage.

Kiean pushed Linette onboard. "Syriah!"

Syriah grabbed Mandin's hand. Her red curls blurred, and they disappeared again.

What on Eamine was happening to the children?

A faint smile pulled at Kora's lips. "They're like us."

Alina's heart skidded. "Take me instead." She hoped her death would be quick.

"Your air is not the same. Nor do you have their powers to give." The kronosapien bent under the hovercraft, carefully making her way to the children's last location.

The children reappeared, huddled behind Kiean, clinging to his thighs.

"Halle!" He waved his arm. "Threat!"

A shattering crash pierced the air. A silver dynamo bolted through the glass doors. Kiean swept the children in his arms as Halle hurtled past him.

Halle stood between them and Kora. The bot thrust

the heel of her palm into the kronosapien's chest. Sparks flew from Halle's hand, stunning Kora. The creature's skin thickened.

Kora backed away and shook her head. Glaring, she lunged. She wrapped her arms around Halle's shoulders, but the bot gripped her waist. Halle's legs blurred as she hoisted Kora in the air. Below the tarmac, Kora bounced off the ground. The kronosapien appeared dizzy.

Satisfied, the bot returned to their side. "I must say, my new upgrade has proved worthy."

Alina touched Mandin's face. "Are you hurt?"

He shook his head, brown eyes large. No signs of seizure or injury from him.

"Get onboard!" She gave him a nudge, and Kiean lifted him.

After loading the children, Kiean turned to her. Alina thrust herself into his arms. Clutching him, she pressed against his strong body, inhaling his scent of fresh rain.

A wide grin spread across his face. "Finally found you."

She choked out a laugh. Seeing the children cloistered against her pale mother in the back of the hover-jet, she squeezed his arm. "Jakob's still down there." She checked the edge of the LZ.

Kora was shaking her head. She lurched up, a hand to her thigh. Her mouth was slashed tight. "You!" She pointed at her. "I will bury you!" As she took a step forward, her skin hardened.

A blast from behind—Kora staggered.

Behind her, Jasmine's arm was extended, a microwave pistol in her hand.

Kora circled the doctor with caution, arcs of

electricity dancing on her curled hand.

Chance towered behind Jasmine. "You and I will finish this." He pointed his baton at Kora.

A sharp whistle sounded in the distance.

On the river bridge a short distance away, Ash waited. A sheet was slung around his torso, and two small heads peeked out from it. His offspring's bumps held snugly against his body.

Kora scowled at the doctor and Chance, then sprinted down the riverwalk.

Jasmine thrust the pistol at Chance and crouched by Jakob.

Dark rage overcame Chance's face.

"Chance!" Alina hopped, waving at him.

He bolted after Kora, his arms pumping. A lead weight sank in Alina's chest.

Gulping, she pulled Jakob and the doctor up the ladder. As they boarded the jet, Alina moved to the front of the tarmac for a better view.

Upriver, Kora stepped onto the bridge. Ash disappeared into the woods. As she crossed the river, Chance raised his pistol. Kora swiveled around and threw out a jolt. It singed the pistol, knocking it from his hand.

Yelling, Chance swung his baton, and Kora grabbed it. They wrestled over the weapon, moving to the bridge's center.

Wincing, Alina called out to him again.

Kora bashed her forearm across Chance's face. As he staggered back against the bridge's railing, she thrust him over. A cracking reverberated through the air—the ice collapsed under his weight. In a flash, Kora fled into the woods.

Kiean grabbed her shoulder. "Get in the jet. I'll make it back to the penthouse with Halle."

"I can't."

His voice deepened. "I said get in!"

Halle said, "The threat has been disposed of. I like my new neutralizer." The bot held up her hand.

A horrible emptiness filled Alina's chest. "Please, help me with Chance! Kora has thrown him into the river. He's underneath the ice and won't make it."

Kiean's jaw clenched. "Halle, protect the family."

"Right away." The bot climbed onboard. Kiean slammed the door shut. He unplugged the power unit and waved at the pilot to take-off.

Bypassing the ladder, Alina leapt off the LZ.

"Wait! Let me get the tool bag!" Kiean called.

After passing a few buildings, she was winded, but dared not stopping. She raced alongside the frigid, unforgiving river.

Finally, her boots pounded onto the bridge planks. Over the railing, she peered at the hole in the ice. Under the dark water, there was no sign of Chance. She swung a leg over the bridge.

"Alina!" Kiean called out from the riverwalk.

Taking a deep breath, she jumped.

Ice water seared her face like fire. Her head throbbed as if it would explode. But the suit kept her torso and limbs temperate. She kicked and dove into the darkness.

Chapter 41

The river current tugged at her body. Instead of resisting, Alina followed it, peering through the murk. *Save Eamine, don't let Chance be lost.* A shadow appeared before her. She swam closer, the suit warming her chest. Recognizing Chance, she swam behind him, reaching for his back. He was limp.

Chance was heavy, and she fought to keep a hold of the fabric around his shoulder. Frantically, she kicked up. The ice remained solid above and bubbles streamed out of her nose. Cold pounded her head. The rest of her limbs still moved.

Feeling underneath the ice with one hand, she pushed off it while still clutching his suit. Dizziness blurred her vision. A freeze pressed her temples inward, and ice-hot needles penetrated her scalp. She nearly screamed from the pain.

She was suffocating. Her arms trembled as she pushed again underneath the ice. Shaking her head, she fought from passing out in the darkness. She choked on a gulp of water. They were both drowning.

A glow beckoned in the water a little further ahead. A light wand waved, the kind that led a hovercraft through a taxiway. Clamping her mouth shut, she struggled to swim toward it.

Her lungs burned. Her arms ached as she gripped Chance's suit. Reaching for the wand, she grabbed it. A force pulled her up.

Her head broke the river's surface. She sputtered, gasping. Kiean's face was overhead, his upper half dangling from the bridge.

"I've got him. But he's heavy." She heaved with all her might, and Chance's head broke the surface. His eyes were sealed shut, his lips blue.

Kiean grabbed Chance's collar. In his other hand, he held a rope. Quickly, he looped it under Chance's shoulders. "Hold on." Kiean pulled himself up and threw the rope over the railing. Slowly, he hauled Chance's body up.

Freezing, she treaded water. The suit kept her chest warm, but she flailed, trying to move her numbed hands. The rope dropped in front of her. Her fingers managed to grasp it. Kiean dragged her up onto the bridge.

Gasping, she coughed, laying on the wood planks. Chance sprawled limp beside her. She rolled to a sitting position. "Is he okay?"

Kiean's lips pressed together.

"Chance?" His cheek was clammy to the touch. His skin appeared blanched.

"CPR. Can you do the chest compressions?" she asked.

Frustration plagued Kiean's expression, but he nodded. He braced himself over Chance and placed his hands on his sternum. "You count."

Alina counted aloud as she knelt by Chance. At the correct interval, Kiean paused, and she tilted back Chance's head. His lips were deep winter on hers. She blew two breaths into his mouth. They waited. No sign of life.

Kiean kept doing chest compressions. Sickness took

a hold of her. As she counted, her body trembled. She blew twice again. Chance remained motionless.

Both suns shone overhead, warming her back. She rubbed her face and eyes. On the third try of compressions, she whispered. “Please Eamine. Please bring him back.” She bent over and blew two more breaths. Her knees ached as she sat back.

A flicker of movement appeared under Chance’s eyes. His head slowly turned to the side, and he coughed up water. Kiean rolled him over, and Chance’s body shook from coughing.

She pushed her hair back. “Yes! Thank you!”

After a few more coughs, Chance rested back. His dark eyes opened, looking up at her. “Alina?”

“Yes, it’s me.” She smiled and cupped Chance’s head, quivering all over.

Across from them, Kiean’s hazel eyes rested on her face. He didn’t say a word. Instead, his hands curled by his thighs, and his forehead wrinkled.

Chapter 42

The ceiling lights glared in the exam room. Through the glass window, Chance's gaze followed an employee sweeping debris from the hospital floor. His hands rested on hot packs atop his thighs, and the table exuded heat into the back of his calves.

The doctor removed the blanket from his shoulders. "Can you give me a deep breath?"

Although his hospital clothes were dry, Chance's mind remained numb. He vaguely remembered someone loading him into a GATV. It must have been another Guardian who transported him to the ER.

The doctor, a soft-spoken man, repeated his request.

To rid himself of the pest, Chance did as he was asked and deeply inhaled. Next, the doctor shone a pen light into his eyes. "Can you read the first line of that chart on the wall?"

"I'd rather not."

"You may still be in a state of shock, but your speech is clear, which is a good sign. At least you're not slurring your words." The doctor scribbled on his crystal tablet. Around him, a nurse shifted to check the readings on the exam table's monitor. She read them off to the doctor.

They were talking about him, but Chance didn't bother to listen. His mother was dead. All because of that beast—Kora had killed her. He squeezed the hot packs tight. The memory of him chasing her down the river bridge returned. After that, he drew a blank. The doctor informed him that he'd fallen into the river, below the ice. All Chance recalled was when he regained consciousness, Alina's green eyes hovered above, calling his name.

Through the room window, near the corner of the ER counter, a man handed Alina a hot drink. Her hair was wet, and she wrapped her hands around the cup. Upon scrutiny, Chance recognized him. That fellow, Kiean, who she pretended was her fiancé. He must have returned to Alpheios for her.

The doctor prodded Chance again. "Your core temperature is returning to normal. Just relax. I'm going to move your arms now."

Chance allowed the doctor to touch his elbows, bending his arms.

"If you remove the hot packs for me, I'll check your legs."

Pushing them aside, Chance continued to watch Alina in deep conversation with Kiean. The doctor moved his lower leg at the knees. "Do you feel any pain or tingling?"

"No."

"Your muscle tone is good."

"Can I leave now?" Chance picked at his hospital smock. He despised being an invalid.

"Not so fast. You're very lucky." The doctor dimmed the crystal tablet. "Another minute in that water temperature, you could have suffered brain damage. I'd like you to rest here before we release you." He left the room.

"Can I get you anything?" the nurse asked.

"My clothes, please.

"They're still drying." She exited.

Out in the hall, Alina inserted her comm bar by her earlobe and took a call. As she listened, her face filled with hope. She relayed the information to Kiean.

Chance reclined back and closed his eyes. The heat emanating from the table was bringing back his blood circulation. He pictured it scalding him, his skin sizzling as he yelled out and thrashed. How he wished he could feel pain to remind himself he wasn't dead. He may as well be.

A click sounded, and noise from the hall spilled through the door. Chance exhaled, ready to tell the doctor to get lost, and that he wasn't needed. But striding toward him was Kiean. Chance angled up. What did he want?

"How are you feeling?" Kiean asked.

"Better." Chance regarded the man in front of him. He granted that Kiean didn't appear weak, and had Chance not known better, Kiean could have been another Guardian if he ditched the longish haircut. The expeditionary suit that he wore, though, was second-hand. Certainly, he couldn't provide for Alina or Mandin in a better manner than Chance himself could.

"I wanted to thank you for helping Alina with her mother."

"Don't mention it. How is Linette?" Chance asked, wary. Did Kiean want something?

"Sounds like Alina's mother is doing much better. Doctor is reporting her recovery is underway."

"And Alina?"

Kiean glanced out the window, watching her speak during her call. "Relieved, you can say. She mentioned that you saved her life."

A spike rankled Chance. "Yes, I suppose I did help her in that way."

"Anyway, thanks for keeping her safe. I'll tell her that you're feeling better." Kiean turned to the door.

"Of course I kept her safe. I mean, I think she prefers it that way." Chance paused, choosing the right words to slice open his mark. "That's why she spent the night at my place."

Kiean stopped mid-stride before turning back. "What did you say?"

"Didn't she tell you? She stayed the night with me." Chance nodded toward the window. "You can't really blame her. I am, after all, Mandin's father." He watched with pleasure as Kiean's face tightened.

"I see."

His nemesis left the room.

Chance snickered to himself. Out in the hall, he watched Alina end her call as Kiean strode over. While Chance couldn't hear the conversation, Alina's eyes widened, and she spoke with intensity. Kiean's back was to the window, but their voices grew louder. She touched his arm, but he stepped back, shaking his head, and stormed off.

Alina's mouth was open.

Laying back on the table before she could glance his way, Chance folded his arms behind his head. He closed his eyes, smiling to himself. One small victory he'd salvaged for all his efforts.

Finally, a twinge grew in his chest. He shut his eyelids tighter, and his arms tensed. His back teeth ached from being squeezed together. One way or the other, he would hunt Kora down and kill her.

Chapter 43

Medical personnel buzzed around the ER. Alina sipped at the hot cider drink that Kiean had fetched for her. Her hand still shook slightly at what transpired on the LZ.

After they resuscitated Chance, Kiean had carried him off the bridge as she flagged down a GATV. Chance lapsed back into unconsciousness during the ride. When they arrived at the ER, she noticed Kiean scrutinizing her. She'd tried to explain how Kora and Ash were Genodyne's creation. Somehow, her explanation felt inadequate.

Kiean raised an eyebrow at her. "You went into the river after him. Without any rope or anything."

"It's this suit." She held out her arms. "The Commandant gave it to me, and its temperature tolerances are much higher than the old ones." That part was true.

Kiean took in a deep breath. "Still a huge risk." His hazel eyes flitted to her neck. And on her hand, searching for the ring.

Swallowing, she patted back her wet hair, her scalp freezing. "Mandin has grown close to him since our stay here. Chance watched him while I was recovering from the bone marrow transplant." Again, partially true.

Kiean's chin dipped, but he listened. She informed him of how Chance had helped her obtain the cure for her mother, and how he defended her from Kora. As she explained, she could feel a thawing between them, of an invisible boundary dropping. They'd had little opportunity to connect since his arrival.

Her link buzzed. Jakob rarely called her, but his number flashed on the screen. Her comm bar was in the zippered compartment of her upper arm. She placed the drink on the counter and retrieved the earpiece.

She smiled at Kiean. "Doctor Bellamy gave my mother the serum."

"And?"

"So far, so good. The kids are at the penthouse with them."

Kiean glanced back at the exam room. "I'll check on him." He motioned with his head in that direction.

She paused. "Are you sure?"

"Yeah, it'll only take a minute." He walked away.

Returning to her conversation, Jakob said, "I want to thank you. For all you've done."

Alina clutched the counter. "Is the serum working?"

"Linette is already feeling better. Come see for yourself."

At the thought of how she'd treated Jakob during her stay, Alina steadied her voice. "Thank you, too. For everything you've done for my mother."

"Tidewater is still in the picture. Would you like to join us?" Jakob asked.

The question lingered. She stood there while the voices of the trauma staff filled the hallway. "I can't right now. Gordo is also attending training camp. But I'm glad that if anyone is going with my mom, it's you."

"If you change your mind, you and Mandin are more than welcome. Kiean, too. He's an exceptional man who rescued us."

After she ended the call, she tucked the comm bar away. Maybe she could bring up the trip with Kiean. They could stop in Tidewater for a weekend. Eamine knew they could use time together. Glancing up, she spotted Kiean returning. Winter overtook his usually warm eyes.

"Did you spend the night at Chance's place?"

"What are you talking about?" Heat crept up her neck.

"I asked you a question."

She gulped. "There was a riot. I couldn't go home. The streets weren't safe."

"Would you have told me?"

"It wasn't that big a deal." How could she convey that in that moment, Chance was the only one in Alpheios who could help her? "Nothing happened between us!"

Kiean lowered his voice. "Are you sure?"

"Yes, I…" *Crap, did he know about their kiss?* Not once, but twice, Chance had kissed her. And she'd kissed him back. She couldn't move.

A glint of realization appeared in Kiean's eyes. "So something did happen?"

She pushed back wet strands. "It was…" Her voice went hoarse. "Just a moment. Nothing more."

He turned his back to her.

"Where are you going?" She swirled to the side, trying to face him.

His chin tilted down. "Hawk is dead."

Goosebumps pricked her arms. *Hawk?* "How?"

"He went missing in tunnel four, and we found his body. That's why it took me so long to get here. Between that and the blizzard." He frowned. "I guess you didn't get my earlier messages after all."

Questions rippled through her. Tunnel four led to a bottomless pit. "No, I didn't. How's Ione?" All her friends were at Evesborough. And poor little Hudson. No father to hold him.

"Mourning back in Evesborough. Which is where I belong." He placed his hands on his hips. "I have to find Syriah." His voice was gruff.

"She's at the penthouse with Halle and Mandin."

"I know where it is. I looked for you there." His mouth twisted down again. "I have to get outta here. The window for clear weather will close soon. Are you coming with me?"

"You're leaving now?"

"Yes, now!" A flare charged his eyes.

"No, I can't leave yet." Things hadn't fully settled out. She reached for him "Kiean—"

He pulled away. "Then stay. Maybe, then, you can at least be honest with yourself."

Her face stung as he walked out of the hospital. Her feet rooted to the ground.

Medical personnel chattered softly around her. They flitted in the halls, tending to patients.

Alina found the washroom in a far corner of the trauma ward. Sickness stirred, and she fought it away. What on Eamine had she done? She splashed water on her face, trying to stir herself. Kiean was gone.

****

In one of the rooms, Chance waited. His color returned, much better than when they hauled him out of the river.

"How are you feeling?" she asked.

His dark eyes traced her movements. “Been better.”

“I’m glad you’re awake.” Her breathing constricted as she approached the exam table. “Are you sure you’re okay?”

“Tired. I’m not used to failure.” His throat bobbed.

Up close, she observed the slight creases around his eyes. “Chance, I’m sorry about your mother.”

His face went blank, and his gaze fell to the floor.

She touched his arm. “Can I do anything?”

He glanced at her hand on his arm and covered it with his own. A deep exhale escaped his lips. “You’ll have to forgive me, but there’s a matter I must resolve.”

“You can tell me.”

He took her hand and laid it over his sternum. “Allow me this leave. I can’t rest until it’s done.” His shoulders settled back in determination.

The thump of his heartbeat stirred under her palm. A fire grew in his eyes, burning.

Her breath caught. He was going after the kronosapiens. She wanted to comfort him somehow, to take the agony of his loss away. If she could douse his rage in that moment, it might rescue the both of them. But she recalled what happened on the front steps of the building.

A knock on the door sounded.

Her hand slipped off his chest.

Lieutenant Harding entered, carrying a crystal tablet. “Sir, if you’re feeling better, Commander Zinyon wants a statement. But I can come back—” he glanced at her “—if there’s a better time.”

Chance straightened. “You know it’s best to take a statement as soon as possible.”

The lieutenant approached. Slowly, Alina backed

away as Chance watched her. Twilight masked his face. But he turned to the lieutenant.

Alina slipped out.

Chapter 44

The first sun was sinking below the horizon, and the breeze was ice on Alina's cheek. Her feet were heavy on the sidewalk.

Maybe you can at least be honest with yourself. Kiean's words remained. She revealed herself on the bridge earlier. When Chance opened his eyes, she nearly choked from relief. Fear had filled her that they would remain shut forever, and she found the thought intolerable.

Her mother's familiar building came into view. Alina took the elevator up.

When the lift doors opened, the gilded hallway sparkled, opening in front of her.

"Alina!" Half-expecting Halle, it was Dr. Bellamy who greeted her instead. "You finally made it."

"Where's Mandin?"

"In the kitchen with Halle. She's making dinner." Jasmine tucked back a blonde curl.

"And how is Linette?" Alina held her breath.

"Recovering fast with the potency of stem cells I gave her. I knew it would work when I saw the sample under the scope." Jasmine slung her messenger bag over her violet climate suit. "I'll check on her again tomorrow."

"You're leaving?"

The doctor rested her hand on the bag strap. "I have

to tell Genodyne about using Ash's blood instead of Kora's. Your balm furthers the healing process for skin as well. They're so many sick people in the city." A genuine smile appeared on her elegant face. "Linette will be back to her old self in no time."

"You'll stop in even after she gets better, won't you?"

"Yes." Jasmine squeezed Alina's arm. "I won't be a stranger."

"I look forward to it." Conviction filled her as she spoke.

"Me too." The doctor entered the elevator and pressed the button. She waved and beamed at Alina as the doors closed.

Alina raised her hand back. At least she found a new friend.

A musical note sounded from behind the wall. In the living room, her mother perched at the keyboard. One of her fingers lightly pressed a key. Alina slid next to her on the bench.

"Dear, I'm so relieved you're home." Linette gave her a gracious smile. Hints of peach were returning to her mother's skin. The gray patch was a mere outline. Her countenance was completely different from the pale woman she was at the office.

"Are you playing now?"

Her mother pressed the note again. The front of her hands held no dark spots. "I've been thinking about taking it up again." She touched a different key. "I never did thank you for what you did for me." A thoughtful expression fell over her face. "You were always so brave. Even as a child."

"So you're feeling better?"

“I am.” She played another note. “I spoke with Kiean while he waited for you at the office. He’s such an admirable man.”

A grain lodged in Alina’s throat. She stopped breathing.

Her mother’s green eyes searched hers. “But he showed up about an hour ago and left with his sister in a hurry. I asked him to stay for dinner, but he said they had to leave. Is everything okay?”

Alina raised her shoulders and let them drop. Her gaze fell to the keyboard. A burning seared her eyes. Bowing her head, she tilted her chin away.

“Alina, what’s this?” Her mother wrapped her soft arms around her.

Clinging, she buried her crumpled face into her mother’s shoulder.

Her mother’s voice proved soothing. “I’m here.”

“I just wanted you to heal.” Alina struggled to talk. “I couldn’t bear it if—”

“Now, now. My lovely girl, all is better.” Linette stroked her back.

Alina sniffled. She stayed in her mother’s arms, gasping deep breaths. Wiping her eyes, she said, “I’ve ruined everything.”

Linette placed a finger under her chin, gently lifting it, meeting her gaze with a lovely face. “That’s unlikely. We all stumble for a moment.” She brushed Alina’s hair back.

Closing her eyes, Alina allowed her mother to caress her cheek.

“You’re so much like your father. Smart and courageous. You’ll find a way.” A luster appeared in her mother’s green eyes.

Her voice trembled. "But I'm not sure how."

Her mother gave her a sympathetic smile. "I think you need a break. Why don't you and Mandin come to Tidewater with us? We can leave tomorrow after Dr. Bellamy stops in. The ocean will help put you at ease."

She bit her bottom lip. "Okay." A pressure released within as she inched closer.

Her mother played a key again, stronger.

"Mama!" Mandin called. He raced across the living room and leapt into her arms.

Cuddling him in her lap, she hugged him. His warm body sapped away her remaining strain. She thought of how Halle had to search for him with her IR sensors that morning by the river. Then this afternoon, he didn't have a seizure at the LZ; he grabbed Syriah's hand, which displayed her giltspar ring. His powers were always stronger around the mineral. "How's my invisible little man?"

Her son hunched his shoulders. "Sorry, Mama. I scared. I had to go bye-bye."

"Is that what you call it?"

He shrugged. "I don't mean to. I scared." He pouted. "You sad, Mama?"

"A little." Alina let out a sigh.

"Kiean and Syriah left." His dark eyes became long. "They gone. When they come back?"

She pondered his inquiry. The information about Kiean's birth parents lingered. She owed him at least that. Closing her eyes, she'd find a way to tell him. But right now, she didn't want to leave her mother. "I don't know."

Mandin touched her forearm. "I think we see them again."

"Do you?"

Her son nodded. "They come back. I have feeling."

Alina kissed his forehead. "I hope you're right."

Linette smiled at her grandson. "Did your mother ever tell you that I used to sing to her as a little girl?"

A grin spread across his face. "A song?"

"You remember?" Alina asked.

"Of course. You used to love to hear me play." Both of Linette's hands found the keyboard, and she played a chord. Alina smoothed Mandin's curls and inhaled his sweet scent. He smelled like he'd been eating vanilla pudding. Her mother sang, soft and lyrical:

Come back to me
So I can hold onto you my lovely
You're my hope and my pride
My darling by my side
As long as you come back to me.

Acknowledgements

While I believed that Alina's story as a young mother trying to navigate through a tangle of familial relationships would resonate with readers, the novel itself would not have been made possible without the support of many talented individuals. I'm indebted to those who provided editorial feedback to include Morena Stamm, PJ Hoover, Mrs. N., and Ray Murphy. The artistry of Teddi Black gave rise to a breath-taking cover design. I could not reach readers without The Wild Rose Press's dedicated production and release team.

I'm fortunate in my worldbuilding research to have a partner with aviation and space exploration acumen. Dan's background as a former NASA employee and pilot has made him invaluable for lending realism to the creation of Eamine as well as the flying scenes.

And to my dear readers, I'm grateful you've taken the leap with me into this imaginary world. I envisioned an exciting environment that humans could inhabit with new, complicating factors for the characters involved. Your support has been immeasurable, and I look forward to sharing more speculative stories with you.

Reader reviews are invaluable to others in deciding if this book is right for them. I invite you to share your own review at:

https://www.amazon.com/stores/author/B0BQGWQRVP

or

https://www.goodreads.com/author/show/23290645.Diana_Fedorak

A word about the author...

Diana Fedorak is a speculative fiction writer from Las Vegas, Nevada. Born in Saigon, South Vietnam, she grew up in a Pan Am Airways family who frequently traveled overseas. Her prior career was serving as an intelligence officer in the United States Air Force. She enjoys writing complex characters in high-stakes science fiction and fantasy worlds.

Diana's 2023 debut novel, *Children of Alpheios*, has won numerous awards to include the Firebird Award for Speculative Fiction, Science Fiction, & Dystopian. When she's not writing, she spends time in her own universe with her husband, two children, and their German Shepard.

For updates on Diana's work, please visit her website and sign up for her newsletter:

https://www.dianafedorak.com

Thank you for purchasing
this publication of The Wild Rose Press, Inc.

For questions or more information
contact us at
info@thewildrosepress.com.

The Wild Rose Press, Inc.
www.thewildrosepress.com

Printed in the USA
CPSIA information can be obtained
at www.ICGtesting.com
LVHW020742221124
796914LV00003BA/4

* 9 7 8 1 5 0 9 2 5 9 0 2 1 *